"MOLLENE," HE SAID SO QUIETLY SHE COULD BARELY HEAR.

She turned slightly to reach up and touch his cheek, a touch as light and fragile as a winter white snowflake. She knew he was going to kiss her. She desperately wanted him to and yet she was mortally afraid. Afraid to want, afraid to fall.

His was the strongest character she'd ever seen in a man. He was intelligent and industrious. She suspected his passions ran deep and strong. And he would be a ruthless enemy. He already despised the fact she'd been an actress. He would never forgive her if he found out she worked for the Rockwells.

"No," she said softly.

Also by Catriona Flynt

One Man's Treasure

Available from
HarperPaperbacks

Harper Monogram

Lost Treasure

CATRIONA FLYNT

HarperPaperbacks
A Division of HarperCollinsPublishers

This is a work of fiction. The characters, incidents, and dialogues are products of the author's imagination and are not to be construed as real. Any resemblance to actual events or persons, living or dead, is entirely coincidental.

HarperPaperbacks *A Division of* HarperCollins*Publishers*
10 East 53rd Street, New York, N.Y. 10022

Cover illustration by Jean Monti

First printing: June 1993

Printed in the United States of America

HarperPaperbacks, HarperMonogram, and colophon are trademarks of HarperCollins*Publishers*

❖ 10 9 8 7 6 5 4 3 2 1

To our parents:

John and Freda Banta
and
William and Marian Flynn

ACKNOWLEDGMENTS

Summit, California, exists only in the pages of this book. It is based on a small community called Mosquito and a logging company located at Pino Grande.

We wish to acknowledge the invaluable contribution made to this novel from the diaries and reminiscences of Donald E. Morton, who lived in Mosquito, California, during the fight over the Treadwell legacy, on which this story is based.

Special thanks also goes to Mr. Morton's daughter, Cecelia Hill, for her friendship and contributions, and to Robert Darr for being our mountain guide.

We also wish to acknowledge the Mount de Sales Academy of the Visitation of the Blessed Virgin Mother Convent School in Baltimore, Maryland, for their information about boarding schools in the late nineteenth century.

The idea for the revolutionary log-carrying cableway, which we attributed to Winslow Fortune, actually belonged to D. H. McEwen. The cableway was constructed through the combined efforts of a number of businessmen and companies. Work was started on it in 1901 and completed in 1902. It stretched 2,600 feet across the gorge to meet a narrow-gage railway on the other ridge, which carried the logs to a nearby sawmill, and it continued to be used until the 1950s.

Prologue

February 1897
Tucson, Arizona Territory

"I'm told I'm a rich man's bastard," the letter began. "And you are that rich man."

Seamus Blade stared at the elaborate swirling script in utter disbelief.

Moving his tongue from his suddenly dry mouth over his bottom lip, he took a deep breath and cast a nervous glance around the private parlor, which had been set up for his breakfast, to see if anyone was nearby.

Blessedly, he was alone. He shook his head and wished for a glass of water to wet his throat. Or a stiff drink.

This was never supposed to happen. He had paid dearly so this wouldn't happen.

His hand shook as he ran it over his clean-shaven chin and forced his eyes back to the paper. The beginnings of a headache began to throb in his temples. A tiny flash of silver and blue blinded one eye for a second.

"I discovered your name in my aunt's papers after she died. I wanted nothing from you—I *hated* you so much!

"But I want something now, rich man. I want you to keep your thugs away from me!"

A sudden stab in his head made Seamus gasp.

Outside in the courtyard of the elegant hotel a mourning dove sang its wistful melody. The morning breeze stirred the glass windchimes in the palo verde tree. A cow lowed somewhere in the distance.

In the primrose papered parlor, Seamus Blade pulled another, larger piece of paper from the envelope and stared at it.

It was a handbill for a theater production.

Seconds passed before he recognized the woman on the theatrical poster. The throbbing in his head cut through his muddled thoughts like a razor-sharp knife.

It was her. His child. The one he'd never seen or even acknowledged. His big mistake. His mortal sin.

He didn't notice the Mexican woman come in to refill his coffee cup. He didn't see her leave. He was intent on the likeness of his daughter, Mollene Kennedy.

Moll Kennedy.

It struck him odd that a daughter of his would bear another man's name.

But, of course, that was one of the terms his lawyer had set down when the money was sent. Seamus had never intended to know a thing about the child, including her name.

She was beautiful, he realized. Truly breathtaking, if the poster could be believed—dark and shapely, with the face of an angel. Better looking by far than her mother. Better looking, he admitted grudgingly, than his other two daughters—although they were fine-looking females, especially Josie.

"I always did sire handsome children," Seamus said aloud without an ounce of false modesty. "Must be something in me blood."

His eyes went back to the letter.

"There have been too many accidents, too many scares, too damned many close calls. Since I have no enemies but you, I know you're the bastard responsible for my troubles."

Seamus couldn't believe his aching eyes. The pain in his head pounded in his temple as he reached for the bell.

"Carlo," he said to the lad who answered the ring. "Bring me a pen, some writing paper, and an envelope."

He waited silently till the boy returned with the fine, white hotel stationery. Then he finished reading Moll Kennedy's letter.

"Why are you trying to kill me, old man? I never did anything to hurt you. Except to be born. That was your fault, you son-of-a-bitch, not mine."

"I wonder where the little tart learned such bloody awful language?" he said to himself.

His own letter to Patsy Murphy, his enormous, burly bodyguard in Denver, was short and to the point. It instructed Murphy to protect this woman at all costs. He included her letter, the envelope with the postal mark, and the theatrical poster along with his own clipped message.

"Carlo!" he bellowed. "Take this down to the post right away. I want it mailed this morning."

The boy palmed the tossed gold piece like a pro and hustled out of the hotel.

Neel Blade walked into the room several minutes later, as was his habit, to share the first meal of the day with his father. A tall, handsome, impeccably groomed blond in his mid-twenties, Neel was the only one of Seamus Blade's children who managed to get along with the feisty, aging fortune hunter. But then, Neel got along with everyone.

"Good morning, Poppa. Where was little Carlo going in such a toot?"

Sweating profusely, Seamus Blade tried to answer his son. He barely managed a groan before crumpling out of his chair and falling to the wooden floor.

1

**October, 1896
California**

Winslow Fortune pulled his watch from his vest pocket, flipped up the gold cover with practiced ease, and scowled as though he had expected the time to have changed appreciably since he had last consulted it two minutes before.

Damn! he swore silently. The train was running twelve minutes behind schedule, and they were still an hour out of Oakland. At this rate he'd miss the 3:45 ferry across the bay to San Francisco. And by the time he caught the next one he would be too late for his five o'clock meeting with Sampson Levine. He ran his hand through his dark hair, and shrugged his wide shoulders, trying to ease the tension in them.

It was probably a good thing he didn't have the dapper,

ginger-haired lawyer in front of him right now, because the chances were he'd throttle him.

He had sent Fortune that mysterious summons without giving even a hint as to the purpose of this unscheduled meeting. Sampson's behavior was enough to rile a man's temper, even if he didn't have to travel a hundred miles to satisfy his lawyer's whim!

And if Winslow Fortune hadn't been in desperate need of a woman—which the lawyer had been charged to find—he would never have caught the train in Placerville at 6:45 that morning for the damn near all-day trip to San Francisco. He had a logging company to run. There were a thousand things that needed to be taken care of before winter set in. He didn't have time for this foolishness.

If time wasn't enough of a problem—and it was his most drastic concern—he'd just learned from the man in charge of blasting the boulders out of the river that an overzealous powder monkey had shattered every window within ten miles of the blast.

Damnation! Didn't he have enough worries without having to replace window glass and lace curtains for half the women in El Dorado County?

His life seemed to be one headache after another. He had spent four long, obstacle-riddled years fighting his enemies for an objective he'd questioned from the very beginning. But he owed the old man. His best childhood memories came directly from his grandfather, and there had been many. What was a little hard work compared to that?

Because if he failed, his two cousins—the dukes of double-dealing and wickedness—would win the legacy. And that thought galled him to the depths of his soul.

With a final scowl Fortune slumped his long, muscular

frame into the plush seat, extending his legs out into the center aisle, and closed his eyes. These last few years he'd learned to grab snatches of sleep whenever he could, because it was seldom that he was able to sleep a whole night through.

Men need to dream magnificent dreams and then follow them to their fruition. Fortune honestly believed that. But the whole process was very wearing, and what made it worse was that the dream he was following wasn't even his own to begin with.

Within seconds he was sound asleep, so he didn't see the wiry, dark-haired boy in the fussy nut-brown velvet Norfolk jacket and short pants sneaking along the aisle toward him, hiding behind each successive seat. The imp had the look of trouble about to happen as he threw little furtive glances over his shoulder. Fortune slumbered away in unsuspecting repose, oblivious to all that was around him.

The boy took a peek out just as the door at the far end of the car opened. It was that mean old Miss Fitzgerald. The boy forgot about swiping the sleeping man's hat and instead dived behind the seat facing Fortune.

"Timothy Cantrell, I know you're in here somewhere, you scamp! Come out this instant." Even when she tried, she couldn't erase the shrillness from her voice.

The boy backed even farther behind the seat, hoping she would miss seeing him as she stepped over Winslow Fortune's outstretched legs. He knew he was in for a licking, but he wasn't about to come out till he was forced to do so.

"Stop this foolishness, and come to me!" the woman's imperious voice commanded. "May the Good Lord be blessed that your mama and papa died and can't see the way you're behaving, ya wee limb of Satan that you be. 'Tis thankful I am that your uncle Jedediah is meeting us in San Francisco. What you need is the spank of a strong hand on your bottom!"

The woman swayed with the movement of the train as she made her way down the aisle. Her shriveled cheeks were scarlet with anger.

The boy crouched in the corner between the seat and the window, trying to make himself as small as possible. But he knew the game was up. Miz Fitz would find him, no doubt about that. Then she would probably grab him by the ear, march him smartly back into the other car, and box his ears good before depositing him back in the seat next to his little sister.

How he wished something—anything—would save him. His young heart pounded. He hated Miss Fitzgerald. She was a very mean woman. She pinched and smacked him as if he was her own kid, but he wasn't.

In fact, he'd never seen her before she arrived to deliver him and Sarah to their uncle in San Francisco after their parents were killed. He knew Uncle Jed had sent lots of money to Miss Fitzgerald—he'd seen her count it—but he couldn't understand why she was so mean.

It wasn't Sarah's fault that she threw up all over Miss Fitzgerald's best dress the first day of their trip. And it wasn't his fault that he laughed, really. He'd tried real hard not to. But the giggles just snuck out.

He could hear her shoes stomping down the aisle. Just as she came abreast of the seat where Timmy was hiding, the train gave a sudden lurch. She fell, grabbing the back of the seat. When the car swayed drunkenly to the right she tripped over Winslow Fortune's long, out-stretched legs.

The sudden impact and the violent sideways motion of the car toppled Fortune right out of his seat. His head cracked against the floor as Timmy came sliding over him. Miss Fitzgerald was on her back like a beetle, with her feet and arms waving in the air.

Timmy might have laughed again, but at that moment the train came to a screeching, stop, raining boxes, baskets, and packages down from the racks above the seats. Passengers were thrown out of their seats. Screams of fear, cries of pain, and roars of anger rent the air. All the excitement delighted young Tim.

Then he remembered Sarah. Miss Fitzgerald must have left her alone in the forward passenger car while she chased after him.

Sarah was so little—only two—and she would be scared. She'd been scared a lot since their parents died.

Timmy scrambled under Winslow Fortune's seat and crawled over several other unseated passengers in his haste to get to his sister. Intent on his rescue mission, he didn't even realize he was bleeding steadily from a wound near the hairline on his left temple.

It was the noise that roused Fortune—a tremendous din, where before there had only been the rhythmic *clack clack* of the train.

He groaned, mumbled a curse, and slowly leaned back until he contacted the sturdy side of the train car. What the hell had happened? he wondered.

He realized then that the train was no longer moving. Evidently they'd derailed, or struck something.

Anger boiled in him. It was all Sampson's fault, Fortune thought. Otherwise he could be home bargaining with irate housewives over broken windows and shattered pisspots!

Timmy hurried toward the door. All he could think about was getting to Sarah.

Two weeks ago their parents had been killed in a freak accident when their buggy overturned on a trip into Vandalia. Timmy hurt inside just thinking about it. Sarah had cried and cried for their parents to come back, and she was still waking up in the night crying for Mama. At least then he had been there to comfort her and protect her from Miz Fitz's slaps. He had taken her to bed with him each night since their parents died.

Timmy planned to talk to Uncle Jed when they got to San Francisco about sending Miz Fitz back to Illinois. They didn't need to waste any more money on her, he'd say. He'd watch Sarah.

He sighed as he pulled the heavy door of the train open. He would be very glad to see his uncle. Being the head of a family was a heavy responsibility for an eight-year-old, and he would be relieved to share it with Uncle Jed as soon as they got to San Francisco. But right now he had to get to Sarah.

Timmy found her standing up in her seat, screaming at the top of her lungs, with huge tears rolling down her pale cheeks.

When she spotted Timmy making his way through the rubble toward her, she gulped in great quantities of air and stopped wailing. She used the sleeves of her pink, sprigged-dimity dress to wipe the tears from her face, then held out her chubby little arms. "Timmy? Timmy!" she cried.

He climbed over two satchels and a large, round hat-box to reach her, then closed his arms around her protectively while she clutched his hair with her baby hands.

"Hey, Sarah, it's okay. I'm here. We're together. Ouch! Don't pull my hair out."

She released her painful grip on his hair and began to run her hand through the blood on the side of his head. Her enormous blue eyes filled with tears again. "Timmy hurt?"

"Nah, I'm fine. What a great wreck! Stuff and people flew all over. And Miz Fitz ended up looking like a witch who fell off her broom." He chuckled in unholy glee at the memory.

Sarah held her bloody hand up for Timothy to see. Then pointed to the spot where his temple was still oozing blood.

Timmy followed her motions with his own hand and looked perplexed. "Oh! How did that happen?"

"Timmy hurt?"

"No. I didn't feel a thing. Let's go see about Miz Fitz. Get her on her feet so she can yell at us."

He swung Sarah up with ease and placed her astraddle his hip, though he was small, then started back toward the next car and the indomitable Miss Fitzgerald.

In the next car Winslow Fortune had dragged himself to a more erect position and was holding his head in both hands to alleviate the throbbing pain.

"What in the name of God happened?" he asked no one in particular.

He pushed himself to his knees and crawled to where he could see around the seat. He wasn't convinced his head would allow him to rise to his full height yet. Maybe he'd just sit down again and stay on this dusty floor forever.

The sight that greeted him at the aisle startled him out of his musing. Satchels, boxes, people, miscellaneous articles of clothing, and odds and ends of food left over from packaged lunches were strewn about all over the car.

To his right was a skinny, homely, middle-aged vixen dressed in black, waving her arms and legs in an aimless manner, obviously trying to get up but hampered by the voluminous skirts and petticoats. He almost laughed, until he caught sight of the glare she was sending him from beneath her skewed hat.

"'Tis a sorry state we're in when a young man comes upon a fallen lady and doesn't even offer to help her to her feet!" she snapped.

Not half as sorry as the fact that the first woman I've found on her back in far too long has to be an ugly old crow with a tongue like a razor, Fortune thought. But he did manage not to voice the sentiment aloud. His mother had raised him to be a gentleman, and some vestiges of her training still remained.

"Madam, as soon as I can get to my own feet, I will attempt to help you to yours. But in the meantime I would appreciate it if you would keep a civil tongue in your head—since my head is already splitting."

"Well!" Miss Fitzgerald was thoroughly affronted, and every rigid line of her scrawny body announced that fact.

Just then Timothy Cantrell wrenched open the door of the car and stumbled in, clutching Sarah to his side.

"There you are, you brat!" Mrs. Fitzgerald exclaimed. "And it's a merry chase you've led me, too. What's that blood all over the both of you?" She struggled to a sitting position, her anger at Winslow Fortune forgotten.

As much as she disliked these wicked children, she didn't want them to be bloody wrecks when she handed them over to their uncle, or he might not pay her the rest of the money he'd promised.

Fortune struggled to his feet and reached a hand down to assist the woman. "Are these your children?" he asked.

"May the saints preserve us, no! I'm just accompanying them to San Francisco."

"Our Uncle Jed is going to meet us there," Timmy said. He wiped his right hand on his knickers to make sure it was clean before offering it to the big man. "I'm Timothy Cantrell. This is my sister Sarah. And that is Miss Fitzgerald you're helping up."

"Winslow Fortune. I'm pleased to make your acquaintance. May I help you with your sister?"

Timmy grinned. "Nah, she better stay with me. She's scared of strangers. But I thank you anyway," he added with a quick glance at Miss Fitzgerald, not wanting another pinch for bad manners. "We came all the way from Illinois. We've been riding the train for days and days. Where are you from?"

"That will do, Timothy. Just because your poor Mama is dead does not mean you can ignore the manners she surely taught you."

At the mention of their mother, Sarah's lower lip trembled, and tears filled her enormous blue eyes. Fortune winced at the woman's insensitivity. How in the hell did she get charged with delivering these kids?

With a gentle smile, he pulled a snowy linen handkerchief from his suit pocket and began to dab lightly at Sarah's cheeks, absorbing the tears. "What a little lady you are, Sarah! Would you like to stand here in the seat and hold your brother's hand while I look at that gash on his head? I'm sure it would make him feel better."

"It's nothing," Timmy began, then realized the man was using his wound to distract Sarah. So he stood her on the seat, then sat beside her and offered her his hand to hold. Sarah grasped his fingers.

Fortune turned to the woman. "Do you think you can find something to clean and bind the wound with, so it won't get infected?"

"Why, yes, I'm sure I can," she stammered, awed by this man's looks and sudden charm. Without another word, she headed off to the next car purposefully.

Her way was impeded by the throng of other passengers trying to collect themselves and their belongings, but she did not let that deter her. She might have been skinny, but she moved people out of her way like a bull.

As soon as the woman left, Fortune turned to the other passengers. Several had obviously been banged around, and there were a few serious injuries.

"Can you watch your sister? These folks need my help."

"Sure," the lad answered. "I watch her all the time."

Miss Fitzgerald returned with clean cloths, a tin cup of water, and some antiseptic—only to discover Sarah taking a nap on the bench seat with Winslow Fortune's suit jacket folded under her head for a pillow.

Fortune and Timmy were busy helping the other

passengers—separating out the injured from the merely
shaken up and getting the uninjured to aid those who
needed help.

Miss Fitzgerald eyed Fortune with growing respect.
She loved strong men who could handle things. She
cast a smile in his direction, though he didn't appear to
notice.

Timothy didn't want to have his head seen to, but
Fortune insisted, and the boy did not argue. He, too,
recognized authority when he saw it.

Finally the conductor came through to announce
that the train had struck a cow on the track. As soon as
the remains had been removed from the track, they
could proceed.

Then he clasped Fortune on the shoulder. "I want
you to know I'm grateful for what you did here, Mr.
Fortune. A boy broke his leg two cars ahead—he's hurt
real bad. I can only be in one place at a time, and I
couldn't have kept all these folks from panicking while
I handled that."

Fortune shrugged. "We're all in this together. Glad I
could help. Can you tell me what time we'll be arriving
in San Francisco?"

The conductor pulled out his large watch and squinted
at it. "Between six-thirty and seven, by the time the
ferry gets across the bay."

Fortune groaned.

"Is that going to be a hindrance to you?"

"I have a five o'clock appointment with my lawyer in
his office on Market Street. Do you suppose I could
send him a wire, saying I'm going to be late?"

"Certainly. You write out your message, and I'll take
care of it myself at the next stop."

"And I understand the Cantrell children are supposed

to be met by their uncle. Could we send him a message, too? Surely he'll be wondering what's happened. I believe his name is Jed Cantrell."

"Absolutely, Mr. Fortune. I'll see to it right away. The Southern Pacific Railway insists on the best for its passengers."

It was 6:37 P.M. by the time the hansom cab pulled away from the ferry terminal in San Francisco. Fortune had stayed until he made sure Timothy and Sarah were safely in the hands of their uncle, and then he grabbed the first available cab.

After giving the cabbie the address of Sampson Levine's law office, he took a moment to survey his appearance. His jacket was badly wrinkled, his white shirt smudged with dirt, and he needed another shave. He hardly presented the image of a successful businessman on his way to an appointment with his lawyer.

Sampson would just have to put up with him. After all, he was the one who had insisted on this mysterious meeting.

When the cab arrived at Market Street, Fortune climbed out and looked up to the third floor of the triangular building that housed Sampson Levine's office. Only a faint light shone through the window.

On a hunch, he asked the cabbie to wait, then took the stairs three at a time. He arrived on the third floor, with hardly a change in the tempo of his breathing, to be greeted by Jenkins, Sampson's male secretary.

"Oh, Mr. Fortune, I'm so glad to see you! I was just about to go home."

"Is Sampson inside?"

"No. He's gone for the day."

"Well, dammit, didn't he receive my wire?"

"Oh, yes, sir. He was sorry he couldn't wait for you here, but he left a message—and had me send another to the St. Francis. That's where you usually stay, isn't it? Anyway, he wants you to meet him at the Majestic Theater at eight o'clock. He's reserved a box."

Then the secretary donned his hat and coat and left. Fortune couldn't believe it. He stomped down the flights of stairs. After the day he'd had, the last damned thing in the world he wanted to do was go to the theater.

The stage lights in San Francisco's Majestic Theater had already dimmed when Winslow Fortune quietly slipped up the stairs and into the heavily draped box, halting in the deep shadows behind the man who had invited him to the production.

He stood in silence, watching the curtain rise on an opulent view of Mount Olympus, in a play he didn't want to see. Sampson Levine didn't acknowledge his tardy arrival. In fact, Sampson didn't even seem to notice his towering presence.

Fortune wasn't in the mood for coyness any more than he was for the mystery of why he was there. "What the devil is this foolishness, Sampson?" he demanded in a whisper that rose above the din of the orchestra.

The dapper little man didn't bother to turn his face away from the stage—from the woman on the wispy cloud to be exact—or in any other way greet him. He'd come to see the most lavishly produced comedy of the season, and he didn't want to miss a line.

"I thought you could use a little diversion," he murmured, as if the meeting was of little importance.

"Damnation!" Fortune's much-tried patience was suddenly at an end. The very last thing he needed in his already frantic life was another diversion. He certainly didn't intend to be amused by this tasteless, noisy excuse for a stage show.

"Did you find a woman for me or not?" he asked his attorney. "At least answer me that. I have a simple problem, Sampson, and I need a woman. I'll pay anything you say, just find me one. In fact, at this point, I'd settle for a man!"

Sampson raised a startled, red brow, turning at last toward the tall man in the shadows. "I'm glad nobody but me heard that remark, Winslow. Someone might doubt your masculinity."

Fortune's eyes grew stormy, but his cheeks flushed. "You know what I mean."

The lawyer nodded. "If you don't relax more, you won't live long enough to collect your grandfather's legacy."

"If you didn't find a teacher for my school, why the devil did you send for me?"

Sampson stroked his neatly waxed moustache. "This production seemed the perfect place to meet. With the goddess dressed like that, nobody will notice if we talk a little business. Sit down and enjoy yourself. I was lucky to get the tickets. You should be grateful I'm sharing them with you."

Fortune dropped into the chair next to Levine's and raised his tired eyes toward the lush female form in lights. The female, who billed herself as Aphrodite Zenos, Goddess of Love, was the heroine of a comedy farce he definitely didn't want to watch.

The Goddess of Love. Thunderation!

Laughter rolled through Sampson's slender body at

Fortune's shocked gasp, but somehow he managed to contain himself, almost strangling on the chortles. So the bold and bawdy humor shocked the big woodsman! It delighted Levine's sophisticated sense of humor to have the upper hand for once. He could already imagine Win's startled face when he introduced him to the lovely goddess after the show. Sampson had tipped her manager handsomely to arrange the meeting.

Fortune worked harder than ten ordinary men. Sampson thought he needed time off to relax. What better way was there for a man to forget his troubles than in the soft arms of a willing woman?

And Winslow Fortune did have troubles. His only relatives, two cousins, were trying every way to Sunday to rob him of a legacy worth more than eight million dollars.

It wasn't money that claimed Fortune's attention at the moment, however. It wasn't even work. For once his thoughts were thousands of miles from his logging camp.

They were in ancient Athens—or, at least, Athens as presented on the stage of the Majestic Theater. Marble pillars and nude statues, Mount Olympus in the apricot mist towering above the flaming torches, and a goddess come to earth.

Win tried without success to tear his hungry eyes away from the scantily clad enchantress on stage. She was nearly naked!

There couldn't have been more than a yard of the filmy, white material in her entire costume, a brief draping toga. He felt certain Sampson's silk handkerchief would cover more.

Controlling his shaky breathing, he tried to concentrate on the words the luscious actress spoke. Lord, she was beautiful! From the mass of thick black hair coiled atop her head to the tips of her sandled feet, the woman was perfect.

He wanted her, and the thought shocked him. He'd never lusted after a woman on a stage in all the years he'd attended the theater. Such behavior was for boys, and he was a grown man. But a hungry man at the moment—so hungry that he was ready to climb onto the stage and take her amidst the pillars and flares.

As his eyes took her in, a few of the lines she spoke penetrated his brain. The play had been billed as a comedy farce. Win mulled over the lines. They weren't funny.

"Why the hell am I here?" he demanded to his attorney. "I didn't come all this way to see a bad play! What's so almighty important you couldn't write it down?"

Sampson Levine was too smart to goad him any further. The game had ended. With a sigh, he turned his eyes from the lovely goddess onstage. She'd have to wait until later. He rose and beckoned Win to follow him into the shadows.

"It's the legacy," he said quietly into the curtained darkness. "The fourth year is coming to an end soon. With only twelve months left to carry out the terms of your grandfather's will, you'd better be prepared for trouble. One of my sources has informed me the Rockwells are planning to have you murdered if you continue with your goal."

"My God—they're my cousins!"

"They want to win."

"I won't let them win!"

"How can you stop them? Every time you turn around you trip over another of their spies. And now they're inquiring about a killer."

"I won't be defeated, Sampson. All I need is a practical way to get my timber to market."

They moved farther back, away from prying eyes. The noisy comedy should have kept the audience occupied, but they weren't taking any chances on being observed. Millions of dollars were at stake. They couldn't be too careful.

For nearly four years Winslow Fortune had worked day and night to carry out the terms of his grandfather's will. "Find a way to use the American River for commercial purposes," Aaron Winslow had challenged, "and all that I own will be yours. Otherwise it will go to my sister's worthless spawn."

Win had tried his damnedest. In the process, he'd built a land and timber empire in California's high country. Now all he had to do was get the timber to the waiting market. The only obstacles standing in his way were a great yawning gorge and the Rockwell brothers, his *dear* cousins.

Sheldon and Harlan Rockwell were the descendants of Aaron Winslow's sister. Win had always known they disliked him and scorned his rough ways, which somehow offended their citified manners. But he hadn't realized how much his cousins hated him until his grandfather died. The day the will was read, there was no doubt as to the depth of their hatred.

From that day on Winslow Fortune had made his grandfather's dream his own. He'd adored old Aaron, who was so different from his own father, a stiff, stern preacher. He intended to do everything in his power to make his grandfather's last request a reality.

The Rockwells had sat on their cosmopolitan backsides in San Francisco and done nothing except harass him and cause him every conceivable type of woe.

Though he was normally a peaceful man, Win felt a flash of righteous anger as his attorney elaborated on the kinds of schemes he expected the Rockwells to plot. Fortune seldom lost control, but when he did his temper rivaled the fires of hell in intensity.

Neither man paid the least attention to the screams from the stage. They'd all but forgotten the Love Goddess. The play seemed unimportant compared to the real drama of Winslow Fortune's life.

For a startling moment, Sampson thought he smelled smoke, and he looked questioningly at Win. The smell was far stronger and closer than what had previously drifted upward from the stage torches. He jerked his head toward the stage the same instant another scream split the air. Athens was ablaze!

"Godalmighty, Win! The place is on fire! Let's get the hell out of here!"

2

The newspaper on the pillow beside her rustled as Moll turned onto her side, jolting her awake.

All through the night—a night she'd planned to spend in joyous celebration of her triumphant stage debut—she had tossed about in the starched, white sheets, her much needed sleep tormented by dreams of flame and smoke.

She had heard every footstep in the hallway beyond her door, every hushed word, every breath of muffled laughter. The minutes had crawled past as she dozed and drifted in and out of her nightmares. Deep sleep had eluded her until dawn, when she was finally overcome by exhaustion.

Coughing raggedly, she propped herself up against the fat goose-down pillows and reached for the paper. The newspaper had slipped off the crisp white pillowcase and was resting halfway beneath the blanket. The theater section lay there.

Fear made her hands tremble.

"Damn," she whispered. "This was supposed to be a good morning."

But all the triumph, joy, and earth-jolting reviews had gone up in flames—incinerated by one carelessly placed torch.

She wanted to ignore the newspaper, but cowardice wasn't in her nature. Neither was patience.

"Thank you, Arthur." Her voice was hoarse and sarcastic. "It was *so* kind of you to bring me the good news and place it on my pillow."

She scanned the page and then read quickly, but the words barely registered. Again she scrutinized the review, just to make sure. Then she gasped.

Holy Hell! It wasn't just bad. It was ghastly.

FUNNY FIRE ENDS COMEDIC DISASTER! MAJESTIC THEATER DAMAGED IN BLAZE: THE LOVE GODDESS OUT OF WORK.

Aphrodite Zenos has been heralded as being so beautiful she drives men wild. Actually, it's her deplorable performance which makes men wild . . . to rush for the nearest exit.

The only laughable part of the comedy farce called *The Love Goddess* was the vision of Miss Zenos scampering off her pedestal when a torch toppled over and set the scenery ablaze.

Part of the stage at the Majestic Theater was damaged in the fire. The theater has been closed for repairs.

Tears streamed down her face, tears of humiliation, and disappointment, of anger and fear.

The storm came fast and furiously. Moll never held back her feelings, and now she wept uncontrollably. Then it was over, but the fury lasted.

She mashed the paper into a tight ball and hurled it across the room. It dropped harmlessly to the carpet before it hit anything. Moll threw herself out of the bed, flew across the room, and stomped on the wadded sheet.

She stooped over, meaning to rip it to shreds, but then she changed her mind.

Instead, she smoothed the wrinkled mess and leaned it against the bed lamp.

"Moll Kennedy," she said aloud, "this isn't the first time you've faced disaster. You're not a foolish, dreamy girl anymore. You've got a little money stashed away. And, for what he's worth, you've got Arthur. You're better off than you were in Panama, or in the orange groves. So quit your belly-aching and get dressed."

The words sounded far more brave than she felt. She was actually scared down to her pretty white toes.

She had never gotten herself in so deep that she couldn't get out, she thought as she stripped off her lace-trimmed nightdress. "You'll be okay. You were born lucky."

She chattered to herself as she washed, swept up her midnight-black curls into an artless twist, and put on her undergarments. Chattering was a childhood habit she'd never gotten over.

When life appeared especially grim or threatening, Moll made a little noise. The words weren't important, just the sound. Because without a bit of clamor and chaos, she was faced with the silence of her own lonely terror.

"You were born lucky," she told herself again, repeating the words Aunt Beebee had always written at the conclusion of her infrequent letters.

Apparently, Aunt Beebee had seen her mission in life as impressing Moll with how fortunate she was not to have been abandoned at an orphanage or in the street.

Moll had gotten the point of that message at an early age, since she was bright as a monkey and twice as cute. But she did wonder why, if she was really so damned lucky, that her mother couldn't love her enough to keep her around and her father wouldn't even acknowledge her existence.

But philosophy wasn't Moll's strong point. Action was. She yanked a dress from the wardrobe and tossed it on the bed. She was hungry, and if she was going to get anything to eat, she had to make an appearance downstairs.

"It can't be any worse than facing Mother Superior," she mumbled as she fastened her petticoat. "And I did that often enough."

The dress she chose to wear for her initial confrontation with the world after last night's fiasco was the same one she'd originally planned to wear for the celebration luncheon for her triumph.

"Damn good-looking dress!" Moll resorted to profanity whenever her spirits needed boosting. Naughty words had shocked her classmates and galled the nuns. They made her feel incredibly wicked and powerful. And on a day like this one, she needed every ounce of power she could muster.

The emerald-green velvet molded Moll's hourglass figure. Its lace-over-satin bloused bodice was deceptively modest, but the deep, square neck, which had been inset with nearly transparent white silk mull, was quite daring.

Pinning a soft, green velvet togue adorned with only two feathers and a rhinestone buckle onto her shiny black hair, Moll inspected her appearance impassively.

"You were born lucky," she reminded herself as she reached for her black silk bag.

The most famous hotel on the West Coast, the Palace was where anyone of importance stayed. Its lobby was an enormous beehive of bustling activity. A full eight stories of indoor balconies were open to the world-famous court below, where the royal, rich, and powerful met for meetings and pleasure. The lobby was so big that a circular driveway came inside, so that carriage passengers could disembark without braving the often chilly San Francisco weather.

Until now Moll had relished staying at a hotel that could truly have been a palace. Today she wished she was housed in a meager boardinghouse where nobody knew her name. She hoped she could sneak past the main reception desk without notice, but that was not to be. Moll was not an anonymous woman.

She heard her name called and came to a halt beside a full-sized palm tree growing in a white marble urn that was taller than she was.

Before she could blink twice, a long piece of paper was stuck under her nose.

"Your hotel bill, Miss Zenos."

A pulse beat wildly in Moll's temple. That alone betrayed her agitation, her lovely face being a mask of unconcern. All around her in the opulent white and crimson hotel lobby, people went about their business with normal morning briskness, oblivious to her turmoil.

She stared at the outstretched paper in horror. The amount of the bill made her reel in disbelief, since it was far more than she had in her emergency stash.

Where was Arthur? Vain little soul that he was, he generally managed to have every hair pomaded into place in plenty of time to escort her out to breakfast.

Maybe the debt was in error.

Moll glanced at the desk clerk. One look at the stony set of his face told her that was a pipedream. She stifled a groan and looked around. Arthur was nowhere in sight.

She'd met him more than a year ago in San Diego while she was singing at the Del Coronado Hotel. It was the best job she'd had since she had landed on the California coast after the Panama catastrophe, but Arthur quickly convinced her that she could do better.

Moll had seen no reason to mention her stint of singing and dancing in a saloon near the railroad station in Los Angeles, or worse, of picking oranges in the groves simply to stay alive. If he thought she was meant for better things, she wouldn't disagree.

Arthur Smith had accepted her story without question. What he saw in her was a beautiful face and figure, a passable singing voice, and a chameleon talent for playing roles. To Arthur, the woman was a gravy train!

Moll could feel the clerk's gaze upon her now, particularly on the transparent silk mull inset of her dress, and on the white curves beneath the silk. The undisguised longing on his face told her he wished his hands could touch what his eyes rested on.

Maybe because of his youth or maybe because of the incongruous situation, she felt embarrassed by his attention. She raised her chin, peered down her aristocratic nose, and waved the bill aside with an annoyed flick of her gloved hand.

"The bill goes to my business manager, Mr. Smith," she murmured in a cultivated from-somewhere-in-Europe voice. "He handles all the money. I never soil my gloves . . ." She let the sentence trail off, wondering if the youth accepted her explanation—and wondering where the hell Arthur had wandered off to.

The clerk, still having a great deal of difficulty averting his greedy eyes from her breasts, cleared his throat noisily and swallowed, loathing the blockheads who forced him to embarrass this beautiful creature.

"Mr. Smith . . ." The boy made a production of clearing the squeak from his throat. "Mr. Smith left the hotel very early this morning in a hired carriage."

The bastard! Only Moll's considerable talent at masking her feelings prevented her from screaming her head off. If a situation ever deserved a shrieking tantrum, this was it!

That rotten little shiv artist! she thought. *He had run out on her and let them see him do it! At least he could've had the decency to sneak out, so I could get away, too.*

Moll darted a glance at the white marble desk. The manager, three clerks, and a blue-clad policeman stood watching her.

The throbbing in her temple grew by the minute. Inside her stylish gloves, her palms were slick with sweat.

"Left the hotel?" she said incredulously, her china-blue eyes wide in feigned disbelief. She hoped the quaver in her voice sounded like shock instead of red-hot rage. She ached to thrust a knife in Arthur's fat back, just like he'd done to her. How in the name of God was she going to wiggle out of this mess?

The clerk, who had a kind if somewhat randy heart, squirmed in his ill-fitting suit. He hated the men who were watching him, who were forcing him to be so ruthless to this poor woman. Yet he needed his job, as his big family needed the income he brought home. He couldn't whisk her off to safety as he longed to do—as some dime-novel hero would.

Unable to meet her trusting eyes, he looked across the elegant lobby toward the indoor carriage entrance and wondered how to phrase the unpalatable truth a bit more mercifully.

"The night clerk told me Mr. Smith waited in the lobby until the paper arrived. Then he went upstairs, and a few minutes later he came back down the elevator with his grip and got into a hack."

The boy looked as devastated as she felt. Moll wanted to say something to comfort him. But what could she say?

Arthur had built her up all out of proportion to her talent or experience, put her on public display, created a mountain of fanfare, plastered her face all over town, and charged an enormous amount on credit. Then when the success of the play quite literally went up in smoke, he had run like a rabbit.

Her full-blown fury faded into panic. She only had a few dollars in her bag, no more than the price of a decent meal. Her stash upstairs wasn't nearly enough to cover the hotel bill, and it was only the first of many. Arthur had been so certain *The Love Goddess* would make them a fortune that he had convinced lots of other people, too.

Clutching the silk bag so tightly that the fabric began to fray, Moll faced the pathetic clerk without a thought of guile. She knew her pretended international fame and lavish goddess name didn't add up to a nickel that she could pay toward the debts Arthur had incurred on her behalf.

Nothing but the truth would do. Moll Kennedy was a

very frightened young woman, but she was no coward. She took a deep breath.

"I'm sorry," she told the clerk. "Mr. Smith handled all the revenue, for the theater production and for me personally. If he is gone . . ." Moll's smoke-damaged voice faltered while she fought against genuine tears.

This was even more difficult than she'd expected. She clenched her jaw tightly, and her tears subsided. She would be damned if she'd bawl in public! She had pride, if nothing else.

"If Mr. Smith left for good, I fear I am completely without funds."

The clerk looked at her, and she looked back. Neither was anxious for whatever came next.

Moll felt downright sorry for the boy. He appeared to be only sixteen or so, and not particularly well fed. Right now he was probably scared because he was being forced by his older, merciless superiors to do a rotten job nobody else wanted. It made her want to scream obscenities at those men watching and waiting.

Instead, she laid her gloved hand gently on the boy's arm and gave him a sweet smile.

In her not-quite-definable European accent she said, "Don't worry, I won't embarrass you, or the hotel. If I am to be arrested, I'll leave like the lady I am. I'm not angry with you. I understand. This is not your fault."

He felt like he had jagged rocks in his throat. He couldn't have spoken even if he'd known what to say. His heart ached for this brave and beautiful creature.

He was just turning to summon the hotel manager when two men in their thirties strode up from the carriage stop. Both men were talking at the same time, arguing with each other. Neither bothered to acknowledge the clerk, but they looked directly at Moll.

She'd never seen either of them. Fearing they were more creditors, she stepped back quickly.

The clerk immediately stepped in front of her, shielding her from the men. Feeling quite protective toward the woman he considered the most exquisite morsel alive, he spoke in his deepest voice. "May I help you, gentlemen?"

The taller, immaculately groomed blond man, in a biscuit-colored wool suit, answered in a cold voice, "We're here to see the actress, boy."

The other man, a smaller, dark fellow in dandified striped clothes, and sporting a natty hat, grabbed hold of his companion's sleeve and tugged.

"That's her," he said, ripping off his hat and jabbing it in Moll's direction. "She's the one. I'd know her even with her clothes on."

From the murmur around them, Moll knew many people in the elegant lobby had heard the remark. She wondered if things could possibly get worse.

The hotel manager, his three faithful toadies, and the uniformed officer all began to descend upon them.

After a brief grimace at the wrinkle his companion had put in his woolen sleeve, the taller man turned toward Moll and favored her with a smile. He had very straight white teeth and the smile of a barracuda. "Aphrodite Zenos?"

"Yes," Moll answered like the superior being she portrayed. Right now her talent for pretense was the only thing she had going for her. "I am Aphrodite."

He inhaled deeply, as if preparing to jump into a frigid mountain stream. His pale face looked as cold as marble. "Your beauty, Madame, surpasses mere mortal description. No wonder they call you a goddess."

She'd heard it all before, but never had it been

uttered with less enthusiasm! Moll wasn't overly vain, but this dolt galled her. Why, even the boy would have expressed more passion!

She frowned for a moment, hoping his infatuation with her wouldn't cause him pain. She hated to hurt nice people.

Then she turned her attention back to the blond man.

"Is there some quiet place where we can talk, Miss Zenos?" he asked. "We have a proposition for you."

It hadn't occurred to her that she'd be fending off would-be lovers as well as creditors this morning. Two of them, no less! No woman, however wicked, should be forced to endure so much grief before breakfast.

"Sir!" squawked the clerk. "Miss Zenos is a lady, and a great actress. You can't talk to her like that!"

The hotel manager, his flunkies, and the cop stepped up to the group. Moll closed her eyes in a moment of silent prayer.

"You mistake me!" the blond man snapped at the red-faced clerk. "I'm here to discuss business with Miss Zenos. I need her to perform a very important role for me. Though I don't intend to discuss it in front of the entire city of San Francisco."

He looked pointedly at the hotel manager and his cohorts. "This lobby is more public than the ferry terminal."

Chagrined at having embarrassed himself in front of his newfound heroine, the clerk quickly sought to mend his error. "Sir, I'll find you a discreet place immediately."

A role. The man wanted her to perform a part, naturally, as she was an actress.

Moll tried to calm herself, to slow the blood that sang through her veins. She wanted to shout for the sheer joy of living and climb upon the desk and do her famous Pedestal Dance. She wanted to hug the stammering young clerk for his patience and compassion.

"Sir," the clerk was saying to the man. "We have a library available . . ."

"What about the dining room?" Moll interrupted. "I was on my way to breakfast. I haven't had a thing to eat since early yesterday. Perhaps we could talk there."

"I'll see that you get a private table," the manager said. "Miss Zenos, would you honor us with your presence at a repast? As our guest?"

Only the brief flash of annoyance that skittered across the blond man's smooth face belied his deferential words.

Moll pretended to ponder his suggestion, not wanting to appear too desperate, either for a job or a meal.

The hotel manager glanced at the uniformed cop, who was looking rather hopeful. Maybe there was a chance of getting the huge hotel bill paid after all.

The manager looked at Moll. When she inclined her dark head in agreement to the gentlemen's invitation, he reached out and retrieved the bill from the young clerk's nervous fingers.

"Enjoy your meal," he said to Moll. "We can talk when your other business is finished."

She gave him the briefest of nods, hoping that he didn't see her relief.

The young clerk had turned away. Moll caught his arm. "Wait," she said softly.

Then she addressed the two strangers. "Gentlemen, would you kindly excuse me for a minute? I need to speak to the desk clerk."

The men had no other polite recourse. They nodded and started to walk away.

Moll turned quickly to the youth. "Perhaps fortune has smiled on me after all."

He nodded enthusiastically.

"I intend to ask for a cash advance," Moll continued. "Whatever the part, I must take it, even if it's not the lead role. Do you know if they're part of the regular theater crowd?"

The boy admitted his ignorance. "I don't get to the theater much."

Moll brushed the matter aside with a shrug. "A part is a part. I'll be able to take care of this little obligation to the hotel." Moll took his hand and pressed it. "Thank you for being so kind and understanding. I'll never forget you."

His high cheekbones went pink with admiration. His heart had never felt as full.

When she withdrew her hand, he saw the gold coin in his palm. "I can't accept this," he said.

"Take it. For your immense kindness to a poor player." She bestowed a radiant smile on him. "Now I must go. My destiny awaits."

She'd only walked a step or two when she turned back and whispered, "I'll be back soon."

He watched her, blushing from his starched collar to his carefully combed hair.

Moll had almost reached the dining room door when she heard her name called. She was utterly astonished when a portly, red-faced man in herringbone tweed grasped her arm and practically dragged her to a surprisingly secluded spot behind several burgundy leather winged-back chairs.

"What are you about, sir? Unhand me!"

He did so quite promptly "I need your help, Miss Zenos," he told her.

Moll tried to sidestep his whiskey breath. She caught sight of his watch fob dangling from the heavy gold chain stretched across his scarlet waistcoat.

What sort of man wore a gold coffin as a fob? Dear God, there was even a tiny gold shovel!

So intent was she on the fellow's gross lack of taste that she nearly missed his question.

She blinked, certain she'd misunderstood him. Surely he didn't really expect her to do that to him!

He made the proposition even more explicit.

Moll's eyes widened and then narrowed menacingly.

Had the portly man been smarter, or less intoxicated, he would have seen the danger coming.

She quickly sized up her enemy. The fool was still enumerating the lurid pleasures he hoped they'd share.

"I'd jump in the bloody bay first!" Without warning she stepped forward, stepped down hard on his foot, and shoved him away.

Caught completely unaware, the man yelped in both pain and astonishment. Then he tumbled backward, hitting his head against a marble urn.

Raising her voice to stage projection, Moll uttered, "You, sir, are no gentleman!" Then she straightened her toque and sailed into the dining room with the regal grace of a tall ship.

The dining room of the Palace Hotel was ornately decorated in shades of crimson, rose, butter yellow, and ivory. Moll figured there was enough velvet, linens, garlands, and flowers for a dozen rooms. But Victorian muss and fuss weren't to her taste.

The two men waited for her at a table. When she spotted them, the darker man was talking animatedly to the blond one, but he stopped when he saw her.

The blond rose quickly to his feet; his companion got up reluctantly.

Not for the first time, Moll wondered if she'd thrown herself headfirst into another mess. Well, at least she was in a public place. They couldn't do much to hurt her in the dining room of the Palace Hotel.

"Miss Zenos," the tall blond man said as she approached. "I sincerely apologize for not properly introducing myself, but the thrill of seeing you in person . . ." His voice trailed off. "We feel as though we know you from all your publicity, and from your delightful performance last night—before the fire. But, of course, you've never heard of us."

She nearly asked if he'd read the morning paper but quickly thought better of it. He wanted her for a role and naturally assumed she'd be available following the fire, which had destroyed the props and scenery of *The Love Goddess.* But if he read the critic's vicious column, he might change his mind.

She couldn't afford that. She forced another smile.

"My name is Sheldon Rockwell," the blond man said in a tone indicating that the name meant something. "And this is my younger brother, Harlan."

Harlan clicked his heels together like a Prussian and bowed from the waist.

Moll nodded in his direction, wondering if he was merely an idiot or something more dangerous.

At that moment the waiter came over to the table and presented them with engraved menus. Even as her greedy eyes scanned the wondrous delights, Moll needed to know this wasn't a ruse. Some men went to ludicrous extremes to be seen with a famous woman.

"You mentioned a part, Mr. Rockwell."

"Yes. Of course," Sheldon Rockwell said. "My brother and I are desperate for you to play a role. But first you must order something to eat. To keep up your health, you know. You ladies are so delicate."

I'm as delicate as a locomotive, you windbag.

She kept her thoughts to herself as she studied the menu. She ordered more food than she wanted, simply to keep her nerves from unraveling.

"A rasher of bacon, eggs baked in potatoes, fried oysters, a graham muffin with honey, spiced fruit in heavy cream, and black coffee."

Harlan Rockwell groaned, but Sheldon ignored him and ordered tea and hot rolls with crabapple jelly for the two of them. "We breakfasted earlier," he said to Moll.

Their stilted conversation dwindled to nothing while they ate. Moll couldn't recall ever having had such an uncomfortable meal.

She was beginning to suspect that the Rockwells were not connected to the theater at all. Above all else, theater folk knew how to talk. These men did not seem like ordinary businessmen, either.

"Do you go to the theater much?" Moll asked them.

"No," Sheldon answered sharply. Realizing he'd been rude, he hastily continued, "I go to the opera. Do you like the opera, Miss Zenos?"

Moll smiled. "The opera is . . . the opera. One either adores it"—she sighed—"or hates it."

Sheldon looked animated for the very first time.

"I love the voice," he said, drawing the last word out, "the human voice. There is nothing like it. You're so right. There is *nothing* to compare to the opera."

Moll decided she'd said the right thing. She'd never seen an opera in her life, but apparently Sheldon Rockwell was a devotee. Maybe she was in luck, after all. Maybe he didn't realize her performance last night was a bomb.

Harlan noisily spooned three lumps of sugar into his teacup, sloshing the hot liquid onto the table linen as he stirred. He made Moll nervous. From the very start of this meeting, he had looked as if he was privy to some hilarious joke.

Moll fairly itched to ask again about the part, but she clamped a lid on her curiosity. Instinct told her to wait Rockwell out. If she appeared too eager, she wouldn't get the cash she needed. She might even totally blow the opportunity.

She contented herself with drinking coffee and pretending she was a great lady with nothing more important to do than spend the morning with friends.

"I haven't had the opportunity to visit the opera lately," she said, hoping Sheldon Rockwell would pick up the conversation. "I've been so busy."

"I'm on the Opera Committee," Sheldon said. "We're on a crusade to resurrect the Metropolitan Opera Company. You probably know it closed several years ago." His eyes glowed with the intensity of a zealot. "That was a sad day."

"I thought San Francisco had an opera theater."

"The Grand Opera," Sheldon growled, his eyes taking on a feral glint. "A veritable cow barn. Utterly loathsome. We'll see its dust someday. The Opera Committee is committed to the Metropolitan."

Sheldon didn't mention that he was the only man on the committee, along with a number of fat busybodies who needed someplace to show off their diamond dog-collars.

"Are you also on the Opera Committee, Mr. Rockwell?" Moll asked Harlan.

Harlan looked astonished. "I prefer Barbary Coast . . . ah, entertainment."

Moll could not respond politely to that remark. Even someone who'd just come to town knew the Barbary Coast offered an assortment of dance halls, gambling dens, and whorehouses. What a wretched little man!

Sheldon stepped in quickly before Harlan's crudeness ruined their plan. "My brother and I were saddened that your theater production has been prematurely closed because of that unfortunate fire."

Harlan's audible snicker robbed Sheldon's words of any sincerity.

Ignoring the impulse to kick the little twirp, Moll nodded sorrowfully.

"Assuming you've accepted no other role at this time, my brother and I wish to offer you employment for a guaranteed period of one year, perhaps a little more."

Moll's curiosity was piqued. What sort of play could be guaranteed to run a year or more? Her confusion kept her silent.

Sheldon mistook her silence for a negative response. He glanced at his brother and decided to sweeten the pot.

"As I said, this employment is guaranteed for a year, and the salary is good. We'll also provide a room for you until you're ready to move, suitable clothing for the part, transportation . . ."

"I won't be working in San Francisco?"

"No."

Then Sheldon specified a weekly wage that was generously high. "Let's see, have I forgotten anything?"

"The bonus," Harlan said.

"Right. There will be a small bonus at the end of the job . . ."

"How much?"

Sheldon raised an eyebrow. He'd been worried she wouldn't accept. Now he realized he just hadn't said the right words. Money. He named a goodly sum.

Moll looked him directly in the eye and for the first time made him aware that she was not a simpleton.

"I'll know if the money is suitable when you tell me about the so-called part you're hiring me to play. I've been on the boards long enough to tell a blue-fizzle when I hear one."

Harlan groaned at her criticism of his brother's honesty. She might be billed as a European actress, but her use of saloon slang suggested something quite different. He ought to know—he had spent many hours in saloons, gambling joints, and bordellos.

This fulsome piece had been around more than the backstage of a theater. She might have come cheaper than they'd planned. Only now it was too late to go back and lower the offer.

"Frankly," Moll continued, "I'm beginning to suspect the role you're offering me is either illegal or immoral. But we both know how much I need a job. So tell me what this is, but don't be so chinny, and don't lie to me. Are you offering me a theater part or not?"

"Not exactly," Sheldon stammered, completely taken aback by her chameleon switch in character. In his world a lady knew her place and kept to it.

Moll started to rise, totally fed up with the game.

"Wait!" Sheldon caught her with a restraining hand. "Hear me out. We need you."

"Yes," Harlan added sullenly. "We're sunk without you."

The panic in Sheldon's pale eyes halted Moll. Now he was telling the truth. Whatever the scam was, he did need her help. And a lot of money was involved—more than enough to pay her immediate bills. Slowly she sat down.

"Continue," she commanded them. The waiter came by with a tray of confections, and Moll chose several. Since her childhood days at boarding school, she couldn't seem to get enough candy. Maybe all orphans were that way, substituting sweets for love.

"I want you to be a schoolteacher. In a school."

Moll burst out laughing, ignoring the heads turning in her direction.

"Hear us out," Sheldon pleaded. It galled him, but he was forced to beg. "We need you."

She didn't bother to hide her impatience.

"Have you heard of the Winslow legacy?" Sheldon asked.

"No."

"The entire state of California knows about it," Sheldon insisted. "It's infamous because of the vanity of Aaron Winslow, our uncle. He made a fortune mining gold on the American River in the early days."

"A big fortune," Harlan added. "He was just a ragged young miner who struck it rich."

Moll nodded in spite of herself. According to the papers her Aunt Beebee had left when she died, Moll's natural father had mined for gold and struck it rich, too.

"Aaron Winslow wasn't satisfied being rich as sin. He wanted his name in history books, along with Marshall and Sutter, Stanford and Crocker. He thought he was one of California's great visionaries. But nobody would listen to his ideas."

"That's 'cause his ideas were dumb!" Harlan slurped his cold tea and belched.

"What does this have to do with me being a schoolteacher?"

"Our uncle died before achieving his dream of utilizing the American River for commercial purposes."

"That's the river where he found gold?" Moll asked.

"The will! Tell her about the will."

Sheldon sighed. "Aaron Winslow's multimillion-dollar estate will go to his only grandson, Winslow Fortune, if he carries out the old fool's dream within five years."

Moll couldn't see where she fit in, but she was curious. "What exactly do you have against this, uh, American River being put to commercial use, Mr. Rockwell?"

"The American River is wild and treacherous. There are granite boulders in it the size of a house. Commercial use is not only impractical—it's impossible."

Harlan interrupted him. "The real reason is money. If Winslow Fortune fails, all the money—all eight million dollars—goes to the old man's only other relatives. Sheldon and Harlan Rockwell."

"I see," she said sagely. "And will the five-year time period be up about twelve months from now?"

"Correct," Sheldon said. "It's been a terrible waste of Cousin Win's time and money, following the whims of a senile old man."

Moll shook her head. "What is my place in this legacy battle?"

"We need somebody inside Cousin Win's operation to keep us informed about his activities."

"A spy?"

Sheldon tightened his thin lips. "That's one word for it."

Moll shook her head. "I'm sorry, gents, I can sing

and dance and recite lines. But I have no idea how to spy on your cousin and make sure he doesn't get the money."

"It would be simple," Sheldon coaxed. "You'd actually work for Win, so you'd be in contact with him and the important people in his organization. He bought up a bunch of timberland on the ridge above the river. He plans to float logs down the American River. Some of the loggers he hired have families at the camp."

"And the kids need a teacher," Harlan finished.

It sounded logical to Moll, but she was certain that nothing these two did was simple, nor honest.

"Your cousin asked you to hire a teacher for his school?"

Sheldon flushed a dull red. "He wouldn't trust us. The attorney for the estate ran a newspaper ad for a schoolteacher. We saw it."

"Will the attorney also get a small bonus next year?" Moll asked.

"Naturally." Sheldon glowered, disliking the actress and her sassy mouth more by the minute. He was doing *her* a favor, not the other way around. If he didn't need her so badly, he'd walk out. He did need someone he could control, though, and Moll's debacle, as well as her debts, put her in the palm of his hand.

"So, if I accept this role, all I have to do is play a schoolteacher at your cousin's logging camp?"

"And send me a letter each week containing all the interesting tidbits you overhear."

"You could get friendly with Cousin Win," Harlan suggested.

Moll's blue eyes hardened. "How friendly?"

She hadn't been so far down yet that she'd been

forced to whoredom, but she was damned sensitive on the subject.

Sheldon exhaled sharply. "Use your imagination and get the information—however you see fit. That's all we ask."

"And that our dear cousin fails," Harlan added.

Moll studied her coffee cup a moment and then nodded. Instinct told her these two were trash, but her gut feeling was that the part was a golden opportunity for her.

"Let's talk about money," she said. "It would be more convenient if I got some of it in advance."

An hour later, Moll waited in her room for the bell-hop, dressed in a quiet gray traveling suit. She was packed and ready to go to the small roominghouse the Rockwells had suggested.

The hotel bill had been paid. Aphrodite Zenos no longer existed.

She reached into the hidden compartment of her hatbox to check her stash of money. If this job was not to her liking, the money would provide her with an escape.

Her fingers hunted for the gold coins, fumbled around, and groped some more. Nothing. The secret place was empty. Dear God, how could that be?

Arthur! Not only had he left her in the lurch with her embarrassing theatrical flop and all the bills, he'd stolen her security money, too.

"Damn you, Arthur Smith! Some day I'll find you and kick you dead!"

She sank down on the side of the unmade bed, stunned and frightened. She was flat broke, with not even a coin in her bag. Now she was truly at the mercy of the Rockwells and their devious scheme to win the Winslow legacy.

There was a knock on the door.

"Are you ready, Miss Zenos?" the bellhop asked as he picked up her bags.

She drew herself up. "Yes. I'm ready."

She walked out of the suite with the grace of a queen and didn't look back.

3

A light fog rolled over San Francisco, blanketing the city, slowing the flow of afternoon traffic. Inside his mahogany-paneled corner office, three stories above the bustle on Market Street, Sampson Levine sat in a brown leather chair, hunched over his desk. His mind was intent upon the large sheet of paper before him.

It was a poster, the eye-catching publicity gimmick for *The Love Goddess,* the previous day's smoky fiasco at the Majestic Theater. Likenesses of Aphrodite Zenos, displayed in all her magnificent glory—and remarkably little else—had hung all over the city. They'd been plastered to walls, stuck on signposts, nailed to trees. Today, with her glory sullied, the handbills seemed to shout her failure.

Sampson shook his head sadly. She was such a beautiful woman. It was too bad her career had gone up in smoke.

He frowned at his mental pun. He'd had such lovely plans for Aphrodite and his friend Winslow Fortune. That one rickety torch had sent Athens up in flames, along with all his carefully laid plans.

Sampson ran his fingers through his clipped curls. Hoping to salvage at least a portion of his plans, he'd gone by the Palace Hotel at lunchtime, but the afternoon desk clerk had informed him that the actress had already checked out, her bill paid by a handsome, well-dressed gentleman.

For a sizable tip, the middle-aged man had told Sampson all the sordid gossip surrounding the actress's situation.

Sampson looked up as the heavy mahogany door to his office burst open—much to the consternation of Jenkins, his nervously conscientious young clerk—and in stomped Winslow Fortune.

"Sampson, I need a woman!"

"Don't we all, Winslow," Sampson replied, nearly sending Jenkins into a fatal blush. "Don't we all."

Jenkins closed the door soundlessly, leaving the lawyer alone with his client. Sampson noted Winslow's rumpled suit and careless tie and wondered if Win had ever bothered to pick up the clothes he'd purchased from Sampson's own very expensive tailor the last time he was in the city. In any event, it had obviously not occurred to the younger man to have the valet at his hotel press the clothes he was wearing.

"Nice day, Winslow," he said. "Have a seat."

"It's a miserable day," Fortune muttered. "Fog's as thick as mare's milk. I'll stand."

"Suit yourself." Sampson's gaze returned to the woman on the poster.

"I just talked to the editor of the *Daily News,*" Fortune said. "Nobody answered this last ad for a teacher. Nobody! Not even an inquiry."

"I know." Sampson said, wondering if Fortune always behaved like a caged beast when he was inside a building, or only when he entered the law offices of Morton and Levine.

"Why?" Win practically shouted.

"Many reasons, the main one being a lack of suitable teachers willing to brave the treachery of the high country with winter approaching. I suppose you've tried Auburn, Placerville, and Georgetown?"

"And Sacramento, Meyers, Coloma, Kelsey, and Jackson," Win said. "Suddenly there isn't a school-teacher available in the state of California. Now, why the devil not?"

Sampson looked Fortune straight in the eye. "Nobody wants to work at the Summit School. And not just because it's way the hell and gone up on a lone-some ridge miles from any town, either. The word on the street is that your school is jinxed, that it scares teachers away."

"They weren't all scared away! Two got married—"

"Eight women, Winslow. I've sent eight women up there in the last three years, and all of them quit."

"But two got married," Fortune repeated.

"And six didn't! Six left during the term, for one reason or another. And to make matters worse, nobody ever heard from the last one again."

Fortune fixed his bleak gray eyes on him. "I know that. I had men out looking for her for days, but they found nothing. Surely she left with a man. There's no other logical explanation."

"But still—"

"And, Sampson, if I can't find a schoolteacher soon, my men will take their wives and children elsewhere. I'll lose my timber cruiser, the woods boss, a sawyer, and one of the best truckers I've ever seen. Plus I'll lose my reputation as an honest man, because I gave my word on this."

He slumped down in a brown leather winged-back chair. "I gave my word to those men when they hired on that there would be a school for their children. And I mean to keep that word. I'll take anybody who is good with children."

Sampson watched the change in his friend and, as he'd done so often in the past, silently cursed Aaron Winslow's legacy.

The old man's egotistical dream to be in the history books with all of California's great men had all but ruined his grandson's youth. At times Winslow's determination to fulfill the old man's wishes had bordered on mania.

Win's own dreams and goals came second. The legacy had even pushed love aside. The girl he'd planned to marry before his grandfather died broke off the engagement because she refused to live in the high country. Win let her go, and she married a banker from Oakland.

The five years stipulated in Aaron's will would soon be up, the bills paid, and the money finally awarded. Frankly, Sampson would be damned relieved when it was all over, and he wondered if Fortune wouldn't be, too.

"You can't be too particular who you get at this point, Winslow. There aren't that many women to spare in California."

"I'll take a man!"

"A man can get better wages at other work."

"I'll pay more." His voice cracked with desperation.

"Dammit, Win, can't one of the mothers teach? The gossip here in the city says the last teacher was abducted in the middle of the night and thrown into the river!"

"Suffering Christopher! Where did you hear that?"

"From the editor of the *Daily News*. Yesterday morning. Didn't he tell you?"

"No. I doubt he had the guts to tell me."

Sampson chuckled. "I doubt he did, either. But he told me rumors have been floating around the city for more than a month."

Win ran a hand through his thick brown hair. "Agatha Powell was still in Summit a month ago. This stinks, Sampson!"

"The whole mess smells remarkably like the Rockwell brothers, don't you think?"

Win nodded. He had already suspected the Rockwells were behind his teacher problem, too. They were waging what they called a "civilized" battle to win the legacy. Fortune didn't think that hiring men to bully his loggers, foul up his supply shipments, sabotage his timber outfit, and scare off teachers was civilized.

The only thing that made Sheldon and Harlan different from common thugs was that they always hired someone else to do their dirty work.

"My only relatives," Win said. "Makes a man wish he was an orphan."

"We can arrange that," Sampson teased. "In San Francisco a man can buy anything he wants."

"Except a schoolteacher." Fortune grinned. "But I

wouldn't want anybody else to take care of those two. That's a pleasure I've reserved for myself—once this is all over."

"You're right," Sampson said. "A man should have the privilege of throttling his own pesky relatives."

"I'd only throttle Sheldon. Harlan I'd squash like a bug. And then—" He broke off and stared at the piece of paper on Sampson's desk. "What is that?"

"A small memento of San Francisco's hottest show."

He held up the handbill for Win to see. "I thought I might keep it as a reminder of the disaster. These were all over the city, but most have been torn down by now. This was on the wall downstairs."

"How bad was the fire?" Win asked finally, unable to think of anything more intelligent to say. He felt himself flush and hoped Sampson didn't notice his reaction to the woman's photograph.

"Not bad at all. The backstage crew had buckets of water handy. A smart move, I'd say. Probably saved the theater. After the disasters in Chicago and Brooklyn a few years ago, people are terrified of stage fires. The props burned, of course, or were ruined with water, and the scenery, too. I guess you could say Athens burned. But the critics did more damage to *The Love Goddess* than the blaze did."

"That bad?"

"You didn't notice?" Sampson teased, though he'd paid little attention to the acting, either.

"No, I didn't. She's a deuce of a good-looking woman."

"That she is." Sampson nodded. "That she is. But today she's an unemployed actress. The Majestic is cleaning up the charred remains of *The Love Goddess* and bringing in another production for the weekend."

Win looked back at the poster. "I wonder if she could teach school? I know a place that would even hire an out-of-work goddess right now."

Sampson burst out laughing. Then he began to roll up the poster.

"Sorry, Winslow, you can't get the goddess, either. She's already disappeared." He tied the roll with a string and handed it to Fortune. "Here's something to keep you warm on those cold winter nights in the high country."

Fortune reached for the handbill. "Thanks. Where do you suppose she went?" He didn't try to hide his interest from Sampson this time.

"Where do you think? She found a man to look after her and was out of the Palace by noon. Her act was over, and her manager had skipped town. So she did what any actress would do."

A glum aura settled over both men as Sampson's harsh words hung in the air. Win didn't dispute them, because they were undoubtedly true. He only wished he'd been able to offer her an arrangement first.

Sampson's thoughts were more complicated. He didn't want the lovely Aphrodite for himself. He had all the woman he wanted in a charming widow named Mrs. Freeman, a woman of considerable passion and great independence. Since his wife had died six years ago, Mrs. Freeman had taken care of his every need in bed, but she'd forced him to rely on himself in other ways.

Sampson had grown to appreciate this quality more than he would have believed. Their loving wasn't a crutch for either of them; it was a gift given freely and thoughtfully. Neither wanted anything more.

Sampson's mind returned to the problem at hand. He was certain that Fortune would not win the legacy. In darker moments he wondered if Win would even live to see the matter resolved.

He genuinely liked Winslow Fortune. He hadn't planned on liking the young woodsman any more than he liked his obnoxious cousins or his arrogant grandfather. But he did, and he hated like hell to see a couple of degenerates like the Rockwell brothers beat him. Alas, the deck was too heavily stacked in their favor.

In an attempt to lighten the atmosphere, he asked, "Do you want to do something wild and wicked on your last night in the city?"

Win nodded. "Actually, I was just thinking about having a night on the town. I'm ready to be led astray."

"Not in those clothes, you aren't. First you have to visit my tailor. Then we'll do the town."

"Your tailor? Damnation! That's what you told me last spring, and he made me some clothes I never picked up. I wonder if he still has them. I think I even paid him."

Sampson laughed. "Get yourself over there and find out. I'll pick you up at your hotel about eight."

"You'll never be satisfied," Win grumbled, "until I start looking like a city dude."

"Never fear, Winslow, even Mendel's not that good! You'll always look like a savage, no matter what you wear. I just want you to resemble a *tamed* one. Now, get out of here. I have important work to do, people to see—"

"And a teacher to find for my school!"

"Yes, and perhaps even that."

* * *

Harlan's expression as he looked her over made Moll feel like a horse on the auction block. She was surprised he didn't open her mouth to check her teeth.

She clenched her jaw and awaited comment on the suit he and his brother had purchased for her. Finally he gave her a short nod.

"Does that mean it's all right?" Moll had shed her exotic accent when she left the Palace, and her tone now bespoke Baltimore. "Well, it isn't. It's awful. It's ugly!"

She gestured toward the severely tailored black wool kersey suit trimmed only with a single silk cord on the cuff and collar, worn over a white silk fitted shirtwaist. Even the hat, a black castor velvet toque, was simple to the extreme. Her uniform at the convent school had been more attractive than this!

"I can't wear this. I look like a nun in it."

"The hell you do, sister. Even if you wore a veil, you'd still look like the cheap tart you are. Cheap and easy." He took a step toward her.

Moll didn't flinch. In a flash she removed the huge jet-jeweled hatpin from the toque and held it poised for action.

"Just try it, duck-butt," she said. Being well acquainted with the saloon scene, she called him the latest common slur for a short man. "Try it, and you'll be worthless to your Barbary Coast trull or any other woman."

Already Moll had learned to loathe Harlan Rockwell and his prissy brother Sheldon. If it wasn't for the money, she'd have slammed the door on them. A duck-butt and a sweet man—what a combination! Could she have done worse by letting some man set her up as his mistress?

At least I'll be free doing this job. One year. That's all it would be. One year, and she'd leave California with her pockets lined and her head held high.

Then she'd take the East by storm! *The Love Goddess* would live again, and she, Aphrodite, would be adored by millions.

Sheldon Rockwell entered the room without bothering to knock. Since he'd paid the cheap roominghouse fee, he felt he had a right to walk in.

He didn't seem to notice the confrontation—Harlan red-faced and angry and Moll clutching the lethal hatpin—as his mind was elsewhere.

"You're dressed. Good. Let's get you to Levine's office. You have an appointment in a half hour. I sent a note in your name, applying for the job in this newspaper." He handed her a two-day-old copy of the *Daily News*. "I've hired you a cab. Levine will be anxious to look you over."

"I'm sure he will." Harlan gave a nasty laugh. He knew how desperate Winslow Fortune was for a teacher. He also knew exactly why the last teacher had left, and where the rumors about the Summit School had started.

Sheldon cast him a quelling glance. One of his worst fears was that Harlan's loose mouth would give their whole game away.

"But we don't want Levine to see us or know that we're connected to you in any way. We don't want him to suspect you aren't the real thing."

"I can't go visit your lawyer looking like this," Moll

said. She was appalled at the thought of appearing in public, and even in a dusty lawyer's office, wearing the dreary black suit. Who would hire such a dowdy-looking woman? "This suit is all wrong."

Sheldon pulled a heavy, gold pocket watch from his vest and checked the time. Then he snapped the engraved lid shut.

"It will have to do, even if you don't like it. You'll be late for your appointment if you don't leave now."

"Why rush?" Harlan said. "Nobody else is going to take the job."

"I can't go anywhere looking like this," Moll said.

"You're going! Now! I want this stage production on the road as soon as possible, and I want my life back in order." With that, Sheldon flung open the door and strode out of the room.

"Into the carriage, fancy lady," Harlan ordered, his day now completed by seeing his dull brother in such a state of fuss. "Let's see if you can at least manage to *act* like a lady."

Harlan's words were bravely insolent, but he was careful to stay at arm's length from the flashing-eyed tartar and her hatpin. He'd thought about tumbling her, but he recognized her survival instincts.

He guessed that she'd use the deadly hatpin, or any other weapon at hand, if she had to. In a way, he respected that trait in her, but he'd be damned glad when she left San Francisco so his world could return to normal.

Harlan liked life fast and nasty, and he resented any-body who interfered with his routine. He slammed the door of the carriage. "When the interview is over meet us at the Poodle Dog Cafe. We'll be waiting."

*   *   *

The law offices of Morton and Levine were exactly what Moll had expected: large, wood-paneled, and crammed with books.

She steeled herself for the interview with the lawyer, praying that she looked the part. Her displeasure with the black tailored suit abated somewhat when she saw the moonstruck expression on the law clerk's face. She hoped the handsome youth's fervent gaze meant approval.

Her heart rate accelerated when the clerk opened the heavy door to announce her, and her hands turned icy. She took a deep breath and entered.

Known around San Francisco as a lawyer of considerable eloquence and style, Sampson Levine saw himself as something of a thespian—an actor, a player of parts. He seldom was at a loss for words or actions, and he had a marvelous ability for thinking on his feet.

But he nearly ruined his image when Jenkins ushered Aphrodite Zenos into his office. Totally astonished, he stared in silence at the lovely woman.

Fortunately, the blushing Jenkins overturned a brass umbrella stand by the door, allowing Sampson time to regain his composure.

He walked around his desk to greet her, noting the tasteful suit she wore.

"Mr. Levine," Jenkins said formally, "may I present Miss Mollene Kennedy of Baltimore, Maryland."

"Miss Kennedy," Sampson said, taking the gloved hand she held out to him. He could hardly believe his luck!

Moll relaxed a bit at the pleased expression in the

lawyer's eyes. Maybe this wouldn't be so bad, after all.

"Mr. Levine," she said demurely, in her best teacher's voice.

"Mr. Levine," Jenkins said, "Miss Kennedy would like to apply for the position of teacher at the school in Summit."

"Ah, yes. Please be seated."

Moll sat with grace, feeling more in control now. At least her knees wouldn't give out while he interviewed her.

"How long have you been in San Francisco, Miss Kennedy?" Sampson asked. He decided the best approach was to simulate a real interview. She didn't need to know how desperate they were.

He listened carefully to her rehearsed answer. She'd been in the city nearly a month and was living with an elderly relative. She wanted the teaching job because the old woman had unexpectedly taken sick, and Moll wished to help out with finances.

Sampson felt a wave of admiration. The girl's motives were perfect. She sounded so noble and caring. Now, if she could convince him that she could perform in the classroom, he'd hire her. He had some interesting plans for Miss Mollene Kennedy of Baltimore.

Whenever Sampson spoke to her, Moll lowered her thick lashes shyly and paused in order to give herself plenty of time to respond with her rehearsed answers. Would he really consider her for the job? She wanted the role so badly she almost believed her spiel herself. Had she convinced him?

Nobody had told Moll how desperate Winslow Fortune was for a teacher, so she thought she had competition. Nobody had mentioned the numerous other teachers who had been sent to the school but hadn't stayed.

Moll was under the impression that Summit was a normal little town, similar to the small towns in Maryland where she had been raised. She also imagined the Summit school to be like the one she had attended— not a convent school, of course, but a large, strictly run institution. The thought of teaching in such a school worried her.

So did Sampson Levine. Moll watched him stroke his moustache and saw the expression in his brown eyes grow humorous. Had she said something amusing, or stupid?

Actually, Sampson was contemplating Winslow Fortune's reaction when the love goddess arrived on his doorstep and announced that she was his schoolmarm. His quick mind worked furiously as he asked the actress questions and listened to her pat answers.

"Have you much experience as a teacher? You look very young."

"I'm twenty-two, Mr. Levine. Not young at all," Moll answered. Sometimes she felt very old, indeed. She'd led a precarious life in the past four years.

"So you've taught before?"

"I've taught some, but actually not a great deal." Like all successful liars, Moll stuck closely to the truth. "I worked for over a year in a convent-run orphanage. I taught there. I even taught some children to speak English."

"The name of the school?"

"Our Lady of Hope," Moll answered, translating the name of the Panamanian orphanage into English.

She's damned good, Sampson thought. He wondered if Win would dismiss him if he hired her. He realized the moment of truth had come, for both of them.
"How did you meet Sheldon Rockwell?"

Moll blinked in astonishment, but her lovely face
was controlled in an instant. "Pardon me?"

"I asked how you met Sheldon Rockwell, the man
who wrote the note for your appointment."

She froze.

"Dammit, I'm sick of all the nonsense! Doesn't the
fool know I'd be bound to recognize his script? Now
what is your connection to him?"

"I don't understand what you mean."

"Do you actually want this job? Or is this all a sham,
a performance?"

Moll wasn't sure what had happened, but she recognized the steel in the lawyer's voice. "Yes, I want the
job. I need it very badly."

"Badly enough to tell the truth?"

Moll opened her mouth to make a retort, but Sampson's
steely gaze stopped her cold.

"Don't bother to lie. I'm very good at knowing when
people are lying to me. So far your performance has
been excellent, and I've enjoyed it. But the game is
over. I was at the Majestic Theater last night when your
act went up in flames."

A flush crept up Moll's face. Then tears of anger
and embarrassment stung her eyes. He was laughing at
her! She jumped to her feet and started toward the
door.

Once again Sampson's voice stopped her. "I think
the critics were too hard on you. Certainly the play was
untried, but it was delightful in conception. I was
enjoying it before that torch fell."

Moll looked back over her shoulder. "Is that the truth?"

"Yes. I went by the Palace Hotel during my lunch today. I was going to see if there was anything I could do to assist you until you could find another production."

"But—"

"You had already checked out, and I understand your bill was paid by an urbane gentleman."

"Yes—"

Sampson smiled. "I'll admit, Sheldon Rockwell was the last man I'd have expected to become your protector, until you showed up here. And I'll also admit I'm disappointed. From the goddess of love to a treacherous spy is quite a comedown."

Moll's blue eyes flashed. "And what kind of position would you have offered me, Mr. Levine?"

"As a teacher at the Summit School, if I could satisfy myself that you could handle the job. I wanted to know if besides ciphering and reading you could teach the children about the arts—teach poetry and singing. Maybe put on little plays?"

Moll's face lit up. "Oh, yes."

Sampson knew she wasn't playacting now. No one could feign such sparkle, such fire. He could tell that she truly wanted the position he was offering, even if it wasn't on the stage. And she wanted it for herself, not for Sheldon Rockwell.

In that moment Sampson felt certain that Mollene Kennedy, or whatever her real name was, intended to give this job all she had in her. He wondered if he had not misjudged her from the beginning. Being a rich man's toy would be so much easier than teaching school.

"It's a one-room school, Miss Kennedy. The teacher has all eight grades. Do you think you could do it?"

"Yes." The word stuck in her throat. He actually wanted to hire her! "Yes, I can do it."

"Summit is an isolated village, a long ways from any town of decent size. There won't be much social life."

The hopeful expression on Moll's face didn't change at all, so the lawyer continued. "And your employer, Winslow Fortune, is hard and demanding. He'll expect your best and won't listen to excuses for failure. You'll either love him or hate him—but you'll have to respect and obey him. Are you still interested?"

"Yes, I am! And I do need the job."

Sampson didn't know what he'd expected of the woman who had posed for that titillating poster which had been hung on every signboard and alley wall in the city. But it was not honest girlish enthusiasm.

"Very good, Miss Kennedy. The position is yours, on one condition."

Her stomach clenched, but, other than the unconscious straightening of her back, there was no outward indication that Moll dreaded hearing what that condition was to be.

"Winslow Fortune, despite what you have been told by Sheldon Rockwell, is a very good man—perhaps the best and most honest man either you or I will ever meet. I will not have him hurt anymore by the evil doings of the Rockwell brothers.

"Sheldon hired you to spy for him. Oh, don't bother to deny it. I know how his mind works. You aren't the first spy he's sent up there, and you probably won't be the last."

Moll's defenses came to the fore. "If you think I'm going to spy for him, and you also think he's out to hurt your Mr. Fortune, why are you giving me the job?"

"Because you'll also be my spy."

"What?"

"Yes. I want to know the details of everything you tell the Rockwells. That may be the only way I can make sure Winslow Fortune comes out of this mess alive."

Moll's eyes grew large in her pale face. "They only want him to lose the legacy, Mr. Levine—not die!"

"Don't mislead yourself. They intend to have that money. They'll do whatever it takes to get it. Already, property has been destroyed and people hurt. The worst is yet to come."

"Why are you telling me this?"

"Because it wouldn't be right to send you up there without apprising you of the true situation."

"Are you always so honest, Mr. Levine? What is your stake in this?"

Sampson moved the inkwell on his desk a fraction of an inch. Then he looked straight into Moll's eyes.

"I was Aaron Winslow's attorney and am now the executor of his estate. I get paid no matter how this stupid affair is settled."

"So there's no advantage to you one way or the other?"

"Financially, no."

"But you want Mr. Fortune to succeed."

Sampson moved away from his desk, to stand before the window, looking out on Market Street, his hands clasped behind him.

"I would like to see the legacy awarded to Fortune

because he has worked so hard to bring his grandfather's dream to reality. But I don't think it will be. The old man stupidly insisted on thrusting the onus of the whole project upon Win. All the Rockwells have to do is wait for him to fail.

"I tried to convince Aaron to make the heirs all work together to inherit. But he wanted it his way—and no other."

"Perhaps Mr. Winslow was senile."

Sampson emitted a bark of a laugh as he turned back to Moll. "Oh, no! He was stubborn, vain, and arrogant, but definitely of sound mind—unfortunately. If I could have proved otherwise, this mess would never have come about. But it has. And as Win says, we just have to play the hand to the end. It's an ugly situation. Are you sure you want to be involved?"

"I'm already involved. Mr. Rockwell has paid my debts. I cannot afford to renege on the deal now."

Sampson lifted an inquiring brow.

"I'm broke! I have no one to manage my act—if I even had an act. I have nowhere else to go. And besides that, those Rockwells are mean."

Sampson nodded. "You don't know the half of it." He walked to the window and gazed out. Then he faced Moll again. "Have you carefully considered the danger of the situation in Summit?"

"What's a little danger compared to starvation?" she snapped in exasperation.

"Very well, Miss Kennedy. The position is yours. I'll inform Win I've hired a teacher and tell him to meet the Friday train in Placerville. Make sure you're on it. Winslow Fortune would never forgive you if he made arrangements to have you collected and you missed the train!"

Moll frowned. "Any pointers about how to get along with this difficult man?"

He gave her a mischievous grin. "Just be your own utterly delightful self!"

"Wouldn't that raise his eyebrows above his hairline?"

"Well, it's true Win's father was a hard-nosed preacher, but he's trying to overcome that handicap."

Moll laughed aloud and held out her hand. "Mr. Levine, it's been a pleasure meeting you."

Sampson took her hand and raised it to his lips, his eyes twinkling. "I assure you, dear lady, the pleasure has been all mine."

He walked her toward the door. "One more thing. Small-town postmasters are notoriously nosy. Perhaps you should invent two aunts to send your reports to. And send mine to my home address."

The man waiting in Sampson's outer office eyed Moll appreciatively as she swept through it and disappeared down the stairs. Then, when he realized the lawyer was watching him, he jumped to his feet.

"Mr. Levine? I'm Jed Cantrell, and I'd like to see Winslow Fortune. I understand he's a client of yours."

Sampson tilted his head thoughtfully. The day continued to be full of surprises.

"Come in and tell me about it."

Jed Cantrell was a tall, wiry, muscular man in his thirties. His dark blond hair had not been cut recently, and he reached a work-worn hand up to push the hair out of his eyes, which were a startling shade of green.

"I'm sorry to barge in like this, but Mr. Fortune got away before I could properly thank him for taking care of the kids during the train wreck."

This was the first Sampson had heard of Fortune's being a hero.

"My brother's children were on the train with Mr. Fortune yesterday. They're coming to live with me. My brother and his wife were killed a couple of weeks ago, and the kids don't have anybody else but me now. My nephew told me how kind Mr. Fortune was to them."

"I'll tell Winslow you came by."

"Thanks. I'm afraid my manners were pretty rough yesterday. I was upset about the children coming in the first place. And when I heard about the accident, I was a wild man. Losing my job yesterday didn't help."

"What kind of work do you do, Mr. Cantrell?"

"I've been a miner for years. My specialty is blasting."

"How good are you?"

Cantrell eyed the lawyer. "I can lay a charge that takes out exactly what you want, and nothing else."

"So why were you sacked?" Sampson asked.

"I was told to do something that was very unsafe and possibly deadly. I'm no fool. I wasn't ready to blow myself to hell—and I told the boss that. We argued, and he swung at me. He fired me after I knocked him in a mud hole."

"Sit down, please. This may be my day for solving Winslow Fortune's problems."

Cantrell took the chair Sampson offered him and waited for Sampson to go on.

"Mr. Fortune has been having some trouble lately

with his powder monkeys. He may be very interested in talking to you." Sampson glanced at the grandfather clock in the corner. "He should be here shortly, if you'd care to wait."

Cantrell nodded.

"How did you know to come to me?" Sampson did not believe in coincidences.

"The train conductor had sent you a telegram for Mr. Fortune, and he remembered doing so."

"Ah." Sampson reached into the cabinet to the right of his desk. "Would you care for a brandy while we wait?"

Sometime later, Sheldon and Harlan Rockwell left the Poodle Dog Cafe in a hired carriage. They had finished their business with Moll, but not before she had gotten sufficient cash from them to purchase a decent wardrobe for her new role as a schoolteacher.

Actually, Sheldon was so pleased she'd managed to fool Levine that he gave her a generous amount. What were a few dollars compared to the millions they were going to get? He was still in an expansive mood when he told the driver to take them to the Merchant's Exchange.

A block or so away, however, he spied one of Moll's infamous posters tacked to a building.

"Good God!" he exclaimed. "What if one of those disgusting handbills were to reach Summit? Cousin Win would know she's a spy."

Harlan guffawed. "If he saw the damned thing, he wouldn't be looking at her face!"

Sheldon sighed. "Maybe you're right."

"What happens if the lovely Miss Kennedy decides

to sink her hooks into Cousin Win and haul him to the altar, Sheldon?"

"Don't be stupid. What would a preacher's son want with that fulsome jade?"

"The same thing most men would want—normal men, that is." Harlan never let an opportunity pass to remind his brother of his unconventional inclinations.

Sheldon brushed a pastry crumb from his neat linen cuff and let the slur pass.

"Preacher's son or not," Harlan continued, "Cousin Win is a stallion . . . not a gelding."

"Gash it, brother," Sheldon said.

"Bugger it, brother," Harlan replied.

They smiled nastily at each other, then continued their discussion. In spite of their deep and bitter differences, they were devoted to each other.

"A tumble or two could muddy a man's thinking. She could make him decide he needs it so much he'd marry her to keep her around. I know how women think, especially greedy ones like her."

"I doubt that she'll try," Sheldon said. "We're paying her well enough to keep her loyalty."

"Not eight million and Cousin Win's prospects besides, we ain't," Harlan insisted. "There's nothing to keep her from trying."

"There sure as hell is, Harlan. Remember those dirty, lewd posters tacked up all over? Cousin Win would dump her in a minute if he ever saw one of those. A little friendly blackmail should keep our pretty schoolteacher in line."

Harlan laughed loudly. "It should. But what if it doesn't? She's a real greedy bitch."

"If she gets too greedy, she'll just disappear into the night the same way the last one did. Summit is a long ways from civilization, brother. The ridge is high, the gorge is deep, and the river is wild. A woman alone and unprotected could easily have an accident."

4

"Hang on, Teacher!" the teen-aged Eddie Hodges hollered, though the sound of his voice was barely audible above the roar of the raging river in the deep gorge below.

If Moll held on any tighter her fingers would be imbedded in the wood of the wagon itself. She clung to her perch and prayed she'd live to reach her new job. She also tried very hard not to look down for fear she'd fall out of the wagon and plunge over the sheer cliff.

She silently berated herself for her habit of jumping headlong into things and began cursing Sheldon Rockwell for not explaining that Winslow Fortune's logging camp—and the little village of Summit—were a lot more than just rural.

He'd told her it was a few miles north of Placerville, but somehow he'd failed to mention the terrifying drive in a swaying buckboard on a trail blasted out of the side of a mountain.

The road switched back on itself so many times that it was possible to see stretches of the trail both above and below them. The mountain dropped straight down at the outside of the narrow road. There was no leeway for error. As she clutched the wagon and gritted her teeth to keep from crying out, Moll was convinced that the trek down into the American River canyon and back up the next mountain ridge would be the death of her.

If she hadn't been so frightened, she would have demanded to be let out. But where? On the driver's side the wagon almost touched the moss clinging to the granite walls, and on the passenger side the wheels seemed barely inches away from the edge.

Finally, after what seemed like an eternity, the wagon arrived at a narrow bridge that spanned the deep, churning water below. Eddie urged the horses into a tiny turn-out and pulled them to a stop. Moll looked up in astonishment.

"Uh, I thought we'd stop a minute." He blushed furiously. "And stretch our legs a bit. It's the only chance between here and the top. Would you like me to help you down, Ma'am?"

"Ah, no, thank you. I believe I'll just stretch and relax right here. But you go right ahead. You're the one who's been driving."

Eddie shrugged and went off on his own errand, leaving Moll to stare down at the river below and the spray it created as the water struck the mammoth boulders with a mighty force. Then it frothed and foamed as it hurtled downstream toward the next huge barrier.

That this river was to be used for commercial purposes seemed insane!

Eddie returned, climbed up on the wagon, and backed the horses up in line with the narrow bridge. Determined not to act like a ninny in front of one of her students, Moll was silent—until the bridge swayed under the weight of the horses and buckboard.

"It's falling!" she screamed.

"No, Ma'am." Eddie sounded delighted at her reaction. "It's a swinging bridge."

"Oh, my God!" Moll wondered if things could possibly get worse. Then she saw that the road at the other end of the bridge rose straight up.

Her mouth went dry as she imagined the horses and wagon tumbling backward off the sheer incline.

"Don't worry, Miz Kennedy," Eddie reassured her, trying to play the role of the responsible, comforting male. "The worst part is over."

Moll didn't know if he was right or if he was simply trying to keep her from getting hysterical. She had tried clamping her eyes shut to close out what she couldn't bear to watch, but she couldn't tune out the sounds of the wild river below. Maybe the Rockwells were correct in believing that only a lunatic would ever dream that the American River was usable. Maybe lunacy ran in the family.

She breathed a long sigh of relief when she sensed the ascent becoming less steep, but she didn't release her death grip on the wagon seat. She did open her eyes, however, thankful to be away from the yawning canyon and the din of the roaring river before the sun went down. The idea of traveling through this wild country without the sun to guide them was unbearable, even if Eddie did know this country like the back of his hand, as he'd assured her more than once.

He pulled the wagon off the road and into the shade of some tall, sugar-pine trees. "I'm going to let the horses stop and blow here for a few minutes, Teacher. That was a stiff pull for them. Would you like to get down and walk around a bit?"

"Oh, yes, I would!" Moll accepted the boy's help in alighting. When she was firmly on the ground she walked around the wagon a couple of times, twisting this way and that to work the kinks out of her back. From high up in the tall pine trees, a furious outburst came from a blue jay, followed by a concerted chorus from a dozen others.

Moll tipped her head back as far as possible to look up and find the jays, but the brim of her hat was in the way. She pulled out the jeweled hatpin, removed the hat from her head, and resumed searching for the birds.

She watched with interest as a large blue jay made a swooping dive toward the wagon, until she realized its target was her hat! The bird tried to wrest the jewel from her hatpin, but it held fast. With a loud squawk it flew back up into the tree branches and readied itself for another run.

Moll dashed toward the tree, yelling and waving her arms. "Stop that, you thief! That's my only good hat. Shoo! Go away!" The jay made an angry screech, rose straight in the air, and dropped its calling card on the silk hat with a juicy plop.

Moll was furious at the bird, and Eddie Hodges was blushing all the way to the roots of his hair. Without a word, they climbed back on the wagon and resumed their journey, Moll clutching the soiled hat in dismay.

"This is Summit," Eddie told her a couple of hours later as they approached several buildings. The village was even smaller than she'd expected. She hoped that not all of her expectations about this role and this place were overblown.

The wagon bumped along a dusty path and finally came to a halt. Eddie set the brake with his left foot and wrapped the reins around it.

"Well, here we are," he announced cheerfully.

She closed her eyes to offer profound thanksgiving. Surely everything that could happen to her in one day already had.

Before she realized what was happening, she was lifted from the secure wagon seat by a pair of strong arms and placed firmly on the soft, pine-scented earth. Moll's eyes fluttered open, but her knees became weak, and her fingers numb. The hat tumbled unnoticed to the ground.

Damn, she felt so tired. Her mind seemed astonishingly blank.

"Hey, are you all right?" a deep, gruff voice demanded.

"I think the road scared her, Win," the youth said. "She's had her eyes closed most of the way since we started across the bridge."

"Eddie, I told you to drive nice and slow."

"Dang it, Win, I didn't drive fast. She's just a flatlander. City people ain't used to country roads. And then the bird crappin' on her hat didn't help any, either."

Moll heard the words floating around her dizzy head, but she paid them little attention. She was counting her blessings for being firmly on the ground with a pair of muscular arms holding her upright while her weary head rested against a solid male chest. Her senses were lulled by the steady, comforting beat of his heart.

A female screech snapped her out of her safety cocoon and thrust her back into the role she was playing. It was just as well, too, for Moll had only felt safe in the arms of one man, and he had died much too soon.

She stumbled out of the strong embrace and opened her eyes to the real world. She was standing beside the buckboard in front of a white, two-story frame house in a yard with pink and red hollyhocks, but all she could see was the man who'd held her. She could hear the voices of people coming and Eddie talking to the horses. But she stood frozen to the spot, captured by the steely gray stare of the tall, rugged man before her.

His lean face was far from handsome, yet it was compelling, drawing her like a magnet. Moll could hardly breathe. Her instincts told her that the man gazing back at her with the same reluctant fascination could be ruthless and dangerous.

She opened her mouth to say something—anything to break the incredible tension between them—but no words came. Instead, the tip of her pink tongue peeked out between her lips, then instantly disappeared again. The man's gaze followed its motion and remained on her sensuous mouth. One second passed, and then another. A chill touched her heart at the look that passed over his face. Was it annoyance, anger, or disbelief? It seemed like a cynical combination of all three.

What had she done to elicit such a reaction? She'd never seen the man before. She took two steps backward and looked down at the ground.

She heard the chatter of a high-pitched female voice and a soft male reply, one of the horses shaking its head and Eddie reassuring it, footsteps inside the house and the creak of the screen door as it opened.

Then a woman with honey-blond hair burst out onto the front porch. She was hugely pregnant, and the full, loose black dress she wore did little to hide it.

"I'm Cassie Hall," the woman called in a cheerful if somewhat breathless voice as she made her way awkwardly down the porch steps, not waiting for the man beside her to help as she hurried across the small yard to the wagon. "And this is my husband, Sebastian," she said before the man could introduce himself. He didn't seem to mind, but just smiled and nodded to Moll.

Cassie grasped Moll's hand. "Bas," she said, "don't stand there lollygagging—get the girl's trunk into the house. She probably wants to change out of that traveling suit. And you, Win Fortune, stop staring at her! You're embarrassing her. See, she's blushing."

Moll definitely was blushing, fiery red. Win Fortune. Winslow Fortune! This was the man she'd been hired to spy on. She didn't notice the chagrined look on his face, because she was too busy chastising herself for having gazed into his cloudy gray eyes only moments before.

The tension eased when Eddie Hodges opened the back of the wagon so Win and Sebastian could get Moll's trunk.

"I'm so glad you've come!" Cassie told Moll. "I've been so lonely here since I left my mother."

Moll was surprised at the sadness in the other

woman's voice and wondered what it would be like living with her own mother. "Are you new here, too?"

Cassie nodded. "We moved over to camp this summer. But everybody's new here except the McDonalds. Hannah McDonald's father homesteaded this land, and this house belongs to her sister, Mabel Francis. When Win came, he built the logging camp and the town of Summit. 'Course it ain't much—there's only five women over there. I've been so hungry for company!"

Cassie paused long enough to catch her breath and glance over at the wagon. "Would you look at that?"

Moll turned her head toward the two men who were straining to lift the trunk they'd slid down out of the wagon.

"It took four of those baggage handlers at the station to get that in the wagon," Eddie said.

"Now you tell us!" Fortune muttered, the muscles in his arms and shoulders bulging beneath his linen shirt.

"What the devil you got in here?" Sebastian Hall asked, his face flushed with exertion. "Cannon balls?"

"Only my clothes and some fashion magazines," Moll answered, hiding her embarrassment. She was sorry it was so heavy, but everything she owned in the world was stuffed into that trunk.

"What about this, Miz Kennedy?" Eddie asked as he lugged the leather satchel out of the wagon.

"Those are my school books. You can just put them on the porch for now."

The men breathed heavily as they carried the trunk

past the two women and struggled to get it up the five wooden steps to the porch.

"Just put the trunk inside the door, Bas," Cassie said. "If Miss Kennedy has new fashion magazines in there, I want to look at them while we drink our tea. Living in Summit is no excuse for being unfashionable."

Moll was looking forward to the tea and whatever food Cassie had to go with it, but the thought of having to go through her trunk in Cassie Hall's parlor was daunting. The magazines had been packed under her toga and tights.

"Your figure's not very fashionable at the moment, Cassie," Sebastian Hall teased. "I'll bet there isn't one picture in any magazine with a dress for you."

Cassie's face colored. "This won't last much longer, Bas. *Then* I'm going to be the most fashionable woman in all of Summit. Oh, you dropped your pretty hat . . . ohhhhh!" Cassie wrinkled her nose. "Eddie, put that dirty thing on the porch. I'll send it home with Hildy Swensen. Maybe she can get the bird nack off it."

Determined not to let anything interfere with her long-awaited pleasure, Cassie continued to shepherd Moll along. "I have a big surprise for you," she went on as they walked into the house. There was a mahogany spool table in the hallway with a vase of flowers made from seashells.

Moll tensed. She didn't want any more surprises today.

"In here," Cassie said, pointing Moll to the parlor.

Four women, in their Sunday best, sat primly on the red velvet furniture. It was obvious they'd been waiting some time.

"All my neighbors have come for a tea party," Cassie gushed, as delighted over Moll's conspicuous astonishment as a little girl would be.

The other women looked on in silence, watching the new teacher turn a shade paler than when she had gotten off the wagon. They'd witnessed the goings-on outside from behind the lacy curtains at the window, of course, and had only just sat down.

They'd seen the teacher practically faint in Winslow Fortune's embrace, and three of them had exchanged speculative glances, while making a point of not looking to see how Hildy Swensen was taking it.

The girl was shy enough, no use letting her know they were all aware of how she felt about Fortune. They were all for the match, because Win needed a good woman and Hildy would make him a solid, true wife. With so little entertainment available, the best sport of all was minding everybody else's business.

Moll's courage faltered. She hadn't expected a welcoming committee. She wasn't prepared to sit through sweet tea and small talk with strangers.

"How nice," she mumbled. This was going to be awful.

"Cassie, this girl is wobbly from her ride," said a plump, round-faced woman with graying brown hair. It was an Irish face, no doubt about that—ivory skin, rosy cheeks, and hardly a wrinkle despite her fifty years. She wore her hair knotted beneath a sensible blue hat and had a dress that matched her cornflower eyes. "She needs some mint tea to settle her stomach."

"Oh!" Cassie flitted off, and a young blond woman followed.

"Have you eaten, girl?" a bulky, buck-toothed woman with a strident voice asked. The huge scarlet hat on her coarse gray hair bobbed precariously and clashed hideously with her maroon dress.

"No."

"Well, I'm starving," the woman said. "We've waited nearly an hour." She rose stiffly, because of her tight corset, and strode toward the kitchen.

"I'm sorry," Moll said, feeling responsible for their wait.

The rosy-faced woman looked exasperated. "Don't pay any attention to Selma, dear. That's just her way. Sit down here and rest. We'll get something to eat in a moment, and you'll feel better. I'm Hannah McDonald, by the way, and this is Mildred Franklin."

"How do you do?" Mildred said.

Mildred was a thin woman in her late forties, elaborately dressed in a plum boucle suit trimmed with heavy black lace, and an expensive hat. She looked out-of-place and uncomfortable in the fussy parlor with the other women.

Selma came back into the parlor with a heavy tray. Before Moll knew it, she was eating tiny, triangle-shaped, chopped-egg sandwiches and little biscuits filled with ham.

"I'm Selma Stoneleigh. This here is Hildy Swensen." She nodded toward the young blond woman, who set down a plate of jelly tarts. "She's from Sweden. And you met Cassie, a' course. We're the only women who live within ten miles of this godforsaken place."

Moll sank back into the sofa with a sigh. Then she shivered. The room was chilly in spite of the autumn warmth outside. Cassie, who'd just brought in a spice cake, noticed her guest's discomfort immediately.

"Bas, be a darling and build me a little fire while I get the tea. No, no, everybody, stay put. That's what husbands are for. I'll only be a minute. Bas, come help before you start in there."

Moll wished she had a few moments alone to gather her wits. Being so tired and unsettled was not like her. She blamed the noisy roominghouse where she'd spent the week, as well as the train trip and the harrowing wagon journey to the logging camp—not to mention the other catastrophes she had survived recently. But it would be ungracious to sit there silently.

"The sandwiches are very good," Moll finally said.

"Have more—they're dinky."

"Selma!" Hannah McDonald said.

Fortune sauntered past the parlor door, nodding to the women but not stopping, and went into the kitchen. He and Sebastian laughed about something.

Moll tried to ignore the nagging confusion in her mind caused by Fortune's presence. She would worry about that later. For now, she needed to concentrate on befriending the only women she might meet all year.

Fortune entered the parlor and dropped the leather satchel on the hardwood floor with a thud, and Moll gasped.

"Sorry, I didn't mean to startle you." He walked over to where she sat. "I forgot to introduce myself. I'm Winslow Fortune. I own the Summit Logging and Lumber Company."

Moll's pounding heart hadn't yet calmed itself, but she managed to effect a chilly reserve about her as she held out her hand. "I'm pleased to meet you, Mr. Fortune. I'm Mollene Kennedy."

"Yes, our new teacher. As head of the school board, I'm also your employer." He took her slender hand in his and held on to it. His gray eyes carried an almost insolent glint, as though he were laughing at her. And as he continued to hold her hand captive, anger washed over Moll.

Three pairs of curious eyes watched the exchange, and one pair filled with consternation and jealousy.

"Would you pass the scones, Mildred? They're excellent," Hannah McDonald said.

The clatter of teacups jostling on a tray brought them both back to their civilized manners. Win dropped Moll's hand and stepped away from the sofa just as Cassie walked in with the tray.

"Oh good, Win, you didn't leave," she chirped. "I brought you a cup. Stay and have some tea with us."

"Sorry, ladies, I can't. I've got to get back to work. Besides, afternoon tea isn't my strong point." His eyes barely touched Moll's, then ricocheted away. "You'll have more fun without any men around. Bas, are you coming?"

Sebastian was liberally helping himself to some of the cookies heaped on a hand-painted plate. "As soon as I get a few more of Cassie's special chocolate cookies." He stopped to throw a final log on the blazing fire, then turned to leave.

"Miss Kennedy," Fortune said politely, "it has been a pleasure making your acquaintance. Ladies." The performance was for everyone else's benefit, and

Moll well knew it. She recognized a good act when she saw it.

Cassie beamed like a proud parent, and Moll wasn't about to spoil things for her hostess. She smiled demurely at Fortune and met his gaze.

"The pleasure is mine, Mr. Fortune. Thank you for hiring me as Summit's schoolteacher."

"I'm sure you'll find it a challenge," he said.

For a second Moll felt uneasy. Surely he didn't know she also worked for the Rockwells. That she was an imposter, a spy instead of a teacher. No, of course he didn't, he couldn't possibly know. She was imagining things.

Moll hadn't been invited to very many tea parties in her life. At school she'd heard other girls talking about them, and her feelings had been hurt because she'd never been invited. But if this one was any indication of what she'd missed, she'd had a better time with the convent gardener, learning to roll cigarettes and swear.

Cassie Hall giggled, and Hildy Swensen blushed. Selma Stoneleigh talked too loud and too much. Mildred Franklin barely talked at all. Hannah McDonald was the only one Moll took to immediately.

Hannah had been right about the effects of food and mint tea on her. Moll felt better and was able to slip into the role she was playing—charming, refined, and educated, though demure enough to be a model schoolmarm.

"What about those fashion magazines?" Cassie demanded as soon as the other women had left.

"Could we leave them until tomorrow?" Moll asked sweetly. "They're at the very bottom of the trunk, and I'd rather not unpack it here in your lovely parlor. But I can tell you what the ladies in San Francisco are wearing."

Win dismounted, dashed up the wooden steps of the house which served as both his office and home, unlocked the door marked Summit Logging And Lumber Company, and stormed inside. The door slammed behind him, but he didn't notice.

His mind was awhirl with suspicion, confusion, and anger, as well as several baser emotions he wouldn't admit to.

"Damn you, Sampson!" he shouted. "How could you do this to me? All I wanted was one ordinary schoolteacher."

Maybe it was only his imagination, and Aphrodite Zenos was not sitting there drinking tea in Cassie Hall's parlor.

He threw himself into his desk chair without even noticing the accounts ledger in front of him. He was blind to anything other than the vision of the woman whose trembling body he'd held in his arms for a moment. Thunderation!

She was a very attractive woman, well formed, neat, and trim. She did look like all the other teachers who had come to Summit. At least her clothes did, except they were new and better fitting than most, as if they'd been made especially for her instead of purchased by mail order.

Still, the uncanny likeness nagged at him. He leaned far back in his chair, stretching his lean muscles, and tried to settle the question logically once and for all. Aphrodite Zenos, the actress, and Mollene Kennedy, the schoolteacher were strikingly similar. Or were they?

He'd only seen the actress once, briefly, and from a theater box. But he'd held Mollene Kennedy in his arms, inhaled the delicious violet scent of her body . . .

Win stopped himself right there. If Mollene Kennedy was to be his employee, he had to treat her the same way he would any of the other women who lived in Summit or at the logging camp. He would have to forget how his blood had churned when he'd held her luscious body in his arms.

He'd been celibate for so long, his mind was playing tricks on him. He'd imagined the teacher looked like the actress, the same way he'd imagined the teacher's reactions to him. Any fool could see that she was just a girl. He had to keep control of himself. It was up to him to set the example for the other single men.

He caught sight of the big black ledger, opened it up, and peered at the figures on the page, but he couldn't concentrate. Finally he slammed it closed. He'd work on the books later.

Ever since he'd returned from San Francisco, Win's sleep had been continually interrupted with tormenting dreams of the love goddess walking through flames, and he burned whenever he thought of the earthy dreams.

Thrusting the ledger across the desk, Win fought to get his thoughts in order. Why torture himself over wanting a woman he'd never see again? What good did those ideas do him?

He pulled at the metal cashbox from the deep bottom drawer of the oak desk, took the key from his pants pocket, and unlocked the box. He opened the battered lid to reveal the dull beauty of gold coins.

Tomorrow was payday, and he always liked to have

the exact number of coins available for the paymaster. Not a man who trusted script, Win always paid in gold.

Midway through the count, however, his mind slipped back to the brief second when a tendril of inky black hair caught by a sudden breeze had stroked his mouth, and the sweet odor of violets after a spring shower had assaulted his nostrils. The stack of gold, scattered by the jerk of his fingers, fell noisily to the pine-board floor.

Win barely had time to retrieve the coins before he heard a heavy tread on the steps leading to his house. He quickly closed the lid of the cashbox, shoved it back into the bottom drawer, and shut it. Then he eased open the top desk drawer just enough so he could reach the pistol inside.

California no longer had the reputation of being the lawless frontier. The time of the wild Gold Rush was gone forever, and a new era, one of civilization, had replaced it. But men were men, and the lure of easy money would always tempt a few from the path of righteousness.

Winslow Fortune took no chances with his payroll. Even at this time of year, when he employed only a skeleton crew, the payroll was substantial enough to merit caution. Just in case, the pistol was loaded. Win was ready.

He answered the loud knock with a gruff "Enter."

Mark Danbury, the mill boss, stuck his dark head through the door. "Mr. Fortune, are you busy?"

"Not really. Come on in and pull up a chair. What's the problem?" Danbury didn't come to the office unless there was a problem he couldn't handle. Win suspected it was the steam donkey again.

Danbury was old-fashioned to the core. He didn't believe steam engines saved time and labor, and because he didn't understand mechanical devices, he feared them.

"The donkey's acting up," Danbury said gravely, his bony face lined with concern.

"Dammit!" Win didn't know which annoyed him more, the man or the machine. The steam donkey was a simple piece of machinery that hauled the huge, heavy, sugar-pine logs to the wooden chute, which plunged a couple thousand feet down the ravine to the river below. The little donkey engine saved a tremendous amount of manpower, but it caused Win endless headaches, mostly because of Mark Danbury.

"What's the matter this time?"

"I don't know, boss. It's snorting and a'bucking. The men are scared it will blow up." Mark raised his dark bushy brows. "'Course they always think that. These new-fangled machines are a plague to both man and beast."

Win wanted to laugh at the man's foolishness. Still, hardheaded as he was about any method that hadn't been used for a hundred years, Mark Danbury was an excellent mill boss, being particularly patient with the whims and superstitions of loggers.

"Check the pressure valve, Mark. I'll be down the hill shortly, as soon as I finish up my work here. Try to keep the donkey going."

"Sure, boss. I'll try."

When the other man was gone, Win got up and locked the front door. He didn't want any more visitors until the cash was counted. Again he pulled the cash-box from the desk drawer and started to count the money. He came out twenty dollars short, but after looking around, he spotted the coin standing on its side, stuck in a crack in the floor.

That task finally completed, he wandered into the living quarters of the house to look for a bite to eat. Hannah McDonald kept his cookie jar filled, knowing his love for sweets.

He spotted the rolled-up poster on the ledge above the green-painted, dry sink the moment he walked into the kitchen. He'd laid it there when he arrived home from his trip to San Francisco and resisted the urge to unroll it ever since, because his infatuation with the actress disgusted him. He was a thirty-year-old man, not some pink-cheeked boy who got excited looking at naughty pictures.

He knew he was going to look at the handbill now, however. His hunger for sweets momentarily forgotten, Win told himself he owed it to Miss Kennedy to settle the identity question once and for all. He also owed it to himself to end forever his ridiculous attraction to the actress from the fiery Majestic Theater.

He crossed the room and took the roll in his hands. His fingers trembled as he pulled the string, dropped it on the floor, and began to unroll the poster.

Inch by inch, Aphrodite appeared to him. From the tip of her high-heeled sandals, as she perched upon a marble pedestal, the goddess grew into a remarkable, full-bodied, well-rounded woman. Win became totally engrossed in unwinding the publicity bill.

Up the trim ankles he went, to the slender calves, the graceful knees, and beyond. His body tensed as he revealed her thighs. His breathing stilled when the hem of her toga dropped into sight, barely in time to cover her most intimate treasure.

His mouth went stone dry when her wide hips narrowed to a tiny waist, which flared upward into full breasts—the kind that more than filled a man's hands with softness. Win stifled a groan. The bodice of the minuscule toga dipped low enough to reveal a shadowy valley between them.

Sonofabitch! He took a deep breath to steady himself and then quickly exposed her face. The oath he swore this time was one a preacher's son shouldn't know.

Staring back at him from the poster, tilted provocatively atop a body that made his own ache with longing, was the face of his new schoolmarm.

Win threw the poster down and stormed to the door. Then he stopped.

"Sampson Levine! This is all your doing." Win's fingers itched to wring Sampson's scrawny neck. "I'm sending you the woman you wanted," Sampson had written in his note. Win never dreamed it would be *her*. Damn her! Damn Sampson!

He turned and went back to retrieve the poster from the floor. He laid it flat on the kitchen table, and it started to roll up, so he set the sugar bowl and a jelly jar on two corners, a coffee cup and a Havana dish on the others. Then he looked at her for a long time.

"Listen, Goddess," he said, "you are made of pure, brass-plated presumption! It's amazing to me no one has strangled you yet! But if you think the flames were hot on your backside in San Francisco, just wait until I get through with you. You're lying to me with this little game of yours, and I hate liars. I'm going to scorch you for even trying!"

Then he stomped out of the room, threw himself on his horse, and headed down the hill to check the steam engine.

5

So this is Summit.

Moll wasn't certain what to think. After being inspected by all five women in town and discovering her new employer was as grouchy as he was gorgeous, she doubted she'd gotten off to a good start.

She walked over to the window and looked out at the logging camp. Cassie was out in the kitchen, checking on the roast and putting in some Irish potatoes.

She couldn't see much because of the slope of the land—only the roofs of a few buildings. A small orchard of fruit and walnut trees on the eastern side obscured the rest. But she knew she'd have plenty of time in the months ahead to see everything within miles. Probably there would be a lot more time than there would be things to see.

The parlor felt too warm, now that a big fire roared in the fireplace, so Moll opened the front door to get a breath of air. Summit had a fresh, wholesome smell, different from any place she'd been before.

Outside, the shadows were getting longer, and the afternoon light was growing dim. Soon the sun would set, and that meant Cassie's husband would be coming back home for dinner.

Even though she'd eaten at the afternoon tea, Moll was already hungry. It must have been the mountain air.

But she knew it was more than that. It was nerves. She was nervous about carrying off the role, about spying on Winslow Fortune. Now that she'd seen him up close, and even touched him, she realized what a formidable man he was.

The wafting smells of roasting pork tantalized her like the beckoning fingers of a belly dancer. She closed the door and went to the kitchen to ask Cassie if she could help. She'd never before had the opportunity to help in another woman's kitchen. It could be an interesting experience, and perhaps Cassie would be a good source of information for her to cultivate.

At the log yard, Win and the boss mechanic, Buckley Brooks, had solved the steam donkey problem. Win felt certain one of the men had caused it. He'd dealt with so many small acts of vandalism and sabotage by now that they were easy to spot. They were also costly, time consuming, and often dangerous.

He'd stopped taking the incidents personally, but he hadn't stopped getting angry. He scowled as he led his horse back up the hill to the company office. The smell of fish frying in the cookhouse told him the McDonald boys had been out fishing again today. They belonged in a schoolroom, and not down by the creek, but the loggers would be glad to have a break from regular cookhouse fare.

Win, like most of the company supervisors, foremen, and other bosses, paid for his meals at Hannah McDonald's house. She put out a big spread of excellent food, and Win was thankful for the homey atmosphere.

He sighed when he thought of Hannah McDonald. He loved her as one loves an older sister. She'd taken him under her wing the minute he arrived in Summit and had bossed him around outrageously ever since. She wanted a decent school for the children, and he'd promised to get one.

Some teacher he had gotten—off the hottest stage in San Francisco.

Win pondered as to how he would break this news to Hannah and Bill McDonald. What the devil could he tell them? That the prissy teacher who had sipped tea in Cassie's parlor this afternoon had been parading her wares for all to see on the stage just last week?

As he walked, he caught a glimpse of Hildy Swensen heading toward the McDonalds' place. Hildy, the town seamstress, helped Hannah serve the meals, so it had to be close to suppertime. He swung up on his horse, knowing this matter couldn't be delayed. He might as well get it over with.

Hildy called and waved. He waved back, but he didn't stop as he normally would have done.

He liked Hildy and admired her tireless ambition. She'd supported herself and her ten-year-old daughter since the death of her ornery, much older husband. In her late twenties, though not especially pretty, Hildy still could have had her pick from the many unattached men around, but Win suspected she wasn't ready to marry again.

Win's thoughts strayed to the new unattached woman in Summit, Mollene Kennedy. It was a damn good thing he was sending her packing. Wouldn't she cause a stir among the throng of randy bachelors in camp?

His frown deepened. He could just imagine the men lining up to call on the teacher. There'd probably be a riot the first day of school, what with all the loggers trying to get seats.

She was a fraud, a beautiful imposter, and yet, in spite of all rational thought, he desired her. It shamed and embarrassed him, but he lusted after the woman.

Drawing his gold railroad watch from his pocket, he saw that it was almost quitting time. He would talk to her before Sebastian got home. For his own peace of mind, Win needed to be rid of her as soon as he could.

He'd drive her in to Placerville himself in the morning and see that she got on the train. East or west, he didn't care, as long as she went away from him.

"How in the name of God did she think she could fake being a teacher?" he asked the gelding.

Glancing up the hill toward Sebastian Hall's place, he thought about how excited Cassie had been to have a visitor. A twinge of guilt nudged his conscience. He kept watching the house for a glimpse of the actress.

Over the years, the land between the McDonald house and the one the Halls rented had been cleared of timber and brush. The white house, which had been built by Hannah McDonald's parents after they had homesteaded their land, was the only one in Summit with the extra bedroom space for a roomer. The last teacher, Agatha Powell—the one who'd disappeared in the night—had stayed in a small house adjacent to Franklin's Emporium. Jed Cantrell and his niece and nephew lived there now.

The late-afternoon sun shone brightly on the big, old white house. It looked strangely barren, sitting up there on the hill by itself with nary a tree or shrub around it. The upstairs windows reflected the bright orange sunlight so completely that they appeared to blaze like fire.

Win stopped the horse for a second and sat back in the saddle, staring at the house. The bay shifted uncertainly beneath him, suddenly nervous and fidgety.

"Oh, Christ! The house is on fire!"

A window shattered, and black smoke billowed into the autumn sky. Orange flames leaped at the shutters and licked hungrily at the dry shake roof, which slowly surrendered to ravenous tongues of fire.

Fortune spurred his nervous horse and raced back to the log yard, yelling at the top of his voice, "Fire!"

Wheeling around, he galloped the horse back up the hill. In the distance the steam whistle at the yard blew the alarm, men hollered, and dogs barked furiously. Flinging himself off the wild-eyed bay before it even stopped, he dashed toward the porch.

"Cassie! The house is on fire!"

The screen door flung open, and Cassie Hall lumbered out, carrying her hand-painted teaset on the large tray in front of her swollen stomach. Win grabbed the tray from her hands, rattling the china.

"Don't drop that!" she screamed.

He quickly deposited it on the dead grass twenty yards from the house and sprinted back to where Cassie was struggling clumsily down the steep steps. Gently he gathered her in his arms, carried her over to her precious dishes, and set her down.

The old house was completely ablaze. Fortune could feel the heat from where he stood.

"Where's the schoolteacher?" he yelled at Cassie.

Sobbing hysterically, she pointed toward the house.

Fortune lunged back toward the burning building. Aphrodite! He couldn't help but think of her as the goddess surrounded by the torches and fire of hell.

Suddenly he saw her silhouetted in the doorway against the backdrop of a boiling orange glow.

"Oh hell! That damned trunk!" Nobody knew better than Win how heavy it was. He and Sebastian Hall had nearly broken their backs getting the damned thing into the house, and now that fool woman was tugging it back out by herself.

The elegant leather and steel-ribbed travel trunk was the heavy-duty model, weighing well over seventy pounds when empty. And Mollene Kennedy had packed it solid. Win didn't know why it hadn't occurred to her she might have to carry it out of a burning building. It seemed that everywhere she went, something caught on fire.

As Moll wrestled the leaden weight into the doorway, it got caught on Cassie's prized Turkish carpet. Moll strained and tugged, but the trunk refused to budge.

Win could feel the intense heat as he ran toward her, bent on hauling the woman off the porch before she ignited. That damned trunk wasn't worth dying over!

"Leave it!" he yelled.

Moll paid no attention to him but gave it one last furious tug. The handle was scorching her fingers, but her life was in that trunk—her possessions, her history. She wasn't going to let it burn.

The thread that was snagged on the rug ripped off

with a jerk. The trunk lurched heavily out the door, teetered on the edge of the steps, and then tumbled down the steps, pulling Moll—who was still hanging onto the handle with both hands—over with it in a cascade of lacy white petticoats.

She leaped to her feet the instant Fortune reached her side.

He wanted to take her in his arms, but he yelled at her instead. "You damned fool! You could have been killed!"

"I wasn't." She bent over the trunk and seized the handle. "Help me with this."

"Are you hurt?" The heat from the burning house seemed unbearable to him as he grabbed the other trunk handle.

"I'm fine." She looked up and smiled, her eyes gleaming with excitement.

Fortune grinned in spite of himself. Mollene Kennedy was a real trooper.

Together they hauled the blistered trunk to safety and then went back to Cassie. With one arm around the pregnant woman and the other around Moll, Win helplessly watched the house burn. It had been only a couple of minutes since he'd galloped into the yard, but the house was a roaring inferno.

"My baby things!" Cassie cried. She twisted out of Win's grasp and lumbered toward the seething, flame-reddened hell.

"No!" Moll screamed. She raced after Cassie before Win could even move and grabbed her.

Cassie fought like a wildcat, crazy with grief and anger. Moll was strong, and she hung on till Win got there to help drag the maniacal woman back from the blaze.

The roar of the fire was so loud, they didn't even hear the others who arrived to help. Everyone within shouting distance was coming up the hill to watch the shell of the building twist and collapse.

Moll handled Cassie, and the other women didn't interfere. Earlier that year Cassie had made no secret of the fact that she had hated to leave her wealthy mother's home to follow her husband. She'd put a lot of effort into making her home and possessions the envy of any woman within ten miles, and now all she and Sebastian owned was a pink tea service with a wild rose design.

Every woman understood her grief, yet none of them would have put on such a spectacle. Life on the mountain was especially hard on women, so far away from civilization. But they had learned to bear the hardships with dignity. When the women went to pieces, life went to hell.

Finally a wagon was brought up the hill, and Sebastian carried his wife to it. Hannah McDonald offered to take Cassie home with her for the night, and then Sebastian would drive her to Placerville the following day.

"What'll we do with Miss Kennedy's trunk?" Jed Cantrell asked Win. Cantrell had just arrived from San Francisco earlier that week with his brother's orphaned children.

Win looked thoughtfully at the smoke-darkened luggage and then glanced at Moll, who was waving good-bye to Cassie as the wagon pulled away.

Thunderation! He couldn't very well discharge her right here in front of the entire community. Not after she'd acted with such courage and kindness toward Cassie. He'd overheard enough snatches of conversation already to know that people considered her a heroine. The men, especially, were awed by her bravery. He would look like a monster if he fired her tonight.

"Get another wagon up here and take the trunk to the office," Win said. "We'll decide about sleeping arrangements later."

Hildy Swensen walked over to them. "Hannah wants you to bring Miss Kennedy to the house for supper."

Win nodded. "Thanks. We'll be down shortly."

"I'll tell Hannah." She glanced at Jed. "Matty is watching Sarah. Timmy's with the twins." She looked at Win again and walked away.

"She's keeping my kids while I work," Jed said. "She's the only one who can."

Adjusting to his lively new family wasn't easy. Rugged, blond, and attractive to women, he'd lived a full bachelor's life of travel and adventure. To his credit, he was making a valiant effort to accept the responsibility of his dead brother's children. He was also accepting the help of every woman who offered.

"Nice woman," Fortune said. He wondered if Hildy's concern for Jed was of a personal nature. Then he saw Moll standing by herself and excused himself. "I gotta talk to the teacher."

"Sure. I'll take care of the trunk. Buckley and me will be down to dinner as soon as we take it up to the office. Tell Hannah not to wait."

"We've got a problem," Fortune told Moll when the men had gone.

She smiled weakly, suddenly drained after all the excitement. Taking a deep breath, she tried to get into her role but failed completely. "We certainly have."

Once the turmoil was over, everyone else had been anxious to get to their own homes, eat supper, and feel thankful about being passed over by misfortune. The evening air was heavy with smoke, and the rubble from the house glowed red in the approaching darkness.

Fortune noticed that Moll's smooth hair had come unknotted and had tumbled down around her shoulders. He reached up and wiped a sooty smudge from her pale cheek. Her warm skin was satiny soft. One touch was a mistake.

Dammit to hell! He should do the job he'd planned to and fire her right now, but he couldn't. Not here. He wasn't normally so indecisive, but this woman made him crazy. At this moment he had an insane desire to protect her.

Sensing the direction of his thoughts, Moll reached a dirty hand to his sleeve. "I want to stay in Summit, Mr. Fortune. Anyplace will be all right. I *do* need the job. More than you know."

Even in the onsetting darkness, Win could see the candor on her face. He believed her, because he knew she wasn't a good enough actress to fake wholehearted sincerity. This made his position more difficult. She was a liar and a cheat, but she obviously needed this job.

He tugged her arm. "Let's go get cleaned up and eat. We'll talk after we have some food. Hannah's a great cook, and she sent you a special invitation."

If Moll hadn't been so tired, she might have seen some humor in standing with her new boss beside his bed while he fiddled with a kerosene lamp looking so grouchy.

Humor was the farthest thing from her mind, however. She just wanted him to leave, so that she could fall on the thick, heavenly looking quilt and sleep forever. Still, the manners taught to her by the sisters at the Mount de Sales Academy were not to be ignored. It *was* his room, and his bed.

The nuns, however, hadn't taught her the type of etiquette necessary when a person had to throw a man out of his own bed. But the good sisters couldn't have predicted many of the other situations Moll had found herself in during the last few years, either, most of which had been objectionable, if not downright shady.

"I feel bad about inconveniencing you, Mr. Fortune."

Win could see how pale she was, even in the dim lamplight. She'd endured the strain with dignity, and she hadn't uttered a word of complaint. In fact, she'd shown a lot of gumption. Despite wanting to dislike everything about this woman, he couldn't help admiring her grit.

"I'll be fine until the cabin is ready," he said. "Some of the loggers have already left for the winter, so there's plenty of bunks."

He set down the small bundle she'd packed from her trunk. The cabin had been Hannah's suggestion. He'd nearly had a stroke when she mentioned it, and before he could swallow the mouthful of ham he was chewing, everybody else had volunteered to help fix up the little place. Now he was in a worse predicament than before. Mollene Kennedy was the town's favorite heroine, and he was beginning to wonder if he was going to get rid of her without getting hanged.

"I'm sorry it won't be as luxurious as the room Cassie prepared, but it will be adequate." That was all he could think of to say.

Moll turned her gaze from the bed. "Will Cassie be all right?"

"Once Sebastian gets her to Placerville so her mother can take care of her, she'll be fine."

"Will that be safe?" All Moll could think of was the wooden bridge swaying dangerously over the gorge.

Fortune chuckled. "Contrary to your opinion of our road, Miss Kennedy, it is perfectly safe. Sebastian will leave first thing in the morning, and Cassie will be with her mother by noon."

"Will she come back?" Moll thought how hysterical Cassie had been and how she'd raved about hating Summit and everybody in it.

"Maybe after the baby is born. Cassie wants Sebastian to be a storekeeper in town, but he's a darned good camp supervisor. I'd hate to be looking for another one I can trust come spring. I've got enough trouble without that."

"The school books . . ." Tired as she was, Moll had the jitters about beginning school the following Monday without books, which had been burned in the fire. Sampson Levine had recommended the texts to aid her limited teaching abilities.

"Surely you can teach a day or two without books."

For a second Moll wondered if Fortune was mocking her. The thought unsettled her already frazzled mind.

Drained by the events of the day, she began to notice how the lamplight brightened and faded in flickering waves. Little bursts of starlight appeared before her eyes, and her ears began to ring. She ran her tongue over her dry lips and wondered what her new employer would do if she simply keeled over on the bed.

"Sebastian will have books for you when he gets back Monday night. Do the best you can until then."

He was frowning again, and his voice was sharp.

Moll wondered if he ever smiled. She'd love to make him smile!

"All right," she murmured.

"You look exhausted, Miss Kennedy. Best you get some sleep. Hannah serves breakfast at six-thirty on workdays. Sunday breakfast is at eight."

"I appreciate you giving me the extra salary to cover the meals at the boardinghouse."

"Board and room was part of the original agreement," he said. "I'm a man of my word. Remember that."

Moll stifled the impulse to laugh. Fatigue, in combination with excitement and fear from the afternoon, had apparently altered her brain, for the situation seemed humorous to her now.

Pale and shaky though she was, Moll managed to get control of herself. "Thank you for walking me here," she said.

Fortune turned to leave, then stopped. He felt uncomfortable in the small room with her.

"No one bothered to thank you for your help this afternoon," he said. "With Cassie . . . and everything. A man doesn't know what to do when a woman goes to pieces like that."

"Her possessions were important to her. Especially the baby garments."

"I guess men don't understand about things like that."

Fortune watched Moll for a couple seconds more, torn between the overwhelming desire to comfort her and the need to confront her. But he wasn't so heartless as to challenge a woman who was swaying on her feet with fatigue.

"Well, good-night," he said.

"Good-night, Mr. Fortune. I know I'll enjoy sharing your bed."

Moll flushed with embarrassment the moment the words left her mouth. Here she was playing the role of some chaste spinster, and she sounded like a strumpet!

Fortune's unchecked laughter increased the heat in her cheeks. "I . . . didn't mean . . . *that,*" she stammered, for once in her life at a complete loss for words.

"We're both so tired we're not thinking straight, Miss Kennedy." Fortune moved slightly closer. "It was rude of me to laugh."

For the first time since they entered the building he gave her a genuine smile. It stunned her. Who'd have ever thought such a sourpuss could be so handsome? Why didn't I meet you when life was simple? she thought.

Taking her by the shoulders, he guided her to the washstand, poured some cool water into the plain, white washbowl, and bathed her hot cheeks.

"You're welcome to my bed tonight," he said softly. "Get in it right now. I'll knock in the morning when it's time to get up."

Without another word, he left.

Moll was asleep within minutes.

In the dark, smoke-spiced night a man wrestled with a fiery demon. Sleep eluded him, as it did on so many nights. Burning sexual hunger tormented his body. But the inferno in his body was minor compared to the conflagration in his mind.

He hated it! Hated his own masculine response with almost as much venom as he loathed the female species that caused him so much pain.

He walked, oblivious of the whispering pines and the midnight chill, until he stood right outside the dark window at the back of the company house, where the new teacher slept in ignorance of his presence. He'd seen her earlier in the day at the fire.

He recalled her wild black hair, which had escaped its tight knot, and her face, smudged with soot. Several buttons had been torn off her tight jacket, and her blouse had hung out of her skirt. She had looked as reckless and untamed as the flames reflected in her wide excited eyes.

His body had reacted disgustingly to her wanton behavior. Even as other men crowded around her, he'd felt the filthy pull of lust. *Bitch!* He knew he wouldn't sleep comfortably as long as she stayed on the mountain.

6

"Hannah said you wanted to see me."

"Sit down, Miss Kennedy. I'll be with you in a minute."

Win had spent the past hour making out his weekly expenses for Sampson Levine. At the rate he was spending money in attempts to turn his grandfather's dreams into reality, he wondered if there'd be two cents left when the project was complete. He closed the ledger, glanced up at her, and reached under his desk.

He unrolled the theatrical poster with a snap and held it up in front of Moll Kennedy's shocked white face.

"Oh, bloody hell!"

Outside, someone was hammering. A rooster squawked, and a milk cow announced it was milking time. Inside the office it was deathly still.

"That wasn't the comment I was expecting," Fortune said, "but I think it sums up the situation."

"Where did you get it?" she stared at *The Love Goddess* handbill in disbelief.

"San Francisco. I watched you incinerate the Majestic. It was quite a performance."

"So you knew right from the start. That's why you acted so strange and crotchety."

His brows lifted at her description of him, but he shrugged. No sense telling her how tense he felt around her, even now, when he was attempting to humiliate her. And doing a good job of it, if her pinched face and watery eyes were any indication.

"I wasn't sure until I checked the poster," he said. He owed her that, at least.

"When was that?"

"Right after you arrived. I was on my way up the hill to discharge you when I saw Hall's house burning."

"Real peachy of you not to can me that night," she said, sitting straighter in the chair.

"I thought so. I even gave you my bed to sleep in."

She sniffed and turned her eyes away. "So I'm sacked?"

"I already wrote a letter to Sampson Levine asking him to advertise again."

A flutter of hope assailed Moll's dejected spirits. She'd learned from Hannah what a hard time he'd had filling the position. Maybe all was not lost.

"What happens to me?"

"That depends."

"On what?"

"How you answer my questions. The students in Summit need to be in school. I might let you stay till another teacher comes."

For himself, the sooner she left, the better, but he knew getting another teacher in the dead of winter would be nearly impossible.

She crossed her arms in front of her, warding off the chill in the room. "Ask away."

"Who are you?"

"Mollene Kennedy. Really."

"Not Aphrodite?"

"Not anymore. Aphrodite left the Palace Hotel the morning after the fire and disappeared into the fog."

"Are you really from Baltimore?" He watched her carefully.

"Yes. I was born there. What I told Mr. Levine was basically true. As far as it went."

"You were in a convent?"

"Mount de Sales Academy. I lived there till I was eighteen."

"Then what?"

"I got married."

That stunned him. He had definitely not expected a husband lurking in the woods. "So it's Mrs. Kennedy?"

"No. Mrs. Bercier." She gave the name its French pronunciation. "And I'm a widow. Étienne Bercier died in Panama more than two years ago."

"You're young for a widow."

She shrugged. "Étienne was young for a corpse."

Fortune frowned at her attempt at levity. "Was your husband in the theater?"

"He was an engineer, working on the canal to connect the Pacific Ocean with the Gulf of Mexico."

"Where?"

"In Panama." She sounded cross. "Aren't you listening?"

"All these new facts are confusing me, Mrs. Berc— What's your name?"

She jumped to her feet, furious at his sardonic tone. "Moll Kennedy, dammit! Are you going to let me teach school here or not?"

"Moll Kennedy." He chuckled. The name fit her. Earthy and Irish. A woman born for pleasure. Until she left, his life was going to be hell. He glanced down at the poster. If he teased himself about taking her to bed, he'd surely lose his mind. He began to roll up the handbill.

Moll sat back down and waited.

"You can stay till your replacement comes simply because I promised the townsfolk I'd get them somebody. But I'll keep close tabs on you. And as soon as another teacher is found, you leave. No argument." He tied the rolled handbill and laid it in front of him.

The arrangement wasn't great, but Moll decided he wouldn't back down. His face was stony.

"You teach basic school subjects. Reading, arithmetic, history. No bawdy songs. No dancing around fiery pillars . . ."

"You sonofabitch!" She grabbed the neatly tied poster and hurled it at him.

She shocked him. Every woman he'd ever known had been demure, and none had ever dared yell at him, let alone launch an attack. Annoyed as he was, he was even more fascinated. He had to clench the arms of his chair to keep himself from hauling her down to the floor. "And no dirty language. The kids hear enough of that around a logging camp."

Having missed him with the poster, Moll was damn near attacking him herself when he finished the sentence. Then she remembered just how broke she was and how much she needed this job.

She whirled around, turning her back on him for a second, trying to contain her fury. She took a deep breath, then another. She could put up with him, she told herself. After all, she'd put up with fat, preening Arthur Smith for over a year.

When she turned back around, she was relatively calm. Although she was icy pale and her hair had a wild, Medusa-like look to it, she appeared to be in control of her fearsome temper. Win marveled at her. What a woman!

"Do we have an agreement?" he asked. "You teach here till the next teacher arrives."

"Yes, Mr. Fortune." She turned toward the door and then stopped. "Does anybody else know?" Her voice contained only the slightest quiver.

"About your act at the Majestic? Nobody who lives in Summit. You shouldn't have plastered up so many handbills if you wanted to keep it a secret."

"You remind me of Mother Superior. She was always saying stupid things like that, too."

He didn't quite manage to turn the sudden laughter into a cough. "If you do a good job with the children, nobody will ever see the poster. I promise you that."

"And if I'm a *bad* girl," she taunted, "you'll nail it to a tree?"

"Hannah McDonald's dining room wall."

The door slammed so hard that the men who were lugging her trunk into the cabin looked up in surprise.

The children stared at her like birds scrutinizing a worm, simply waiting.

As she looked back at them across the smooth, pine desktop, Moll was terrified. She suspected this was the most hostile audience she had ever faced.

"Good morning, class," she said with all the dignity she could muster, ignoring her sweaty palms and knocking knees. "I'm Miss . . ."

For a brief, horrifying moment she couldn't recall

her name. She'd used so many aliases in the past months, the role she was now playing flitted right out of her mind.

". . . Kennedy," she finished.

The high-necked shirtwaist threatened to strangle her as the little beggars sat at their desks, waiting for the opportunity to ambush her. But she understood them. In her day, she'd been the best prankster in the school.

"Good morning, Miss Kennedy," they answered.

The enthusiasm in their high-pitched voices couldn't have been lower if they'd been marching to the gallows.

Moll had a theory about children. They weren't bad, but merely uncivilized. They loved what was lovable, and attacked and devoured anything that wasn't. If they weren't sure, they simply waited until they could distinguish the difference.

"My books burned up in Mrs. Hall's fire," she said quickly, "so today we won't have ordinary classes. I hope you don't mind."

The children were too busy exchanging glances to answer, but she knew they didn't. Kids loved thinking they were getting away with something, like escaping expected work.

"First, because it's a nice day, we're going outside to observe nature. Then we're going to discuss what we observed. Listen carefully. There will be prizes this afternoon if everyone participates and behaves. Tomorrow, of course, regular classes will be held."

The morning passed quickly, and after the noon-time baseball game, her eleven students settled down to listen to her read from a copy of *Treasure Island* she'd found in the desk. She read well, with expression and verve, and her charges were utterly entranced.

By day's end, when she passed out lemon drops to the delighted children, Moll felt a smidgeon of her self-confidence return. Even the older children were smiling when they left, at least ready to give her a chance. Maybe she could pull this off, she thought, leaning back in the teacher's chair. Maybe she could be a teacher.

But she knew the test wasn't over yet. Fortune would watch her day and night.

That thought didn't displease her as much as it should have. She wished she'd met him before her life had gotten complicated. The few times he'd touched her, all her senses had gone crazy. It was dumb to daydream about a man who hated her, who was her sworn enemy. But she was a healthy young woman, and sometimes fantasies were difficult to suppress.

After a moment's deliberation, she wrote out a simple schedule for the rest of the school week. Staring out the open door at the tree-covered hill across the road, she made up her mind to try to make learning fun. The lemon drops worked, so other forms of reward might also stir her students to greater efforts. She thought of little Timmy Cantrell, who seemed so serious about being good but wasn't very successful.

She'd heard at the dinnertable Sunday afternoon that Timmy and his sister were recent orphans now living with an uncle. She knew the boy was trying his best to adjust to the new arrangement, and she could sense the little fellow's fear of failing—and she understood the impish impulse that had earned him more than one scolding.

A dog barked somewhere in the distance, breaking the silence of the empty schoolhouse. This was a long way from the constant bustle of the city.

Moll thought of her own childhood. She knew what it was like to be alone at such an early age. An outcast and an unwitting troublemaker most of her life, she reflected on the few times a teacher had praised her efforts. She recalled the warm feeling of achievement and how she'd worked to repeat the experience.

Moll walked the half-mile from the schoolhouse into town in order to go to the post office before she went home. She had to post a letter to the Rockwells letting them know what had happened since she arrived.

Well, not everything. She didn't mention that Winslow Fortune had the Aphrodite poster. Why worry them and give them reason to doubt her?

Moll already despised them. Spying offended her sense of honor, and she felt she was betraying everyone who lived in Summit.

Summit was a tiny village consisting of two buildings, not counting the school. Franklin's Emporium housed the grocery store, as well as the post office, and served as the general meeting place for the town's permanent residents. The Franklin family lived in rooms over their store. Across the street stood Stoneleigh's Blacksmith and Livery.

Mark Danbury watched the new schoolteacher come down the dirt road and enter the Emporium. He'd bought a bottle of liniment for a sore elbow and was outside rolling a smoke when he spotted her. A man didn't often see a new face in a place like Summit.

She didn't seem to notice him leaning against the rust-colored curling bark of a madrona tree, but he was close enough to see her take a letter from her pocketbook. Close enough, too, to see in the afternoon sun that she was a lot better looking than the last teacher, the one who had been in Summit such a short time. Danbury ran his wet tongue along the side of the cigarette to seal it and lit a match.

A burly red-faced man with thinning hair approached him from across the dusty road. "Good-looking woman," the man said as he passed.

"Yeah," Danbury agreed. Then lowering his voice said, "There was a letter from *them* today."

The red-faced man continued to walk toward the Emporium without acknowledging Danbury's comment. He had a passion for horehound sticks and bought several each afternoon after work. He was a timber cruiser and finished work about midafternoon.

Fifteen minutes later Danbury and his burly friend met again in a grove of trees southwest of Summit. The afternoon shadows were beginning to get longer, and there was a cool nip in the autumn air. A deer watched them from behind a nearby cluster of poison oak and then silently moved on.

Mark Danbury ripped the letter open and scanned its contents. The other man waited patiently, sucking on the end of his candy. He had no choice but to wait, since he couldn't read a word.

Danbury enjoyed the power of being able to do something the bigger, stronger fellow couldn't do. So he reread the missive, making the waiting period twice as long.

"We have a new partner," he said at last.

"Who?" The big man coughed and spit.

"Someone *they* want us to keep an eye on."

"Who?"

"I guess the new pard ain't so trustworthy."

"Who the hell is it, goddammit?" He'd been on the wagon for the past few days, and his alcohol-starved nerves were on edge. He bit into the candy and ground it noisily with his teeth.

Mark managed to hide his glee. He relished being able to pull the strings of this big oaf, but he had to be careful. So far, Hodges had been loyal, but Mark knew that C. J. Hodges was a man whose hatred was as strong as his loyalty. He'd watched him beat a man to death with his bare hands. Mark would never forget that power and fury, nor did he let C.J. forget he knew his secret.

"A new twist." Danbury laughed, wrinkling his homely face into a grimace. "They've sent somebody to warm Fortune's bed."

The burly man's round face turned red with surprise and embarrassment.

"They sent a woman," Danbury added, in case C.J. hadn't figured it out. Mark did think he was a bit dim.

C.J. opened his eyes as wide as his puffy lids would allow. "A woman?"

"Just the sort to twist Fortune's secrets out of him. And twist him into knots."

"They sent a woman?"

At times Mark's patience with C.J.'s muddled brain wore thin. "Yes," he said. "Only they don't trust her. And that's where we come in."

"Yeah ... how?"

Danbury let out an exasperated breath. "There's a lot of money involved, see? And she just might decide she wants to double-cross, uh, our friends, and hook up with Fortune. If she does," he put his hands to his own throat to demonstrate, "we kill her."

"Oh." Hodges thought for a minute. "How will we know if she's hooked up with Fortune?" He'd known

Fortune for years, and they had once been good friends. He couldn't imagine Win getting waylaid by a hussy.

Danbury's laugh was ugly. "We'll know."

"Oh."

"It's getting late. We'll miss supper if we don't hurry." Mark turned to walk back toward the road.

"Who is the woman?" C.J. was so nervous with all this double-crossing and throttling that he was attacking another candy stick. The medicinal smell of horehound hung thick in the air.

"The only new woman in town, you fool."

The bigger man looked belligerent, then stupefied. "The schoolteacher?"

Moll felt awkward sitting in the dining room with a dozen men, and it occurred to her that her discomfort was exactly what a real schoolteacher would feel. A week or two ago, in some elegant San Francisco restaurant, she would have considered dining with a crowd of admiring men simply her due.

Now, with Winslow Fortune's eyebrows raising every time a man spoke to her, she tried to become invisible.

Jed Cantrell and Buckley Brooks sat on either side of her. Brooks, a good-looking, slender, rosy-cheeked man with brown curls and a small moustache, was a tad too friendly for Moll's taste. He was the type of man who fancied himself irresistible to women.

As Hildy removed the large bowls which had held chicken and dumplings, Sebastian Hall burst through the front door.

"It's a boy!" he shouted, his face glowing with

delight. "Born this morning. His name is Stanford Allen. Cassie is just fine."

At least five minutes of shouting and pandemonium passed before Sebastian was seated and a plate brought for him. Hannah came into the dining room to get the details while Hildy set two sour-apple pies and a pound cake on the table and refilled the cups.

"Doc said the baby might have arrived a week or two early because of Cassie's distress after the fire, but he weighed more than seven pounds. I sure am glad I wasn't driving her in from Summit. He came so fast I might have had to deliver him on the swinging bridge."

Moll shuddered in horror at that thought, and beside her Jed gave a chuckle.

"Not much like the city, is it?" he whispered, reminding her that he saw her in San Francisco, when she was leaving Sampson Levine's office.

"No!" she answered. "But I like it. Do you?" She noticed he'd gotten his hair cut. His shiny, dark blond locks looked good with his deeply tanned skin. Jed wasn't an especially handsome man, certainly not as boyishly good-looking as Buckley Brooks, but there was something appealing about him—though he was certainly not as attractive to her as her boss.

She looked up to see Fortune watching her, his lids narrowed over his eyes. She gave him a brilliant smile, one of her best practiced-before-the-mirror, knock-you-on-your-fanny-Jack heart-stoppers. He blinked.

"Isn't it wonderful about Cassie, Mr. Fortune?" she purred.

He still looked stunned. "Ah, yeah . . . just wonderful."

It was after seven by the time Moll shut the door to her little cabin. Sebastian Hall had only ridden in to

Summit to deliver the package of new school books and give everyone the news of his son's birth. After eating, he'd stayed for a short time to relax and assure everyone that the doctor in Placerville had given Cassie and little Stanford Allen excellent reports.

She locked the door, dropped the books on the bed, and started a small fire in the pot-bellied stove before carefully unbuttoning her fitted navy jacket and five-gored skirt. As unappealing as she found the garments, she had to take care of them, because most of the outfits in her big trunk were totally inappropriate for Summit.

After she pulled the muslin curtain over the small window, Moll looked around at her new home.

The men of Summit had renovated the cabin on Saturday. First they'd removed the large hornet's nest, before anybody got stung. Then, all day long, folks had stopped by to meet her and leave things to make her life a bit more comfortable—a rocking chair, a reading table, a braided rug, the curtains. The carpenters had knocked together a bed frame, and Hannah McDonald had donated a feather mattress. By sunset on Saturday the stove had been polished and the window washed, and the cabin was downright homey.

"Summit's not so bad," she told herself as she applied the pearl-handled buttonhook to her black hightop shoes. While it was neither as large nor as exciting as Baltimore or San Francisco, it didn't present the problems of a city. And compared to the disease and squalor she'd witnessed in Panama, the tiny little mountain village was heaven. A safe haven for her world-weary soul. Here all she had to worry about was making Fortune happy.

Rolling down one lisle stocking, she let her mind

drift back to Panama, to the brief happiness she'd known with Étienne, to the passion. God, how she'd loved him! Étienne Émile Bercier was the first and perhaps the only man she'd ever loved. She'd given herself to him, body and soul, which was why the end had been such a bitter agony. His death had nearly destroyed her.

Moll stood up and quickly removed the rest of her clothes. She didn't allow herself to dwell on the past. It still hurt too much.

The kettle on the stove had begun to hiss gently. When the water was hot enough, she poured some into the large glazed earthenware washbowl Selma Stoneleigh had sent over, careful not to scratch herself on the big chip on the side.

She bathed as thoroughly as a person could from a bowl and then donned her blue wool robe and felt Romeo slippers.

Unbeknownst to her, a big, burly man was watching the shadows on the curtain, breathing roughly as his lewd mind suggested what his eyes couldn't see. Damn it, he was horny. He'd almost decided to join her in the cabin when he heard the sound of someone coming up the path. Fortune!

He stepped away from the window and faded into the shadows at the back of the building. The lamplight inside stayed on for quite some time, and in frustration, he finally gave up and left.

Inside her snug cabin, Moll poured herself some tea and looked over the school books, deciding she was pleased with them. Any books would be a help, but these were excellent texts. Then she climbed into her featherbed, feeling ever so safe and secure. Whatever could harm her in such a tranquil setting?

* * *

Young Tim Cantrell had put the mouse in the teacher's desk right after lunch on Friday while she was in the privy.

He hadn't thought of the idea himself, of course. All the older boys had egged him on. But after the furry little gray critter jumped out of the drawer where *Treasure Island* was kept and tried to scurry into the folds of Miss Kennedy's lace petticoats, Timmy was the only one who admitted doing the dreadful deed.

It was a sad day in Summit.

It never had occurred to Moll that she'd have to discipline one of the children. She'd been on the receiving end of the strap so many times in her misbegotten life that she'd never thought about doling out punishment. Yet she realized immediately that the mouse episode was a test.

If the school year was going to amount to anything more than one long nightmarish episode of pranks and mischief, she was going to have to get a grip on things. She picked up that message as the mouse was beating his chops to get out the door.

"I am so disappointed." She was wracking her brain to think of a punishment befitting the crime other than swatting Timmy's little backside.

First she announced in her sternest voice that there would be no treats that Friday afternoon. This brought a groan from the students. That's when she knew she had them.

Theatrically, she plopped the candy sack in the top drawer and shut it with a bang. Ila Fisk laid her head on her desk and sobbed, because she'd been looking forward to the treat all day. Matty Swensen doubled up her fists and vowed to clean up on the boys, even the biggest ones.

"And furthermore, there will be no reading today of *Treasure Island.*"

After assigning them to write *I will behave in class,* one hundred times in their best penmanship, Moll sat back and gave some serious thought to discipline.

Timmy wasn't the problem. In her heart she admired the little guy's courage in taking all the blame. Eddie Hodges, Bert Stoneleigh, and Otto Fisk were the ones she had to clamp down on, because if she lost control of the school, she'd lose her job. She wasn't going to give Fortune the pleasure of telling her she'd failed.

When the day ended, Moll walked home with Timmy. She could see by his trembling chin that he regretted ever having seen that darned mouse. They walked in silence to the small house near the McDonalds', where Timmy stayed till Jed picked him up for supper. Hildy Swensen met them at the door, holding little Sarah.

"I've come to see Mr. Cantrell," Moll told her.

Hildy didn't look pleased. "He's not home."

"I'll wait," Moll said, wondering at the chilly reception. "This is important."

"Timmy, take Sarah outside and wait for Matty. She took a dress I mended to Mrs. Franklin."

"Is Mr. Cantrell working down on the river?" Moll asked, hoping to ease the tension.

"No, he's out with Mr. Fortune. Is Timmy in trouble?"

Moll looked around to see if Timmy had gone out. "The big boys put him up to a trick today. He admitted doing it, but the other boys didn't. I want Mr. Cantrell to know what happened, so Timmy won't be led astray again."

Hildy shrugged and rolled her eyes. "Jed don't know much about kids," she said.

Moll didn't either, but she wouldn't admit it to anybody. "I'm sure Mr. Cantrell wouldn't want his nephew making trouble at school."

Hildy nodded a bit reluctantly. "Matty's home," she said abruptly. "I gotta go help Hannah with supper. You come back some other time."

Hildy knew that Jed Cantrell needed her and so did his children. She'd already seen the way Winslow Fortune had acted the day Moll arrived. She didn't want Jed falling all over himself about Moll, too. The schoolteacher was beautiful, but not the right woman for either Jed or Win.

"There's Mr. Cantrell now," Moll said. "You go ahead. I won't be long."

Hildy scowled but left. Unsure of herself where men were concerned, and uncomfortable with her own possessive feelings, she had no idea how to deal with Moll.

The talk with Cantrell had been short and simple.

"Tim, come over here. I want to talk to you."

Jed wasn't mad. In fact, he was having trouble not laughing, but he managed to be stern and understanding at the same time. Moll liked him for that.

Timmy agreed tearfully to leave all manner of rodents outside the classroom and never again be coaxed into doing bad things for the bigger boys.

"He's a good boy," Moll told Jed. "And he's becoming a good student."

Jed shrugged. "I was a hellraiser myself. My brother John was perfect, though, never in trouble. Guess the little fellow takes after his uncle."

"I think he misses his father," Moll said quietly.

Jed got a faraway look in his eyes. "So do I."

Hildy was still scowling when she served Moll's supper. In fact, she was almost rude. Win was the first man Hildy had given any thought to since Old Olie Swensen died, and that was because he was such a good man—kind and thoughtful. She was only fourteen when Olie Swensen had paid her passage to California. She was a sensible girl, but also sensitive. She'd come with stars in her eyes, expecting a husband who wanted to love and cherish her forever.

What she'd found instead was a cantankerous old buzzard who wanted a young girl to work her fingers to the bone all day and then welcome his rutting all night—like a sow for a boar. And a boar was what he smelled like, too.

But Winslow Fortune was altogether different. He was a man a woman could pin her hopes and dreams on. Hildy did not want his head turned or his heart broken by a pretty woman who wanted *every* man's attention.

For reasons she didn't exactly understand, Hildy didn't want Jed smitten with the teacher either. The whole evening long, she frowned and wished Moll was as homely as the last schoolmarm.

If Hildy had asked, Moll would have told her she didn't want a man in her life at all. What with the Rockwells, Sampson Levine, the absent but fondly remembered Arthur Smith, and her glowering employer Winslow Fortune, Moll wasn't very keen on the male population.

Why on earth would she want to go after a man who loved to play with dynamite? Hildy was welcome to him—and his newly acquired children, whom he was always pawning off on somebody else because he didn't know what to do with them. All Moll Kennedy wanted was to finish this little job, collect her bonus from the Rockwells, and take herself to Broadway.

She'd have to deal with Hildy, though, or it would be bloody uncomfortable for the next six months. A plot began to develop in Moll's fertile brain. She was going to apply herself to becoming Hildy's best friend. She smiled sweetly when the coffee Hildy poured slopped on her sleeve. It was going to be a challenge.

"You're quiet tonight, Miss Kennedy," Fortune said. "Did the mouse incident dampen your spirits about teaching?"

"You heard about that?" Moll asked.

Hildy plunked a salmon loaf with creamed onion sauce at one end of the table and looked longingly at Win.

"Six times before I even got here tonight."

"I heard the mouse ran up your bloomers!" Bill McDonald teased.

"Bill, be nice!" Hannah yelled from the kitchen.

"Not quite," Moll laughed, only blushing a little bit. "I'm fast on my feet."

Win walked her home.

"So how did the week go?" he asked as they stepped off the McDonalds' wide porch into the darkness.

She chuckled. "Fine until this afternoon. I guess I should have expected something like this."

"I once put a snake in the teacher's desk."

"You! I can't believe that. You're so . . ."

"What? Dull? Boring?" he teased, feeling more

lighthearted than he'd felt in months. Tonight he wanted to forget everything and simply enjoy a walk in the moonlight.

"Perfect," she answered quickly, managing to make the word sound like an insult.

His deep laughter carried through the night.

"I'm definitely not perfect. What about you? Were you a sugar-and-spice little girl? Or were you a little bit bad?"

"I was a lot bad. I gave the sisters more trouble than any other girl in school!"

"What about your parents? Did you give them fits, too?"

"They died when I was young," she lied smoothly as she'd often done in the past. "My mother's sister was older and unable to keep a lively child, so I went to the Academy when I was six. The sisters raised me."

Win wondered if it was true. With Mollene Kennedy he was always skeptical. "How did you get to California?"

"I came here from Panama."

"Helping build a canal?"

"Étienne believed in the canal. But he and others died of malaria. After that I moved on. Oh look! There's a shooting star!"

Fortune took her hand. "Make a wish, Miss Kennedy."

I wish my life was normal. Just once before I go I want to kiss that marvelous mouth of yours.

"Did you make a wish?"

"Yes. That nobody puts a snake in my desk."

"Good! Keep watching Eddie Hodges."

"I am. It's hard shaking your finger at a boy a head taller than you and acting like you expect him to mind."

"Tell me if you have trouble."

"Thank you," she replied. "I'll remember that."

This time Win clearly didn't believe her. Something about her tone, despite the polite words, told him she wouldn't call on him for help even if Eddie Hodges and his friends hung her by her bloomers from the flagpole.

A distinct rustle in the bushes caught their attention, and any further discussion about school was instantly forgotten.

"What was that?"

"Probably just a dog, or a raccoon." Win took her firmly by the elbow and hurried her up the path. "To be on the safe side, though, you should stay in your cabin with the door latched."

"Why?"

Win sighed. Mollene Kennedy was not a woman who automatically did what she was told simply because a man did the telling. Somehow, this intrigued him. His mother had always acquiesced to his stern father, until she seemed to have no personality whatsoever. Yet she remarried three months after his father died. Win's fiancée had had the same compliant way about her—until she found somebody else.

He knew without question that Moll would lead a man a merry chase. Yet, deep inside, he felt that if she loved a man, she'd be loyal to the core.

The noise in the manzanita bushes started again.

Moll gasped aloud. "That's bigger than a raccoon."

"I think so, too. Look, I don't mean to frighten you, but some of the men have seen cat tracks. This is wild country. Be careful."

He stayed outside her cabin until he heard the bolt slide into place. Then he walked all the way around the cabin and the company office building. He hadn't lied to her exactly. He just hadn't told her all the truth.

Yes, some of the men had spotted cat tracks, but they were out in the woods. The tracks he'd seen near the house and outside the window of her cabin had not been made by a cougar. Or any other animal for that matter. They were human.

Somebody was watching Moll Kennedy.

In his San Francisco office Sampson Levine was working late. He glanced at the letter from Winslow Fortune and wondered if it was still steaming.

"Mr. Fortune wants a new teacher," Sampson told Jenkins when he brought in some papers to sign. "Miss Kennedy doesn't satisfy him."

Jenkins blushed from his collar to his hairline.

Sampson enjoyed making Jenkins blush. It proved that the young man had some very male thoughts, in spite of his prim demeanor.

"Send Winslow Fortune a letter telling him I'll take care of everything."

"Yes, sir. And I'll contact the newspaper and run another ad."

Sampson shook his head. "No. Don't bother with the ad. I don't want to interview any more skinny old maids. We'll simply let Winslow cool off."

He got up and looked out into the night. "Fortune has the right woman. He just doesn't know it yet."

Jenkins nodded skeptically. He didn't understand his employer, but he admired the lawyer tremendously. "Do you need anything else tonight?"

"Not tonight, Jenkins. Go on home. I'll lock up when I leave."

Sometime later the office door opened softly. Sampson looked up and smiled at the slender Chinese youth standing in the doorway. "Come in, Leong. I'm glad you could make it."

The young man walked quietly into the office, closed the door, and took a seat.

They looked each other over carefully.

"Your message intrigues me," Sampson said, his fingers stroking his moustache. "I think working together could be most interesting."

"You know what I want. Can we work it out?" Leong asked softly. Nothing in his refined manner betrayed his nervousness.

"Oh yes," Sampson said. "You keep me informed about the Rockwells, and I'll find the girl for you."

7

Mark Danbury leaned against the crumbling stone wall near the burntout ruins of the old Simms place and waited for the others to arrive. He was nervous about what he had to say to the men, and waiting made him edgy.

C.J. Hodges was down the road a ways, bent over the back leg of Edgar Fillmore's black horse, examining a loose shoe. Standing straight, he hooked his thumbs in his suspenders and motioned his head toward Danbury.

"What's eatin' him today?" C.J. asked. "He's cranky as an old maid."

Fillmore shrugged. Danbury was the least of his worries. A normally pleasant man with a ready smile and warm brown eyes, he'd wondered over the last few years what he'd done to deserve such a terrible life. His wife Pearl's many miscarriages had been bad enough, changing her from a happy, loving girl to a silent, gaunt creature he barely knew. But worse, three years ago their first son had died from an infected rat's bite, and now Teddy, their only living child, suffered so badly from asthma that Pearl had taken him to the desert.

Fillmore also owed numerous debts. That's why he started working for the Rockwells in the first place. He had no idea what skullduggery Danbury would tell them the Rockwells were planning, but he had no choice except to go along with it. He was desperate for the extra money.

Leland Ames and Buckley Brooks rode in a few minutes later from Summit. Ames was talking about a three-day poker party he'd attended and bragging about his winnings. Brooks went along with the story, although he doubted the truth of it. He'd never known Ames to end up the winner in any game.

The last to appear, having made the trip to Kelsey to buy food for the gathering, was Potty Simms. A long-faced gent with hard eyes and a drooping moustache, Simms had a personal reason for aiding the Rockwells. His grandfather, like Winslow Fortune's ancestor, had made a strike in the gold fields. Not only had the Simms family squandered their gold, they'd also lost the land they'd bought.

The land—this very place where the men were meeting—had belonged to his family. While Simms acknowledged that his father's mismanagement had cost the family the land, he refused to recall that he'd been too lazy to buy it back. Now it had been bought for back-taxes by none other than Winslow Fortune. Potty Simms hated Fortune for his money, his luck, and his ambition, and so he had gladly joined the Rockwells to work against him.

Mark cleared his throat noisily as Simms and Brooks

passed out the bread, meat, and beer to the others. "Our employers have a new job for us."

The men, having worked hard all day, dove into the meal like starving dogs, tearing at the food and stuffing their mouths.

Mark scowled, waving aside a tin cup of beer, and continued. "They're disappointed Fortune ain't taken the hint and quit."

"Some hint," C.J. crowed. "A runaway team, a falling tree, mechanical breakdowns, and a house fire. An' that's just this month."

Danbury frowned. "The fire was an accident. We had nothing to do with it. Remember, the Rockwells don't wish to hurt anybody else. They simply want Fortune out of the way."

That got their attention fast.

"Out of the way?" Brooks asked cautiously. "How?"

"He's been too stubborn and too stupid to be scared off by what we've done so far," Danbury said. "We've got to get rougher—do something permanent."

"They want him hurt?" Ames asked as he chewed a hunk of hard bread. "Crippled?"

"They want him dead!"

"No!" C.J. was instantly on his feet, wild-eyed and angry. "He's my friend."

"Don't be an idiot," Simms said. "A rich man like Fortune can't be friends with a working bum like you."

"He's been my friend for a dozen years," C.J. persisted. "Since his grandpa first brought him up here."

"The Rockwells want him dead," Mark said, as if he hadn't heard the other exchange. "They don't want to take the chance he might win the legacy."

"He can't win," Brooks said. The thought of killing

somebody almost spoiled his appetite, but not quite. He grabbed a pork chop and took a huge bite. "There are too many of us."

Leland Ames agreed, rubbing a greasy hand through his sandy hair. "We're not hired killers."

"If the Rockwells want him dead," Mark screamed, his face ugly with rage, "we kill him. C.J. . . ."

"No! I won't do it." C.J. threw his tin cup at the charred wood near the fireplace and stalked off toward his steed. He mounted, spurred the horse, and sped away, without looking back.

"Stupid bastard," Simms muttered. "What do you want me to do, Mark? I'll take care of Fortune."

Win stared into space.

The letter he'd started writing to Sampson Levine, inquiring about his ad for a teacher, lay half finished on the desk in front of him, forgotten.

While he was trying to rephrase a sentence, an idea of how to get logs from one high mountain ridge to another without floating them down the river had popped into his mind. It was so simple, he didn't understand why he hadn't thought of it years before.

It was also so damned revolutionary, people would think him crazy. But what the hell! People already thought he was insane.

He quickly sketched out the idea in bold black strokes on a blank piece of paper. His heart was beating like crazy. Sweet Holy Lord, was it possible? Could it truly work?

He ran his tongue over his dry lips and stared at the drawing, his head buzzing with excitement. It could be the perfect answer to getting the tall timber out of these mountains.

The clock on the wall struck seven.

Win crumpled up the unfinished letter and hastily wrote another, asking Sampson to locate a good engineer. As an afterthought, he asked the lawyer to find out who owned the land beyond his timber claim. If this crazy notion worked, he wanted to own enough timber to make the venture profitable.

Then he grabbed his hat and turned down the lamp. He was late for a town meeting.

Before he closed the door, though, he remembered the drawing. He ran back inside and locked it in the desk with the cashbox. The drawing could be more valuable than the gold in the box.

The logging company was the lifeblood of the little village of Summit. The summer workmen, as well as the year-round residents, kept the little businesses in operation—not only the grocer and the blacksmith, but farmers who supplied meat, eggs, and vegetables for the cookhouse, the ranchers who raised the stock the company used, the local men who did odd jobs, and the women who baked and did laundry and sewing. A number of families counted on the logging company for extra income.

Until this evening, Win had often worried how the town would survive if he failed to get his logs to a sawmill downriver. And guilt had driven him onward when he'd been so tired and discouraged he simply wanted to quit. Tonight, as he prepared to talk to the townsfolk about the future, he felt younger than he had in several years, lighter in mind and spirit, and full of hope for his future as well as theirs.

George Franklin, a New Englander with a weathered face and a bald head, stood up and cleared his throat. "I propose we build a town hall."

"We need a place where a man can get somethin' ta drink around here," C.J. Hodges said. Like many of the men crowded into the Emporium, he was there because he didn't have anything else to do. "What the hell we need a town hall for?"

Win was also surprised by the idea. In the past, the twice yearly meetings had always begun with the suggestion of opening a saloon, which was always promptly vetoed, and ended with the discussion of there being no regular church services.

"What goes on in Summit that can't be conducted here in the Emporium or the schoolhouse?" Win asked.

"The town's a'growin'," Albert Stoneleigh, the glum blacksmith, answered.

"The town is good-sized in the summer when all the loggers are around," Bill McDonald said, "but when the snow falls it's the same bunch of us that's been here for years."

"It's a'gonna grow," Stoneleigh persisted.

"Will it, Win?" McDonald asked. He was smart, and doing very well financially because of the logging company, but he was cautious. More than any of the rest of the people, McDonald understood how much they had to lose if Fortune was unable to commercialize the American River.

"Right now I'm confident about Summit Logging and Lumber Company being in business at the turn of the century . . . and far into the future," Fortune said, meeting McDonald's penetrating stare. "I would also expect the town to grow in accordance with the business."

"What about the town hall?" George Franklin asked.

"What about a saloon?" C.J. echoed.

Win ignored the latter. C.J.'s drinking had already ruined his marriage and had put their long-standing friendship in jeopardy. "Have you thought about what you want?" he asked Franklin.

George had it written down. He gave Fortune the details and an approximate cost.

Win looked over the proposal and nodded. The plan was impressive and not terribly costly.

"If the town donates the land," Win said, "the logging company will pay all the shipping costs and contribute some material. You folks will have to come up with the rest."

"Why cain't you pay it all?" Stoneleigh asked, sounding annoyed.

"The logging company has a lot of expenses. More than usual because of the sabotage we suffered last summer by the men my cousins employed. I'm trying to pay as I go—to make sure everybody gets their money if I fail. I simply can't afford to build your building at this time. Besides, I think your meeting hall will mean more to you if you share in the cost and the labor."

Stoneleigh looked unconvinced. He always tried to get something for nothing, and he resented anybody he perceived to have more than he did. Franklin didn't offer any comment, but Bill McDonald agreed with Fortune.

"If we contribute, we'll work harder to keep the town going if Summit Logging and Lumber Company clears out," Bill said.

"How much are you puttin' up?" Stoneleigh asked. He knew McDonald's land had originally been homesteaded by Hannah's parents, and he still resented it. Besides, Bill McDonald had graduated from the Placerville Academy, and Stoneleigh didn't trust educated men.

"I might just have a better idea how to raise the money than each of us just putting up a share. I'd like your opinion on this." Bill glanced around at his friends.

At the back of the room, C.J. Hodges pulled a flask out of his coat and passed it to Buckley Brooks and Leland Ames. Edgar Fillmore shook his head, worried what Stoneleigh would charge to shoe the black. He put great store by that horse. It was all that remained from better times.

C.J. grabbed the flask again and drank. The odor of raw liquor hung in the air. Mildred Franklin and Selma Stoneleigh exchanged looks of disgust.

"My kids were asking the other night about a Winter Fair," Bill McDonald said. "Seems Miss Kennedy was reading to them about things people do in other countries. I think we might do that to raise money. If we tell folks, I think they'll come."

"Who would want to drive to Summit?" Stoneleigh grumbled. He was still irked because Win wasn't going to pay for the building.

"Lots of folks from Kelsey and Georgetown and around here, if we let them know when," George Franklin said. "If we had something to eat and things for them to buy, folks would come just to see what we could do."

"You could have a dance, too," Win suggested. "Everybody will come to a dance. People would even drive out from Placerville."

In the back of the store, Mark Danbury leaned against the table with the bolts of yard goods. He wondered if he could trust Potty Simms to carry through with their plan. Simms might hate Fortune, but he was unreliable as hell. Mark cursed C.J.'s sudden scruples. He shifted impatiently and shot a glance at his cohorts.

Mark didn't mix much with C.J. in public because of their other association, and while he worked well with Ames and Fillmore, he didn't like Buckley Brooks. Brooks's being a crackerjack mechanic irritated him, but the dirty stories Brooks was always telling made Danbury loathe him.

Mark ignored the horseplay in the back and wondered what the Rockwells would make of this latest development. Mark wasn't hot on the idea himself—he didn't hold much with dancing and festivities—but sometimes his San Francisco employers were pleased by the strangest things. Maybe this could be a smoke-screen for the killing. He decided he should at least inform them.

An hour later, after the meeting had broken up, Win was standing outside Moll's cabin before he had any idea he intended to stop and talk to her. It was late, but the light inside was still lit. He knocked sharply before he could change his mind.

When he saw her through the curtain, he remembered the footprints he'd seen by the window. He realized they were probably made by somebody from the log yard or the town. Maybe the fellow wasn't so much a danger as a Peeping Tom out for a few thrills. But Win didn't want any other man leering at what he was more and more thinking of as his.

Even though she'd be leaving soon, he'd get her some thicker curtains as soon as he could, something heavy that would protect her from prying eyes and evil minds.

When she pulled open the door, he saw that her hair hung down her back in black shining curls and she was wearing a soft blue robe and slippers.

For a moment Fortune didn't know what to say. He knew it was late, but somehow he'd expected her to be fully clothed when she answered his knock.

"Mr. Fortune? Is something wrong?" Moll looked out into the cold night, wondering why he always frowned when he saw her. Then she thought he might have found another teacher, and her heart sank.

"I know it's late, Miss Kennedy, but I need to speak with you."

"Come in."

He knew it was a mistake the moment she shut the door. The cabin was too damned small. Mollene Kennedy was soft and lovely, and smelled sweetly of violets and recently washed hair. All he could see, no matter where he looked, was her enormous bed with the thick turned-back quilt and the mussed sheets.

She'd been in bed. His body tightened at the thought.

It hadn't occurred to him she might have been reading in bed.

"Is something wrong?" She told herself her heart was thumping because his visit surprised her. Not for a second would she admit how uncomfortable she was entertaining him in her bedroom. The cabin was, for all intents and purposes, simply a large bedroom. "Is there a problem?"

Yes, Moll Kennedy. I'm lonely and tired and I want you in that bed.

"No, ah . . ." He cleared his throat and tried to remember why he'd come. "I just wanted to talk to you before school starts tomorrow."

"Sit down." Having been a child who was called before Mother Superior a hundred times or more, she knew she'd been caught at something. But what? Playing baseball perhaps? She would not apologize for knocking the ball through the privy door. It had been one hell of a home run!

There was only one chair, and Fortune reluctantly sat in it. The rocker was small and too close to the stove. But then he wasn't planning to stay long. His gray eyes strayed to the bed.

Moll plopped herself on the wrinkled quilt. Her robe scooted up when she sat, and her ankles showed. In her attempt to straighten the blue wool she'd loosened one slipper, which dropped to the wooden floor.

With difficulty, Win pulled his thoughts from her shapely white foot, the smoothly buffed toenails, the slender ankle.

"Bill McDonald told me you read to the children about the winter and Christmas fairs they have in other countries."

"Yes?"

"I'd like to borrow that book." He wondered if the room was stiflingly hot or if his own thoughts had raised his body temperature. "Do you mind if I remove my coat?"

"I'm sorry. I should have taken it when you came in." She hopped off the bed and in three steps stood in front of him. "The stove really heats up the place."

Win was on his feet, too, less than a foot from her, pulling on the sleeves.

She purposely avoided touching him when she took

the garment. While other unattached women so often played flirtatious little touching games with him, Moll Kennedy was being noticeably circumspect.

Sitting back down in the chair, he wondered if he was disappointed or relieved.

The beauty of her wild black curls and her gently draped figure nearly struck him dumb. Win had never seen such a fine, clean complexion, or such wickedly innocent eyes. Who would believe that such angel blue eyes could belong to a woman who had danced and cavorted half naked onstage?

The urge to taste her full lips was almost too much to resist. If she'd shown even an inkling of expectation, he would have been lost to his baser instincts.

"You wanted to read about country fairs?"

He sighed and began to explain about the town meeting, and the plans to build a town hall between the Emporium and the school.

"How exciting!" she said, instantly enchanted with the idea of a winter fair as a fund raiser. "My students and I will help."

Her show of enthusiasm bewildered him. He hadn't expected a woman as cosmopolitan as Moll to show any interest in such a bucolic endeavor.

"I know Hannah and Hildy will love the idea of a winter festival, too. They'll help, I'm sure."

"Albert Stoneleigh says it will snow that day."

"Oh? What day have you picked?"

"No specific day yet, but whatever one we choose, Stoneleigh thinks something will happen to ruin the fun."

Her laughter filled the tiny cottage. She went over and grabbed some books from the top of her trunk and began to thumb through them. Her energy was infectious, and

Win couldn't help being excited about the project, too.

Maybe it was just getting his mind off his duties that made him feel so good, or the incredible idea he'd had about getting the logs to market. Maybe it was sitting shoulder to shoulder on a lumpy quilt with a laughing woman, planning a party for anybody within thirty miles who would show up. Or maybe it was simply being normal for an hour, being without any responsibility other than that of choosing the right band for the dance. Whatever the reason for his lightness of heart, he savored it.

At the breakfast table the next morning, Win brought up Bill McDonald's idea of having a winter fair in Summit to raise enough money to build a town hall. Then he suggested several dates in early December.

"I looked at Miss Kennedy's books, and I think we could sell meat pies and roast potatoes to the people who come, as well as charging admission to the dance."

Hildy had just put a platter of ham on the table and looked up in time to see Bill McDonald wink at his wife. Hannah glanced from Win to Moll and smiled before she turned back to the kitchen to bring back more oatmeal muffins. It dawned on Hildy, and anybody else who was paying more attention to the conversation than to the potatoes and eggs, that Win and the teacher had been alone together sometime between supper and breakfast.

Hildy didn't like the idea of him in Moll's cabin. Win needed a woman who could tolerate this lonely mountain or be a lady if he managed to become rich. Hildy fancied herself as that woman. She'd be a good wife for him. She'd work hard and make him proud of her. She could adjust to being wealthy. She might even like having him touch her in bed, though she wasn't certain about that.

"Hannigan has a cider press and a bumper crop of apples," Bill told them.

"The abandoned Simms property has five or six persimmon trees. The boys could go after school and bring back a wagonload for cakes and cookies." Hannah refilled the dish of potatoes.

"What about a Gypsy?" Charlie Wells asked. "My mother said the Gypsies always came to the fairs in England. We need a fortune-teller."

"I can do that," Moll said, without thinking. "I've got a great costume from . . ." She broke off and glanced at Fortune. "I went to a costume party once in it."

Win hoped it covered more than her last costume. He could just see her prancing around Summit in a toga. His scrunched eyebrows told her he didn't approve.

Moll colored and went back to her plate.

"Would you like more coffee, Miss Kennedy?" Hildy asked a few minutes later, having served everyone else twice.

"Why, yes, Mrs. Swensen, I would." Moll smiled sweetly. "Have you ever been to a fair?"

Surprised at being addressed, Hildy colored and answered honestly. "Yeah. Back home, when I was a girl. People brought their market goods and sold them. And women sold brooms, baskets, needlework, and cheese. And wonderful things to eat."

"May I come over after school?" Moll asked. "You could give me some details."

Hildy readily agreed, pleased to be included.

* * *

By the time Moll got to school, there were many plans afoot for the most exciting event that had ever happened in Summit—so many plans, in fact, that Moll nearly forgot about the trouble she was having with Eddie Hodges and young Bert Stoneleigh. For the first time in her life, she felt a twinge of sympathy for the nuns who had raised her. Maybe she was reaping what she had sown.

Moll had sent a note home with Eddie Hodges asking to talk with his father at some convenient time, but there had been no answer.

"Eddie, your father hasn't come to see me yet."

"I guess the old man's too danged busy to bother with you," Eddie replied.

Bertie snickered.

The other children, remembering the great mouse episode, were far too wise to join in with Bert Stoneleigh's guffawing.

"Eddie Hodges will stay after school today to scrub the outhouse," Moll said. "Bert Stoneleigh will stay in at recess. Both boys will apologize to the school."

Hannah brought up the subject while Moll drank tea in her kitchen the following afternoon. "I hear Eddie has been disrupting class."

"Where'd you hear that?" Moll asked. She had forgotten how folks in Summit had nothing to do but talk.

"Matty mentioned it last week. The twins told me about Eddie's antics yesterday afternoon. How bad is it?"

"Bad enough. Sometimes he sits and looks out the window. Sometimes he's unruly and smart-mouthed. So far I'm handling the problems as they crop up, but he isn't doing his schoolwork. And I don't know why."

"C.J. is why. He drinks, and it's raddled his liver and pickled his brains." Hannah expertly rolled out the dough she was making for steak-and-potato pies.

"That fits most drunks I ever encountered," Moll said, inwardly shuddering as she remembered some of those men and their actions from her saloon days. "But how does C.J.'s drinking affect Eddie?"

"C.J.'s a crazy man when he's boozing. He gets into fights. He disappears for days, picks up with loose women, spends all the money. The boy thinks he has to take care of him, because the mother left two years ago."

"She left?" Moll asked, incredulous. "I assumed she'd died."

"Nope. She left because she couldn't stand it any more. C.J.'s gotten even worse since then. Poor Lorna. I don't think her life is much better than it was. She's working as a hasher at a little cafe in Kelsey. I don't know how she can take care of herself on what she makes there."

Moll thought of what many women did when forced to support themselves. "At least she found honest work."

Hannah frowned. "She looked so tired and thin the last time I saw her. I heard she was also taking in laundry. Life is rough as a cob for a lone, unschooled woman."

"It can be tough for an educated woman, too." Moll reached for a sugar cookie. "Anyway, I sent Eddie home with a note asking his father to come in and talk to me."

"He'll never come, Moll. He can't read or write." She crimped the edges of the first pie and then reached for the second. "Never had a chance to learn, because his own father was a drunk, and he was put out to work when he was real little. He's ashamed he's illiterate. He'll probably do most anything to avoid talking to you. Ask Win for help with the boy. Eddie respects him."

"Maybe tomorrow," Moll said. Surely the boy wouldn't be so unruly if his mother came home. She wondered what she could do to reunite Eddie's family.

It wasn't to be the next day, either. Coming in from the play yard after lunch, Moll caught her skirt on a loose nail on the doorjamb and ripped the seam. Instead of looking for Win after school, she went straight to Hildy's house to see if the skirt could be mended.

Hildy spent every afternoon at her sewing machine, and folks stopped by as they needed to. She welcomed Moll enthusiastically. Moll couldn't help wondering what had brought on the change of attitude, but she decided Hildy must be as lonely for friendship as she was.

Hildy Swensen's two-room house wasn't much bigger than her own cabin, but every inch of space was arranged to afford the slender blonde convenience of movement and area to work. A sewing room had been made out of a screen and curtains.

Before Moll had a chance to explain her problem, Hildy was stripping her out of her suit.

"Easy to fix," Hildy assured her as she sat down at the sewing machine.

"You tore your petticoat, too," Matty pointed out.

Before Moll knew it, she was standing behind the

wooden privacy screen in nothing but her lace-edged combinations.

"Combinations!" shrieked Matty, who knew everything there was to know about ladies' garments. This exciting revelation proved Miss Kennedy was the most wonderful, glamorous woman she'd ever known. Matty wanted more than anything to be glamorous.

"Pretty, pretty." Hildy smiled, admiring the demure one-pieced undergarment. She'd seen a picture of combinations in a magazine, but she'd never seen a pair up close. More practical than a chemise and pantalettes, the capped-sleeve, scooped-neck, cambric undergarment, which buttoned down the front, barely reached Moll's thighs. Lacy white garters peeked from beneath the combinations and fastened to long clock-patterned silk stockings.

"I like that. I'm going to make a pair."

No one heard the footsteps on the porch or the knock on the door. They were all three talking at once, exchanging frank opinions on how Hildy's underwear should be fashioned and laughing at some of the more absurd suggestions. And Moll, of course, was twirling around, modeling her own, perfectly at home in the limelight.

It never occurred to any of them that somebody might walk in. Until somebody did.

"Hildy," Winslow Fortune called as he pushed open the door and stepped inside, as he'd always done—as everyone did who visited the town seamstress during the afternoon hours when she worked at her sewing machine.

Fortune stopped dead in his tracks. A rumpled shirt hung limply from his fingers. His gray eyes went as stormy as the winter sea, and his face froze in shock at what he saw.

To her absolute horror, Moll stood before him in glorious dishabille, her hair escaping its twist, her clothes tossed on the Singer. She gasped at the sight of him, her hand clasping her throat.

Fortune wondered why the hell she was covering her neck when her legs were completely exposed, from ankle to crotch, and her deeply shadowed cleavage was stripped to his view.

"Miss Kennedy tore her skirt," Hildy explained. She was surprised to see the anger in Fortune's eyes and felt the need to defend the schoolteacher.

"And her petticoats," Matty added. "At school . . . on a nail by the door."

Moll finally regained her senses and darted behind the wooden screen. She was shaking. Her employer's anger sparked a matching fire in her. Where was the man who'd been so pleasant the other night? That apparently had been an aberration of his normally surly character.

Her anger was steeped with embarrassment. How could she have been so stupid as to have been caught in her underthings? And by the one man she needed most to impress, who was already looking for any excuse to get rid of her! She wanted to kick something, or throw herself on the floor and scream. But she did neither.

As she stood with her head averted, she again saw the mixture of hunger and condemnation raging in his eyes. She'd seen that look in men before, when she was on the stage. In men who had wanted her and hated her for it. A shudder went through her trembling body.

Tense silence filled the room.

Fortune cleared his throat. "Sorry. I should have knocked louder. I pulled the button off this shirt, Hildy. And another one is loose. No rush." He tossed the crumpled shirt on a chair and turned on his heel.

"Uncle Win," Matty yelled as he stomped across the wooden porch. "Miss Kennedy's the best teacher I ever had!"

Fortune's shoulders stiffened, but he didn't answer, just kept walking toward his horse. In the mood he was in, it was a miracle he noticed how the horse blanket was wadded into a bunch and that there was a wicked knot of rose thorns under it.

"Damned kids," he muttered, tossing the thorns to the ground.

Sheldon Rockwell lay unmoving amongst the soft silken pillows, trying to blot out the discomfort of awakening, trying to will himself back to his heavenly cloud of euphoria. But it was too late. Reality had come to claim him.

"You are awake," a hushed, foreign-sounding male voice said. "Bath being made ready."

As the fragrant, lingering odor of opium smoke taunted him, Sheldon gave himself over to the gentle hands that would wash and massage his body back to normal. Later he might be able to take tea and beef broth. And then he'd rest—he needed lots of rest.

The drug acted as a stimulant, enabling him to forgo food, water, and even sleep for many hours as he sought pure, delicious ecstasy. While the poppy-induced haze of bliss clouded his mind, nothing else existed for Sheldon but pleasure. Now he must endure the hell of returning to earth and the responsibilities of life.

He wasn't an addict. He simply smoked opium to relax. He didn't wander around Chinatown seeking his pleasures in the opium dens like the habitual users did. He wasn't that kind of man. And he knew he could quit any time he wanted. In fact, this probably was his last journey to the sweet celestial paradise.

Nobody knew about this small decadence except Leong. Sheldon had hired the handsome Oriental youth more than seven months before and had never been so completely satisfied with a servant. Leong made his life infinitely comfortable, and when Sheldon had expressed curiosity about smoking opium, Leong had presented him with a pipe.

Now, awakening to the reality of lost time, jangled nerves, and aching flesh, Sheldon wished his brain was numb again. What if somebody found out? Even Harlan didn't know about this adventure, though his brother had made numerous suggestive remarks about his relationship with Leong.

Snatches of luscious but foggy memories skidded around in his head and collided with the remnants of his morality and the fear for his yet untarnished reputation.

This can't go on! The thought jarred painfully.

He wouldn't slip again. He promised himself he would stop now, before this foolish recreation became a habit. Before his reputation was damaged. Before the Opera Committee discovered his sins. He needed the respect and acclaim of the Opera Committee as much as he needed air to breathe.

"Bring me some strong tea," he said sharply.

The decision had taken all his strength. Then he gave himself up to Leong's clever hands. The boy helped him into the bathtub. Warm water lapped up and soothed him.

When he was able, he'd make a decision about Moll

Kennedy. God, how he loathed the woman. Only for eight million dollars had he endured her company and the subsequent letters.

Hiring her had been Harlan's idea. Naturally Harlan would think about putting a woman spy in their cousin's bed. But she wasn't working out. Her letters were full of nonsense he cared nothing about, and his other spies had already reported Cousin Winslow visiting her cabin. Either Cousin Win didn't indulge in pillow talk, or Moll Kennedy was worthless as a spy. Maybe she was even dangerous.

It was her fault he'd been on this binge, Sheldon decided. That week in her company had nearly undone him, and her constant bickering with his brother had been unbearable. Harlan was dreadful enough without some slut baiting him. Sheldon thought he would go crazy before he got her off to the woods.

Once she was on the train to Placerville, Sheldon had gone straight home to Leong. He'd felt an irresistible urge to smoke his magic pipe. Leong understood. Everything was waiting, as it had been repeatedly since then.

Soon he must decide about the woman. Perhaps they should forget the investment they'd made in her. Maybe they should simply terminate her.

8

Harlan Rockwell read the words so neatly written on sheets of heavy, cream-colored paper a second time and swung around to challenge his brother. "What sort of horseshit is this?"

Sheldon sliced a delicate sliver of abalone steak, forked it into his mouth, and chewed it thoughtfully. "I thought you might know, brother—you're the one who understands women."

Harlan flung the letter down on the table and glared. "I thought you told the bitch what you wanted."

At that moment, Figaro, Sheldon's long-haired white cat, ambled into the dining room. When he spotted Harlan, he came to a halt, arched his back, and hissed all at the same instant. After two disjointed steps backward, the cat spat and fled the room.

Sheldon tossed his fork onto the plate and pushed it away, his appetite utterly spoiled. "Maybe we should just kill them both."

Leong came into the dining room to clear away the food. After pouring tea for the men, he quietly exited with the large silver serving tray. He'd learned the hard way to keep his long, braided queue out of Harlan's reach.

"He's real nice," said Harlan, mockingly sweetly.

"Yes. He is." Sheldon's tone indicated he'd tolerate no insolence about his servant. "Sugar?"

"Brandy. What if she ain't in Cousin Win's bed yet?"

Sheldon looked at his brother as if he'd lost his mind. He stood up and reached for the brandy decanter, forgetting he had a servant to fetch and carry. "Of course she's in Cousin Win's bed. She was hired to crawl between his sheets."

"No, she was hired to teach school."

Sheldon's eyes closed as the truth dawned on him. "I hired a spy," he whispered.

"You hired a schoolmarm! You took a half dressed strumpet off a burning stage and put her in plain clothes. Then you told her to talk softly and walk without wiggling her butt and think pure thoughts. You put her on a train and sent her up to the mountains and told her to teach little kiddies their ABC's. And sure as hell, that's just what the silly bitch is doing!"

Sheldon groaned. "She must be sleeping with Cousin Win."

Harlan waved the crumpled letter at him. "Where does it say that?"

"C.J. saw Win go in her cabin."

"Maybe it was on fire—the stupid slut is real good at setting places ablaze."

"C.J. told Mark he saw Win go in the cabin and stay nearly an hour."

Harlan snorted. "C.J.'s a sot. A woman like that would take more than an hour . . ."

"That kind of talk turns my stomach."

Harlan smiled. "You do look a little peaky, and you've lost some weight. Haven't you been feeling well lately? I've been by several times the last couple weeks, and Leong informed me you were resting. Are you sick?"

"I'm fine. We're talking about our expensive but nonproductive spy, not me. Since she didn't understand what we wanted from her in the first place, I think you should drop her a note. It was your idea to hire her."

"You do the writing, Sheldon. I'm not good at that sort of thing. You just tell her that Winslow Fortune will become a fountain of information, once she gets his drawers around his ankles."

Harlan took a loud slurp of his brandy and then continued. "And, for the record, it was your idea to hire her. You saw the ad in the goddamn paper, and you thought it would be real keen to get a female to worm secrets out of dear Cousin Win. *You* tell her how to squeeze the worm."

"I'd rather eat poison. You're the expert—you write the letter." Sheldon hated this kind of argument. Harlan got mean when he was losing.

"She doesn't like me."

"Neither do I."

Harlan's eyes gleamed wickedly. "Shame on you, brother. You're so testy lately. Smoking dope will do that to you."

Sheldon became as pale as the linen tablecloth. "I haven't—"

"Horseshit! The lovely little Leong makes lots of

runs to Chinatown these days. You're an opium addict."

"I am not—"

"What about those old whiffle-tits on the Opera Committee? What if they find out their 'dear boy' spends half his time in poppy paradise? What if Sampson Levine finds out? He hates us! Christ, we've got a fortune at stake here, and you're unconscious half the time, you dumb sonofabitch!"

Sheldon knocked over the chair as he stood up. "Go to hell, Harlan!" He stormed out of the room to the sound of his brother's laughter.

Fortune sat astride his horse and looked at the clear blue sky. For the third day that week not a puff of cloud marred the brilliant blue. There wasn't a drop of rain in sight, even though it was the middle of November. While most folks were enjoying the pleasant autumn days, he wished for cold weather and storms.

He thought of the rockslide that had occurred the previous day while he was inspecting the log chute—the first overt act of violence directed solely at him. In spite of Sampson Levine's warnings, Win never really expected his cousins to hire men to attack him. But there was no doubt that the sudden rockslide had been deliberately set off.

Win had not only heard a yelp of pain and some curses just before the rocks tumbled, he'd also found a blood-smeared sack of tobacco beside the tool which had been used to start the avalanche.

He'd easily avoided the tumbling stones, but the incident had both angered and saddened him. The idea that his kin wanted him dead was hard to stomach. He found it easier to ponder the weather.

His was a seasonal business. During the past few summers, vast numbers of sugar-pine logs had been sent down the chute to the river below, where they sat behind holding ponds before being sent downriver to the mill at Folsom. Sugar-pine logs were often eight to ten feet in diameter and astonishingly heavy.

Win prayed for rain. Come spring, he hoped, the winter snow would melt, and the river would rise above the boulders. If water in the river was low, running the logs downstream could be dangerous.

As Win sat there, wondering if nature would cooperate at all this year, he heard the shrieks and laughter of children and knew that school had ended for the day. Perhaps he'd catch a glimpse of the teacher on her way home—though his last glimpse of her had put him in misery for hours.

Last night he had almost gone to visit Bella Strong, a woman who had a select clientele. But the McDonald twins had showed him their new puppies, and Hannah gave him a batch of cookies to take home. One of the men stopped him on his way up the hill to tell him about more cat tracks. Then the temptation to see Bella passed. She wasn't the one haunting his dreams.

For several days, Win had seen Moll walking into the woods and out of it. He wanted to caution her again about snakes, which hadn't denned yet, and other animals . . . and, yes, even men. He was still uneasy about the footsteps he'd seen near her cabin, and he'd noticed new ones again today.

Loggers were a hard-working, hard-living, hard-drinking lot. Fortune suspected that a few were as wild as the animals in the woods where they worked. A city girl like Mollene Kennedy wouldn't know that. He felt obliged to bring it to her attention.

And, hell, he wanted to see her again, away from the crowd of Hannah's boarders. His gray eyes brightened when he saw Moll strolling purposefully down the dirt path, her paisley shawl draped over one shoulder.

A faint, cool breeze touched Moll's flushed cheeks and ruffled her dark hair. She closed her eyes for a brief second and relished the pleasant sensation of the bright afternoon sun shining on her face and the fragrances of the green depths of the forest wafting out to her. She was tired. Nothing she'd done on the stage had ever taken as much energy as teaching school did.

Being alone in the shadows of the enormous sugar pines quickly revived her stamina and zest for life. Walking along the paths and dusty logging roads, listening to the birds, smelling the pleasant odors of pine and shrubs restored her mind and humor after a day of being cooped up in a room the size of a chickenhouse with eleven children.

Actually, she liked teaching. After the first harrowing week ended and she discovered the little darlings hadn't done her in, she settled down to her duties with competence. She felt a sense of pride about her accomplishment, though she couldn't explain it to anybody. How could she admit she was damned proud she hadn't made a fool of herself in front of a bunch of kids? Or that the little beggars hadn't murdered her?

Tromping along the logging road, her hightop shoes sending up puffs of fine dust with every step, she was lost in her thoughts and totally unaware of the man who was following behind her.

Her mind went back to that day at Hildy's house when Fortune caught her in her combinations. She recalled the tears, which had come so suddenly when he stomped out, and remembered how kind and sympathetic Hildy had been. For once, Hildy hadn't treated her like an enemy.

Muttering despicable things about men in two languages, Hildy had made Moll a cup of ginger tea and wrapped her in a blanket till the clothes were mended.

What Hildy hadn't understood, of course, was what had caused the tears. It wasn't just anger, but disappointment, frustration, and confusion. Dammit, she liked Winslow Fortune—more than was safe for her wayward heart.

He was big and rugged and grumbly, and all she dreamed of was making him laugh. She wanted to take the burden of his problems from his broad shoulders and give him one whole happy day. She wanted to see him relaxed and smiling. She wanted to be the woman he smiled at.

The heat in his gray eyes ignited a similar fire in her heart. Who the devil was she trying to kid? She wanted him relaxed and smiling, all right—in her bed.

With Étienne it had been different. He'd been a nice man, concerned about her comfort, seeking her approval, soothing her fears—on the days when he wasn't too preoccupied with work to remember she existed. He'd instructed her in the art of love, but the heat between them had never grown into a raging forest fire.

In many ways Étienne had acted as young and insecure as she, although he was twelve years older. Small, slender, and thoroughly continental, he had taught her to be a sexual woman but had failed to show her how to be a mature adult. During the months they were together, he spent too much money—buying her gifts, entertaining her, trying to fulfill her every whim. She loved it, naturally, because nobody had ever catered to her whims before, but it was all make-believe. It was playing at life, playing at love. They had had only a honeymoon, not a marriage.

Alone and terrified after Étienne's sudden, awful death, Moll had to grow up. In Panama, before she got passage on a ship to California. In the orange groves, where she worked while waiting for money from her aunt in Baltimore. And later, after learning her aunt was dead, in the saloons where she sang.

She came to understand that love wasn't a man buying a girl presents, or a girl spending the whole day getting dressed up and deciding what new presents she wanted. Real love was living with someone day to day, even when life got rough.

"Miss Kennedy!"

Moll jumped, startled to be caught daydreaming in the woods. Raising her hand to shield her eyes from the orange afternoon glare, she saw that the rider silhouetted against the sun was her boss. A rosy flush touched her cheeks.

Fortune had been aloof since the incident at Hildy's house. He hadn't apologized or criticized. If anything, he'd been downright stuffy and correct. Perhaps he didn't know how to discuss the matter any more than she did.

Once, though, in an unguarded moment in the McDonalds' parlor when he thought no one was watching, he let his gaze linger on her, burning hot and hungry.

The look seared her mind. So did the memory of her body's answering flare of desire. Fortune was trouble.

Now, as he approached, Moll told herself not to

react to him in any way. She didn't need this man in her life in any capacity except as an employer. She had a job to do, and she damn well meant to do it. Getting involved with Winslow Fortune would ruin everything—if she was dumb enough to let that happen.

No, she wasn't that stupid. She had a history of following her emotions instead of her brains. This time she planned to do things right, because this man was more dangerous to her well-being than any other she'd ever known.

Her pulse quickened at the sight of him on his magnificent steed, and she set her facial features in the pose appropriate for a timid teacher meeting her employer.

"Good afternoon, Mr. Fortune."

She felt herself tremble as she gazed up at him. Her body was betraying her.

Fortune wanted to fling himself off the horse, pull her into his arms, and kiss her senseless, but he fought for control.

His words sounded harsh and surly. "Stay out of the woods. My men can't work with you sashaying amongst the trees. This isn't a stage, and they aren't your audience."

Moll recoiled from his blunt order, and the warm flush that had tingled through her before now grew hot with anger. She'd taken care not to wander anywhere near the loggers. She had been seeking solitude, not company, and definitely not the attention of men. Fortune's accusation was unfair, and untrue.

She straightened her shoulders and squared her jaw. "You hired me to teach school, and I am doing that. Quite well, I might add. But my free time is my own. I will go where I want, when I want, and it's none of your concern . . ."

"This isn't a pretty park in Baltimore," Fortune interrupted her. The bay tossed its head and rolled its eyes.
Fortune automatically shifted his body to the horse's
movements without thinking. He was ashamed of the
way he'd spoken, but his anger was riding atop other,
more dangerous, emotions. "This is the wilderness—
wild animals live here. If cornered, they will attack you.
I can't protect you from them any more than I can
protect you from some man who thinks you're out in
the bushes looking for a little fun. Unless a tussle in the
brush is what you're looking for."

She sucked in her breath. "How dare you!"

The horse sidestepped skittishly, moving up an
incline. Win had his hands full controlling the restless
animal.

"Don't walk in the woods . . ."

Whatever words came next were cut off by the deaf-
ening roar of a shotgun.

Fortune's already high-strung horse screamed and
went into a frenzy. Caught completely unaware, Win
barely had time to tighten his grip on the reins before
he was tossed into the air by the fear-crazed bay.

Stunned by the sound of the gun blast, Moll didn't
react till Win hit the ground.

"Win!" she shrieked, rushing to where he lay, fearing the worst. She was vaguely aware of the horse
galloping away down the road.

He lay as still as a rag doll in the pungent-smelling
mountain misery, trying to get his breath. He groaned
in disgust as well as pain. No man liked to be unseated
in front of a beautiful woman.

"You're hurt!"

"No," he moaned, feeling like he'd been run over by
a train.

"There's blood on your pants!"

Win bolted upright and looked at the side of his pants. A little more investigating assured him he wasn't wounded. "Shot musta hit the horse," he said. "I better go find him."

"Who was it?" Moll asked as she put her arm around his waist. It was a long walk to Summit, and she didn't want him to faint along the wayside.

"Hunters, I guess," Win answered, enjoying her closeness in spite of his fury about the gunshot. His gaze lingered on her face for a moment, and then he led her out of the woods and went in search of the horse.

"Three tries, you fool, and all you done was hit a horse in the ass!"

Potty Simms burned at the criticism but kept his mouth shut. It wasn't his fault the damned horse decided to hop around just as he pulled the trigger. None of it was his fault. He'd tried real hard to kill Fortune, but he'd had a run of bad luck.

"If you can't do it right the next time," Danbury said, "you're through."

"Yeah, Potty," Leland Ames put in, annoyed at how much he'd lost to Buckley Brooks on Potty's third try. "Hit Fortune, or hit the trail."

The next time Moll went walking in the woods by herself, a few days later, she got lost.

Somehow she'd gotten caught up in her thoughts of Win and wandered into the thick of the forest. She'd completely lost her way. Normally she had a good sense of direction, but today everything had gone wrong.

Suddenly she skidded on some pine needles and fell down on her rump. "Oh, damn!"

On previous walks, she'd loved the feeling of wild majesty of this Sierra mountain ridge—the stately sugar pines with their incredibly long cones, the beauty of the red-barked madrona, the fragrance of the cedar. She'd been in complete communication with nature, as if she were a living, breathing part of it, the same as a doe or a blue jay or the wild, winding honeysuckle.

But today she'd somehow gotten lost.

She tried to clear her head, to get her bearings. She looked around.

The tall spires of green threatened her somehow as they reached to the sky, blocking the sun, casting her in deep shadows. Thick clumps of manzanita, buckbrush, and poison oak further obscured her view. The loamy smell of the earth beneath the pine needles reminded her suddenly of an open grave. When something rustled the dry grass not far away, she gasped in alarm.

Someone was watching. She'd been jumpy since the shooting last week, when some fool hunter had lacerated the flank of Win's horse, but it wasn't her imagination this time. Someone was out there.

Moll glanced around but saw no one. Slowly she got to her feet and dusted off her skirt. Her shawl had fallen to the ground, and she carefully brushed off the pine needles, all the while holding her panic at bay.

An icy shudder slithered up her spine, and cold chills crawled past her ears and across her cheeks. She fought to control her hysteria.

The eyes continued to watch her. Deadly eyes. Moll could sense the evil emanating from them.

She forced herself to look around the landscape, while another part of her listened.

She forced herself to recall the name of each kind of tree and bush. Once identified, the huge trees seemed less ominous, the vegetation less encroaching. She observed the chartreuse-green moss hugging the tree trunks and the brownish white mushrooms peeking out of the ground.

Her heart rate slowed to an almost normal pace.

She heard the sound of silence. Nothing moved. Nothing scurried, twittered, or squawked. Nothing cried out. The forest was utterly, terrifyingly silent.

But the menace was still there.

Moll licked her parched lips with a tongue as dry as sandpaper. She listened, and again there was nothing. Holding tightly to her apprehension, and refusing to panic for even the briefest instant, she forced her trembling body to identify the direction of north.

She'd get out. She'd walk out. Common sense and logic would save her.

With more than a little bravado, Moll surveyed her position and charted what seemed to be a sensible course out of the woods, far from whatever was watching.

"This isn't the first time you've been watched, Moll," she told herself, somewhat relieved at the sound of her own voice. "You've strutted your stuff in front of hundreds of people and loved every minute of it."

With that, she launched herself forward—not running, though. To run would be to panic. No, she walked briskly in the direction she'd chosen, like a lady out for a constitutional.

She'd taken about fifty steps out of the grove of trees when a scream tore the air like rending cloth, the most gruesome sound Moll had heard in her entire life. It shrieked on and on, the beastly cry of a woman in terror—or in ghastly pain.

At the first wretched sound Moll froze. But as the horrifying sound went on and on, she felt her body react as if it was controlled by a force beyond herself. Blood pounded in her head. Shudders racked her frame. With her composure shattered, she succumbed to hysteria.

In her madness and fear, Moll gave little thought to direction. She simply ran.

Mindless, she dodged trees and plants as she fled. She had no idea how long she ran. By chance, she stumbled upon a path. The screaming had died away. But, winded and exhausted, she still kept running.

She couldn't stop. Having given in to her panic, she'd lost all control. Finally she crashed headlong into something solid and unmoving. And smelly.

The impact shook her to her shoe buttons. Before she had time to react, something ensnared her, catching her arms to her sides and squeezing tight.

Moll tried to shriek but barely managed a squeak from her parched, winded throat. Her weak knees buckled, and she collapsed, inhaling the strong odor of tobacco mixed with unwashed clothes.

It was only then that she realized her captor was human. Above the sound of her own racing heart, she heard the sound of another loud heartbeat.

Finding a reserve of strength, Moll forced her head up and stared into a pair of dark, angry eyes.

A tiny cry escaped her throat.

She knew the man, though his name momentarily escaped her. Matt? Mark? That's right, it was Mark. She'd heard his name from Win or Bill McDonald at the stables on the day of the shooting, but she couldn't recall what they'd said about him.

She managed to gasp a few words, "Someone . . . forest . . . screamed."

The dark, violent look faded quickly from Mark Danbury's eyes, and crimson crept over his face. He loosened his iron grip on her arms and stepped back. After apologizing for grabbing her, he explained that he'd heard a cry. "I came to see if there was trouble."

"Thank you." Instinctively, Moll moved out of his reach. She saw something flash in his face at her movement, but he made no attempt to touch her again. She inched farther from him. She couldn't help herself, the man repelled her. She had to get away from him.

"I must get home ..."

Thundering hooves drowned out the rest of her words. Winslow Fortune and Bill McDonald galloped up and quickly dismounted.

"What the devil's going on?" Win demanded.

Only then did Moll realize her clothes were torn and her hair had fallen down. The way Win's look swept over her left Moll with no illusions about her appearance. Her clothes were in tatters, and her pride wasn't much better.

"I heard a woman scream," she said, still breathless.

"You heard a cougar, Miss Kennedy. A mountain lion. A very dangerous animal. I've warned you about animals, and hunters. Why are you out in the woods?"

"You didn't say a word about that kind of danger."

Win looked at Bill and shook his head. Then he thanked Danbury for helping Moll. "She looks like she's had enough for one day. I'll take her back to the cabin on the horse."

A muscle in Danbury's jaw twitched, but his voice was soft when he spoke. "Sure, boss. Hope you weren't too scared, Miss Kennedy."

Moll shuddered as he walked away. The man made her feel as dirty as he smelled.

She caught Win watching her. "Don't say a word."

"I don't plan to." He couldn't understand why this female always made him want to throttle her or smother her with kisses. Ignoring Bill's knowing smile, he lifted her into the saddle and climbed on behind her. They rode in silence. For once they were content and at peace with each other.

9

Buckley Brooks joined Harlan Rockwell on the steps of the finest whorehouse in Placerville at three o'clock on Friday afternoon. Brooks had faked an injury that morning in order to provide himself with an excuse to go to town. Now he and Harlan waltzed inside like gents on their way to do legitimate business.

Harlan seldom liked other people, but Brooks was a man he got on with. He didn't tower over Harlan as most other men did, and they shared an appetite for the same type of lewd entertainment. They both singularly lacked scruples, and, unlike most of the other people who worked for the Rockwells, Brooks was solely motivated by greed.

"So how is Cousin Win getting on with the teacher?" Harlan asked as they watched the parade of prostitutes flaunt past.

A young Oriental girl caught Buckley's fancy, and then a redhead with a big bottom. It took him a minute to answer. "She don't like Fortune much. She's got the hots for Jed Cantrell."

"What?" Harlan was squeezing the nipple of a bleached blonde who was leaning over him, and nearly pinched it off. She shrieked, smacked him, and stormed away.

"I'd bang her myself, but she's got eyes for Jed. Your cousin don't like it, but she don't care."

"Well, I do, by God. I ain't paying her to screw anybody but Cousin Win. She's meeting us tomorrow. Sheldon and me'll set her straight." He waved a fat brunette forward. "You stay outta her pants, too, Bucky. Cousin Win won't tell her secrets if he thinks he's one of a crowd."

"Sure." Brooks smiled and shrugged. Rockwell was paying him plenty to see that the machinery kept breaking down. There were always other women. "Why don't we try a threesome?"

If there was one thing Moll hated, it was a man who wanted to chat before the sun came up. Jed Cantrell was ready to leave for Placerville before daybreak, and he was disgustingly cheerful. Moll preferred to drink coffee and ease gently into morning, but anxiety about the trip to town and her upcoming meeting had already destroyed her serenity. So, without complaint, she climbed into the high wagon seat in time to see the eastern sky turn pink.

It had been easy to convince folks that the trip was necessary. The Winter Fair was two weeks away, and Moll needed props for the Gypsy tent. Before long, she had an enormous list. Everyone in the village wanted something or another.

The summons had come on Monday. The Rockwell brothers would be in Placerville over the weekend and wanted to see her Saturday. There was no please or thank you, just a time and place to meet. Moll's first reaction was fear.

"The Ghost of Mother Superior," she'd told herself as she gripped the note, trying to laugh off the anxiety clenching her stomach.

The truth was that as she'd settled into her new home and her new job, she'd sort of forgotten about the two men in San Francisco. They were so far away and so unpleasant to think about. And she couldn't tell them that Fortune had seen her at the Majestic and had her poster as a momento. That would be the end of her!

She'd kept up her end of the bargain about writing them a weekly letter, the same as she'd written to Sampson, but in reality she'd spent little time scouting for details about Winslow Fortune's operations. In the dead of night, when she lay awake reviewing her behavior and her letters to them, she admitted she was a very poor spy. She figured she could bluff her way through it, unless they discovered she was also working for Sampson Levine. Then she would be in trouble.

More than once lately, Moll had yearned for a confidant. She'd thought about divulging her role to Hannah, as nobody else was as intelligent or discreet. Hildy told everything she knew to either Hannah or Win, Mildred was too standoffish, and Selma was too obtuse. Hannah was the only one Moll trusted—but Hannah was Win's friend.

By the time the wagon pulled away from Summit early Saturday morning, Moll was so nervous about the meeting at the Cary House that she'd didn't give much thought to the drive.

But Jed wanted to chat.

Actually, Jed wasn't originally scheduled to be her driver. Win had asked C. J. Hodges to make the trip, but he'd gone on a drinking spree. And since Win had an appointment in Auburn to meet the engineer that Sampson had found, Jed got to drive.

Moll clung to the wagon seat and pretended to listen to Jed's stories and contemplate the scenery. In truth she was saying every prayer the sisters had ever taught her. She even made up a few.

"You a flatlander, Miss Kennedy?"

"Yes, I guess I am," she answered. "There's nothing like this in downtown Baltimore." Moll didn't believe there was anything like it on the rest of the whole damned planet. She had decided that he had the horses and the wagon under control—until they reached the bridge.

The bridge creaked ominously the moment the horses stepped onto the narrow wooden structure, and then it began to sway. The roar of the river surging over the granite boulders matched the roar in her ears. Blood thundered in her temples, and silvery white lights sparkled before her eyes. Beads of perspiration appeared above her lip, mixed with a fine spray of water from the river.

"The water's low this year," Jed told her. "We need rain. If Fortune's going to get his timber to the mill, we need lots of rain. Miss Kennedy, are you okay?"

"I'm fine." Her voice sounded thin and reedy, but her elocution was perfect. The sparkling lights faded, her head cleared, and her heart rate slowed. She was aware of the cold, damp air swirling up from the churning river. "It's cold down here."

"No sunshine." Jed guided the horses off the bridge and onto the path carved out of the mountainside.

In an effort to keep her mind off the drive up the steep grade, she looked over her shoulder at the moss and green ferns growing in the cracks of the granite wall. She was so close to the side of the cliff, she could have reached out and stroked the velvety moss and tiny sprigs of dark green plant life.

"Are you originally from California, Mr. Cantrell?" she asked after a moment.

"Born in New York, raised in Ohio. I've spent the last fifteen years drifting from one place to another. I was in Colorado for a spell before I came to California."

For the first time since she'd climbed in the wagon, Moll was truly interested in what he was saying. "Were you in the Denver area?"

"Off and on. Mostly I worked outside of Denver, at some of the mines. But I visited a lot." Cantrell had lived with a woman in Denver more than three years, but he didn't mention that. Some things a man didn't tell a woman he was trying to impress.

Her heart gave a little bump. "Did you ever hear of a man named Seamus Blade?"

Jed laughed. "Who hasn't? That old man's as rich as he is crazy."

"Oh?"

"Old Blade's one *lucky* Irishman." Jed had been trying to get her attention since they left, so he was going to make the most of the opportunity. He didn't know a great deal about Blade, but he didn't intend to tell her that. "Everything he touches turns to money. They say he has a nose for gold—he can smell it in the ground. Anything he invests in, he comes out a winner. He's rolling in money."

Jed rounded a corner, spotted an approaching rider, and pulled the wagon into a narrow turnout to wait. The rider was Buckley Brooks. They spoke briefly, and then Brooks rode on. Jed didn't mention how early he thought it was for a man to be on the road from Placerville, or where he suspected Brooks had spent the night.

"Seamus Blade brags that he's lucky at cards *and* love. Heard he really likes the ladies. Are you okay?"

"I'm fine." She took a deep breath and smiled. "Does he have a large family?"

Jed gave her a look of pure speculation. Was she angling for a rich husband? He admitted, with her looks, she might catch one. "Can't really remember," he answered, thinking how unfair it was that he hadn't been born rich.

Sheldon Rockwell surveyed Placerville from the second-story balcony of his suite at the Cary House and sipped brandy from a silver flask. Like so many other mining towns in California's Mother Lode, it was long and narrow, located at the bottom of a deep ravine and spreading up into the surrounding hills.

It was a glorious autumn day, but Sheldon was too hung over to appreciate the weather or the quaintness of the bustling town. He considered it hopelessly provincial and fervently wished that he hadn't accompanied Harlan and his friend Brooks last night to the card room at the Round Tent.

Not only had he gotten disgustingly soused, he'd lost three hundred dollars to a laughing gambler in a pink brocade vest. Then Harlan and his chum had gone off looking for a brothel and left him behind.

He took another swig from the flask and wondered if he felt well enough for breakfast. Below him, on the street, a large spotted dog came running out of the alley and spooked an old horse pulling a milk wagon. The wagon lurched unsteadily as another dog, which was chasing the first, ran toward the horses, and the milk wagon almost knocked down a portly lady in plaid who was wearing an abominable purple hat.

"Now I've seen the entertainment of the week," Sheldon murmured to himself. "I think I'll try breakfast."

He wandered back to his room. The three-story Cary House advertised itself as being the most elegant, modern hotel in Placerville and boasted a complete change of bed linens after every customer. Sheldon was not impressed. By his standards, it bordered on shoddy, but at least the brick building was fireproof. With Moll Kennedy coming to town, a man couldn't be too careful.

Sheldon hoped breakfast would be edible. Food might improve his mood. It also might help him to gain back some of the weight he'd recently lost and take his mind off the ten o'clock meeting with Mark Danbury. The homely, morose man was more depressing than Harlan. Sometimes Sheldon wished he'd never hired Danbury, but the man knew everything that was going on in Summit, as if he never needed to sleep.

Jed stopped at Placerville Hardware and helped Moll down from her perch. Like Moll, he had a list of supplies to get for the Winter Fair, and he needed some dynamite and blasting caps.

"Hannah said to remind you to place an advertisement about the fair in the *Mountain Democrat*," Moll said.

"How could I forget? She and Hildy told me about a dozen times. Do you want to have lunch with me?"

Moll hadn't expected the invitation. "Thank you, but I've already got plans."

"Okay. I'll meet you at the bell tower at two. We can drive around and pick up your packages. I know there's a lot of things on your list. No need to be trudging them all over town."

Warmed at his consideration, Moll thanked him. "Why don't I have them delivered to the Cary House and meet you there instead of the tower? That's where I'm eating."

A nice man, she decided as she walked off, but not the man for her. Not that she was looking for a man. But whenever she thought of men, the image of Winslow Fortune popped into her mind.

She glanced at a store display of hats and remembered the tragic demise of her last decent hat the day she had arrived at Summit. Fortunately, Hildy Swensen had transformed her other hats beautifully.

Now Hildy was a very eligible widow, she thought. Of course, Hildy was always casting glances at Winslow Fortune, but Moll knew Hildy wasn't right for him. She might be perfect for Jed, though. Absorbed in thought, Moll walked away, leaving the anxious storekeeper, who'd been certain he had a sale, frowning in disappointment.

As she continued down the street, Moll wondered if she could do something to make Jed see what a kind, caring woman Hildy was. The girl could use a little sprucing up, she decided. There wasn't anything terribly wrong with her looks, but her clothes were shabby, and her hands were work-worn. And, more often than not, her hair was in disarray.

The wonderful smells of a bakery, wafting toward Moll from down the street, interrupted her matchmaking thoughts. Within minutes, she was sitting at a tiny table, eating hot apple pie and drinking coffee, while Mrs. Buchanan, who was eating one of her own cookies, inquired about Summit. Moll invited her to the upcoming Winter Fair. After a second cup of coffee Moll went on her way.

The first stop on her list was Simon's Clothing Store. Hildy had given her instructions to buy fabric to replace the flared skirt she'd torn when running through the woods. Mrs. Simon, a brisk, gray-haired woman with spectacles, found a bolt of wool that went well with the skirt's jacket as well as a quiet trim for both. She also showed Moll a bolt of blue-violet wool crepe.

"This would make a lovely dress for you, my dear. It would compliment your coloring beautifully."

By the time she left Simon's Moll had bought several of the things on her shopping list, plus seven yards of the blue-violet crepe and a bottle of rose water hand lotion for Hildy. She told herself it was just a little something extra to give Hildy for all the sewing she was doing. She didn't consider it the first step in getting Jed Cantrell's head out of his powder box.

Moll suspected Jed had a powerful way with the ladies if he was in a courting mood, or a bedding mood. And with his tanned skin and blond hair, he was quite good-looking. She was sure Hildy would succumb to his charm, if the darn fool ever started being charming.

By noon, Moll had accomplished all her tasks and left the packages with the merchants, telling them to deliver everything to the lobby of the Cary House. The meeting with the Rockwells loomed.

Her nerves began to quiver ominously. She had to do something to keep her mind occupied for the next hour or she'd go crazy and run shrieking down the middle of Main Street.

She decided to look for a bathtub to replace the chipped hand-me-down bowl in her cabin. She asked a stranger on the street and learned that the place to find a bathtub was O'Keefe's Furniture Store and Undertaking Establishment, several blocks down.

O'Keefe's displayed all its furniture at the front of the store. No one seemed to notice Moll when she walked in, so she strolled around, examining what was for sale as if she had a pocketful of money and a whole house to furnish. In a small room at the back of the store, with large marble vases of paper lilies on either side of the door, Moll saw several coffins. After catching a glimpse of some people in black standing near one of them, she turned away.

Over in the far corner she discovered the bathtubs. In the midst of hip baths, sitz baths, foot tubs, and plunge tubs, stood one white, enameled-canvas portable bathtub with a nosegay of purple violets painted on the side.

The dapper salesman, with his hair slicked down, wearing a somber funeral suit and smelling of lily of the valley cologne, had seen her from the other room. Believing that his obligation to help a live customer outweighed his duty to the dead, he slipped out to wait on her. After several minutes of his sales spiel about the tub's comfort and easy assembly—no different from a folding cot—Moll decided to purchase it.

Digging out one of the gold coins she'd received

from Sampson Levine, Moll told the salesman to wrap the folded tub and deliver it to the Cary House by two o'clock. Then, feeling utterly giddy at having found such an unexpected treasure, she practically skipped out the door, only remembering decorum when she passed another mourner coming in.

A glance at her pendant watch told her she still had more than thirty minutes before her meeting, so she wandered up Sacramento Street to do some exploring. When she encountered a steep hill she could not possibly climb in the type of shoes she wore, she changed directions. At the corner of Pacific and Gold-ner there was a stone building with the sign See Yap Co. Intrigued by the name, Moll pushed open the heavy door. The fragrance of incense greeted her.

A tiny, dark-haired girl in a pink silk tunic and trousers shyly welcomed Moll to the elaborate temple. Feeling like an intruder, Moll had no intention of stay-ing, but the girl invited her to explore.

Wooden friezes of intricately carved vines and flow-ers, as well as birds and fierce dragons, decorated the room. A dainty wind chime tinkled above a charcoal brazier. Mysterious fragrances beguiled her, and a sense of tranquillity she'd seldom known settled over her. For the first time since she'd received the com-mand from the Rockwells, Moll relaxed and indulged herself in the peacefulness of the moment.

She'd learned more about her father today than she'd ever known before. She'd finally met somebody who knew enough about him to make him real. It gave her a strange sense of satisfaction to know that Seamus Blade was more than a signature on a legal document.

Forgetting about the time, Moll continued to peruse

the delightful, fragrant temple, allowing an inner peace and the beauty of another world to touch her mind and spirit.

She was late.

She took a deep breath and marched into the Cary House. Sheldon Rockwell, impeccably attired in wheat-colored worsted wool, was waiting for her in the lobby. He didn't look at all happy.

"I don't know about you," Moll said brightly, "but I'm famished. It's a long drive from Summit."

Ushering her to the table he'd reserved, Sheldon wondered why the woman didn't weigh a ton. Every time he saw her she ate enough to feed a family of four. "Please order," he said with a sigh.

Moll decided to try a Hangtown Fry, a local specialty of oysters and eggs made famous during the Gold Rush, and Sheldon seconded the order. After all, there was little to do in Placerville besides eat. The waiter scurried to bring champagne glasses, a silver wine chiller, and French champagne, which always accompanied the special dish.

Sheldon and Moll eyed one another warily. She wondered if she was due to be sacked—or shot.

He only knew that every time he was around this woman, he ended up being sorry that he had come. And where the hell was Harlan?

They silently saluted one another with the champagne glasses, each waiting for the other to attack.

"Your teaching position is all right?"

"Better than I anticipated."

"Cousin Winslow is satisfied?"

"I believe Mr. Fortune is pleased with my methods and the children's progress."

Sheldon refilled his glass. Moll had barely touched hers. "And the parents?"

Moll smiled prettily, forgetting that her charm did nothing for Sheldon. "Both Mr. Fortune and I have received compliments by the parents. I only have one problem student. His father drinks, and his mother has left them."

Sheldon didn't give a royal fig about the children's problems. This wasn't the place to tell her, though, because she was clearly ensconced in the role of Miss Prim Schoolmarm, and the restaurant was full. He cursed Harlan for being late and leaving him with this crazy actress.

The food arrived, and the waiter topped their glasses. They ate in relative silence, giving their attention to the food. The delicately seasoned oysters and fluffy eggs were delicious.

Moll frowned, realizing she was a trifle tipsy from the champagne she'd consumed. It had been some time since she'd touched any alcohol. "Did you come all this way to inquire about my teaching?"

"No." Sheldon downed his fourth glass of champagne. "Are you sleeping with Winslow Fortune?"

Although the words were softly spoken, Moll just knew everyone within three blocks heard them. An angry flush tinted her cheekbones, and fire blazed from her blue eyes.

"*I am not,*" she answered slowly from between clenched teeth. How foolish to let herself be lulled by the good food and drink. Moll glanced around, looking for his brother, but Harlan Rockwell was nowhere in sight. He was the one she had expected to be nasty.

Sheldon knew he'd started off wrong but was determined to carry it through, in spite of how angry he'd made her. It was a public place, and he felt relatively safe. He was certain that this outrageous woman would have stabbed him with a bread knife if they'd been alone. Licking his pale lips, he continued.

"Harlan and I hired you to do a job, and we're paying you handsomely. You'd be in jail if it wasn't for us."

"I'm being paid for information only." Moll trembled with rage, but thanks to her acting talents she managed to control her voice and her movements. Even the people at the nearest table didn't realize anything untoward was going on. She signaled the waiter for coffee.

"So far, the information you've sent us is useless garbage," Sheldon told her when the waiter left. "We don't give a damn about the school or what Hannah McDonald serves for dinner. We need something we can use to destroy Winslow Fortune!"

"I'm doing the best I can." She hated having to defend herself, but she was in fact delighted that she hadn't come across any information that could help them harm Win.

"No, you're not. You're not coming up with one damned thing that will help us collect the money."

"I'm trying!"

"Not hard enough. Not the way we want. Cousin Win likes women, but he's particular. He's not like my brother, who would crawl off with any sow who'll toss up her skirts." Sheldon realized he was raising his voice. He poured the last of the champagne into his glass and drank it.

"I won't do that. You're not paying me for *that!*"

"Winslow is a man of strong passions. I know he's not sleeping with any other woman at the moment. I also know he can't keep his greedy eyes off you. Cousin

Win is a hungry man. He'll fall into your bed with little argument."

Moll's patience was at an end. Rockwell was not paying her to prostitute herself, no matter what he said. Without further thought, she upended the wine cooler, spilling icy chunks and chilly water into Sheldon's lap.

Harlan chose that moment to walk in.

Moll brushed by him without a word.

"Well, brother," Harlan said with malignant glee, "I see you have the situation under control."

To Harlan's utter astonishment, Sheldon lunged to his feet and hit him squarely on the chin, knocking him to the dining-room floor.

Jed Cantrell was waiting outside with the wagon when Moll hurried outside. Neither of them noticed Winslow Fortune untie his horse from the hitching post across the street, nor saw him ride out of town ahead of them.

Jed, who had been tasting hard cider and ale at Pearson's, was quite cheerful as he loaded Moll's packages, including the portable bathtub, into the wagon. He carried on a stream of chatter nearly all the way home, not noticing that she'd been drinking or that she was furious.

Moll was so angry that she hardly said a word. Jed just continued telling her about his brother's children, a subject that concerned him greatly.

"What am I gonna do with those kids?" he kept asking her.

Moll wondered about her own children, the youngsters who filled the Summit School. Was she still going to teach them, or would she lose her job now that she'd poured icy water on Sheldon Rockwell's privates?

It wasn't until the wagon was halfway across the swinging bridge that Moll noticed just how happy Jed was acting. And how he smelled.

"You brought a heavy load," she commented. "What's in the back?"

"Three kegs of steam beer, some ale, some soda. Lumber and canvas for the refreshment booth. A few odds and ends. Oh yeah, and a box of dynamite."

Moll almost jumped off the wagon. "Dynamite?"

"Don't worry, Miss Kennedy," Jed said. "I'm the best powder monkey in the state of California. You're as safe with me as in your dear mother's arms."

That didn't comfort Moll one bit. Her dear mother had tossed her out into the cold world soon after she was born.

"Dynamite can't blow without blasting caps," Jed assured her. Then he began to sing "A Bicycle Built for Two," and she joined in moments later.

They would have been perfectly safe if it hadn't been for the hogs. A number of years earlier a homesteader had died, leaving several barnyard pigs to run wild. The porkers had bred freely and multiplied, and now their descendants roamed the mountains, creating havoc wherever they went.

Noticing that the afternoon shadows were getting long, and anxious to get home and unload the wagon, Jed urged the horses up the steep grade toward Summit. Suddenly, an enormous white sow and three half-grown pigs thundered down an incline, right into the path of the oncoming wagon.

Frightened by the snorting hogs, one horse reared while the other leaped and started to run. Jed yanked on the reins to control them, but not before the wagon swayed sharply and the back wheel slipped off the narrow road.

Moll fell.

Screaming in terror as her worst fear was being realized, she was pitched sideways out over the yawning canyon. Jed couldn't help her; he had his hands full controlling the horses. She grabbed the thin armrest on the wooden seat as she was hurled off the wagon. Only her quick thinking and strong grip saved her from falling down the mountain.

Ahead of them on the trail, Winslow Fortune heard Jed's yell and Moll's hair-raising scream.

He'd left the afternoon before for his meeting in Auburn with the engineers Sampson had recommended. The early morning meeting had been short and surprisingly successful. They had promised to get back to him with some drawings and figures by spring.

Having the rest of the day to himself, Win decided to ride back through Placerville. He might just visit Sebastian and Cassie and admire the baby. Of course he ought to stop and get a gift first. Not for a moment did he admit that his real reason for going to Placerville was to check on Moll and Jed.

He had a steak and a beer at the saloon across from the Cary House, and then decided to have another beer. New babies weren't that interesting. They all looked alike to him. He was feeling very relaxed when he walked outside. It was a beautiful day. His life was going relatively well. Nothing dangerous or untoward had happened recently.

He damn near fell over the hitching rail when he saw Harlan Rockwell saunter into the Cary House. What the hell was Harlan doing in Placerville? And where was Sheldon?

10

"*Have you ever seen* a Gypsy?" Hildy asked.

"I had my fortune told once. I think the woman was a real Gypsy." Moll laughed softly, recalling the incident. "My school friends and I went to a tea room in Baltimore, and this woman read palms and cards in the back room. It was a spooky place—dark with yards of dusty material draped around. Lots of flickering candles. And the woman smelled like gin."

Hildy chuckled. She was adding a black layer of taffeta beneath the scarlet handkerchief-style skirt of Moll's costume. She hadn't even raised an eyebrow when she first saw the brief gown, nor said a word beyond suggestions to make it warmer for the fund-raising event.

"I saw a Gypsy before I came to this country." Hildy knotted the thread and snipped it. "She told me I'd take a long, hard voyage. And when I arrived where I was going I would cry and wish I hadn't come. But later, I would be very happy. I would be with a good man who loved me, a big house and ten healthy children . . ."

"Ten? How awful! That's almost as many as I have at the school." Moll was carefully sewing black ribbon on the inset Hildy had added to the tightly laced bodice.

"I like kids. I want more than just one. What did the Gypsy tell you?" Hildy took the skirt over to the machine.

"About the same thing—except for the ten kids. That's probably standard Gypsy stuff. She said I would marry and he would take me to a foreign land. I would be happy at first, but then I would have many tears. Later a strong man would give me my heart's desire, and we would live a long, happy life together."

"Some of mine came true," Hildy said. "You're still waiting." She shook out the skirt and examined the sewing critically. "Don't get serious about any man who wants to take you to some foreign country."

Moll laughed. "I won't." Everything the old Gypsy had said had come true before she was twenty— except for the strong man offering her heart's desire. She suddenly felt melancholy. "When we get through here, I'm going to trim your hair," she said, to change the subject.

Her campaign to spruce up Hildy had been joined enthusiastically by Hannah McDonald, who gave her a shawl and several pieces of yard goods and lace trim. It wouldn't be long before Hildy would rival any woman around.

Now, if only Jed would pay attention and do his part. He apparently hadn't figured out what his part was yet. Moll was giving serious thought to writing him a script.

Later, when she hung the now-modest fortune-teller's costume on the hook behind the door in her

cabin, Moll's thoughts wandered back to the day she
and three other girls had sneaked away from the convent school to visit the back-street tea room. They'd
been so nervous, they had giggled their way through
two cups of weak tea and some stale bread before getting up the nerve to ask to see the Gypsy.

The other girls had been told about handsome young
husbands, and the names of their first babies, and the
kinds of houses they'd have. They thought they'd gotten their two bits' worth.

Moll's turn had left her unsettled and frightened.
The woman had told her about the sound of clapping
hands and several encounters with danger and death.
And men.

"There are many men, my lovely. Some will desire
you, some will hate you. Two will love you until death.
And one powerful man fears the secret you carry."

The other girls thought Moll's "fortune" was more
exciting and romantic than theirs, but the immediate
risk of getting caught by the sisters on their way back to
the convent overshadowed the entire episode.

Moll closed the heavy drapes and locked the door. It
seemed strange that Fortune was so set on her leaving,
yet thoughtful enough to supply heavier drapes to keep
out drafts. He was a complicated and confusing man.

After building up a fire to warm up the cabin, she
unsnapped a couple of locks and opened the bottom
drawer of her trunk. Bundled in the folds of the only
decent dress Aunt Beebee had ever sent her was the
packet she'd received two years ago from the Baltimore
lawyer, informing her of her aunt's death.

She'd been in Panama when her aunt died.
Because the mail service was so erratic and her personal situation so desperate, she'd somehow missed

the first letter from the lawyer. She'd written to him from California and later received his final missive about Aunt Beebee.

The thick package included several old legal documents, a half-dozen photographs, financial records, her mother's death certificate as well as her aunt's, and a sealed letter from Aunt Beebee.

Moll unwrapped the papers. She glanced at the pearl-gray merino dress and decided it would look good on Hildy. It no longer fit her, not since her figure had fully developed. The color wasn't right for her either; it was too dull.

And it reminded Moll how Aunt Beebee had spent nearly the entire endowment from Moll's father on herself. That money was the only thing he'd ever given Moll, except life.

Slowly she read the legal agreement signed by her parents. For quite a substantial settlement, her mother had agreed to raise Moll in a proper manner and as a Catholic, never make further legal or financial demands on her father, and never reveal her father's identity.

If giving her to Aunt Beebee immediately after birth and later putting her in a boarding school was a proper rearing, Moll guessed her mother had carried out the terms of the agreement.

Moll picked up a yellowing photograph. She wouldn't have known her mother if *Mary Rose Kennedy* hadn't been scrawled on the back. As far as she could remember, Mary Rose Kennedy never came to Beebee's house while Moll was there. Moll was a burden of shame her mother didn't want. She was only seven and already living at Mount de Sales when her mother died of consumption.

Aunt Beebee felt no compunction about revealing all the lurid details surrounding her niece's birth. The letter, written during the last year of her life, and perhaps meant as an apology for stealing her inheritance, told everything she knew about the "terrible sin" that had brought Moll to life. How Mary Rose Kennedy, a widowed nurse, had taken care of this man after a serious accident, and how he'd seduced her with his wicked, wanton ways.

Moll, she said, probably took after her father—a gold miner and a gambler with the devil's own Irish tongue—because her mother was a "good woman" in spite of her one mortal sin, for which she had suffered the rest of her life.

And in this letter, Aunt Beebee had divulged the name of Moll's sire—Seamus Blade, a wealthy businessman who lived in Denver. He was an immoral sinner, Beebee stated righteously, who was married and had a family.

"I wonder, Seamus Blade, if she thought I'd walk up to your door and announce myself?" Moll said aloud as she sat on the wooden floor of her cabin, pondering the papers strewn about her.

Seamus Blade had been only a name in that letter from Aunt Beebee, until Moll asked Jed Cantrell about him. It seemed odd that from the few things Jed had said, she now felt she knew her father. Now he had breath and blood and bad habits, like every other living man.

She wished she had a photograph of her father. What kind of man was he? Her aunt's version was undoubtedly biased. Jed's version probably was too, as she had detected in his tone a note of envy over Blade's wealth.

Did she look like him? Neither her mother nor her aunt had been especially attractive. Could it be that she took after her father? She imagined him tall, handsome, and elegant, his black hair turning silver now. Then she remembered the Gypsy's words about a powerful man fearing the secret she carried.

"Don't worry, old man," she said softly. "I won't bother you if you don't bother me."

A noise outside the cabin interrupted her thoughts. Was it a cough? She put the papers back into the trunk and locked the drawer, waiting for a knock. Was it Hildy? Or Winslow Fortune?

She lay the gray dress on the foot of the bed and went to the door. After a moment's hesitation, she opened it and glanced out into the darkness. She saw no one.

"Hello? Is somebody there?"

A shiver touched her spine. Holding the door open, she called out again. Nobody answered.

"Guess it was the wind."

But just as she closed the heavy door, she heard another cough, muffled this time, but loud enough to distinguish. And not far way.

Heart pounding, she shot home the bolt and leaned against the locked door. She didn't hear another sound, but all through the night she kept waking up to listen.

Sheldon Rockwell poured his brother a brandy and returned to his own comfortable seat in front of the fire. It was foggy and cold outside tonight, and the blazing fire felt good.

"Leong pointed something out to me," he said.

"I'm sure he did," Harlan replied.

Sheldon frowned at his brother's innuendo. "He read over all the letters from our dear actress."

"I thought you hated her after she iced your nuts."

Again Sheldon frowned. He loathed the woman, but he wasn't so shallow that he couldn't see her value. "Leong says she gives us a lot of information in her silly, female way."

"What, for instance?"

"Oh, C.J. Hodges has been drunk for several weeks and can barely do his work. Danbury is always in a dither over some confounded machine, and he's not really competent. Leong showed me how Danbury's information is very inconsistent."

Sheldon wet his lips and continued. "The teacher says Leland Ames gambles his pay away. Potty Simms stole Edgar Fillmore's horse last Tuesday and hasn't been seen since. And Buckley Brooks—your dear friend—is gone half the time. Probably to some whorehouse, though the teacher didn't mention *that*."

"So what the hell does it all mean?"

"Our many spies aren't reliable or available! And Cousin Win is still alive and well."

Harlan spat into the fire.

"Our lady spy also told us a man named Jed Cantrell was hired as an explosives man a month or two ago, and Cousin Win is pleased with him."

"Buckley Brooks said Jed Cantrell is trying to screw the teacher."

"So is Buckley, no doubt. The point is, Cantrell could do us a lot of good—or more to the point—do Win a lot of damage with his dynamite."

Harlan smiled and got up for more brandy. "A toast, brother, to our new employee—Jed Cantrell."

* * *

The scent of wood smoke mingled with the aroma of cooking meat and a barely controlled sense of anticipation and excitement. The day of the Winter Fair had arrived, and Summit was ready to celebrate!

It was a perfect, clear morning. There was a nip to the air, but for the middle of December, the weather was exceptionally beautiful.

Moll was up before dawn, gaily dancing around her cabin, singing as she dressed in her modest but exotic black-and-scarlet dress.

Even Winslow Fortune, who had worried about the lack of rain for over a month, was delighted with the clear skies.

"Looks like a nice day," he said. "Albert Stoneleigh is going to be disappointed."

"He's such a gloomy Gus," Hannah said as she laid out platters of bacon and scrapple. "Always expecting the worst of everything."

"And everybody," Bill said, helping himself to a stack of flapjacks.

Everyone had worked on the event for days—even Albert. Women had sewed and baked. Men had built booths. They'd sent word out as far as Tahoe and Sacramento. Fortune donated enough lumber for the floor of the town hall, and he and the others had worked far into the night building a foundation and laying down the floor, which was to be used for tonight's dance.

After school, the children had gone to pick apples, walnuts, and persimmons to sell. They'd made garlands with toyan berries and cedar boughs. Eddie Hodges and Willard and Wendell McDonald came upon some of the wild hogs on the way home from the persimmon orchard. After the ensuing savage hog-and-dog fight, the boys shot two big pigs. So Summit was going to offer its guests roast pork as well as other culinary treats.

Farmers began to arrive at around seven o'clock. For a small contribution to the building fund, they could sell their produce and poultry. One farmer brought three cows, another brought a lively young goat, and a horse trader had a whole string of fine riding ponies.

Moll was astonished and delighted to see so many people already in town. She'd never seen more than four people there at one time.

Her Gypsy tent was located next to the booth selling the fragrant holiday garlands, candy, fruit, and nuts, and just across the road from the cider-and-ale stand.

The Gypsy tent, made of feed sacks haphazardly sewn together and stretched over poles, had a certain barbaric appeal. The tattered maroon brocade curtain at the front would add mystery and intrigue to her performance.

She had barely settled herself in her chair when Winslow Fortune pushed the curtain aside and entered her little den. After depositing a coin in the empty lard tin painted just for the occasion, he sat stiffly on the chair facing her.

They stared at each other. An attack of nerves caught Moll right in the middle of her self-confidence. "Can I tell your fortune . . . Mr. Fortune?"

He grinned. "Will I win the *fortune*, Gypsy?"

They laughed at the silly word play, though more out of nervousness than humor.

She took his hand. It was warm, the palm smooth and firm. The lines were strong and deep. His steady pulse beat a powerful life force in the vein at his wrist, and Moll found herself in awe of his vitality. He was a strong man, in body and character.

She said the first thing that popped into her head. "You have a bold love line, sir."

Amazed at what she'd just said, she blundered on, telling him of good health and wealth of his own making.

"Are you saying I won't win the legacy?" To his surprise, he believed what she was saying. He also realized how much he enjoyed her touch. He wanted to turn his palm over and close his fingers around hers. And pull her into his lap. And kiss her ripe, red mouth.

Moll frowned, studying his hand. "I'm not sure. There's lots of trouble ahead. Even danger! But you're young and healthy, and you'll make your own way. You might not win the legacy, but you'll beat your enemies."

His brows raised, but he didn't seem displeased.

Moll relaxed and slipped completely into her character. She continued to tell her employer whatever thoughts entered her head. Thoughts about his children and his numerous grandchildren, about a home full of love. "You've always wanted warmth and love in your life, but it's evaded you. Not to fear, true love is in your near future."

She found herself blushing at his direct stare, at the stormy sea in his gray eyes, at the quiver in her own body. "Anything else you want to know?"

"No." He stood up. "You're very good, Gypsy." He tossed another coin in the lard tin. "Good luck today. The people of Summit appreciate your efforts."

"Thank you, kind sir. May good luck go with you."

She gasped at the line of people she saw waiting outside when Fortune pushed aside the curtain. But she took a deep breath and greeted her next customer. "Come in, come in. Let me tell your fortune."

Moll closed her busy stall at lunchtime and wandered up and down the street. It was amazing! There were stalls and booths and wagons lined up all the way down to the schoolhouse. Twirling as she walked, she danced to the music in her heart. She was thrilled for the town.

She stopped at a farm wagon to buy an exquisite length of Renaissance lace and pay lavish compliments to the farmer's red-cheeked wife.

Up the street, by the madrona tree, a man sipped hot spiced cider and watched the blond seamstress. He knew she wanted him. She was like the teacher—a sly, wicked harlot. He'd been warned against such women. He had no intention of touching her. She was a foreigner, and he hated all foreigners. He hated her accent and her strong blond looks. He also hated what she did for a living. Who would want a woman who put her hands on the flies of other men's trousers?

"Hildy?"

Hildy Swensen looked up from the fancy apron she was folding. She'd made a number of aprons, fancy towels, and tablecloths for the fair. "Hello, Moll. Did you get tired of your tent?"

"My throat is already sore, and I have all afternoon yet to go. I was thinking about getting some lemonade. Do you want to go with me?"

"Yeah. I want some meat on a stick. I'm starved. Folks have been waving those sticks at me all morning."

Moll hadn't had so much fun in ages. "I want a meat pie. Some farmer's wife brought them, and they smell wonderful. By the way, you look swell."

Hildy dipped her head in embarrassment. She wasn't

accustomed to compliments. "The dress is pretty."

She wore the pearl-gray dress Moll had given her and a dusty-rose shawl. Her hair was clean and shiny, and the bangs and tendrils Moll had cut for her softened her thin face. She simply glowed.

"Do you think Win will ask me to dance?"

"He's a fool if he doesn't," Moll answered honestly. "And all the single men."

A half-hour later, Moll again opened her tent for business. She was quite good at playing the role of clairvoyant, she decided. Fortune-telling was just for fun, of course, but she couldn't help thinking that some of her comments were truly inspired. People seemed pleased, and a number of them dropped extra coins in the can.

A large, burly man stumbled in and plopped down on the chair, which creaked ominously. Moll could tell from the flush of his cheeks and the squint of his eyes that he'd been imbibing quite heavily. As soon as he opened his mouth, the tent reeked of beer. She wished she could open the curtain.

"I'm C.J. Hodges," he said.

"Let me tell your fortune, Mr. Hodges."

"That's what I'm here for, toots."

"Then put your money in the can."

"Oh." He dug through his pockets, dislodging his shirt from his trousers and exposing a fat, hairy navel. After asking her the price several times, he threw two bits into the lard tin.

"You gotta lot of money in there?" he asked.

"Not much," she answered, picking up his sweaty, work-worn hand. It had three lines on it, all etched with indelible grime. What the devil was she going to say to this big gorilla?

An inspiration came to her as she opened her mouth. "You're a very hard worker, sir. You've always worked, even when you were a small boy."

A pleased expression spread over his angry red face. He nodded.

Warming to the subject, she continued. "You had to work, didn't you? It was necessary for the family."

"Tha-at's right. We needed what I made to live on 'cause there was so many a' us. I couldn't go to school, 'cause I had t'work."

"So it's important to you that your son gets an education," Moll said slyly. She was determined that Eddie Hodges stay in school. "You and your wife are good people and both want the best for your family."

"Right! Eddie's smart. Me and Lorna didn't get much schoolin'." He scratched himself contentedly, pleased at hearing himself praised. It was a pleasant change from all the criticism he'd gotten lately.

"You might not have gone to school, but you're very smart at certain things. You learned skills in your youth that help in the job you do now."

"I went to the woods when I was twelve. I learnt my job good."

Moll nodded sagely. "But some people don't appreciate you. You don't get enough credit for the job you do."

"Damn right! Thas goddam right."

When he lurched out of the tent, he believed Moll was the wisest all-seeing creature on the face of the earth.

Toward late afternoon, Moll had Matty Swensen bring her some hot lemon juice for her throat, and she took a short break to look outside. She couldn't believe the number of people milling around now, shopping, talking, laughing, and generally having a wonderful time.

Around dusk Moll began to close her tent. She was unbelievably tired and felt the beginnings of a headache. Her throat was raw. She wanted to get some supper and then go to her cabin to rest a few minutes before the dance. From inside her tent she could smell potatoes roasting, meat grilling over open fires, spicy warm cider, and at least a hundred other edible temptations. She reached for the lard tin.

"I want my fortune told."

Moll stepped quickly away from the source of whiskey odors. She recognized him as the man she'd seen in the woods the day she'd heard the mountain lion, but she'd forgotten his name. What she hadn't forgotten was how uneasy he made her, as if something about him wasn't quite right.

"I'm closing up," she said.

"I'll give you four bits—for the building fund."

Moll did not want to be inside the tent with this man, but she saw no choice.

"For the building fund," she said hoarsely. She sat back down, holding the money tin in her lap.

The man sat down too. And stared at her.

"Let me tell your fortune, sir," she said through stiff lips. More than anything she didn't want to touch his hand, but she forced herself to turn his palm over.

All day she'd had clever thoughts come to mind, but now all she could think about was her throat closing up so tight that she couldn't breathe. She reached up to the neckline of her bodice and gave it a little yank. Even though it wasn't even close to her throat, she felt the need to loosen it.

The man watched her, not blinking, while she waited in vain for the inspiration. "My throat is sore," she apologized. Then she gave him the old Gypsy routine about finding his true love and having a family. The thought came to her to caution him about traveling over water. "I see troubled waters ahead," she said vaguely.

The more she talked, the more he stared, and the more her unease grew. By the time she finished, her skin had begun to crawl. She smiled too brightly. "Thank you and good luck. The town appreciates your contribution."

He continued to stare at her, and then he nodded, pushed open the curtain, and walked out.

Moll nearly collapsed with relief as the evil cloud left with him. She quickly closed up her tent, found Bill McDonald, and deposited her money tin with him. Then she went into the crowd in search of sustenance.

Edgar Fillmore nervously sneaked out of town. Danbury had promised him a new horse if he'd take care of Fortune tonight during the festivities. It had sounded simple when Danbury described it. Sneaking up behind Win, hitting him over the head, and stealing the money tin to make it look like a robbery. Now Fillmore questioned the plan. What if he failed, as Potty Simms had?

Fillmore had already decided to join his wife and son in the desert. That new horse would help. He might even keep the money he stole from Fortune. As he slipped into the darkness toward the company office, he made up his mind about one thing. He was leaving Summit before morning whether Win was dead or not.

* * *

It was already dark when Moll walked the worn path to her cabin. Perhaps it was foolish to change from her Gypsy costume, but she wanted to wear the new blue-violet crepe dress Hildy had worked nights to finish. And Moll wanted to be herself, not a painted Gypsy.

A bath would have felt wonderful, and she looked longingly at her portable tub folded up in the corner, but she couldn't spare the time. She didn't even bother to light a fire, because she knew she wouldn't be home till daylight. They would be serving breakfast at the schoolhouse in the wee hours before folks drove home.

She washed herself in tepid water from the basin and hastily redid her hair. She hoped that a little dab of violet perfume would cover the smell of wood smoke that clung to her. Soon she regained her stamina and was ready for the dance. A glance in her mirror told her she looked soft and feminine. Like Hildy, she hoped the man in her dreams would ask her to dance. Like Hildy, she dreamed of Win.

She knew that if Jed Cantrell didn't show Hildy some attention soon, the situation was going to be complicated, and painful for somebody.

The whisper of wind in the pines caressed her. She glanced up at the dark sky. The half-moon floated lazily against the velvet darkness, and a silver veil of clouds slid past. In the woods an owl hooted, but its call was muffled by the sound of the band as it started to play.

Moll stepped up her pace. It had been months since she'd danced, and she was giddy with excitement.

Would Win ask her? If he didn't, she'd just have to ask him.

She was so intent on the idea of being in Win's strong arms that the noise of someone stumbling and cursing behind her startled her. She screeched and bolted for town. The ominous thud she heard next did nothing to slow her down as she raced toward the light and the music.

She was breathing hard and shaking when she reached the schoolhouse. This time, she knew for certain that someone had been behind her. Not a dog or a raccoon or some wild critter. That had been a man's voice cursing the darkness.

The only man who lived up by her cabin was her boss, and she could see him on the platform, with a mug in his hand, watching the band. Bill McDonald stood by his side, talking. Hildy was dancing with Albert Stoneleigh. The gloomy blacksmith seemed to be having fun for once.

Who could have been behind her? Nobody had any business being up there besides Win. Unless, of course, he'd sent somebody to the office for something. Or it could have been somebody meeting his sweetheart for a tryst under the stars. But as she stood in the shadows of the school waiting for her pulse to slow, she saw no one come out of the woods. Either the man had been seriously hurt when he fell, or he'd sneaked around the other side of the building.

She had to mention the incident to Win. The proceeds from the fund raiser were being kept at the company office over the weekend, and most of the people in Summit knew it. What if somebody was trying to rob the office and steal all the money they'd made today?

"Win?"

Win had just stepped off the platform. He inhaled sharply at the sight of her. Even if he'd wanted to, he wouldn't have been able to avoid going to her.

"Win," she said again in a softly rasping voice, "I need to talk to you!"

"Why are you talking that way?" The husky tone of her voice sent shivers up his spine.

"Too much fortune-telling. I'm losing my voice." She grasped him by the arm and practically dragged him through the crowd and into the shadows. "I need to talk to you."

Win had hung around the beer tree that afternoon, talking business and politics and weather with a large group of men who got more philosophical as time wore on. Win wasn't much of a drinker, but he'd had more than one beer. So now he felt more than willing to glide off into the darkness with the most beautiful woman in town. As soon as they reached the back of the crowd, he slipped one arm around her and a minute later the other, pulling her against him.

"You are so lovely." He bent his head.

Moll gave him a shove and stepped away. "Wait a minute!" When he tried to capture her again, she shoved harder. "I didn't come out here for that. Somebody was near the office a few minutes ago. Did you send anybody up there?"

Win realized she had changed into a demure gown, something that fit her curvaceous figure snugly. He took a deep breath to control his desire. "You saw a man?" he asked.

"No. I heard him. He tripped and fell. And cussed. He was behind me."

"Did you ask who it was?"

"I ran." His arms were still around her waist, and she relished the warmth. It had been such a long time since she'd been with a man she cared about.

"Why?"

"Somebody was outside my cabin a few nights back. I heard the bushes move . . ."

"An animal."

". . . and I heard a cough. No, two coughs. A man's cough. I called out then and asked who it was. Nobody answered. So I locked myself in and shut off the light."

"Why didn't you come get me?"

"You were over working on the floor."

"I'll go take a look. Maybe it was a visitor taking a tour. If he broke his leg in a gopher hole, it would be inhospitable to let him lie there all night and freeze. I'll get a lantern. Have you seen Jed?"

"No, I just got here."

They looked around for a few minutes. Jed was nowhere to be found. Win picked up a lantern and decided to take several of the buckets of money up to the office.

"I'm going with you," Moll told him as he started down the path."

"Go to the dance. That's what you're wearing that new dress for. I know the way to my own house, Miss Kennedy."

"It isn't safe for you to walk up there by yourself with all that money."

"Announce it to the world, Moll!"

She ignored the sarcasm. "Besides, I know where the man fell."

"If there's a man lying on the path, I bet I'll find him."

"Don't be such an ass!" she snapped.

The words hung in the air between them, louder than the fiddles, the horns, and the drums on the stage.

Win cleared his throat. "Mighty salty words for a schoolteacher, Miss Kennedy."

"I beg your pardon, Mr. Fortune."

She couldn't recall when she'd been so mortified. Even when he'd whipped out the goddess poster, she'd been more angry than embarrassed. Why was it that when she wanted so badly to make a good impression on him, she always messed things up?

A smile tugged at his lips. He handed her the lantern. "We'd better get going."

They walked in tense silence.

"Where does a girl who was educated by nuns learn such language?"

"From the gardener," she answered stiffly.

"How did you happen to be in the company of the gardener?"

"I liked him better than anybody else," she said. She did not mention what a lonely, scared little girl she'd been. "He gave me lemon drops."

"How old were you when your parents died?"

She didn't answer. "This is about the place where the guy fell."

They looked around for a few minutes but didn't find a body anywhere. They did, however, discover a recently unearthed stone lying in the path.

Edgar Fillmore huddled behind a little clump of brush less than twenty feet away, his heart palpitating. Ignoring the pain in his badly twisted ankle, he thought only of fleeing. He had promised himself that he'd crawl to the nearest horse and ride like hell, if only he escaped detection.

"There's nobody here," Win said. "Let's go lock up this money."

"All right." She hesitated a moment. "My mother died when I was seven. And as far as I know, my father is still alive. I believe he lives in Denver."

Win glanced at her. Hadn't she told him before that both parents were dead? Even in the faint light of the lamp, he could see that she was distressed. "Moll, I'm sorry . . ."

"I'm a mistake. Nobody talks about bastards in polite society, but I am one." The darkness made her bold. She'd never admitted this to anybody.

"My biggest sin was being born. My aunt told me what a lucky girl I was not to have been abandoned on the streets."

He didn't know what to say. For the first time he had some insight into this beautiful woman who danced so wickedly onstage.

"Are you going to dismiss me for telling you such horrible things?"

"No. I'm going to take you back to town and try out that new dance floor. Did I tell you I'm a good dancer?"

She smiled into the darkness. "No."

Sometime after midnight Jed asked Moll to dance.

"Win and I looked for you earlier," she said.

"When?" he asked as he twirled her around.

"Right after the dance started."

"I might have been eating." He changed the subject quickly. "I remembered a couple things about Seamus Blade, if you're still interested."

"Of course I'm interested!"

"I saw Blade in San Francisco a year or so ago. Can't remember exactly. He was with his son—the big, red-headed one. What's his name?"

"I don't know," Moll said. She had a brother! A big, red-haired brother.

"It just came to me that I'd seen 'em. And then I got to remembering. I heard a couple years back that his oldest boy—the redhead—got arrested for murdering his wife."

"What?" That certainly did not fit into Moll's picture of her father's life.

"Yeah—somewhere in the south. Seamus musta bought him out of trouble, though, because he was with the old man when I saw them. And he didn't have no jailhouse pallor."

Moll didn't know what to say. Had Aunt Beebee been right, that she had taken after a whole family of scoundrels? "Does Blade have a big family?"

"Big enough," he said. "Two girls, I think. The kind who make the newspaper's society pages. Blade's wife died quite some time ago, so he's always escorting other women to parties and the theater. The paper's full of that sh . . . stuff. I think I heard there was a son that didn't get along with the old man so he ran off to sea. Maybe there's more kids than that."

George Franklin asked her to dance, and Jed went off to dance with Hildy. Moll would have been delighted at Jed's move, but she was too busy mulling over the newfound information.

"May I cut in?"

Win's voice penetrated her thoughts. "Yes."

"Are you getting tired?"

"I never get tired of dancing." But for once she was weary, and she wanted to go off by herself and do some thinking.

He pulled her into his arms. "When you do get tired, will you let me take you to breakfast?"

"Are they serving now? I'm supposed to help."

"Let somebody else help—you worked all day long. I'm asking you to have breakfast with me."

She nodded, suddenly shy and unsure of herself. "Yes," she said softly. "I'll go with you."

11

A few weeks later, tiny flickering lights blazed in a wondrous pyramid on the darkened porch. Moll thought it was the most beautiful sight she'd ever seen.

An evening breeze blew gently, and the dainty candles flickered in their tin holders and then flared bright again.

"Happy Christmas to you."

Elias and Bertha Dietrich stood beside their gift, beaming with pleasure, as the others stood in the twilight chill and admired the Christmas tree. Each year they presented the McDonalds, their closest neighbors, with this symbol of Christmas tradition. Afterward, for safety's sake, the candles were extinguished and the tree was taken into the parlor. Then Hannah served everyone oyster stew and salmon cakes, foods traditional to her heritage.

Moll, who'd never known any sort of family tradition, felt fortunate to be included in the festive celebration. Last year she'd sat alone in a less-than-auspicious hotel in a crummy little town, drinking watery, hot spiced ale from a battered cup and waiting for Arthur Smith to take her out to dinner. He had never showed up, since he had gotten side-tracked at an all-night poker game. Although he'd won enough to get them to a better hotel in a better town, Christmas had been miserable.

It had never been her favorite holiday. As a small child she had become caught up in the church activities, growing more excited as the days drew closer. But the cruel letdown came when the other girls went home to their families, and Moll would remain—sometimes all by herself, sometimes with other sad girls who also had no one to take them home and love them. Although the nuns had been kind, Moll was certain it wasn't the same as having a family.

The candles suddenly blinked out, and Moll realized that the children were carefully blowing on them. She smiled and went to join in.

From where he stood at the far end of the porch, Win watched Summit's mysterious schoolteacher. She was wearing the same blue-violet dress she had worn to the Winter Fair dance. Her hair was pulled back from her face and secured with mother-of-pearl combs on the sides. It cascaded down her back in a soft black cloud. Long gold-and-pearl earrings hung from her ears, and she wore a pearl brooch at her throat. She looked more beautiful than he'd ever seen her, but sur-prisingly remote and sad.

Win had given up getting another teacher for the Summit school, but he hadn't told Moll. He didn't plan to tell her. The threat of being replaced kept her on her toes.

Fortune was a hard man. Raised by a cold, stern, uncompromising father, and a loving but determined grandfather, he had learned early that power depended more on wisdom and leadership than brawn. His decision to let Mollene Kennedy stay at Summit had been a gamble, but with the knowledge that he was watching her every move, she'd turned into a better-than-average teacher. Unorthodox, perhaps, but concerned and competent. The youngsters clearly adored her.

As he watched her troop in with the children who were following the tree, he thought of the things she'd told him about her childhood. He guessed that there were many children like her in the world, unwanted and unloved.

He'd never liked his sanctimonious father and had considered his mother a trivial creature, but never for one moment had he felt his parents weren't happy that he was alive. His grandfather had adored him, and he had returned the sentiment. He wondered how it would feel to be told you were a mistake.

"Hey, Win, don't stand out in the cold! Come in and join the fun."

"I'll be right there, Bill."

The Christmas Eve supper, in accordance with Catholic tradition, was plain and almost sparse, but the holiday entertainment was lavish. First the children recited verses they'd learned at school. Then Willard and Wendell McDonald, who had the voices of angels, sang for them. Jed Cantrell read about the birth of Jesus from Matthew's Gospel. Elias Dietrich told a story of his childhood in Germany, and Bill McDonald told the tale of a gold miner's Christmas.

The unlit Christmas tree filled the house with a pleasurable fragrance. At the end of the evening, Hannah passed out persimmon cookies and coffee. Buckley Brooks played his fiddle to the accompaniment of Bill McDonald on the pump organ, and everyone sang.

"This is the way Christmas was meant to be spent," Moll said.

Hannah smiled. "Come early tomorrow. Our Christmas dinner is a feast! Ham, roast beef, and goose—everything you can imagine to eat. And we light *the tree.*" She rolled her eyes as she uttered the last two words.

Moll laughed. Hannah had already made it clear that she considered the Christmas tree a threat to hearth and home. But the German folks were so pleased to share the custom, that Hannah didn't have the heart to tell them.

"So what do you think of the blazing tree, Miss Kennedy?" Fortune asked. He'd just slipped into the kitchen for another handful of cookies.

"I think there's been enough blazes in my life," Moll answered, her blue eyes snapping.

Hannah looked from one to the other, curious about the undercurrents she was sensing. Until recently she'd thought Hildy was the girl for Win, since they were both such serious and hard-working people. Then she'd watched him with Moll.

The passion between Win and Moll was impossible to miss. Hannah had lived with Bill McDonald for thirty years and married off three grown children. She'd learned to spot kindling love often before the lovers realized what was happening between them. She smiled. This combination would be interesting to watch.

Now all she had to do was look around for the right man for Hildy. Maybe Hildy didn't need somebody as steady and hard-working as herself. Maybe she needed a little more excitement in her world. An idea occurred to her.

"Moll, tell Jed to bring the children over early tomorrow to look in their Christmas stockings."

An hour later, Moll stepped out onto the porch. The night was cold and clear. Stars filled the night sky.

"I'll walk you home."

She inhaled sharply. "I thought you'd already gone up the hill. You left some time ago."

Fortune leaned against the porch rail. "I needed some air. Bill put quite a slug of whiskey in my coffee, and in that warm room it went to my head."

"I didn't think you had any weakness."

A flicker of desire ignited deep inside him and threatened to blaze, even though he immediately resisted it. Perhaps she hadn't meant to flirt, but the soft words tantalized him. He yearned for her as he'd never longed for any other woman, but he knew that it was impossible.

"I have many weaknesses." He quickly moved away from the railing, took her arm, and guided her down the steps.

Win didn't need a lantern. The pale starlight was bright enough for him to see, even if he hadn't known the way by heart.

"You're beautiful tonight in your pretty dress, but you seem sad."

"Oh, no!" she said quickly. "I enjoyed the evening."

"Tomorrow will be better."

"I'm looking forward to it."

"But you don't like Christmas."

"It's a time for families."

"And you never had one. Would you like a family?" He didn't know what lunacy made him ask that. She was an actress who lived for adulation and applause. She couldn't be expected to desire what other women wanted—a home, a warm family, and the love of one man. Could she?

Not that it mattered to him. He was merely curious. She attracted him deeply on a physical level, and he felt a great need to discover what she was like on other levels.

"Since I was a little girl, I dreamed of having a family. I even made one up."

Win caught his breath. He wanted to believe a woman like her could want a man like him for something more than a diamond bracelet or a quick roll in the sheets. Yet he was afraid to hope. He'd already failed abysmally at love once. He wasn't sure he had the courage to try again.

"Moll."

A shiver of anticipation went through her at the sound of his deep voice. Win drew her closer, draping his arm around her shoulder. She snuggled into his warmth.

"It seems strange seeing the logging camp dark," she said, to cover the thrill that shot through her as his arm tightened on her shoulder. Strangely enough, she felt young, awkward, inexperienced.

"Nobody wants to work on Christmas. The men deserved a few days off. So do I."

They walked the rest of the way to the cabin in

silence, savoring the starry night, the physical closeness of their bodies, and the warm attraction tingling between them.

Win decided that Christmas was a dreadful time to be without a mate. He'd spent many years in a lonely bed, touching only emptiness in the night. He realized how he wanted warmth and another heart beating next to his. Surely Moll was as lonely as he. Surely she ached for love the way he did.

But this line of thinking was dangerous. It was not the time to let the season rule their hearts, simply because they both were vulnerable and alone.

Not since Étienne had Moll been so aware of a man.

Not since his fiancée left him had Win felt so tender toward a woman.

The wind had picked up over the last few hours. A fragrant melody played in the cathedral of the sugar pines, as if a choir of angels serenaded them as they walked. One thin cloud drifted on high.

"Oh look—an owl," she said when they reached the clearing in front of her cabin.

"I can't look," he whispered. "I'm watching you."

Moll stopped and gazed up at him, her eyes wary and wide with expectation.

"Mollene," he said so quietly that she could barely hear him.

Her fingers brushed his cheek, a touch as light and fragile as a snowflake. She knew he was going to kiss her. She desperately wanted him to, and yet she was mortally afraid.

She suspected his passions ran deep and strong, and she knew he would be a ruthless enemy. He already despised the fact that she'd been an actress. He certainly would never forgive her if he found out she worked for the Rockwells.

"No," she said softly, but she didn't move away. She could feel the heat from his big body, and her whole being strained toward him. God, how she needed him!

His arms tightened, pulling her against the length of his hard body, feeling her softness melt against him through the thickness of their clothes as if she belonged there.

"It's Christmas," he said. "This is a Christmas custom."

His soft and gentle lips barely whispered over hers, once, twice, and again. She couldn't believe such a strong man could be so tender.

"What Christmas custom?" she murmured, clutching the sleeves of his coat, holding on for dear life.

His mouth found hers again, and his warm tongue traced the line of her bottom lip. "Our custom . . . yours and mine. To be repeated every year."

"We can't have a custom," she breathed as his lips again found hers. And she groaned as she answered the kiss.

Several minutes later, he asked, "Why not?"

"Because . . ." She trailed off as she gave herself up to his caress. She was starved for him, starved for his affection.

A dog barked somewhere in the distance and barked more fiercely a second time. There was a holler, a yip, and a slamming of a door. The dog uttered one more defiant bark and was quiet.

"I'm home," Moll finally said in a voice that didn't sound like hers at all.

"Yes." He sounded as shaken as she when he opened

the cabin door for her and waited in the doorway until she lighted a lamp.

"Thank you for walking me."

"My pleasure." He touched his fingers to his mouth. "Moll . . ."

She looked at him, waiting for whatever came next, her heart racing, blood rushing, and brain adrift in a sea of desire and utter confusion. She could see her emotions echoed on his bleak face.

The room grew tense as the silence dragged on.

". . . you better build up the fire. You'll catch cold."

He shut the door and was gone.

She slumped against the wall for support.

"That can't happen again, you fool," she mumbled as she opened the black door of the stove to put some kindling inside and then watched it catch fire and burn. "Not till you've told him who you are. He's an honest man. He deserves honesty in return."

As she unbuttoned the sleeves on her dress, she knew she could never tell Win she was a spy for the Rockwells. She was too much of a coward. He wasn't the kind of man who made gigantic mistakes, and he certainly wouldn't forgive hers. She might have a hundred excuses for whatever she did, but the truth was that Moll Kennedy was a failure. And an actress down on her luck. And a lousy spy.

Christmas Day arrived cold and clear—and very early for Moll, who had dreamed of candlelit trees and warm Christmas kisses. And Winslow Fortune in her bed.

She wasn't prepared for the excitement at Hannah's house. The children were wild. Matty, the twins, and Jed's two had all left stockings by the big brick fireplace. Santa Claus had been generous. Each child got an orange and a bag of hard candy. The girls got ribbons for their hair and pretty gloves, and the boys got thick mittens and stocking caps.

Moll was helping in the kitchen when Win walked in.

"Eddie Hodges is down at the house all by himself."

"Alone?" Moll asked. She spooned spiced peaches onto a glass relish dish.

"I thought he went to visit his mother." Hannah frowned, disappointed for the boy. Eddie had told her how much he was looking forward to seeing Lorna.

"Something must have happened, because he's back already. C.J. isn't around," Win said.

"Naturally." Hannah wiped her hands and gathered cookies and fruit together. "Win, you go down and get Eddie. Bring him back with you. No argument. He's coming to dinner." Nobody argued with Hannah, anyway. "Bill, you go get one of your socks. And that cap and scarf I knitted for you. I'll fix a stocking for him."

"I like that cap—it matches my eyes," Bill teased.

"I'll knit you another one."

Bill stopped at the door. "I love you, old woman."

Hannah turned very pink. "Go on!"

Moll went outside on the porch to be alone and cried. It was a brief storm but a turbulent one. She stopped when a rough hand patted her shoulder.

"It's a sad thing," Bill McDonald said, "when a child is more grown up than his parents. Eddie is a fine lad."

Christmas dinner was every morsel the feast that Hannah had promised. The house was full of people. Eddie came with Win. Sullen and angry at first, he quickly relaxed and joined in the festivities.

Moll had never seen so much food in her life! She ate until she was stuffed. Then she went for a long walk with the rest of the guests, who were as miserably full as she was. And then they went back and ate more. It was gluttonous and sinful and utterly marvelous.

"When I was a kid in Colorado," Buckley Brooks said as he shoveled in a spoonful of mincemeat pie with a hard sauce, "we were so poor, the winter after my father was killed, that we ate our Christmas supper at a soup kitchen. You know, the kind of place where they give you a bite to eat and want your eternal gratitude? I swore I'd never be so poor or hungry again that I had to take that kind of charity." He was silent for a minute. "My mother found another husband right after that, so we ate better."

Something in the way he said it made Moll think he hadn't been happy with his mother's choice of men.

Win sat watching Moll. At times, her expressions were transparent. He wondered what Brooks had said that had caught her attention.

"Did you always live in Colorado?" Moll asked.

"Until I came here," Brooks answered, looking at the dessert table, marveling at the variety of things he hadn't yet sampled.

"Denver?" she asked.

Win relaxed. She wasn't interested in Brooks as a man, simply as a source of information.

"Telluride, mostly. But I've been to Denver lots of

times." He got up and excused himself. "Win, d'you wanna play some horseshoes?"

"I would, Bucky," Eddie Hodges said, grabbing his new cap and scarf.

Later Moll remembered that she hadn't finished asking Brooks about Colorado. She saw him watching some of the other men pitch horseshoes, so she set down her teacup and walked outside.

"Mr. Brooks, do you have a moment?"

He glanced around from the game. "Sure."

"I was wondering . . ." Moll didn't know what to ask.

Buckley Brooks had been on his best behavior around Moll since his friend Harlan had told him to keep away from her. But if she was going to offer, he sure as hell wasn't going to refuse. This could be an unexpected holiday treat.

"I heard you mention you'd been in Denver."

"Yep."

"Were you there long?"

"Off and on." He'd spent a singularly unpleasant time in jail in Denver, but he doubted if she'd be interested in that. And he wasn't planning to tell, since his release had come when some other inmates had broken out and he'd decided to follow the crowd.

In spite of his friendly air, Moll didn't especially care for Brooks. He was too cocky, too sure of his prowess with women, and she suspected he had a mean streak. He'd been nicer lately, but the look that flashed across his face now made her uneasy. She stepped away from him.

"Hey, Miss Kennedy! Watch me!" Eddie had gotten into the game. He held up a horseshoe.

Moll moved over to where she could see him better. He was a fine-looking lad when he wasn't surly or mad. Right now he was having a great time, laughing and joking with the older men.

He pitched the horseshoe with practiced ease, and it landed with a resounding metallic clank. Moll clapped at his performance and shouted encouragement, and the boy preened at the attention.

Behind her, Jed leaned over to Brooks and asked, "Did she ask you about Blade?"

"Who?"

"Seamus Blade of Denver."

To say that Brooks was surprised was an understatement. "No. She didn't ask me nothin'."

"Do you know him?" Jed was curious. Buckley had a peculiar look on his face.

"Heard of him." Brooks scowled. "Who hasn't? One of them rich crooks who made his money and then looked down on us poor folks who work for a living. I heard of him, all right, but I never socialized with his type. I wasn't good enough."

Jed knew that Brooks had a chip on his shoulder about his poor upbringing. He figured Buckley's lack of ethics resulted from his childhood. But it was Christmas, and he wasn't going to let his festive mood be spoiled by the other man's memories. "I think the teacher is angling for a rich husband," he confided.

"That lets you and me out!"

"Right." Jed just shook his head, but Buckley was determined to pout.

"I thought she was running after Win," Brooks said a moment later. "It must be real cozy up on the hill with her cabin so close to his house."

The idea didn't make Jed happy. He still entertained a few ideas about Moll, though not too many
since he saw how possessive Win was about her. Moll
was an exciting woman, and he wished himself in Fortune's place, but he sure as hell didn't want Win's
headaches.

"The girl is smart to be thinking about Blade," he
said, "if she wants a rich husband. Fortune can't possibly come out on top in this fight—not with everybody
working against him."

"Yeah," Brooks said. "What did you decide? Are you
accepting the Rockwells' offer?"

"It's a lot of money," Jed said.

Brooks smiled. "Can't afford not to take it, can
you?"

Jed's attention had wandered to the shouting over
by the horseshoe pit. Buckley followed along behind
him.

Win frowned from where he stood watching in the
kitchen. What was it with the woman? Now she was in
the middle of the game, trying her hand at horseshoes
while Eddie and Jed gave her pointers. He'd already
seen her make a point of following Brooks. Was she
after every man in camp?

"She's a very pretty girl, Win."

"Don't start, Hannah. I'm not in the mood."

"I can't believe you're jealous of Buckley. A man
like that? No woman would ever take him seriously.
Or is it Eddie you're worrying about? He *is* growing
up."

"I'm not sure what she's after. Or who. I think she
wants every man in camp running after her."

"You really have it bad for her, don't you?"

"Hannah!" He was embarrassed, trying to deny his

attraction for Moll, trying not to smile at Hannah's pointed gaze.

"I already warned Moll and Hildy to keep Buckley at arm's length." She was using her most motherly tone. "I told them his intentions were not honorable. When a woman reaches my age she knows those things."

"Moll didn't listen. Or maybe she isn't looking for an honorable man."

"Maybe she was just asking him for the time!" Hannah said.

"I don't think he can tell time," Win snarled back.

They both burst out laughing.

It was unusual for Hannah and Win to have a few minutes alone without somebody wanting something. Both of them valued the friendship they shared.

"She's a fine woman, Winslow."

"She's not everything she seems."

"Who is?" Hannah shook her head at him. Sometimes the man was so naive.

"She's not a teacher."

"Of course she's not, dear. She's a pretty girl down on her luck who answered Mr. Levine's ad. And, glory of glories, she's teaching those youngsters more than any of the other teachers ever did. My boys love her. So does Matty."

"I can't."

"Of course you can." Hannah poured them some coffee and sat by him. "Right from the first, there was a spark between the two of you. I saw it out Cassie Hall's window when you helped her out of the wagon."

"Hannah, were you spying on us?"

"Of course. All the town ladies were. What else is there to do around here?"

He ran a nervous hand through his carefully combed hair. "I don't have time for a woman."

She shrugged. "Men never do." She picked up a piece of a macaroon and popped it in her mouth.

"I can't get involved with a woman till this year is over. And if I lose this place, what do I have to offer?"

"Yourself, you big ninny. That's all a good woman wants."

"I think Moll's one of the Rockwell spies," Win said. "I saw her come out of the Cary House that day she went to Placerville before the Winter Fair. She walked out right after Harlan went in."

"Oh. I guess that puts a different light on things, doesn't it?" Hannah felt disappointed, but she could hardly believe Moll would be involved with the shady Rockwells. "Are you sure, Win?"

"Yes. Jed came to me the other night and said they'd approached him, too."

"If I was looking for somebody to do some damage, I guess a powder monkey would be the right choice."

Win agreed. "I told him to take their money. From what he was told, there are some others on my payroll who work for them."

"You already knew that. Did he say who?"

"No. He did say he could set off a blast or two to make them think he was on their side. That way they might not hire somebody more dangerous. To be honest, I don't know if I trust him. I hate this, Hannah."

"Especially about Moll." Hannah patted his hand in

a motherly way and handed him a piece of molasses candy. "I understand your frustration. Still, my instincts tell me Moll is a good woman. In spite of what you think."

"I don't know what to think anymore. I don't know who to trust."

"And you don't know who to love, do you?"

He didn't bother to answer. Hannah had made up her mind about his feelings, even if he had his doubts.

"Come in, come in," Bill called from the parlor, "we're going to light the Christmas tree."

"Grab two buckets of water," Hannah told Win. "I'll take the pail of sand."

Win laughed but did what she told him.

"I saw you outside talking to Brooks."

At the end of the long day, he was walking Moll back to her cabin.

Moll gave him an odd look. "He wasn't much on conversation today and we got interrupted."

"I thought he was real hot with women. At least the way he tells it."

"Oh? I think he must be all talk. He doesn't seem to like me much, and I don't find him at all appealing."

Fortune couldn't imagine any man who didn't want to haul her off into the woods. God, that's all he'd been able to think about since he'd held her in his arms the night before. Kissing her, touching her, loving her. His body responded instantly to the thought.

"So what did he have to say?"

"Very little." She couldn't understand why he was so persistent.

"Moll." His patience was wearing thin.

"I heard him telling today about being from Colorado. I thought he might know about Seamus Blade—my father—so I wanted to ask him, but we got interrupted. It's not important—Buckley probably doesn't know him, anyway."

"I doubt if they run with the same crowd," Win agreed, relieved that her father was the man who concerned her. "Your father's from Denver?"

"Jed told me he still lives there. He's seen him and read about him in the papers. But you're right, he probably doesn't pal around with working men." She looked at the sky, thinking that she was closer to her father than she'd ever been, but in some ways much farther away. "I'm not supposed to contact him, but I want to know what type of man he is."

"Moll, if you want to know about your father, why don't you just write him a letter?"

"I can't do that."

"Why not?"

"My mother signed papers saying we'd never bother him again."

"He was probably trying to protect himself from blackmail from her. It doesn't apply to you, does it?"

"I can't," she whispered.

"How come a girl who always broke the rules wants to play by them now?"

"I hadn't thought of it that way."

He kissed her at the door because he couldn't help himself. "Part of the Christmas custom," he whispered. He wanted to stay. God, how he wanted to stay! But he summoned all his strength and set her away from him.

Moll opened the door and lit the lamp.

And then she screamed.

The cabin had been ransacked. Furniture had been upended. Her pitcher and bowl had been shattered. The trunk had been opened: her clothes were in a heap on the bed, her undergarments had been thrown around and trampled on, and all her papers were lying on the floor.

"It's okay, love. It's okay," Win told her as he gathered her close. But for the life of him he couldn't understand the animal who would do this to her.

12

CHAPTER ELEVEN

New Year's Eve, 1897

"He's the rudest man!" Moll told her reflection in the mirror as she tried to fasten an earring.

Until now she'd been too emotional about the emerald teardrops, her last gift from Étienne, to wear them. But tonight she needed to lift her spirits, and wearing the earrings with her emerald velvet dress to Hannah's New Year's Eve party might do the trick.

Mentally she blessed Hannah for having the party. Moll wanted to dance and have fun tonight. If she laughed enough and flirted a little, maybe she'd forget her anxiety about the break-in, and her annoyance at her boss.

Win had informed her he was taking her to the party. He hadn't asked her, hadn't even been polite. He'd simply ordered her to accompany him.

Moll's wayward temper was none too steady since

she'd discovered her house in shambles. Horrified that some unknown person had touched her things, she'd been plagued with anxiety and nightmares. She felt victimized, vulnerable, and spitfire mad.

Win's presumptuous command, whatever his intentions, had only added to her irritability.

Her fingers finally got the earring hooked, and she turned away from the mirror. A glance at the clock told her that her escort was late.

Moll wasn't the type of woman to wait around for a man. If he couldn't arrive on time, she'd go without him! Or, better yet, she'd fetch him herself.

Throwing a heavy, ermine-trimmed, black velvet cape over her shoulders, she locked the door to her cabin and left. The new outside lock had been Win's idea.

She was halfway up the stairs to Win's office when she heard loud voices.

"You got no right to talk to me that way, goddammit!"

"I have every right—you work for me. You almost got the two of us killed today, C.J.! It was dumb luck that wagon didn't go over the edge!"

"It was an accident!"

"You were drunk! You're drunk all the time. You don't give a damn about anything but whiskey!"

"That's a lie!"

"You went off on Christmas leaving Eddie all by himself. He'd have gone hungry if Hannah hadn't invited him over. Your boozing has already broken up your family. Next it's going to cost you your job! Our friendship is the only reason I've kept you on this long."

"Listen, friend, I don't need yer goddam job!"

Moll retreated down the steps just as C.J. threw

open the door. Shaken by what she'd overheard, she returned to her cabin. Taking a deep breath, she found her key and unlocked the door with icy fingers. Then she sat on the bed and waited for Win. The thought of losing him paralyzed her.

The snow had started before midnight. Hannah's small celebration to honor the coming of 1897 had been more lavish than Moll had expected. There had been music and dancing and wonderful food. And at the stroke of midnight, they all drank a toast to the brand-new year.

It was exactly what Moll had needed. For the first time in a week, she relaxed and forgot to be afraid. Her optimistic outlook had returned, and she took childlike joy in the falling snow.

By the time Win and Moll left the party, the flakes were as big as goose feathers and had begun to pile up on the ground.

"It's so beautiful," Moll said, her warm breath a white cloud in the wintry air.

"Everything is beautiful when I'm with you."

She turned her head in astonishment, unable to believe that Winslow Fortune could utter such sweet words. "Why Mr. Fortune, I do believe you're flirting with me."

"Apparently, I'm not doing a very good job." He sounded a bit chagrined.

Her laughter mingled with the swirling snow.

He kissed her at the door, as he'd wanted to do all evening. She looked breathtaking in the green velvet. He told her so, and kissed her again.

"It's too cold to stand outside," he murmured, taking

the key from her hand. Then he pushed the door open and pulled her inside.

"We need to light the lamp." She was suddenly nervous, but this time it wasn't about intruders. She was nervous about her feelings for Win.

"Not right now." His greedy mouth silenced her.

She forgot to worry, forgot everything but Win. Her fingers plunged into his thick hair, and she pressed herself close, thrilling at the steely evidence of his desire. It had been forever since she'd kissed a man this way.

Heat flooded her loins, a fiery, burning need she'd almost forgotten. A languorous warmth seeped into her whole body, lulling her defenses, drugging her brain. Her world began and ended with Win. She wanted nothing else, and nothing more. She wrapped her arms tighter around him, wanting to give, wanting so desperately to please him.

He brushed her cape aside, running his hands down her back to her tiny waist. She was wearing a corset tonight, he noticed. She didn't always wear one. His eyes had intimate knowledge of her body, in spite of the fact he'd barely touched her.

He hated the thought of the stays digging into her tender flesh. He knew he must remove the offending contraption and replace it with his soothing fingers. He found the buttons on the back of her dress and began to loosen them one at a time.

Cocooned in his warmth she arched against him, loving the feel of his big muscular body close to her smaller, softer one. Loving his sharp intake of breath. Loving the hard promise . . .

"What are we doing?" Moll suddenly pulled out of his grasp. Her head was spinning crazily, her body trembling with unfulfilled desire. She fumbled around till she found the lamp chimney and the matchbox.

The hissing flare and the pungent smell of sulfur dampened the mood. But only a little.

He was very aroused, and very angry.

So was she. The anger only sharpened the hunger. She'd never experienced such ravenous longing. It was all she could do to keep from hauling him down to the rug and finishing what they'd started.

"You've been married," he said. "You know what it's like to be with a man." He stood with his hands clenched, and with his gaze probed the depths of her eyes, the depths of her soul. "It's been a long time for you, hasn't it?"

She nodded reluctantly and dampened her dry lips. She could hardly breathe for the strain of resisting him. She'd never felt such an ache before, never felt such need. It made her feel defenseless, vulnerable, and terribly frightened.

Outside the wind howled through the pines as the storm increased in strength. She shivered at the mournful sound.

"Don't you miss it?" His voice grated.

She shook her head, not in denial but to make him stop.

"You're a passionate woman, Moll." Only rigid control allowed him to stand where he was. His restraint was hanging by a thread. "Don't you miss a man's mouth on yours? You have such beautiful breasts. Don't you miss a man touching them? Don't you miss being pleasured by a man? Don't you miss waking up with a man's body next to yours?"

"Stop it!" Her voice was so shrill it hurt her throat. God, yes, she missed being kissed and touched! And she'd been so lonely since Étienne died. At times the torment was unbearable.

Her passions ran strong and deep. She wanted him. She'd been aching for his touch since he kissed her at Christmas. No—long before that. Since she first saw him.

"I want you, Moll. I've never wanted anybody as much as I want you. Let me stay with you tonight."

"No." She backed away from him till she reached the edge of the bed. In such a small cabin, that wasn't far. "You didn't hire me to sleep with you."

Outrage flared in his gray eyes, and he lunged away from the door and grabbed her by both arms. "You insult me!"

"And you're insulting me! I'm the result of two people's lust. I've suffered for it all my life. I won't do that to anybody else." She twisted away from him and walked to the stove. "Go home, Win. Leave me alone."

Furious, and more hurt than he had believed possible, he slammed the door of the cabin behind him.

Moll went out to the wood pile behind Win's house just before she went to bed. It was after one when she'd calmed herself enough to even think about sleep, and then she realized she was almost out of firewood.

The thought of waking up to the bitter cold and being forced to wade through snowdrifts to bring in icy, wet wood, which would smoke more than burn, had convinced her to make the trip right then. Grumbling to herself, she'd put on her boots and coat and wrapped a heavy scarf around her head.

Win's light was still on, she noticed with a stab of satisfaction. He wasn't having any better luck sleeping than she was, and that made her suffering a little more bearable.

She made three trips from the stack of firewood to her door, piling the sticks under the little overhang to keep them out of the worsening weather.

The snow fell in beautiful white swirls, tossed about by the whims of the wild, north wind, creating a silent fairyland in the woods. Right now Moll wasn't in much of a mood to appreciate the wondrous, crystalline universe beyond the warmth of her stove.

It was some way to start off the new year. She shoved the front door open with her hip, since her arms were loaded with wood.

As she stepped inside, the lamp went out.

Startled, she gasped and felt for the table, trying to fight her sudden vertigo and get her bearings in the dark. The load she carried hampered the search.

"Aahhhhhh . . ." An angry roar assaulted her ears, just before a hard body smashed into her.

She screamed in terror, dropping the wood as she tried to get away.

But her attacker was bigger and stronger than she and seemed intent on hurting her. The malodorous stench of whiskey seemed to emanate from him. The thought occurred to her that he must have attended one of the numerous parties on the mountain.

Then his fist landed solidly on her shoulder, and she screamed in fear and agony. And screamed again.

He hit her a half-dozen times before she covered her face and rolled up into a ball, trying to protect herself.

A few words penetrated her shocked brain. Spoken in the same angry roar she'd heard at the beginning, the words were hard to distinguish.

". . . Blade . . . kill . . . get even."

She was terrified the man would murder her. Instinct took over. Moving slightly, knowing she wouldn't get a second chance, she lifted her booted foot and stomped on his, then raised her knee. Her leg connected with his privates, not hard enough to hurt him because she was off-balance, but definitely hard enough to get his attention. He gasped and swore, then hurled her to the floor.

Believing he meant to further harm her, Moll tried to roll to protect herself. But her assailant just bellowed, "Bitch!" and ran out the door.

She lay on the floor sobbing for breath, her body crumpled over the sharp edges of frozen wood, when the door slammed open again.

"Moll! Are you okay?"

She didn't answer. She couldn't. Winslow Fortune, in his boots, trousers, and the unbuttoned shirt of his woolen union suit, filled the lantern-lit doorway. His suspenders hung at his sides.

"God Almighty!"

He set the lantern on the table, slammed the door against the cold air, and knelt down beside her. As relief seeped into him, he wanted to hold her against his heart. Instead, he pushed aside her coat and made a slow examination for broken bones, careful not to hurt her. Then he picked her up from the floor.

"I'm all right. You can go home."

"Not without you." He carried her back to his house.

"I'm okay," she murmured when he laid her on his bed.

"You're staying here tonight. Tomorrow I'm taking you to Placerville to the doctor."

"Absolutely not!" She pushed herself up on one elbow, winced, and lay back down again. "Being beaten was bad enough. I'll be damned if I make that ride through a snowstorm!"

"You're hurt."

"Not that bad." She was trying very hard not to cry. Fear and anger mixed with pain and ate away at her self-control. She wanted very much to weep in Win's arms.

"First thing in the morning, I'll have Hannah look at you. Then we'll decide about the trip to town." He moved to put some wood in the stove.

She made a face at his persistence, but the grimace hurt her jaw.

"Who was it? Can you remember?"

"My brain's not addled, Mr. Fortune." She scowled at his concerned gaze, then touched her jaw gingerly, wondering if she'd have a bruise. "I didn't see him."

"Why not? Your lamp was lit."

She wondered how he would know that if he hadn't been checking on her.

"My woodbox was empty. I went out to get firewood so I wouldn't have to do it in the morning."

"I'm sorry about the woodbox. I didn't think to look."

The room was suddenly quiet. They'd definitely had other things than stovewood on their minds when he had left.

Moll cleared her throat. "When I stepped back into the cabin, someone was there. He might have been behind the door—I don't know. The lamp went out as I walked in. That's all I know."

"He hit you?"

She gave a short laugh. "He certainly did!"

"Is that all?"

"Isn't that enough? Oh, no, he didn't do anything

else. He didn't rape me, or even try. He just kept punching me till I kicked him."

"Your kicking scared him off?"

"I put my knee in his privates."

"Oh . . . good!"

"Any other questions?"

"Not tonight."

"Then leave me alone."

But he didn't. He built up the fire and sat in the chair beside the bed until she was asleep. Then he got another quilt from the chest at the end of the bed and laid down beside her. He couldn't help thinking how the attacks on Moll began around the time he started romancing her. He wondered if someone was after Moll to hurt him. If so, it was working. He moved closer and gently held her for the rest of the night.

Moll unearthed the writing paper as soon as she was alone, as soon as Win and Hannah and Hildy thought she was fit to stay by herself. It had been two days since the attack.

She was angry, and scared silly, but she was actress enough to fool them with her calm demeanor and her witty charm. They had agreed she was all right, in spite of the bruises.

Hearing the words *Blade* and *kill* was the only thing she remembered clearly about the brutal attack. Everything else was foggy in her memory.

But those words burned into her brain.

Seamus Blade . . . kill.

Why?

Why not? She was a threat to him. He was probably a pillar of his community—adored by his family and nominated for sainthood by the Church. And she was his *secret sin.*

She could see it all now. Her father, her tall, silver-haired sire, surrounded by his flock of spoiled rich children, an entire admiring city, and, naturally, the faithful clergy—nuns, bishops, and a whole slew of angelic choirboys. The only thing standing between him and national acclaim and Eternal Glory was his secret sin.

Suddenly she remembered her conversation with Hildy the afternoon they had remade her skimpy red-and-black saloon costume. They had discussed the Gypsy who had given readings behind the tea room many years ago, and the medium's unsettling predictions for her.

What had the old Gypsy told her about a man of power?

She couldn't recall the crone's exact words, but Moll never let little details like the exact truth get in her way any more than reason and logic did.

Her newly imagined version of the visit to the Gypsy now included thieving pickpockets in the street, villainous characters in the tea room, and a strolling violinist. Moll never skimped on scenery in her daydreams.

But most importantly, the oracle's revelation centered around the man of power.

Moll leaped to her feet and paced around the cabin. Her mind raced in a hundred directions at once. She wanted to scream and kick and throw herself onto the bed. Instead, she sat down in her chair and began to scribble.

Venting her hysteria and wrath in the only way she knew how, she fired off an angry note to the man who had fathered her.

"I'm told I'm a rich man's bastard and you're that rich man," she began. When she had finished, she stuffed the letter into an envelope and, with an impulsive whim of pure devilment, stuck in a folded handbill of *The Love Goddess* from her performance at the Majestic Theater.

"That ought to curl his hair," she muttered.

Without allowing her anger to cool, she threw on her coat, marched out the door, and practically ran to town. The snow had begun to melt, and the path was slippery, but it didn't slow her down. She wanted to get the envelope in the outgoing mail before another hour passed.

A week later, when her temper had cooled, she looked back on her impulsive action with a quiver of trepidation.

Win had told her to contact him, she thought as she pinned up her hair into a chaste coronet for school. An impish gleam sparkled in her blue eyes. "I doubt that's what he had in mind, though."

Her choked laughter was a mixture of anxiety and chagrin. What if she'd landed herself in another mess?

She used the Zodenta Tooth Soap, patted Spiro Powder under her arms, and buttoned the tiny pearl buttons on her white blouse.

Old man Blade was liable to fall over dead when he saw that handbill. She brushed the thought away angrily. She was glad to let the old bastard know his little indiscretion hadn't faded away.

What would she do if Seamus Blade wrote back to her?

When she remembered the lengths her mother had taken to avoid her, she realized that this was very unlikely.

* * *

Days passed, and a cloud of depression settled over Moll, reflecting the turn in the weather. Clouds came and went, but it didn't snow again. Win grew sullen and distant, apparently worrying about the upcoming logging season. Gloom reigned over everything.

Although it was the talk of the town for weeks, nobody in Summit knew who had attacked the teacher on New Year's Eve. Or if anybody did, they didn't admit it.

Moll felt powerless and violated.

It was bad enough to think of some unknown deviant pawing through her clothes on Christmas Day. But the attack on her was far worse than the ransacking. While the bruises on her body faded with the passing days, the bruises to her soul did not. Outrage burned silently within her, and Moll desperately wanted revenge.

Her assailant was still out there, and Moll knew he was watching her. She could feel his malevolent eyes on her, the same way she had felt the deadly gaze of the mountain lion that day in the woods.

He watched her from a distance, sickened by the evil he now knew about her. She was a she-devil, a child of lust, a daughter of sin! He'd seen the letter in her trunk.

He'd touched her clothes, unable to help himself. Then he'd found the papers and the letter.

Now he recognized the reason he was drawn to her. It was so simple that he almost smiled. He had to kill her, to destroy her wickedness.

His hands itched to squeeze around her white throat.

Soon . . . He would have an opportunity soon.

Nearly a month later, a small Mexican boy carried a stack of mail into a private parlor in the Orndorff, Tucson's finest hotel, and laid it on the table beside Seamus Blade.

"Buenos dias, Señor Blade."

"Same ta you, laddie." The small red-headed man began to thumb through the stack as he waited for his son to join him for breakfast.

Neel was late, which was unusual since he was punctual by nature, but he had been moody for quite some time. The elder Blade thought the problem was that the boy needed a woman, but he conceded that maybe there was another reason. Maybe he was homesick. Seamus would consider returning to Denver as soon as their business in the Tucson area was complete.

He picked up a thick envelope addressed with elaborate swirls that had been forwarded by Agnes O'Malley's block printing.

He ripped open the envelope, thinking about the gold mine he'd recently won on the draw of a poker hand. The words flew off the page at him.

"Sweet suffering Jesus!"

The ghost of his past had returned to haunt him.

He read and reread the letter until he understood the meaning. Then he stared at her picture, stunned by her beauty and shocked to his heretofore unknown puritanical core that she—his daughter—had posed before a camera like a common strumpet.

Rigid with judgment and scorn at the sort of woman she'd become, he couldn't escape the blanket of guilt that accompanied the vile pounding in his skull. His daughter, the one he'd never seen nor inquired about from the time he'd been informed of her conception, was alone and in serious trouble. He had to act, and immediately.

He yelled for Carlos to bring him some writing paper.

Within minutes, and without giving the matter any further thought, he had ordered Patsy Murphy, the one man he knew who would protect his child with his life, from Denver to California. Carlos ran off to mail the message.

After the lad was gone Seamus wondered if he should have discussed the problem with Neel. Neel was the smartest of his children, and by far the most level-headed.

But it was too late. The letter was off.

Seamus gasped at the pain in his head.

The parlor door opened, and Neel walked in.

Seamus barely saw his son. His head exploded in a firecracker of light and agony. Trying to speak, and then trying to pray, he slumped and fell from his chair to the floor.

It was snowing when Agnes O'Malley brought Patsy Murphy the envelope. Snow wasn't unusual during this time of year in Denver, where the winter was long and beautiful if a person was fortunate enough to live in a warm, rich man's house.

"Thank you, dear," Patsy said with the easy Irish charm he showed all women, even though Agnes was sixty and built like a feather pillow.

" 'Tis from Himself," she said, using the traditional Irish form to refer to the boss.

"Good. I've been a bit bored, with Miss Celestine having the influenza. Maybe he has me an errand."

Agnes snorted. The sort of errands Patsy participated in were enough to make a body die of fright. He was a tough one, he was, in spite of his glib tongue and Irish ways. A fine figure of a man, to her way of thinking, but a bit of a wild one.

Patsy Murphy was built like a beer wagon. Big, brawny, and nearly indestructible, he had the face of a street fighter and the brains of a robber baron. Six-foot-three and made of two hundred seventy-five pounds of iron muscle, he'd been Seamus Blade's bodyguard and aide for four years. Mild-mannered, except in a fight, Patsy was a favorite with the domestic staff at the Blade home.

When old man Blade found out what a dynamite brain Patsy had he wanted to set him up in business and make a gent out of him, but Patsy had turned him down. He liked to be in on the action, he said, in on the brawls and the intrigue.

He ripped open the envelope and scanned his employer's missive. Then he looked at the other note. His brows rose to his thinning hairline.

"Why, the old bastard." He chuckled. "Got himself another chick. That oughta cause a dustup on the homefront. I wonder if she's the only one?"

Patsy unfolded the handbill. "Wooowie! What a bird!"

He reread Blade's instructions and then went to pack. California! He had heard a lot about California but had never had the good luck to go there. It was a rare treat, and looking out for the actress would be a pleasure.

"I hope she's better natured than Celestine. It'll take a strong man to tame that one."

Briefly he wondered who would be coming to watch after Celestine. For a few days she'd still be recovering from the influenza, which *should* keep her out of trouble. He didn't envy the man who got her next. After a lengthy confinement, she'd be a pisser.

But she wasn't his problem this time. Since Seamus and Neel would be back in Denver soon, he figured the girl would be all right.

He knew that was a lie, of course. Celestine Blade was born trouble. How such a pleasant family had produced such a hellion he didn't know, but for a few weeks she was somebody else's problem.

Patsy was on the next train to Sacramento, ready to enjoy the wonders of nature from the first-class parlor car.

13

The last Friday in February was a cold, clear day.

As a reward for an excellent school week, Moll walked her small band of students down the center of the main road to view the new town hall. The building was still under construction, but the children were excited and impressed by the progress.

"How many schoolchildren can say they helped raise money for the new town hall?" Moll said. "You should be proud of yourselves."

Everyone beamed at the compliment.

"Miss Kennedy, when the town hall is built, do we get to go inside?"

"Of course. It's for everyone, including children. There will be meetings and parties held there. And church services once a month."

"What can we do?" Matty Swensen asked.

"Timmy, get away from there. I think that board is

holding up something." Moll took a deep breath. Sometimes Timmy was still naughty, but he was a much happier boy than he'd been in October. "Maybe the students at the Summit School can put on a program. Let me talk to Mr. Fortune about it."

"What sort of program?" Eddie Hodges asked. He hoped he didn't have to get up and recite poetry in front of the whole town. Miss Kennedy was big on reciting, and if there was one thing his dad did not understand, it was poetry reading. C.J. was on the wagon again, and Eddie didn't want anything to knock him off.

"A program to show your parents what you've done this year. A recital or spelling bee. Or perhaps some sort of entertainment. Let me think about it."

They gave the structure a thorough inspection. Eddie said he'd heard there was lumber enough for a stage. He was quieter these days, and often distant, but no longer so much of a troublemaker. Moll wasn't certain what had changed his behavior, but she wasn't questioning a good thing.

"It would be keen to be onstage," he said. "Have you ever been on a real stage, Miss Kennedy?"

Moll almost said "Yes, a burning one," but then she remembered whom she was talking to. "Yes. Perhaps you will be, too."

Bert Stoneleigh and his brother Simon told them that benches were going to be built, and Tilly Franklin said the hall was also going to have tables. Was there no end to the fineries of the Summit town hall?

Moll had discovered that outings away from the classroom insured better all-around behavior. And since Eddie's surly ways had ended, the other boys had settled down.

"Now, because you've all been so good this week, we're going on down to the Emporium. Mr. Franklin is waiting. Each of you can choose your own penny candy from the jars."

That afternoon, as she sat in Hannah's kitchen, sipping tea before the men came in to dinner, Moll mentioned the idea of a children's program to Hannah. "I thought we might put on a play."

"That sounds like fun. We should try to get as much use out of the building as we can, since we put so much effort into raising the money to build it."

"The children are very excited about putting together a program."

Hannah poured herself some tea and sat down. Hildy was still up at her house.

"You're looking better the past few days. Are you still having nightmares?"

Moll didn't deny that she hadn't been herself for quite some time. "I'm not as scared all the time and I'm not having nightmares very often." She paused. "But I'm still so damned mad!"

"Win told Bill he wanted you to move into the house with him—to keep you safe. Bill advised him against it—said it wouldn't look right, and we'd make room here if you were in danger."

"Oh, now wouldn't that have given Mildred and Selma something to gossip about!"

"He meant well, Moll."

"I know." She took a sip of tea.

"He's only a man, my dear. Nothing more. And men aren't perfect."

"I know that, too."

"Are you in love with him?"

Moll slopped the tea out of the cup as she set it in the saucer. "Hildy's the one who's in love with him."

"In some ways Hildy is like a young girl. She was infatuated with Win because he was kind to her. That's all he's ever been to her—a kind friend. He needs a much more sophisticated woman than Hildy can ever be."

"He doesn't need a woman he can't respect."

Hannah gave her a questioning look.

Moll wasn't sure if she should trust Hannah, but she desperately wanted to talk to the older, wiser woman. "I was married when I was eighteen."

Hannah listened curiously. She'd known almost from the beginning that Mollene Kennedy wasn't any ordinary spinster schoolteacher. A woman as beautiful as Moll didn't end up alone and out-of-work in a place like Summit, unless she had a past.

"The nuns had me escort a young girl to her home in Washington, D.C., when school was out that year. The girl's parents insisted I stay a few days and see the city. It was so exciting. I was there on my birthday, and they bought me presents.

"I met a man at a party we went to, and he called on me the next morning. He was an engineer, a Frenchman, and a number of years older than I was. I immediately fell in love and married him within days. And we went off to Panama to his job."

"That sounds very romantic."

"It was. Exciting and adventurous, too. Everything a lonely girl dreams of. But Étienne contracted malaria like so many of the others did down there. And he died."

Hannah had an idea of what came next. "And you were left alone. And broke?"

"Just about. Grief-stricken and terrified. Eventually I managed to get to California. By then I was broke."

"Do you have any family?" Hannah couldn't imagine being all alone and destitute. Her heart went out to the young woman.

"My aunt had died by then." Moll took a deep breath. "I have a father. I'm told he lives in Denver. Jed Cantrell said he knew his name. He and my mother weren't married. My mother was his nurse after he was hurt in an accident. He had a wife and family in Denver."

If Hannah was shocked, she didn't show it.

"Perhaps I should have written him for money, but my pride wouldn't let me do that. I sang in a saloon instead. Later, I sang in better places. Eventually I became an actress with my own production. I took my stage show to San Francisco."

"And Win knows?" Hannah admired Moll's courage. She also understood why Win was in such a bad mood these days. Falling in love with an adventuress had to be quite a shock for a man of his staunch upbringing.

"Win knows. He caught my act in San Francisco."

"And he asked you to come to Summit?" For the first time, Hannah was flabbergasted.

Moll laughed. "Oh, no! No, he didn't invite me here. He was very annoyed when he realized who Sampson Levine had sent to teach his school."

"Sampson's a delightful scamp, isn't he?"

"Win didn't think so."

Hannah's laughter filled the room. She imagined that her dear friend Winslow was quite put out with

Sampson's games. She also imagined the lawyer's delight in tempting Win with such a fetching girl. The only problem was that now some very strong emotions were at stake, and with them, the potential for great pain.

"Moll, you didn't answer my question. Do you love Winslow Fortune?"

"Of course not."

"Hmmmm . . . I would have thought an actress could lie better than that."

"When can you have your students ready for their program?" Win asked, as he sat across his desk from Moll. He wasn't in much of a mood to be planning social events, but maybe the town did need a little diversion.

"I'll need two or three weeks to be certain everyone has his part down pat."

"The town hall should be finished by then. Depending on the weather."

The weather had become a touchy subject of late. It had only snowed once since New Year's and spat rain a few times. Win's grim mood matched that of every other man on the mountain. If they didn't get a lot of rain before summer, the timber simply couldn't be run down the river, and they'd be beaten by nature instead of the Rockwells.

"Then it's all right to go ahead with the program?"

"Yes."

She got up and started to leave.

"Moll, how have you been?"

She shrugged. "I'm better."

"I'm sorry we couldn't find the man who hurt you. I

saw footprints in the snow that night. But I was so concerned about you, I didn't follow the tracks. The next morning, they'd been covered up."

"I know."

"Have you had any more problems?"

She shook her head.

There was a knock on the office door, and Moll automatically opened it. A large man pulled his hat off when he saw her.

"I'm looking for Mr. Fortune." His voice was rich, with an Irish lilt to it.

"Come in. I was just leaving." She stepped outside.

"I'm Patsy Murphy. Sebastian Hall sent me to see you."

"Yes, come on in. Miss Kennedy, will you tell Hannah I'll be late. And that I'm bringing someone with me."

"Yes, Mr. Fortune." She closed the door behind her.

They were already eating when Win arrived.

"Sorry I'm late, Hannah. This is Patsy Murphy. I've hired him to take Sebastian Hall's place."

A chair was brought for Patsy and they all introduced themselves.

"Where'd you say you're from?" Buckley Brooks asked.

Patsy's rough brawler's face was placid when he answered, "Chicago. But it's a tough place. A body ain't safe in his own bed. Thought I'd try my luck in California. The mountains looked pretty, so I came on up."

"He went to the *Mountain Democrat*," Win explained, "and asked to see any ads for employment. They sent him over to talk to Sebastian."

"Fine man," Patsy commented as he piled potatoes on his plate. How he'd come by the job was a bit more complex than his explanation to Win indicated, but Patsy believed in simplifying life whenever possible. "I think Sebastian hated to be leaving this job. He said Summit was a grand place to live because the people were so good-hearted."

That little speech earned him a larger piece of pie than the rest, Patsy noticed. A good, honest compliment was always appreciated—at times as much as a ripping good lie.

He was trying hard to keep from staring at the beauty down the table. She was even better looking in person than on that risqué poster that old man Blade had sent him. Softer looking, sweeter. The kind of woman to keep a man warm on a long winter night.

He'd start on his report to his employer before he went to bed. Blade was an old busybody where his children were concerned. He seemed to think they weren't capable of running their lives without his help. Interference they got from start to finish. Patsy imagined the old rooster crowing with glee at finding a new chick to peck at and annoy. He'd make the report long and carefully detailed—like how creamy her skin was in the lamplight, and what hot looks the owner of the logging company was throwing in her direction. Patsy was sure his report would delight Seamus Blade.

At first the Irishman's intense scrutiny made Moll uncomfortable, but she quickly noticed that he gave the same attention to Hildy, Hannah, and the corned beef on his plate. He was friendly to everyone, yet she noticed he managed to say a lot without really answering questions. She hoped Win had made a good choice.

And she hoped Patsy Murphy wasn't working for the Rockwells.

Patsy lavishly complimented Hannah for the meal and winked at Hildy when she took away his empty plate. Out of the corner of his eye he noticed Jed Cantrell's face show absolute astonishment. Patsy smiled to himself. Like his boss, he liked to keep things stirred up. He thought that plain little blond girl needed some attention.

The air was tense with expectation.

In spite of the high winds and the threat of snow, all the newly built benches in the Summit town hall were filled.

At the back of the hall, a table had been loaded with refreshments for afterward, to celebrate the play's success. The table was so loaded it was nearly groaning.

Moll, who had never suffered much stage fright, was in an absolute stew. She knew there was no reason to be upset, yet she simply couldn't calm herself.

The stage was perfect. Her eleven young charges knew their parts backward and forward and had been in their costumes for at least an hour. At this moment they were bouncing around behind the sheet like rubber balls in perpetual motion. Trying her damnedest not to shriek at them, Moll ordered them to sit on the rug she'd brought and relax. They didn't need the quiet, but she did.

Peeking out from behind the sheet at the audience, she saw beaming parents anxiously awaiting the show. It brought tears to her eyes to know how much these children were loved. Even C.J. Hodges was there, to

Moll's surprise, in a jacket and tie no less, with his hair slicked down neatly.

She took a deep breath and caught the scent of new lumber, and it filled her with a sense of pride at having been part of creating this building. People would enjoy it for generations to come. Suddenly she realized what a special place in her heart the town of Summit had claimed.

The last place Win wanted to be was on the back of his horse with the icy wind blowing in his face. And the last thing he wanted to do was search for Lorna Hodges. If it hadn't been for Eddie . . . He wasn't Win's kid, so why did he feel responsible?

Eddie had walked into his office right after school and asked to talk to him. Before he left, Win agreed to do something about Lorna.

"I didn't wanta tell, Win. I'm so ashamed." His face was red, and his chin quivered. "My mother's whoring for money."

Sick to his stomach for the boy and for the laughing woman he'd known for years, Win had agreed to make the trip. Eddie wanted to go with him, but Win told him that Miss Kennedy was counting on him tonight. The program would be ruined if he wasn't there to do his part.

He cringed when he saw the cabin. It was run-down and miserable, a lonely shack on a lonely road. He wouldn't want his horse put up in such a squalid shanty. A snowflake hit his cheek, icy and sharp. He winced and climbed off the bay.

"Don't worry," he told the horse as he tied him to a moldy post holding up a sagging roof. "I'm not staying."

"Lorna," he called as he pounded on the grimy wood. "Open the door."

Feet shuffled, and somebody coughed. All the lamps in the building were turned out.

A drum began to beat. *Boom-boom-boom. Boom-boom-boom.*

A torch flared at the back of the stage, and then another.

A sheet had been stretched taut across the stage and fastened to decorated poles. Behind the sheet, silhouetted in front of the torches, stood several palm trees, a grass hut, and the tropical sun.

A spear-wielding figure leaped on the stage and yelled. Another figure yelled back.

The audience gasped in unison.

"Oh, my God," C.J. Hodges hollered. "They're naked!"

It was, without a doubt, the most ghastly night of Win's life. He wouldn't have wished such a loathsome farce on his worst enemy.

Lorna Hodges had thought he was a customer.

Not only did he have to dissuade her of that mortifying notion, he had to convince her to shut her door to other men.

Lorna was angry, ugly, and remorseful. At some point during their argument, he realized she was also very ill.

It was hard to believe this was the same happy, pretty girl he'd met when Eddie was young. Now she was worn and feverish, and far from clean. Win was torn between the need to rescue her and the urge to get away from her as fast as possible.

After handing over all the money he had and promising more later to keep her going, Win finally convinced her to take the lantern off the front step and close up business.

"Go to bed, Lorna, and keep warm. I'll build up this fire and make sure you've got plenty of wood inside. Then tomorrow Eddie can go for the doctor."

He had barely mounted his horse again when Buckley Brooks and two other men rode into the yard.

"Well, if it ain't the bossman. Come here to get your banana peeled, Win?"

Fortune was not going to get into a fight over Lorna Hodges. He was not going to wallow around in the muddy horse manure in front of Lorna's crib. "Lorna's not taking callers tonight."

"She'll take me," Brooks bragged. He slid down into the slop and headed for the door.

"She's sick."

"Hell, she don't have to do nothin' 'cept spread her legs."

"I think she's got smallpox . . . or cholera." Win figured Brooks would have heard of one of those contagious diseases.

"Come on, Bucky," one of the other men called. "Let's go to Placerville. I wanta get laid, not infected with somethin' deadly."

As he rode off, Win figured nothing worse could happen that night, but he was wrong. It started to sleet before he had ridden a mile. Icy beads pelted down like devil's pitchforks, chilling and wetting him to the skin. By the time he reached Summit, he was, without a doubt, in the foulest mood of his entire life.

The last thing he wanted to do after finally getting inside his cabin was go back out in the cold, but he knew he was obligated to show up at the town hall. As owner of the Summit Logging and Lumber Company, he would undoubtedly be expected to give a short speech.

After changing his sodden clothes, he went out into the night, feeling ornery, disgusted, uncomfortable, and hungry. Anybody who crossed his path was definitely risking trouble.

The lights in the hall were still off. The play must not be over yet, Win decided. As he got closer he saw Albert Stoneleigh standing under the overhang, puffing on a smelly, smoldering cigar.

"How's it going?" Win asked as he reached for the door handle. He hoped the blacksmith wouldn't detain him. Just one of Albert's depressing thoughts and he might go jump off the bridge.

"Don't know what this world's a'comin' to," Stoneleigh said. "All them kids running around in their birthday suits."

Win stuck his head in the door, thinking he hadn't heard right. Albert tended to confuse things. Probably all those years of pounding metal had somehow loosened a few screws.

Thunderation! Right there onstage, covered only by a sheet, was the unmistakable form of Moll Kennedy in all her glory . . . and nothing else. She was tied to a stake, surrounded by naked, chanting cannibals.

Win backed out and closed the door. He couldn't even think.

"Albert, I'm going over to the schoolhouse. Tell Miss Kennedy I'll be waiting for her there."

"Don't you want some rum cake? Selma baked it special."

"I'm just not up to rum cake tonight, Albert." He trudged away into the darkness.

He was sitting in her chair when she walked in the door twenty minutes later. A candle burned on the desk beside his elbow.

Moll was so excited she wanted to dance. The play had gone far better than she had expected. Even the little incident with the torch hadn't dampened her mood.

"Mr. Stoneleigh said you wanted to see me."

Win sat for a moment, not saying anything. He sat very, very still.

"Mr. Fortune?"

"You always need attention, don't you?"

"What?"

"Attention. Admiration. Excitement. That's what you live for, isn't it?"

"What are you talking about?"

"What the hell kind of woman does what you did tonight? Wasn't San Francisco bad enough? You paraded around onstage and subjected yourself to men's evil thoughts. But that wasn't enough! You had to expose innocent young children to your wicked ways."

"Wicked ways?"

Fortune was on his feet. "Nothing is too depraved for you."

"Depraved? Have you lost your mind?"

"I lost my mind the moment you came into my life, you brazen hussy!"

Inflamed and infuriated, she threw herself at him with upraised fists.

He caught her wrists. "I want you out of here. Tomorrow. Before I strangle you!"

Trying with all her might to pound him, she managed only to bump him with her hipbone and then stomp on his foot.

"Owwwh! You're crazy!" He managed to avoid a savage kick. "You're fired, Miss Kennedy!"

"Go to hell, *Mr.* Fortune!" She was yelling and crying, trying to tear him apart.

He gave her a shove before she could do him any serious damage. "Crazy witch," he muttered as she stumbled away from him and lurched out the door, peppering the night air with expletives. "Good thing she didn't have a gun."

Trying to catch his breath, he leaned against the side of the desk. His foot hurt where she'd stepped on it. He'd have a bruise tomorrow. He sighed, not ready to go back outside.

He was too mortified to face his neighbors. They'd trusted him to give them a competent teacher, and instead he'd hired a thespian. No, she wasn't even that. She was little more than a strumpet dressed up in nice clothes. Except for tonight, when she wasn't dressed at all.

And he'd known about her all along! He'd had no business letting her stay. He should have put her saucy little butt back on the train to San Francisco and not even given her time to blink. But he hadn't, because he'd felt sorry for her.

Hell! Couldn't he at least be honest with himself? He didn't make her go because he'd wanted to get her into bed. That was the truth, plain and simple. He'd wanted that from the beginning, and he wanted it now, even with his foot throbbing with pain.

He rubbed his hands over his face, wondering what the hell he could say to the townsfolk. He'd allowed a woman of questionable character to come into their midst and lead their children down the path of wickedness as surely as the Pied Piper.

He should go talk to them, but he was afraid that Bill, Jed, and the others would lynch him from the rafters.

"Hey Win, are you in there?"

Win sat there awaiting his fate as Bill McDonald walked in.

"God, Win, you missed a good show! That was the funniest damned thing I ever saw!"

Win stared at him in stunned disbelief.

"Miss Kennedy is a very talented woman. She wrote that play, you know. Those kids looked so cute running around behind that sheet in their union suits. They were great. I thought I'd split a gut laughing."

Union suits?

"Albert said they were naked." Win's voice sounded peculiar, even to his own ears.

"The old fool didn't want to go inside. He stood out there in the cold, puffing on that smelly old stogie. But he was the first one in the food line. Was Moll here?"

"A while ago," Win answered quietly.

"George Franklin thought she might want to make a speech."

"I think she was . . . tired. All the excitement, and everything . . ."

Because Bill insisted, there was nothing Win could do but join his neighbors at the town hall. Everybody had to congratulate him on the wonderful entertainment. The spoof was a delight, and Miss Kennedy was a gem. Win forced a smile, choked down cake, and repeatedly looked at the door, waiting for the opportunity to make his escape.

". . . had a little extra commotion when the torch fell over . . ."

Win closed his eyes. Not another torch!

"Miss Kennedy had a bucket of water handy, Jed. She thinks of everything." Hildy turned around and smiled at Patsy Murphy. Then she walked off to see if her daughter needed help with her shoebuttons.

George Franklin slapped Win on the back. "You look a little worn out tonight, boy. Have a rough day?"

"Not any more than normal," he answered, wondering if he was going to start laughing hysterically.

He wanted a stiff drink, but he knew he needed to make this apology without Dutch courage. He took a breath and knocked on the door to Moll's cabin.

It opened to his touch.

A chill touched his heart. Why wasn't the door bolted? Without knocking again, he gave it a shove and stepped through the doorway, calling her name as he entered. "Moll?"

Startled, she let out a little cry and froze where she was, half rising from the bathtub.

Win couldn't have been more stunned if he'd been hit on the head with a two-by-four.

She was naked.

He'd been so worked up about seeing her, it hadn't occurred to him that she'd be busy, let alone that she'd be stripped down to nothing, lolling in the bathtub. In fact, he'd forgotten all about that damned portable tub with those damned violets painted on the side.

"The door was open," he said. "You shouldn't leave it open."

"Well, close it!" She'd sunk back into the water. Her heart began to thud like the tom-tom in tonight's play. She gazed down at the water, realizing she was almost as exposed as when she'd been standing. She heard the door close and lock. Win stood leaning against it, motionless.

He couldn't take his eyes off her, couldn't think.

None of his dreams, none of his fantasies even touched the physical perfection of Mollene Kennedy.

She swished her hand in the water, causing a small ripple, feeling annoyed at herself for her nervousness and vulnerability. She wanted to throw something at him, but the only thing at hand was her precious sponge, and she wasn't going to waste it on him.

"What do you want?" Her voice sounded shaky.

"To apologize. I'm sorry. I was wrong. I made a terrible mistake tonight."

It was hot in the cabin, and he unbuttoned his heavy coat, letting it drop to the floor where he stood. He immediately forgot it.

"Moll . . ."

Before he knew what he was doing—and before she had any idea—he reached down and scooped her up out of the tub.

"My God, Win!" She knew there was no turning back, not now, not ever.

His mouth was on hers, hot, fierce, desperate. She clung to him, her arms tight around his neck, her mouth as frantic as his own—touching, licking, and caressing.

Eventually he found a quilt to wrap her in. He stood

her by the stove and dried her, and then pulled at his own clothes and threw them off.

He was gorgeous, she thought. His shoulders were impossibly wide and muscular. His chest was covered with a sleek mat of dark hair. He reached for the buttons on his trousers, but she stopped him with shaky fingers.

"Let me," she whispered. She'd never been this bold before, but with Win nothing less would suffice. She needed to touch him as much as she needed to breathe.

"My God, Moll . . . hurry."

The bathtub stood in the middle of the small room, crowding them. Win bumped into it, and it swayed precariously, water lapping at the painted canvas.

But they had no time to move it.

He picked her up again and skirted the tub. Laying her softly on the feather bed, he joined her as she sank into the softness.

"Don't make me leave tonight."

How could he even think such a thing? "I can't make you leave because I want you to stay," she said softly.

Outside the cabin the wind picked up, the storm grew ferocious, and sleet beat ceaselessly down on the cabin roof. The outside world was frigid, but inside the tempest was fiery, relentless, and wild.

Moll had known love before, but nothing that matched the power of Win, nothing to match his fury. Or his skill. She touched his cheek with awe. "You make my blood run hotter than fire."

"And you, my love, are fire. One look and you drive me mad." His kiss was hard and possessive. He'd waited forever for her, and now he wanted her forever. "God, how I ache for you."

"And I ache for you, sweet love." She breathed a tiny sigh.

Her mouth was soft and trembling. He savored its shape, its taste, its promise. Pulsing with anticipation, he grasped at the threads of his self-control. She stroked the hard muscles of his back, and he groaned with pleasure. He pulled her closer, pressing against her thigh.

Her clever hands found him, worshiped him, and guided him. Finally they surged together in a passion-filled haze, meeting in the eternal, rhythmic magic of love. And later they discovered the magic again.

And yet again before dawn.

The fire was merely ashes when Win awakened to the bright light of day. He snuggled deeply into the covers, sleepy and content, never wanting to leave the warmth of his bed. And then he realized he wasn't alone.

Dear God, what have I done? He opened one eye. That was all it took to know he'd ruined his life.

She moved, pressing closer to him, and his treacherous manhood hardened. He wanted more than anything to sink again into her warmth and lose himself in the wondrous madness. Instead he threw back the covers and began to pick up his clothes and put them on.

"Hello."

His back was toward her. He snapped up his suspenders over his undershirt and reached for his coat. Dodging the tub, he reached the door.

"Are you leaving?"

She was sitting up, the quilt pulled to her breasts. She looked wild and absolutely exquisite.

Fortune could barely meet her eyes. He could see the hurt, and he ached for her. Ached for them both. "I've put your reputation in jeopardy by being here. I don't want you hurt."

"Are you coming back?" Her voice was shadowy soft.

He shook his head. "This was wrong. It can't happen again."

The alarm clock hit the door just as he shut it.

"Roast in Hell, Winslow Fortune!"

And she threw herself onto the pillow and wept.

14

The screen door of the Emporium slammed shut as C.J. Hodges stepped off the wooden porch. He was just chomping down on his horehound stick when a bony hand clamped onto his arm.

"I wanta talk to you."

C.J. chewed noisily. He wasn't a man who ran from a threat, but this was one confrontation he preferred to miss.

"Behind Stoneleigh's barn—in five minutes."

C.J. continued to crunch his candy as he sauntered past the stable. There were more men in town this spring, so he spat and shuffled before turning back toward the barn.

"You been avoiding me," Danbury accused him when C.J. finally showed up.

"So?"

Danbury was too intent on his purpose to understand the soft challenge. "I'm ordering you to kill Fortune."

"I won't." C.J. quietly put another horehound stick in his mouth and sucked on it.

"You shoulda done it in the first place. Simms and Fillmore aren't killers."

C.J. said nothing but eyed him dangerously.

"The Rockwells are furious at the screw-ups. It's the middle of May, and Fortune is healthy as ever! You could snap his neck with one hand . . ."

C.J. lunged toward Danbury and grabbed his shirt-front, lifting him off the ground. "I said no!"

Fear rushed through the smaller man. C.J. was a monster when he lost control. "I seen you do it before . . ."

His words ended as Danbury crashed against the barn.

"I told ya 'no'!"

"You'll kill him, C.J., or the sheriff learns about the other one!"

Moll stood by the side of the dusty road and watched the huge logging wagon roll past. Pulled by sixteen straining mules, the heavy-duty wagon had been especially built to truck the mammoth sugar pines to the log yard. She counted thirteen logs in the towering pile, held secure by strong chains. The sight was overwhelming.

Eddie Hodges walked beside the wagon, prodding the mules and hollering commands. Bill McDonald, who drove one of the wagons, told Moll that Eddie had the makings of a fine teamster. She waved, and he raised the long prod in reply, grinning with boyish pride.

She knew she had Win to thank for Eddie keeping up his school lessons. The boy was a good student when he applied himself, and somehow Win had convinced him how important a good education was for his future. After a long, hard day, Eddie studied at night to keep up with his class.

School would be out for the summer in two weeks, and she wondered what came next—for Eddie, and for her.

Her walk took her off the logging road and up a well-worn path to a clearing northeast of town. In a grassy clearing beyond a spring-green clump of poison oak was a rusty iron fence surrounding a half-dozen worn headstones, dulled by time and blackened with moss. It was a peaceful spot which Moll visited almost daily after school.

It was safer to walk in the tiny cemetery than in the woods. Here she couldn't get lost in the trees, and she could see anyone who approached. She came here to unwind after the tensions of the day, to get some fresh air, and to think. For the first time in her life, she looked forward to time spent in contemplation.

About Win mostly. About what came next.

He'd only been to her cabin once since the night of the jungle play, since the night they became lovers.

He knocked on the door one evening after dinner and stiffly asked if he could come in. Moll's heart had pounded like crazy.

More than anything she'd wanted to throw herself into his arms and confess her love for him. Instead, she moved several steps across the tiny room and waited.

"Are you pregnant?"

The angry, abrupt question left her speechless.

"If you are, I'll do the right thing." He sounded as though he'd rather be hanged.

She was so hurt that she sagged backward against

the bed. It was all she could do to keep the tears that knotted her throat and blinded her eyes from falling. But her pride asserted itself, and she kept a fierce grip on her emotions.

"Moll!"

He grabbed her and shook her before she could think.

"Leave me alone!" she cried, tearing herself away.

"Are you carrying my child?"

"No! And I wouldn't come groveling to you if I was!"

"Tell me the truth! I want to know if I got you pregnant."

"No, Mr. Fortune," she said through clenched teeth. "You can breathe easy. There's no nasty little reminder of our night of sin. You have no responsibility to me. Now get out of my house!"

He'd left her alone after that. Oh, he'd been polite at meals and even made a point to ask about school— stilted questions to which she gave stilted answers. But she knew that he hated her and he always would. She only wished she could hate him back.

She was listless, and she'd lost weight. And now she had another problem besides a broken heart. Someone had been in the schoolroom, searching her desk.

At first she thought it was Win. The book she'd been reading to the class wasn't where she'd put it. She wondered if he was checking up on her. Two days later, when she found the contents of the desk dumped on the floor, she realized it had to be the person who'd vandalized her cabin on Christmas Day.

Walking a little farther, Moll discovered a lush wild rose covered with sweet pink blossoms. Knowing that Hannah would love the fragrant flowers, she reached for a branch and cried out as a thorn pricked her finger.

A ruby droplet of blood splashed her blouse, making her want to cry. Not because of pain, but because every time she wanted something beautiful she ended up being wounded.

She felt like her heart was bleeding as she inhaled the rich, sultry perfume.

Hannah was delighted with the roses and arranged them in a cut-glass vase on the table. "Win asked me to tell you he wants to see you tonight up at the office. Anytime after you eat is fine."

"Why didn't he tell me himself?" Moll snapped.

Hannah sighed loudly. She thought they were acting like a pair of foolish children. "I just deliver the messages," she said. "I'm not responsible for how either of the lunatics behave. Besides, he's not going to be here for supper. He rode over to someplace near Kelsey."

"To see Lorna Hodges?"

"So you know about Lorna?" Hannah glanced at her.

"Buckley couldn't wait to tell me."

"I'm sure he couldn't. Did he also tell you that Win stopped Lorna from working and gave her enough money to survive without taking in men? Or that Win got a doctor for her and is paying for her stay at a clinic to be treated for consumption? No? I didn't think he did."

It was the first unpleasant conversation they'd ever had, and Moll felt terrible. "I'm sorry," she whispered, not knowing if she was sorriest for being nasty to Hannah, for Lorna's plight, or for herself.

"You're not hurting me, Moll. I love you *and* Win. I

feel bad watching you two keep on hurting each other. Why don't you patch up your misunderstanding?"

"We can't. It's too late. Too many terrible things were said."

"Balderdash! You're both alive and breathing. If you both make an effort, you can work out your problems."

Moll shook her head.

"I'm tired of my dining room being like a funeral parlor. What I ought to do is put the two of you out on the back porch, like I do the kids when they're behaving badly."

Moll smiled sadly. School would be out soon, and that would be the end of their problems. She had a little money saved up now. It would be the best thing for everyone concerned if she left Summit and didn't come back.

She thought more about her future as she walked up the hill after supper. Perhaps she would go to Denver. But she couldn't, since Seamus Blade hadn't bothered to acknowledge her letter.

"Miss Kennedy!"

She turned to see Patsy Murphy behind her.

"Would you be wantin' a bit of company?"

She laughed. How could a person refuse a charmer like Patsy? "I'm on my way up to see Mr. Fortune."

"Are you in trouble, girl?"

"Undoubtedly. Mr. Fortune is always mad about something." She kicked at a rock in the path.

"It's a heavy load he's carrying these days, poor man. What with the troubles on the job and worrying about the river a'bein' so low. To my mind, he needs a bit of cheering."

"You might be the one to do that, but not me."

Since Patsy had been in Summit, Moll had slipped into the habit of talking to him many evenings after work. He was easy to be around and seemed interested in her in a friendly way. His romantic charms he saved for Hildy, and this had Jed Cantrell going around looking as cranky as Win. If Moll hadn't been so lost in her own problems, she'd have been pleased, for Hildy's sake.

Patsy seemed curious about her childhood, and Moll found herself telling him story after story of her life with the nuns. And some of the things that had happened since.

"Are you writing a book?" she had asked him once when his questions got quite personal about her parents. She hedged about that subject. The only people who knew she was illegitimate were Hannah and Win . . . and Seamus Blade.

Patsy had laughed and said, "I'm just a country Irishman, darlin', and nosy as the devil. Did you notice how pretty Hildy looked in that pink dress tonight?"

They trooped up the hill together now, with Patsy muttering about having to walk to keep his figure after Hannah's good cooking. He hesitated at the office steps.

"There's some funny things going on around here, Molly." He looked as if he planned to say more, then stopped.

"I know. Funny things have happened to me lately, too." She was thinking about the intruder in the classroom.

"And they're happening to Win." Patsy was trying to make up his mind what to tell her.

"I know there's been problems on the job."

"Not just equipment tampering. Fortune, himself, may be in real danger."

"No!" Her heart began to pound in alarm. "How do you know?"

He shrugged. "A nosy man sees a lot and hears more. I want you to be careful. It would be a sad thing if you got in the way of something meant for him."

"What are you talking about, Patsy?"

"Ahhh, nothing much, darlin'. An Irishman doesn't need much to talk about. Just be careful up here in your little cabin by yourself."

"Win is close by." She refused to think anything could ever happen to Win.

He frowned. "He is, at that. I best be getting back to me room. All this exercise has me worn to a frazzle."

She chuckled and ran up the steps.

Patsy watched her go. The poor girl was downright moony over Fortune. And between scowls, the boss shot lustful looks her way, too. Patsy had a fair idea of what had happened between them. After all, he hadn't been far from the cabin the night Win had gone in and loudly demanded to know if she was pregnant. That was one fact Patsy had left out of his report to Seamus Blade!

Patsy was a romantic. He didn't think two broken hearts needed to be exposed to the world, or to the infernal curiosity of Seamus Blade. Time might solve the predicament of Moll's passion for Win, if the blighter managed to live that long. Patsy knew for certain that Win had a hell of a lot worse difficulties than those with Moll.

That he would put in his report to Blade.

He frowned at the thought. He'd heard nothing from his employer since he was ordered to California, and he was becoming uneasy about the silence. He'd sent a report back to Denver every two weeks since he arrived and had told Seamus more than once that there was a heap of trouble at the camp, beyond just the attacks on Moll.

For one thing, her lover was on somebody's death list. Patsy was itching to jump into Fortune's fight, but he'd been ordered to protect Moll. So he wrote the old man saying it would be a hell of a lot easier watching Moll if he simply threw a bag over her head and hauled her back home to Denver. When no word came from Seamus, Patsy concluded that Blade didn't want his other children knowing about her.

He never went into his room without checking the yard first. The bunkhouses were nearly full, and there was a number of roughnecks in the bunch. Patsy considered himself lucky to have a tiny cubicle of his own.

He kept his report on Moll in a box behind the chamber pot. Most men, he figured, might search a man's bunk and his dresser to check on him, but damn few would feel around another chap's pot.

Tonight, feeling unusually concerned and glum, he sent a letter directly to Neel Blade asking him what to do next. Was he to help Win, abduct Moll, or just return to Denver? Since Seamus hadn't answered his pointed questions, Patsy felt he could wait no longer. The Irish in him told him that. Something was coming, something big and ugly.

Win wasn't in the office when Moll went in. The door to the kitchen was open. She sat down in a chair and waited, trying not to be nervous.

"I didn't hear you come in." He had a mug of coffee

and a plate of cookies. "Would you like some of these?"

"No thanks. Hannah made a big dinner." She glanced down at her fingernails.

"I noticed you haven't been eating much lately."

She wasn't certain how she should respond, so she said nothing. Surely he hadn't called her up here to comment on her eating habits.

Win closed the ledger on his desk and looked at her. "You've done well this year at the school."

She didn't trust the compliment, not from him. This was a man who could make love to her all night long, drive her wild with pleasure, drive them both over the edge repeatedly, and then walk away from her the next day telling her that the beautiful experience was wrong. She watched him silently, waiting for what came next.

It sickened Win to see the distrust in her eyes. Had he trampled her feelings so badly? The answer was yes, he'd wounded them both. He hadn't slept a whole night through since he'd left her bed. He kept telling himself he'd get over her, but the pain kept getting worse. At times he wondered if it was lethal.

"The school board voted to give you an award of merit for your efforts under difficult circumstances. And a small monetary token of appreciation."

"Thank you."

"And we'd like you to come back next year."

Win found it difficult to make the offer, because he wasn't positive the town would exist next year. The spring runoff was low. The log drive would be dangerous, and if the logs didn't get to market, he would lose. The legacy would go to the Rockwells.

He had enough money of his own to keep the company going only one more year if his cousins got the inheritance. One way or another, his future was very uncertain.

"I thought you wanted somebody else."

He wouldn't lie to her. "I did. At first."

"What changed your mind? Or was it the other members of the school board who asked me back?"

"I didn't want you at first because I didn't trust you. And I didn't think a woman with your background could do a proper job. I've discovered that while your methods may be unorthodox, the students like school and they've learned more than expected."

He ran his fingers over his tired eyes and looked up at her. "I changed my mind about getting another teacher before Christmas. I waited for some time before I wrote Sampson to cancel the ad. Not because I was still looking for somebody else, but when you were attacked, I . . . I wanted you out of here because I wanted you out of danger."

"Did you tell Sampson not to look for a replacement?"

"Yes. Toward the end of February."

"And you didn't mention it to me?"

He picked up the coffee cup, then set it back down again. "After the night we . . . after we were together, I didn't trust myself to be alone with you."

"You came once."

"Not to hurt you, Moll, though you seem to think so. I was driving myself crazy wondering if I'd given you my child. I had to know! And you had to understand I wouldn't abandon you. *Our* child would never be unwanted or unloved."

"I see." She bit her lip to keep her emotions from overflowing. "Were there any applications for my job?"

"Not that I know of."

"You could have had Hannah tell me you canceled the ad. She seems to know all our secrets."

"Not all of them. Besides, I wasn't up to one of her lectures. Hannah has this notion that a few sweet words will solve all our problems."

"But they won't?"

"No." He was thinking more about his uncertain future than her unsavory past.

"You may be right. Was it you or the other board members who wanted me back next year?"

He shook his head, feeling old and tired. "The vote was unanimous. They all wanted you, and I don't think we can find anybody else who will come to Summit."

"You're a hard man, Win." She applauded her self-restraint. Once again he had wounded her, but she refused to let him see her bleed.

"Yes, I am."

"Most other men would have lied."

"I'm not other men."

"No, you're not. And since you've been honest with me, I think I should be as candid with you. Tell Sampson to run another ad. I don't want to work for you next fall." She rose and headed toward the door.

"Moll!" He had his hand against the wooden door before she could pull it open.

She didn't turn around. She simply spoke the words that were tearing her apart. "I can't live close to you anymore, because I can't sleep at night. I can't dine in the same room as you, because I hurt so much I have no appetite. I can't pretend you didn't kiss me and make love to me. You might be so hard it doesn't bother you, but I'm not!"

One hand was on the door holding it closed and the other was on her shoulder, gripping it tight. His emotions were taut, near the surface, ready to explode. "I think about you all the time, day and night. Don't you know I'm crazy, thinking about you?"

She leaned against the door. "This is killing me."

His mouth was on the back on her white neck, nuzzling ever so softly. "Don't go."

She didn't know if he meant don't go tonight or don't go from Summit, but her answer was the same. "I must!"

He inhaled sharply, fighting for control. Then he moved away from her. "It's dark outside. I'd better walk you home."

"That's not necessary. It's just around the corner."

"Are you sure?"

"Yes. In fact, I think it would be best if I went by myself."

He let her go then. When she was at the bottom of the steps, he slowly closed the door. "I think it's for the best, too, Moll. If I went home with you, I wouldn't be able to leave."

The moon hung in the middle of the huge black sky like a big round, yellow plate. It reminded C.J. that he'd forgotten to eat.

"Hol' s'still . . . ya ole moon," he called in a drunken sing-song voice. "Come back 'ere . . . un hol' s'still. I wanna eat . . . sompthin' . . ."

The thought was too complicated for him to finish, so he walked on through the darkness, babbling and feeling sorry for himself. After weeks of being sober, he'd fallen off the wagon with a bang!

It was Fortune's fault—and the woman. What was her name? Lorna. No—that was his wife. What was her name? The teacher—he couldn't remember. It was somebody else's fault—Danbury! He hated the ugly little bastard!

He'd ridden to Placerville to get a bottle of whiskey and decided to get laid. That always cured his problems. So after he got his booze, he stopped in at a place he'd heard some loggers talk about. Not a fancy cathouse—a cheap one. He paid. He remembered giving the whore some money. Then he passed out.

Later he came to and yelled, "You stole all my money. I been screwed."

"That's what we're here for, honey," an ugly woman yelled back, and everybody in the place laughed.

And he had laughed, too, though he had wanted to cry. He used to be real talented at making girls happy in bed. He'd been young and fine looking, and the women couldn't leave him alone. He was a hard-driving man! Lorna had said so too. She'd been crazy about him.

But Lorna had left him, and the dollies laughed at him. Now he was a drunken sot who passed out before he got his hooter out of his pants. Tears streamed down his face.

He weaved drunkenly along the dirt road. "Where's m'horse? I lost m'horse!"

The horse, and the saddlebag with the bottles of whiskey, had disappeared someplace. C.J. couldn't remember when he'd last seen them.

"T'hell with you, horse." He looked back up at the sky. "There s'the moon. T'hell with you, moon!"

The scream barely penetrated his whiskey-fogged brain. At the second scream, he turned toward the sound and slurred, "You shut up."

Above him, on a granite boulder beside the road, a

mountain lion growled and swatted the air with one enormous paw.

"Shut up," C.J. yelled, extending his hand like a child with a make-believe gun, "er I'll shoot ya."

The shotgun blast knocked him to the ground.

The cat screamed again, leaped right over C.J.'s inert body, and disappeared into the darkness.

A wagon loaded with supplies drove up. Two men looked at each other in the moonlight.

"You killed him."

"Hell, I shot three feet over his head. Sonofabitch just fell over."

The teamsters jumped out of their wagon and looked at C.J. lying in the dirt. One of them held out a lantern.

"He's passed clean out. Let's get him in the wagon."

"Who's gonna believe he was standing in the middle of the road waving his fingers at a goddam mountain lion?"

Win had been working on the books almost an hour when there was a knock on the door.

"It's open."

Patsy Murphy stuck his head in. "Would you be having a few minutes to talk, Win?"

Win thankfully shut the ledger. "What's on your mind?"

"I couldn't help noticing how many accidents have been happening around here. A man might think the place was jinxed, if he believed in that sort of thing."

Win watched him carefully. "He might."

"That hook that fell yesterday—one foot closer and your head would have been cracked like an egg."

Win merely nodded.

"And that wire you run into in the dark last week. Funny it being there where it was."

"Actually I didn't think it was funny at all. Much higher and I could have hanged myself on it."

"Would you be needin' a bodyguard, Mr. Fortune?"

For the first time in days, Win felt a spark of life in himself. "Would you be knowing of one in my neighborhood, Mr. Murphy?"

"I just might," he smiled. "I just might."

"You've guarded men before?"

"Men and women."

"Where?"

"Denver. Before I came here."

"I thought you came from Chicago."

Patsy shrugged, "Denver, Chicago, New York, Belfast. A man's gotta work, you know."

"Are you working for the Rockwells?"

"Them rotten buggers? I am not!"

"But you've heard of them?"

"Before I even left Placerville. I don't work for crooks. I don't have to."

"You're that good? Who did you work for last?"

"Seamus Blade."

The name seemed familiar, but at that moment Win didn't place it. "What would you do as my bodyguard?"

"Watch out for you."

"I don't want to be tripping over you all the time. You're as big as a house. I don't want you in my way."

"I won't be interfering with your privacy, if that's what you're saying."

"No, that's not it. If you hang around me like my shadow, folks are going to think it's strange."

Patsy smiled impishly. "If you keep giving potty

looks at Miss Kennedy, folks won't think you're strange for me."

Win choked on a laugh. "Potty looks! You insolent bastard! Aren't you supposed to be respectful?"

"Oh yes, sir!"

"I guess I'm supposed to pay you extra."

"It's better that way. Then I'll be honest and I won't have to steal from you."

"What will you be doing?"

"The same as I'm doing now. Keeping my eyes and ears open. Watching your ass."

He stood beside the cabin door, waiting. The light went out. He groaned aloud.

The pain in his body was excruciating. His head throbbed, his heart pounded, and his innards ached. He lusted to slash and tear. He needed to hurt her like she was hurting him.

She was calling him! Beckoning him to come to her.

He knew. He always knew. Like he knew before—with the other one.

He had to stop it like he did before. He put his hand upon the door. The wood was rough and dry against his palm. He started to give it a push.

A hiss and a cry stopped him. A barn cat shot past him. Another yowling cat followed.

The door to Fortune's office opened, and two men came out onto the porch: Fortune and the burly Irishman.

"Cat in heat," Fortune said.

"Know just how he feels," the Irishman replied.

The man slowly moved away from the door. The noises in his head subsided, leaving only the violent headache. He inched back into the brush as the other men went on talking. The lust died down. The violence faded. A cold sweat broke out over him, and he rushed off to be alone to vomit.

C.J. woke up the following morning lying inside Albert Stoneleigh's barn. He had no idea how he'd gotten there. His horse, still saddled, stood nearby.

"M'head hurts," C.J. mumbled. "Did you kick me?"

The horse ignored him.

C.J. laid back in the straw and closed his eyes. In the darkness, his mind showed him an interesting sight: a mountain lion standing on a boulder looking down at him. There was a scream and a terrible ear-shattering noise. And then he tripped.

The next thing he saw was the big cat leaping over his head.

Sweat beaded on his forehead. "God Almighty! I gotta stop drinkin'."

15

"*What's the real reason* you're in San Francisco?" Sampson asked. "Besides the weather."

It was foggy as mare's milk outside, and the cab was inching along. Although Maison Riche, where he'd made reservations, wasn't too far from the Elmer House, Moll's small but comfortable hotel, Sampson knew they'd be late.

"I had to get away. I thought San Francisco would be a nice city to visit. I was too busy to take in the sites when I was here before, you know. I left in a rush."

"Right," he said. "What did Win say about this trip?"

"I didn't tell him. I just hitched a ride into Placerville and caught the train."

Sampson groaned, shaking his head. She was incorrigible. "I hope the food is good tonight. If that madman from the mountains bursts in and murders me for abducting his woman, I want to be well fed before I die."

"He won't follow me, Sampson. I'm sure he's relieved I'm gone."

He peered at her across the dim-lit carriage. "What did you do to your hair?" He knew he might as well change the subject, since he wasn't going to get any straight answers out of her till she was ready.

"Do you like it? I was able to get in to see André for a trim—he worked me over when I was Aphrodite."

"Did he recognize you?"

"André? Of course! He knew who I was before I was a goddess. He thinks I should come back to the stage." She chuckled. "Theater life has been dull since I left."

"Moll, you make me feel young."

"You are young, dear man. What I want to know is why you were available for dinner on such short notice?"

"The love of my life has gone on an extended journey. She's off to England for the summer. I'm quite beside myself without her." This was, Sampson suspected, a turning point in his relationship with Mrs. Freeman, although she insisted she merely wanted to see England. He was lonely without her, though, and was looking forward to her return.

The restaurant was quaint and charming, the service superb, the food without equal. Moll relaxed as she hadn't been able to in months.

"So why do you think Winslow won't come bellowing into the city after you?"

She grinned at his choice of words, which made Win sound like a back-country savage. "Because he was relieved to get rid of me."

"Are things still that bad between you two?"

"We bring out the beast in each other."

"I can't believe that." He believed something quite different, in fact. He imagined the excitement between the pair was unquenchable, and his sixth sense told him they'd been lovers.

"Win thinks I'm a degenerate, scheming hussy. I think he's a self-righteous, sanctimonious sonofabitch."

Sampson marveled at her passion, her zest for life. She was the perfect woman for Fortune. "So how long will you be in town?"

Sampson realized he was looking forward to a few days of diversion. Moll would liven up his life.

"A week. Maybe two."

"If you need a dinner companion or an escort, I'm at your service."

"Thank you, Sampson. I think I'll take you up on that." She'd only been gone from Summit a short time, and already she was lonely. "Are there any good plays in town?"

"Nothing as hot as your act, Moll."

As she rode down Union Street on her third day of nonstop shopping and sightseeing, Moll spotted Arthur Smith, her gone-but-not-forgotten manager, and emitted an outraged screech. She'd been waiting months to get her hands on the cad! Calling for the cabbie to stop, she alighted from the carriage to follow Arthur into the Pacific Union, a dimly lit club.

"I say, madam," a big, officious-looking chap with a halo of gray hair called as he hurried across the dark, wood-paneled room toward her. "This is a gentlemen's club."

She didn't pause in her pursuit of Arthur. She was going to kill the bum as soon as she caught up with him, and a mere two-hundred-pound bouncer wasn't getting in her way.

The doorman reached out and grasped her arm, bringing her to a sudden halt.

Moll eyed him. "Unhand me, sir."

The man flushed, but he didn't remove his hand. "You can't come in here. Women aren't allowed."

"Fine, I don't intend to stay." She started to walk on but again was detained by the strength of his paw. The fellow was proving to be more of a stumbling block than she'd expected. "Let me pass, sir."

"You have to leave, madam."

"You are bruising my arm, *sir*."

"You must leave, *madam*."

"When I'm through!" Moll's voice had risen to stage projection, and men in the club were beginning to notice the altercation, Arthur Smith included.

He'd removed his neat brown bowler and was about to sit down at a poker table when he heard a voice from his misbegotten past—a voice that had haunted his dreams. He froze like a hunted rabbit, then twisted his head about, hoping against hope that he was mistaken.

His heart dropped to his round belly. The witch was here, and she was chasing him. He searched desperately for a way to escape.

"Mr. Arthur Smith," a solemn voice called. "Would Mr. Arthur Smith please come to the front door."

The men at the table were looking pointedly at Arthur, and Arthur was looking for a way out.

"Arthur Smith!" Moll's voice rang down from the rafters.

He drooped, clutched his hat with sweaty palms, excused himself from the poker table, and shuffled toward the door. He knew Moll, knew her moods and temper. He was certain that nothing had happened over the past months to mellow her. His life was decidedly in jeopardy.

"Mr. Smith. Please escort this lady out of here." The doorman was extremely annoyed to have his sanctuary invaded, especially by this virago. A woman had her place, and in his mind, that place was not in a gentlemen's club.

Moll stood rooted to the floor, her chin lifted in defiance. She wasn't moving till Arthur went with her. The little beggar looked positively sickly. Had he shrunk since the last time she saw him?

"How good to see you, Moll." He wished he didn't sound so mealy-mouthed.

"Stuff it, Arthur!"

The doorman edged them closer to the exit.

"Shall we take a stroll, my dear?"

"Good idea, Arthur. It would be a pity to get blood on the carpet."

He took her arm and led her out. Fortunately there was an empty bench a short distance away. Arthur felt he'd collapse if he didn't sit down.

"I looked for you, Moll," he said after a moment of unusually tense silence.

"At the jail?"

Arthur turned positively chalky. She wasn't going to make this easy for him. He knew that if she'd actually been hauled off to the pokey, he was a dead man.

He forced a weak chuckle. "I left to look for another show," he said. He winced at the viciousness of her laugh. "I was thinking of you."

"You went high-tailing it out of the Palace Hotel and left me there to face the creditors, you sonofabitch!"

"I believed in *The Love Goddess*. I thought we had a hit!"

"If it was so great, why did you run?"

He appeared to be having some trouble with his tongue. It was wallowing around in his mouth as if he was chewing molasses candy.

"Dammit, Arthur, you let them see you go! You marched through the lobby with your leather satchel and climbed into a cab right in front of the whole world. Why didn't you sneak down the back stairs? At least that way I might have had a chance to get away, myself. When I got downstairs that morning, the hotel manager was waiting for me—with a policeman!"

Arthur appeared to be choking. "My heart," he gasped, clutching his chest.

"That old gag won't work with me," Moll said. "I've watched you pull it before. I even scooped up all the money on the poker table when the others carried you over to the doctor's office. Remember?" She hoped he was only conning her. He was the color of a marble tombstone, except for his blue lips.

He coughed several times, and the normal pink began to seep back into his cheeks. "I need a drink."

"Oh, I'm sure you do. You deserted me. You left me with all those debts, and the cops on my doorstep. And you stole my stash! You knew what that meant to me, you rat, but you stole it anyhow."

Arthur slowly stood up and wobbled back down the street to the club. He went in without giving her a backward glance.

Moll thought about following him. He deserved all the terrible things she'd wished on him over the past months. He'd stolen her hope, her trust, and her security.

But she didn't follow him. She couldn't waste her

time on revenge anymore. Arthur Smith was a vain, dis-honest, and pathetic old man. She almost felt sorry for him.

Not far away, in his elegant mansion, Sheldon Rock-well carefully spooned sugar into the odious, herbal infusion he was trying to drink. Leong's Oriental reme-dies were dreadful. They were supposed to wean him off opium, but Sheldon didn't believe him. He didn't believe anything would take away the craving for his magic pipe.

As he drank the noxious brew he picked up the morning paper and scanned over the news. Little inter-ested him these days. He yawned and turned the page. An item on the society page grabbed his attention. Sampson Levine, lawyer and eligible bachelor, had been seen the past two nights around town in the com-pany of a comely schoolteacher from the mountains. A Miss Mollene Kennedy.

"Leong!" Sheldon yelled so loud that Figaro, who had been reposing on an apricot silk pillow in the chair beside him, shot up into the air with a yowl and dashed out of the room.

"Yes, Mr. Rockwell?"

Sheldon thrust the paper at his servant. "She's here! The bitch is in San Francisco."

Leong read the article without any expression. Then he set it down on the table. "You want to see Miss Kennedy?"

"No!" Sheldon's shaking fingers hit the side of the delicate cup and sloshed the medicinal tea all over the table linen. "Yes!" He put his head in both hands in anguish. "I want to know why she's here."

"I will find."

"Yes, you do that. You find out where she's staying. Who's footing the bill? How long she's planning to stay? My God, maybe she's going back on the stage!"

Leong was nodding.

"And get Harlan over here!"

For once Leong's serenity slipped, but Sheldon was too preoccupied to notice.

Harlan Rockwell hadn't been in Sheldon's house for over a month, not since he walked in and found his brother coming out of a week-long poppy orgy. The confrontation between the brothers had been ghastly and violent. Leong marveled that they hadn't killed one another.

Harlan threatened to expose his brother's drug habit to the world if Sheldon didn't take some steps to cure himself. He also threatened to murder Leong for supplying Sheldon with opium. Harlan wasn't against drug use in general, but he hated Sheldon's addiction because it threatened his own security.

"You are sure?" Leong had enjoyed Harlan's absence. Sheldon was pompous and demanding, but he didn't have his brother's evil streak.

Sheldon nodded. "I want him here. He'll help me think. I'm better. Your herbs have helped me. I don't crave the pipe anymore." It was a lie, but right now he and Harlan had more trouble than a simple misunderstanding. "I won't let him near you."

Leong had no faith in Sheldon's ability to control Harlan, but he'd have to risk it because he needed this job. At least for a bit longer. He'd keep Sheldon happy until Mei Ling was free.

"Something is wrong," Sheldon kept saying. "Why is she here?" He knew if the woman was wining and dining with the lawyer, something very suspicious was going on.

"You're quiet tonight, my dear." They were dining at Sampson's hillside house for a change.

Moll smiled at him. "I was thinking about the plays we've seen this week. How I wish my own production was worth revising."

She'd spent the entire day debating what she should do next. She'd decided not to return to Summit, not even for her belongings. She'd have them sent to wherever she stopped next. Her soul searching had led her to one disturbing conclusion—her options were still as limited as the last time she'd left San Francisco.

"I heard some excellent reports about the play you put on in Summit," Sampson teased.

Her tinkling laughter warmed him. She was such a lovely creature, and so incredibly unhappy. As an older and wiser man, he longed to ease her pain.

"Alas, Sampson, my talent is fine for Summit. But not for San Francisco, or any other city, I fear."

"You're being very critical of yourself."

"I'm being honest."

"I thought you wanted to revise your show and take it back East."

"I did . . . last fall. Now, I don't know what I want."

"Don't you?"

She sipped the excellent claret. "Win offered me a teaching contract for next year."

Sampson looked pleased. "I knew he'd come to his senses sooner or later."

"He told me the other members of the school board

wanted me back. And he didn't think they could get anybody else. That made the vote unanimous."

"Winslow always was a charmer." Sampson figured his friend deserved a good thumping. It was damned hard to play Cupid when one lover was such an oaf.

"I told him I didn't want the job." She looked over at Sampson, waiting for his response.

"Life is very complicated when you're young and in love."

The sewing machine needle sped over the cotton fabric as Hildy's feet swiftly operated the treadle. Matty's new yellow dress would be finished in time for Sunday services.

Hildy was alone today. Tilly Franklin had invited Matty and the other children over to her house for a party. It seemed so peaceful to be alone with nobody interrupting.

The knock on the door made her smile. All she had to do was think of uninterrupted peace and quiet, and naturally somebody stopped by.

"It's open," she called.

"Good afternoon, pretty lady." Patsy Murphy's big frame filled the doorway.

"Patsy! What are you doing here?"

"I brought you a birthday present."

"My birthday isn't until next week."

"I know when it is. Hannah told me. I wanted to give this to you today." He held out a red box with carnations printed on the top.

"What is it?"

"Open it." Her luminous eyes gave him a thrill. It

had been a long time since he'd seen a woman so pleased with a simple gift.

"Candy?" She put a small hand to her mouth, overcome with pleasure. "Nobody ever gave me candy before."

She opened the fancy box and marveled at the gold foil and incredible, delicious chocolate aroma. "This is beautiful, Patsy. Do you want a piece?"

He smiled broadly. "I'm thinkin' I'd rather have one of these." He bent over and kissed her on the mouth.

"Ohhh," she breathed.

He pulled her gently toward him, somehow understanding her fear of intimacy. Again his mouth found hers. This kiss was longer than the first, but no more passionate. When he ended the embrace, he saw that she was watching him.

"Would you be wantin' to try that again?"

"I don't know."

"Did you like it?"

She nodded.

"Then I think we should do it again."

"Yes." This time she moved toward him and put her arms around his solid waist. Hildy had no idea she could be attracted to any man, but kissing Patsy was a most agreeable experience. Her body warmed and tingled. She thought she might like doing this all day.

Patsy's motives had been pure when he delivered the chocolates he'd had George Franklin order especially for Hildy. But after the fourth kiss, his pristine motives evaporated into steamy excitement. Hildy didn't have much experience in seductive behavior, but once she decided she liked it she was a fast learner.

And Patsy thoroughly enjoyed being the teacher. He was ready to take the lessons all the way to graduation.

They were so engrossed in their educational experiment that they didn't hear the door open or Jed Cantrell walk in.

"What the hell are you two doing?" he demanded.

"Kissing," Hildy said when she finally raised her head.

"I can see that!"

"Go away, Cantrell—go blow something up." Patsy was still holding Hildy close and didn't seem to be in any hurry to let go of her.

"This is disgusting!"

"Why, Cantrell?" It amused Patsy that Jed was so intense. He knew Jed was making time with some hot young rancher's widow. And the fool ignored Hildy, except when he was dumping his kids on her doorstep. "Are you sore because you're not the one she has her arms around?"

Jed slammed the door without answering.

"Why was he so mad?"

Patsy nuzzled the fine blond hairs on her neck. "He's jealous."

"Oh no . . ."

"He is, indeed. The man's damned possessive of you, darlin'. I'm thinking he'll be giving me a run for me money any day now." He kissed her again. "So I better get a head start on him."

Leong did his work well. By nightfall, he reported back to Sheldon that Mollene Kennedy was registered at the Elmer House. She'd been there for five days and was expected to stay till the end of the week, or longer. She had, according to the night clerk, paid in advance for her own room. This information cost Leong two dollars, which Sheldon reluctantly reimbursed.

Harlan and Sheldon arrived at the Elmer House the following morning just as Moll was leaving for breakfast.

"The ghosts from Christmas Past," she sighed. She'd rather have seen Arthur Smith, even though he would undoubtedly have stuck her with the bill.

"What?" Harlan Rockwell was not a literary man.

"Never mind. What are you two doing here so early?"

"I believe that question is ours, Miss Kennedy," Sheldon said. "Why are you in San Francisco? And why weren't we told?"

She led them to a small cafe nearby, took a seat, and ordered before she answered. This time she was not depending on their pleasure. She was hungry, and she planned to enjoy a late continental breakfast.

"I'm here because I got bored in Summit."

"I told you!" Harlan said to his brother. "I knew she needed more kicks than she'd get up in the hills. A fancy piece like her needs bright lights and excitement!"

Sheldon ignored him. "You didn't ask us if you could come."

"Why should I ask you? You don't own the city."

"You work for us!"

She shrugged. The waiter brought a basket of sweet rolls and poured her coffee. She picked out the Danish with the thickest icing and broke off a piece. With complete concentration she savored the delicacy, licking her fingers when she finished.

She glanced at Sheldon with steely determination. "I think that needs correcting."

"What?" the brothers asked together.

"I don't like either of you. And I don't like working for you. I don't like sneaking around the woods spying on dirty, sweaty loggers or your big, dumb cousin. So I'm not going to anymore. I quit."

They stared in stupefaction.

"I'm not going back to Summit, either. It's boring there—no restaurants, no theaters, no department stores. And the people are," she paused, thinking of all the outstanding people she had met in Summit and how much she'd grown to love them, ". . . they're as boring as the place. Especially Winslow Fortune. He is the most boring of all."

"He fired you," Harlan said.

"No, he didn't. The Summit school board unanimously voted to hire me again, but I declined the offer. I'm moving to . . . Denver." She paused. "I have . . . ah, relatives there."

"So why have you been socializing all over the city with Sampson Levine? Don't deny it—we read about you in the paper."

She shrugged. "I came to tell him to find another teacher."

"You couldn't put that in a letter?" Sheldon asked.

"I wanted to shop. The backwoods are rough on shoes and clothes. My wardrobe needed replenishing before I left California. I needed a good haircut—not some farmer's wife putting a bowl on my head. I wanted to eat in good restaurants, take in a little nightlife— something besides the bears mating in the woods. Teaching school is hard work, you know. I'm here, and I'm ready to have some fun!"

"Get on the train and go back to Summit. Tomorrow. You can take your butt to Denver or any other place as soon as your year is up. But not before."

"I quit, remember?"

"We paid all your debts."

"So sue me!"

"Go back to Summit, Miss Kennedy, and do the job you were hired to do, or we'll do a lot worse than sue you."

Leong was waiting in Sampson's outer office when the attorney got back from his midday meal. Jenkins looked positively scandalized.

"What's wrong?" Sampson asked when they were in his private office, knowing only the most dire circumstance could have made Leong expose their relationship.

"They sent me out to Chinatown to hire somebody to kill her. An assassin."

Sampson nodded. He'd expected something of this nature. He'd tried to warn her against dumping her job with the Rockwells. "Have you done it? Hired somebody?"

"No, I come here."

"Wait an hour. Then return to the house and tell them it's all taken care of."

"You want I hire somebody?"

"No! Just tell them you have. Make up some name if you must—I imagine Sheldon won't want to know the details, though. Simply pretend you did what they told you to do. And, in the meantime, I'll get Miss Kennedy out of the city. Understand?"

"What about Mei Ling?" This was of the utmost importance to Leong.

"It's all taken care of—my friends are getting her out."

Leong had approached Sampson months ago for help rescuing a girl who'd been sold into slavery. Sampson didn't know if she was Leong's relative or lover. He simply knew the youth had been willing to do anything to help the girl escape. Sampson discovered a local mission dedicated to aiding Chinese girls fleeing the bondage of the brothels.

Leong nodded gravely.

"Are you ready to leave on a moment's notice?"

"Yes."

"I'm told it will be fast. When she's out, the two of you must disappear. It's very dangerous. You'll both be killed if they catch you."

"I know. I'm ready." He turned to leave.

"Leong. I might not see you again. Thank you for what you've done for me and my friends. You took a big chance, betraying the Rockwells."

Leong simply nodded.

Fortune stood on his dark porch, looking out across the night toward Moll's cabin. It seemed so small and dark. Funny how he'd become accustomed to looking out and seeing a light in the window. He missed her. In spite of all the aggravating, impossible things about the woman, he missed her like crazy.

Shaking his head, he stomped down the steps and headed for the woods. The night air was warm and so full of life that he thought he'd go crazy. It was a night for lovers, and he was alone.

He was still angry about Moll leaving without even bothering to say goodbye. An image of her face taunted him in the darkness.

He kept telling himself he was thankful she was

gone. In a way he hoped she wouldn't come back. "Sure would make things easier," he muttered.

The way life was going at Summit, with breakdowns almost a daily occurrence, and now the personal attacks, Win was glad Moll was in San Francisco and not anywhere close. He didn't want anything happening to her just because she chanced to be in the way of something aimed at him.

In the city, she was safe. Up there, who knew what might happen to her?

Buckley Brooks had followed him into the woods, thinking that this would be easier than he'd expected. Fortune was obviously unable to sleep and had stepped out for some air. With a little luck Brooks could take care of the problem tonight and be on tomorrow's train to San Francisco to collect his reward.

When Win stopped for a moment to pick a honeysuckle branch, Brooks moved into position behind a manzanita bush, raised the revolver, and waited. Sweat trickled down his neck. As Win came toward him again, Brooks drew a bead on Fortune's chest. Easy as pie. He narrowed his eyes, squeezed his sticky finger on the trigger, and flinched at the loud report.

He heard Win's sudden cry and saw him fall to the ground. He didn't wait around to see more.

Brooks was halfway out of Summit when he decided he didn't want to leave that night. He wanted to stick around town and savor the knowledge he'd beaten a rich man, for once in his life.

What he needed right now was a woman. There wasn't a whore close by except Bella, but she wouldn't take him as a customer. He decided to visit that rancher's woman Cantrell was so hot after, the one he'd charmed into his cabin the evening of the Winter Fair. Maybe she'd put a smile on his face like she did Cantrell's.

"What are you doing here so early?" Moll asked when she saw Sampson in the lobby.

"I thought I could catch you before you left for the day. Where have you been?" Sampson had been waiting for more than an hour, fearing that something had already happened to her.

"Taking in some culture—Mission Dolores, an art gallery, the museum. I left early so I could see a few of the things I've missed since I was in the high country." Actually she hadn't missed them at all. She was merely trying to fill up all the time in her day. "I even watched some people bicycle around the park. One of them was a woman. Do you think I could learn to do that? I'd love to try."

"Let's go up to your room."

His brusque tone startled her.

"It's important, Moll."

When they got to her room, he explained what Leong had told him.

"I don't believe it! They want to kill me? Because I quit?"

"Sheldon ordered a Chinese assassin hired today. Pack your bags. I'm taking you out of here."

"I'm not going back to Summit. I can't stay there any more. Win hates me. It's killing me to be so close to him . . . I simply can't go back."

"Just pack, Moll. You're staying at my house tonight. Mrs. MacDuff is there. Trust me, you'll be safe in my house for one night."

They got all of Moll's possessions down to the lobby in less than an hour. Sampson sent the bellman out for a cab while they waited inside. He wasn't taking any chances.

"Excuse me, Mr. Levine, there's a message for you from your office."

"Thank you." He handed the page a coin, in exchange for a piece of paper.

"What's the matter, Sampson?"

He looked up from the note. "Jenkins said there was a telegram for me. From Bill McDonald. Win was shot last night."

"No!" She put her hand up to her mouth to stop from screaming. "Get me on a train! I'm going back to Summit."

16

"*What are you doing* here?" Win shouted. He'd been sitting on Hannah's screened-in back porch in a wicker recliner with his feet propped up. His left arm was in a sling, and one side of his face was abraded. Seeing Moll worsened his foul mood. He'd thought that she was safely out of the nightmare he was living.

Moll hadn't actually believed he'd be glad to see her. Just because the news of his being shot had terrified her into realizing she couldn't exist without him didn't mean he felt the same way. She'd rushed to his side like the heroine of a bad melodrama, expecting to find him battered, bleeding, perhaps even dying. And she'd spent the train trip planning how she would care for him and make him see that they belonged together.

Instead she found him quite healthy and endearingly rumpled. Why was her reaction to him so tumultuous?

The attraction between the two of them flashed almost out of control, but it didn't seem to please him. If anything he was crankier than usual.

"Thanks for the warm welcome, Winslow," she said. "Sampson said you'd been shot."

"So?" He wanted to pull her into his arms and kiss her senseless, but he hurt too much to move. And his common sense told him she belonged anywhere but Summit.

She tossed an envelope in his lap. "This is from Sampson."

Then she turned on her heel, marched back into the kitchen, and greeted Hannah with a warm hug. "I missed you."

"It seems like you've been gone forever! It was very dull around here without you."

"I'll bet." Moll motioned toward the back door. "How is he?"

"Vile."

Laughter burst from Moll's throat. "I can tell. What happened?"

"Someone shot him when he was out for a late night walk." She shuddered. "If he hadn't stumbled over a rock just as the shot was fired, he'd probably be dead."

"How bad is he?"

"The bullet went through the fleshy part of his arm. He scraped his face when he fell and also sprained his wrist. He didn't see who shot him."

"Stop talking about me like I'm not here!" Win yelled from the porch.

Hannah shook her fist in his direction. "Now that you're back, he has somebody new to crab at."

"I'm going up to change my clothes before I give in

to the temptation to toss him off the porch into your rosebushes."

"Moll." Hannah lowered her voice. "He's happy you're home."

"I can tell. Any more enthusiasm and I wouldn't be able to stand it."

Win was amazed at the contents of Sampson's letter. Even though he'd been certain his cousins had already hit rock bottom, he admitted they'd descended to a new low.

"It's a lucky man who gets to sit around all day while all us other poor bastards are workin'."

Patsy had come up to the house at Win's request, more than an hour before quitting time.

"You're welcome to join me if you bring some cookies with you. I've been in agony smelling them bake."

The Irishman returned moments later with a plate of warm chocolate drops and some coffee.

"Who did you work for in Denver?" Win asked.

Patsy eased himself into a creaky rocking chair and gave Win's question some thought. "Seamus Blade."

"Moll's natural father?"

"The very one."

"That's quite a coincidence—the two of you ending up in a thriving metropolis like Summit at the same time." He ignored Patsy's snort of laughter. "Why are you here?"

"Many a man would call it luck. Or the will o' God. Meself, I've never been much of a believer in coincidence. Not when I work for Seamus Blade, him being a man that makes things happen."

"He sent you?" Win leaned back in the recliner, trying to find a position that didn't hurt.

"He did." Patsy rocked the chair back and stopped. "He wanted the girl protected."

"How the hell did he know where 'the girl' was?"

"Ahhh, she wrote him. A doozie of a letter, it was. She's a hot one when she gets mad."

Nobody needed to tell Win that. She was a hot one at other times too. This thought popped unwanted into Win's head, and he made great effort to shove it out of his consciousness, along with the accompanying surge of desire.

"When did she write to him? She told me she never planned to contact him because he didn't want anything to do with her."

The chair rocked forward again. "Right after she was attacked, she wrote accusing him of tryin' to do her in. He sent me here to protect her. Figured she'd done somethin' to upset somebody, and needed a bodyguard."

Patsy thought for a minute. "He's a proud man, Seamus is, proud of raising himself out of poverty. He's a rich man because of his own hard work and cunning."

"He has a right to be proud."

"Aye. But a man can't think very highly of himself for cheating on his wife. Not when he loved her like Seamus Blade loved his Maggie."

Patsy paused to watch a yellow cat walk across the yard with a rat in its mouth. Then he reached for a sugar-dusted cookie before Win could get them all. "That was years before I met him, but he talks about his dear wife like she was a saint."

"He cheated on a saint?" Win's tone was derisive.

"It's not as bad as it sounds, man. Maggie had a bad

heart. He told me one time how sickly she was the last five years of her life. How the doctor told him not to touch her, for fear of another baby. And he's a randy beggar—still is at his age. Moll's a year older than Celestine—the youngest. Two times, at least, the man didn't abstain."

In a way Win could understand the man's need for sexual release, but he could not understand abandoning a child. Not when he knew how badly Moll had suffered from the rejection.

"Seamus loved his wife. He's mourned her a long time."

"But he got a child on another woman," Win persisted.

"He did that. He gave the baby up and didn't know her whereabouts for years. The minute he found her again, though, he sent me to keep her safe. By the way, did you ever see that poster of her?"

"She didn't send that? Not *The Love Goddess* poster?"

Patsy nodded. "Sent it to him along with the letter. Shocked him, too. He might be a lecherous old goat, but he thinks his daughters are as pure as driven snow."

"I'm sure she meant to shock him." He couldn't help smiling. Moll didn't do anything by halves. "Does she know about you? That Seamus sent you?"

Patsy shook his head. "Lately I've been thinking about telling her. She's a fine girl. Not as flashy as I was expecting."

"The poster does give a man an inaccurate picture of her."

Patsy looked at him closely. "Inaccurate, you say?"

Win's cheekbones reddened. He cleared his throat. "About her character."

"Oh, sure. Sure. She's got a sterling character."

Fortune's lips twitched, but he didn't smile. He wondered exactly what Patsy knew about his relationship with Moll. "How long will you stay?"

"At first I thought a month or two, 'cause we'd catch the blighter right off."

"There's been footprints outside her cabin again. Are they yours?"

"You think I'm such a careless man?"

"I didn't think I was either." Win gestured toward his arm.

"I'm a bit in a lather meself lately. I've been waitin' for the old man to tell me what to do next."

"So you're leaving? I'm asking because we have a new problem. A new element has joined forces against Moll. My cousins have hired an Oriental assassin to kill her."

Patsy shook his head. "An Oriental would be mighty conspicuous in Summit. I won't go off unless I have to. You might be needin' me. I'm a fair hand in a fight."

Win could imagine how good Patsy was in a fight. "Good."

"This is a bloody powder keg you're sittin' on."

Win nodded. "Speaking of powder kegs, I've seen Jed glowering at you a lot lately. Is your romance with Hildy serious?"

"Serious enough, for a man like me. She's a fine woman, she is. Maybe not a prize beauty like Moll, but she is a treasure. A man should let his woman know he values her. If he cherishes her and praises her, she'll be there for him when life gets rocky. Jed needs to know Hildy is more than a drudge. I'm teaching him."

Win considered this. "And what are you teaching Hildy?"

Patsy rocked back and forth, his hand stroking his square chin. "To have expectations."

Abruptly the steam whistle blew at the log yard. Three sharp blasts.

"Emergency!" Win said, starting to get off the recliner.

"Sit still! I'll run over and check. I'll send somebody to let you know."

Win was amazed at how fast the big man could move.

A few minutes later Hannah came rushing out to the porch, visibly frightened, her hands shaking as they clutched the high collar of her dress. "Win, there's been a bad accident up on the logging road. One of the wagons lost a load of logs on the grade."

Outside, a man's cry rose above the yells and shouts of the others. C.J. Hodges screamed something about his son, threw himself on a horse, and raced up the hill. Several other riders followed.

"Eddie's up there," Hannah said, her face ghastly pale. "And Bill."

Win struggled to get to his feet. "I'm going—"

"You can't ride!"

"Somebody can drive me." He lumbered to the door and hobbled, with Hannah's help, across the yard.

Patsy picked them up in a wagon. The twins piled in the back. Moll and Hildy had emerged to see what all the commotion was and joined the people running along the road to the wreck.

The logs lay tossed across the road like gigantic matchsticks, the smaller ones broken and splintered. One wheel had come off the wagon, and it had overturned. The iron tire had rolled into a rhododendron bush and was covered with white petals.

Three of the mules were hurt, and the fourth was dying. Bill McDonald, covered with dirt and grime, lay by the side of the road with a badly broken leg. Eddie Hodges was dusty but otherwise unharmed. He was tending to the rest of the skittish mule team.

"What happened?" Win demanded.

"Chain broke just as we started down the grade, and the load began to roll," Bill said. "And then everything went to hell!"

C.J. stood nearby, listening.

"That's a damned good boy you got, C.J.," Bill said, his mouth etched with pain. "The team went crazy and I was thrown. He pulled me out of the way of the wagon. Then he got the team stopped."

"The chain busted?" C.J. asked, his normal bluster soft and strained.

"On the back." Bill tried to squelch a groan as he was lifted to a wagon. "Damn, I thought this was going to be safer than riding the boat down the river drive."

C.J. slipped away without speaking to anyone.

"I'll drive Bill into Placerville," George Franklin told Hannah. "You better come along. You'll worry about him all night if you don't."

Moll and Hildy assured Hannah they'd take care of the meals, and then they walked back to the house, taking the twins with them.

Win was giving orders to get the road cleared of wagons and people. He'd gotten word that the last of the four logging wagons had left the woods and would be approaching the top of the grade within a half hour. He wanted to get the oncoming wagon past the log spill and into the yard before nightfall.

Suddenly, C.J. came racing from behind the wrecked wagon, yelling loudly and cussing for all he was worth. He jumped up on the nearest horse, which didn't happen to be his, pulled the animal around, and galloped toward the logging camp.

"Want to go see what he's mad about?" Patsy asked.

"I have an idea what he's mad about. I'm curious who he's mad at."

"Get in the wagon."

They got to the yard in time to see the fight. Or, more fairly, the beating.

"I'll kill ya!" C.J. kept screaming. His face was mottled, and his hair was standing on end. He was systematically beating Buckley Brooks into the ground. Brooks was no match for him on a good day, and right now C.J. was insane with rage.

"Can you stop it?" Win asked Patsy as he awkwardly climbed down from the wagon. His head ached, and his shoulder was throbbing. He needed to lie down, but it didn't look like he'd be able to rest any time soon.

"Are you sure you want me to? If Brooks cut that chain, he deserves a beating."

Win watched the fight for a minute. Buckley Brooks would never again be as handsome as he was before C.J. lit into him. "You better stop it. I don't want his death on my conscience."

Patsy hefted a big bucket of water and splashed C.J. full in the face. Mark Danbury had a second bucket waiting. The flood left C.J. gasping for air. Brooks fell face forward into the mud and dirt and lay as still as a rock.

"Let him be, C.J.," Fortune said. "He's had enough."

"He almost killed my boy!"

"I know. But Eddie's all right. Why don't you go home and see that the kid has a good dinner?"

"Okay." He got up and started to leave.

"C.J.?" Win wanted to get at least one good thing out of the day. "Is Brooks responsible for all the breakdowns and accidents?"

"Yep. An' I figger he shot you, too."

Win didn't ask him how he knew. He fished in his pocket and pulled out a coin. "Here's five dollars. Take Eddie to Placerville and buy him a steak on the company."

"Steak don't cost no five dollars."

"Buy him one tomorrow night, too. Both of you take the rest of the week off. You deserve it. But don't go on a toot, you hear?"

C.J. grinned. "Sure. I ain't been drinking." He kicked a clump of grass. "Thanks, Win. Maybe we'll ride over tomorrow and visit Lorna."

"I'm just glad Eddie's okay."

Win turned to Buckley, who was trying to get up on his knees. He was a sorry sight. "Brooks, can you hear me?"

Buckley groaned. His clothes were torn, his nose was broken, and his head was a bloody mess.

"You're fired. You can spend the night at the bunkhouse because I don't think you're fit to ride. You get out tomorrow and don't come back."

Win turned to Mark Danbury. "Help him up. Keep a guard on him till he leaves. You can pick up his pay at the office tonight after supper. If you ever see him back this way again, shoot him."

"String 'im up!" one of the loggers shouted.

"I'll get a rope," another one said.

"No!" Patsy yelled. "There'll be no hanging! Mr. Fortune doesn't want more violence. Somebody bring a wagon and throw him in the back. Drive him to Placerville."

Danbury looked like he was about to argue, but he changed his mind and went over to see about Brooks. He stared down at him for a couple of minutes and then walked off.

Patsy put his arm around Win and helped him back to the house. All the excitement had drained him. "You look like you're about to keel over."

"I can walk by myself."

"Relax and enjoy it, lad. The women love to fuss over a sick man."

Three days later the bicycles arrived with a note from Sampson.

"Moll: You said you wanted to give these a try. Have fun! If you don't like them, some of the children will."

"Don't tell anybody," Moll told George Franklin. The bicycles had come to the Emporium on a supply wagon.

"You can't keep a secret in Summit."

"Please. It won't be for long. Only until Friday."

George finally agreed. "We need a little fun around this place, I expect. Let's put them in the storage room before anybody else sees them."

By working days and evenings while Moll watched Jed's children and helped Hannah, Hildy performed the impossible and whipped together two ladies' bicycle costumes, complete with leggings and hats.

Hildy managed to look quite demure in her cycling

costume of navy blue, consisting of a skirted jacket, vest, and voluminous bloomers, which were gathered and buttoned inches below the knee. The only difference between the split skirts worn by women who rode horses and the bloomers was the safety feature of the gathered cuffs.

Cherry-pink knickerbockers had been Moll's choice. Worn with a pink-and-white-striped shirtwaist and a closely fitted vest, the slender-fitting knickerbockers buttoned at the knee over tight pink leggings. Her jaunty, white straw boater had pink ribbons to match.

"I'd like to wear these all the time." Moll loved the freedom the knickerbockers gave her.

"I feel almost naked," Hildy complained. "Look at my ankles."

"They look good to me. You should show them off more often."

It took them a while to get the hang of the bikes. Out behind the Emporium, they wobbled around and almost crashed a dozen times before either one of them could make the contraptions go straight. But after some practice they got quite daring, and soon they were riding circles around each other, laughing like little girls.

"What are you going to do with those darned things?" Mildred Franklin called from her upstairs window. Despite considering herself superior to the rest of the citizens of Summit because of her eastern background, Mildred couldn't contain her curiosity about the newfangled bicycles. She simply had to know what was going on.

"Hello, Mrs. Franklin!" Hildy called to her. "It's a lovely day."

"We're going for a ride," Moll said. She made a large figure eight, hardly wobbling at all.

"Where are you going?" Mildred wanted to know, as if there was someplace to go in Summit.

"We're riding through Summit." Moll looked at Hildy. "Are you ready?"

"All the way through," Hildy called. She felt incredibly bold. "Ready."

"We'll be the talk of the town."

"I've never been the talk of the town before," Hildy said with a cheeky smile. She felt younger than she had at fifteen.

"Then it's about time." Moll pedaled around the Emporium and out onto the street.

Hildy followed along as they passed Stoneleigh's Blacksmith and Livery. Albert Stoneleigh decided the occasion called for a cigar. He stopped working and lit one up.

By the time they sailed past the town hall they had bicycling down to an art. They were good, they were fast, and—wonder of wonders—they were still upright!

"School's out!" Moll yelled as they whizzed by the empty schoolhouse. She couldn't believe she missed being inside.

Moll noticed a brown-eared rabbit sat by the split-rail fence, munching on some tender grass and watching them.

They zipped down the long slope, managing by sheer luck not to crash. It was slower going by the time they pedaled the dusty road in front of the McDonalds' house, because the terrain was flat. Moll began to question whether her legs would hold out till they got to their destination.

"Ma, quick. Come look!" one of the twins screamed.

"Ma, Ma. Look!" the other twin echoed.

Moll got brave enough to take one hand off the handle-bars and wave. She nearly went out of control and had to concentrate to get the steering corrected again. Hildy simply called out her greetings.

"Oh, no!" Hannah said from the porch. "I can't believe her. And now she's leading Hildy down the dusty path to trouble. I should have known all that help I got this week meant she was up to something."

She went back into the house, muttering and shaking her head. "He'll wring her neck this time. The first day he's back on the job. I think I better make a chocolate cake. That might calm him down."

The road became bumpier as they approached the logging camp. They jogged along on the bikes, their straw hats nearly falling off their heads, as they went over ruts and bounced till their teeth rattled.

"Look at the women!"

From the men in the yard came shrill whistles that challenged the noise of the steam engine. Man after man turned toward the road, watching in petrified amazement.

Moll and Hildy sped past with their ribbons sailing out behind them. The shouts and the whistles grew louder and continued as they raced in front of the cook shack and the bunkhouses. When they came to the last of the outbuildings, they stopped for a much needed breather. They could see men crowding along the road, waiting for them to return.

Uncertainty showed on Hildy's face. Defiance spread across Moll's.

"What should we do now?" Hildy asked. Her hat tipped over one brow, and she raised her hand to straighten it.

"We ride back the other way."

"Are you crazy?"

Moll lifted her chin. "Probably."

"All those men are watching."

"Then let's give them a good show!"

"We'll get in trouble."

"Nawwww." But Moll hesitated for a moment. She could see Win and knew she was already up to her neck in trouble.

Summoning her flagging courage, she pushed off and, after only the slightest wobble, began to pick up speed. The cheers, whistles, and applause drove her onward, straight down the center of the road.

Hildy got brave enough to wave to Patsy, who was clapping like a crazy man, but Moll sped away with her eyes straight ahead, never looking around till she reached Hannah's house. There, she stopped and got off the bike.

Willard and Wendell couldn't wait to try the marvelous machines. It was a good thing there were two bicycles, because the boys would have gone to fisticuffs if they'd had to share.

"Are you all right, Moll? You look funny."

"I'm fine, Hildy. I just need a drink of water. I'm thirsty."

Matty came running down the hill, holding Sarah on her hip. Timmy tumbled along beside her.

"Mama, you went so fast," Matty laughed. "And everybody cheered."

Moll cringed at the thought. She could already hear Win's lecture.

"Come in for some lemonade," Hannah called from the porch. "I'm sure you need it after that ride."

* * *

Moll was sitting out in the big green swing in the lilac grove behind the house when Win rode up on his horse. He swung down, dropped the reins to the ground, and strode over to her. The sling was off his arm, but his shoulder was still stiff and sore.

"What the hell did you think you were doing?"

She rubbed her finger up and down on the cool glass, making patterns in the condensation. She met his glare with cool indifference. "I was out for a cycling excursion."

"And what do you call that getup you're wearing?"

"I call it a bicycling costume." She stood up and pirouetted for him. "Do you like it?"

A bubble of laughter rose up inside him. He tried hard to recapture the feeling of self-righteous indignation he'd had when he rode into the yard, but it eluded him, along with the anger and the jealousy.

The crazy thing was that he did like her bicycling costume. It reminded him of a candy store. And the way it fit Moll's curvaceous body reminded him of how long it had been since he'd touched her.

"Yes." He was trying not to smile.

"What?"

"Yes—I like it. I like you in it."

His answer astonished her. She had gotten herself prepared for a long-winded lecture about her need for applause and attention.

The truth was, she became extremely uncomfortable when the men began to yell and whistle and gather by the side of the road. She would have liked to have ridden home on some other route, but her pride wouldn't let her. She'd forced herself to endure the ride back to prove to herself one more time that she wasn't a coward.

"I like it very much." He walked over to the lilac bush. The spring blossoms were long since gone, but the foliage was still green and lush. "You look grand in whatever you wear. You're a good teacher and a fine woman. Everyone here in Summit likes you."

"Did that bullet graze your head? You're being so nice to me." She watched him suspiciously, waiting for him to return to his old self.

"I just thought of something Patsy said to me the other day."

"What?" She sank back down onto the wide swing. A body couldn't stand too many shocks at once.

Win took off his hat and lowered himself down beside her. He put his arm along the back of the swing, touching her shoulders in a most restrained manner.

"He said a man needs to treasure his woman."

She looked at him curiously.

"My father was a harsh man, Moll. He judged everyone and found them wanting. Especially his family. I never heard him praise my mother. He gave her orders, and she followed them meekly. When he died, she quickly found another husband. I've often wondered if she wasn't secretly glad he was dead. Her new husband is much kinder to her. I'm afraid that I take after my father sometimes."

He put his hand on her shoulder and pulled her closer, moving one finger up and down her sleeve. "I've never told you how beautiful I think you are."

"No, you haven't." She studied his face. The bruise had all but disappeared. "I wasn't going to come back, you know."

"I didn't want you to."

He stopped her when she started to draw away. "You're in danger here, Moll. Now more than ever."

"I thought Buckley left the countryside."

"The Rockwells are after you."

"So you know?"

"Sampson told me about the assassin." He shook his head. "How many women are running from an Oriental assassin?"

"Not many in Summit, I'd wager."

He chuckled and brushed a curl off her cheek, looking intently into her blue eyes.

"Are you going to kiss me, Win?"

"I was working up to it."

"But you want to know about the Rockwells first?"

"I already know about them. I saw you at the Cary House in Placerville last fall. They were in town. The boys don't leave the splendors of the city unless they have a good reason. Their underlings do all the dirty work."

"I was one of the underlings."

"What dirty work did you do?" He unbuttoned the high collar of her shirtwaist, and slipped his fingers inside, touching the pulse at her throat.

"Nothing that ever pleased them. Sheldon gave me a dressing down that day at the Cary House."

"And you let him?" He leaned over and kissed her neck.

"I dumped ice water from the champagne bucket into his lap when he told me I should take you to bed to learn your secrets."

He buried his face in her hair, laughing. "No wonder I love you."

She pulled away, utterly stunned. "Oh? You do?"

He kissed her then. Long and lingering, savoring her

taste, her softness. "Of course I do. Right from the first, I think. You love me, too."

She was unbuttoning his shirt. "I do? How do you know that?"

"Because you're kissing me out here on this swing . . . with Bill and Hannah and Hildy and probably half the kids in your school watching out the parlor window."

"Oh, no!" She tried to jerk away, but he wouldn't let her. He held her tight, and she relaxed, loving the feel of his arms around her.

He kissed her again, so very sweetly, and held her close. He inhaled her essence, wishing he hadn't let the long, lonely months pass so foolishly. Holding his desire in check—he hadn't been lying about the observers—he cherished her mouth and her perfect ears and her eyelashes.

"I want to court you properly. Will you go on a picnic with me Sunday?"

She was having a hard time concentrating on anything but how she felt when his mouth touched hers. She would have done anything he asked of her. "Yes."

"Are you going to loll around out there all afternoon?" Jed called from the side of the house. "Hannah can't get dinner started while she's peeking out the window at you two."

"You're just jealous, Cantrell. You can't find a woman who'll put up with you, and you're jealous."

"Damn right!"

A light breeze fanned her cheek as she lay on the thick gray blanket, gazing up through the spiraling treetops at the deep blue sky. She couldn't recall ever feeling so at peace with the world before.

"I thought you were asleep."

"No, I'm just lazy. It's such a beautiful day." She put out her hand and caught his. "Come down here with me."

"If I lie down beside you, I'm going to make love to you. Right out here in front of the chipmunks." Win had not touched her since she had returned from San Francisco. He'd kissed her hundreds of times, but he'd kept the caresses as circumspect as he could, trying to show by his actions how much he valued her as a person, not merely as a woman who'd shared his bed. The strain was damned near killing him.

"Is that bad?" She wanted him as fiercely as she'd ever wanted anything in her life.

"Moll, I said I wanted to court you properly." He took her hand and pulled her to her feet. "I'm going to take you for a boat ride."

"Down the American?" She sounded horrified. A bouquet of flowers was her idea of courting, not a wild boat ride over the rapids.

"There's a holding pond at the bottom of the hill," he said. "It's deep and still. It's really quite lovely on a day when logs aren't coming down the chute. And there's even a boat down there."

Moll thought it would be a lot more romantic to stretch out under the trees, but she allowed him to convince her to accompany him. He'd never be as spontaneous as she was, but she adored that about him. She loved every inch of Winslow Fortune. In spite of their differences—because of their differences.

Actually, it turned out to be quite tranquil floating on the cool still water. The American River ribboned its way between two mountain ridges. On the north side, a log chute descended nearly three thousand feet from the top of the cliff to the bottom of the gorge.

She reclined in the stern of the boat, trailing her hand in the water while Win rowed. The scent of bay laurel mingled with the liquid fragrance of water, filling her with a glorious sense of peace. Win was explaining how the river drivers rode the boats down the rapids when they made the dangerous log drives, and she tried to listen, but a warm lethargy stole through her body.

A strange rumbling sound disturbed her drowsiness. She opened her eyes and looked around.

"Oh, Christ!"

Alarmed at his tone, she sat up straighter. The noise was a thundering roar.

"Stay still!" he commanded.

Moll realized he was rowing them directly underneath the log chute. She barely had time to notice the heavy wooden structure above their heads when a screaming sugar pine log whizzed out over the pond and dropped into the river with a tremendous splash. The rippling wake almost capsized the small boat.

"It's Sunday," she whispered, hanging onto the bobbing boat. "Nobody's working today."

"Are you all right?" Win asked.

She noticed his hands were shaking as he held the oars. "I'm fine. What about you?"

"I'm furious! Somebody just tried to kill us!"

"Are you sure?"

"Yes! A signal is always sounded when a log is sent down the chute! And you're right—it's Sunday and nobody is working. As soon as I can get around that log, we're going home. I'm going to find out today who's still working for the other side."

Moll looked down into the water, into the green depths where a sinker jutted up from the bottom. Something strange was snagged on the sinker. It looked like . . .

Moll inhaled sharply and screamed!

17

The pool was deep and green, and a large trout swam leisurely through its depths. A long, ragged piece of cloth, caught on a snag, floated outward like a veil in the wind. And jammed awkwardly into the fork of an underwater tree branch was the remains of a human hand and arm. The rest of the skeleton was trapped beneath the sunken log.

Already shaky from the near miss with the log, Win nearly jumped out of the boat when Moll screamed.

"For Chrissake, what's wrong?"

Moll got a grip on her panic and gasped, "There's a body down there."

"Where?" His mind wasn't working too clearly.

"In the water. Caught on a log."

He swung the boat around and, steadying it, peered into the watery green depths.

"God Almighty," he whispered. Without another word, he rowed to the shore and helped Moll out.

It took a long time for them to climb the three thousand feet back up to Summit.

Grim-faced and resigned, Win talked to Bill McDonald about their gruesome discovery.

"Dear God in Heaven," Bill said, shaking his head. "What next? Who do you think it is?"

"There's a long piece of what looks like red plaid material caught on a snag right by the skeleton."

"Red plaid? . . . Not the teacher . . . Agatha Powell?" Hannah asked. "She wore that red plaid shawl every day."

"And she disappeared in the night," Win said, "without a trace."

When he assured Sampson that Agatha Powell had run off with a man, it had seemed a reasonable explanation. They'd looked for her everywhere but found nothing. So the general consensus was that she'd left on her own accord.

But Win had always been bothered by that conclusion. Agatha Powell was homely, smelly, and snappish. Win questioned what man would have wanted her. Now he guessed he'd been right.

"But how did she fall in the river?" Bill asked. "It's a long ways down."

"That's for the law to decide." Win looked very tired. "I'll send somebody to Placerville for the sheriff."

"Nobody's around," Bill said. "The log yard is dead. Even the bull cooks left yesterday."

"Somebody sent a log down the chute," Win told him.

"Today?"

Win nodded. "While Moll and I were out in the boat."

"In the holding pond?" Hannah was shocked.

"Right. I heard the log and managed to row underneath the chute."

"I didn't hear a signal," Bill said.

"There wasn't one."

Bill understood just how close they'd come to dying. "You must need a drink."

"I do. But somebody has to ride for the sheriff."

"I need to go back for the picnic basket," Moll said. "We didn't stop to pick it up."

Hannah walked to the front porch with Moll. "I'll send the twins down to get it."

"Thank you." She didn't relish going alone.

"I thought it was going to be such a perfect day for the two of you."

"It was." Moll smiled, thinking about how much she loved Win.

"When he first came here looking for a place to put the camp, Winslow was different," Hannah said. "Oh, he was steady and determined. I expect he's always been that way. But he was energetic and dynamic. And around our family he relaxed and was so much fun. In the past couple years he's become so harsh and rigid and careworn. You've been good for him, Moll. You got his mind off this stupid war with his cousins."

Moll smiled. "He's good for me, too, Hannah. He is such a strong man—so steady and alive—I admire him as much as I love him. My husband, Étienne, was a brilliant man. He was kind to me, but . . . ."

"You would have walked all over him . . ."

"I would have *danced* all over him, poor man." She shook her head. "It'll take a brave man to love me. Sometimes even I don't understand the way I act. You were right—we've been able to talk out our differences. We want to be together—that's all that counts."

"Are you sure you want to go up to the cabin?"

"Yes. I'm exhausted."

The afternoon sun was hot. Moll walked along the path, looking forward to taking off her clothes and lounging in her bathtub, soaking off the eerie, unfamiliar sensations that had been creeping over her skin since she gazed down at that awful bony hand.

She was glad to reach her snug little cabin. She'd been happier here than any place else in her life. She opened the door and stepped inside, waiting for her eyes to adjust to the dimness. She blinked . . . and gasped.

"What are you doing here?"

From the moment he left, Win wished he'd found someone else to make the ride to Placerville. He kept seeing Moll's pale face in his mind and berating himself for leaving her alone after such a dreadful shock.

He was halfway down the grade when he met Leland Ames coming up the hill. From the glum look on Leland's face, Win knew he'd lost his wages again.

"I'll give you a week's extra pay," Win said when Leland stopped, "if you'll ride to Placerville and bring back Sheriff Hilbert."

"Sure." Leland was always agreeable to extra money. "What's wrong?"

"We've found a body in the holding pond. Tell the sheriff the remains are caught under a snag and might be hard to get out."

"Anybody I know?"

"I'm not sure. The body has been there a long time. It may be Agatha Powell."

"That teacher who disappeared last year?" Leland pocketed the money Win handed him.

Win nodded. "You might as well stay over." He knew Leland would head straight back to the poker tables.

"Thanks." Ames had been laying low since C.J. pounded on Buckley Brooks, avoiding Danbury and staying out of trouble. With a little luck he hoped to hang on to his job and keep out of jail.

Win swung the horse around. The longer he was away from Moll, the more uneasy he felt. Fear pulsed through him. He kicked the bay and galloped toward Summit.

Timmy Cantrell was chasing a rabbit. He was bored and very annoyed with his uncle. He knew Uncle Jed had been to Franklin's Emporium to purchase candy. When Tim saw the striped bag, he thought the candy was for him, but Uncle Jed had yelled at him and told him to leave the bag alone. Timmy had run outside and pouted, angry at the unfairness of the world.

Until he saw the rabbit. It wasn't a very big rabbit, just the right size for a small boy who wanted a dog but couldn't have one. Just the size to hide in his bed and pet. But the rabbit didn't know that Timmy wanted to be friends—it took off with Timmy running far behind. Up the hill it went, all the way to the company office.

That's when Timmy saw his teacher.

He almost called out to her.

Then he saw she wasn't alone. She was with a man who worked at the logging yard. Something was wrapped around her arms and her mouth. The man was dragging her to a wagon, and she was kicking and fighting.

Timmy stood stone-still and watched. He wanted to help, but he was afraid to move.

The man threw Miss Kennedy into the back of the wagon with a thud and jumped up onto the seat, whipping the mules. The wagon fishtailed up the logging road to the woods.

Jed Cantrell sat in the swing on Hildy Swenson's porch, feeling like an absolute idiot in his five-year-old blue suit, clutching a bag of taffy. Across from him, on a spindly chair, sat Patsy Murphy in his tailored black worsted, holding a large bouquet of Hannah's loveliest yellow roses. Hildy had gone off in search of a vase, after giving the Irishman a peck on the cheek for the bottle of French lilac cologne he'd also brought her.

Jed's blond hair had fallen in his face—he'd been too busy to get a haircut lately—but he didn't bother to brush it aside. He was too miserable to care. For the life of him, he didn't know why he was competing for Hildy's affections, especially when the rancher's widow was so hot for his company.

He'd never stood in line for a woman before, but he wanted Hildy. He'd always known she was a good, steady worker. And that she was kind and affectionate with his kids. Sometime over the winter, though, he'd begun to notice other things about her. Her sweet womanly scent when she served dinner. Her gentle curves when the wind blew her dresses flat against her. Her humor when she forgot about being shy.

Hildy was nothing like the ranch woman. She was

honest and decent. She was nothing like Moll. She was more practical, disciplined, and solid. Jed had realized he liked that. A rolling stone for years, he'd decided it was time to settle down. With his ready-made family, he needed a woman he could count on. Someone like Hildy.

He was a dashing man, so his mate didn't need to be as spirited. But he'd hoped for a woman who was friendly in bed. He wasn't sure about Hildy. She seemed so timid—almost innocent. In spite of having a half-grown daughter, she acted like a virgin.

And then he'd walked into her house and found her kissing Patsy Murphy. Not just *kissing* him, but plastered up against the bastard like a piece of flypaper!

"Uncle Jed! Come quick . . . he's got Miss Kennedy!"

The roses fell to the wooden floor. "Where is she, boy?" Patsy shouted. "Tell me!"

Timmy was almost as frightened by Patsy's roar as he'd been by the man who'd taken Miss Kennedy.

About to chastise the boy for annoying him, Jed started in surprise when Patsy hollered. The big man's reaction astonished him.

"Where is she, Tim?" Jed demanded.

"Up the hill. He put her in a wagon."

"Who was it, son?" Patsy lowered his voice.

Hildy came outside when she heard the commotion. "Who would hurt Moll?"

"A man," Timmy said. "He works at the camp."

"Who's in camp today?" Hildy asked.

"I think I saw Danbury," Jed said.

"Where's your horse, Jed?"

"At Stoneleigh's stable. Same as yours."

"I'll find Win!" Hildy was already running toward Hannah's.

"Does Danbury work for the Rockwells?" Patsy asked as they sped toward the livery for horses.

Jed didn't answer.

"Dammit, I know you do . . ."

"I work for Win . . ."

"You're taking a payoff from the Rockwells. Win told me."

Jed stopped a second. "Who are you?"

Patsy kept going. "I work for Win. But Seamus Blade sent me here to keep Moll safe. She's his daughter."

"Oh shit."

They borrowed two steeds from Stoneleigh's stable and mounted up. C.J. and Eddie Hodges rode into the livery yard just as Patsy and Jed charged out of the barn.

"Does Danbury work for the Rockwells?" Patsy demanded.

"Somebody kidnapped the teacher," Jed explained. "It might be Danbury."

"He's crazy," C.J. answered. "He hates women. You better find her quick!"

Eddie raced up the road to save his teacher, and the others trailed close behind.

Win had just slowed his horse to a trot in front of the Emporium when he saw Eddie bolt out onto the road. He immediately suspected something was wrong. Seconds later he saw Patsy, C.J., and Jed on their horses following the lad, and Win felt his stomach clench in dread. *Something's happened to Moll!* He spurred the bay after them.

Further up the trail, the wagon bumped over the dusty ruts, swaying and pitching from side to side. Mark Danbury paid no attention to the careening buckboard. He drove as if the devil was on his tail.

Inside his head the voices babbled and shrieked, louder than they'd ever been in the past, and pain pierced his skull. It was all his fault, the voices said. Simms had run off. Then Fillmore. Now Brooks was gone. C.J. wouldn't talk to him. He couldn't find Ames. The Rockwells would get even—they always did. It was *his* fault.

"It's the woman's fault," he muttered. "Not mine. She's the evil one."

In the back of the wagon, Moll bounced and jostled, with every new bruise and ache silently cussing the man who'd kidnapped her. She fought to loosen her bonds. The struggle kept her sane, kept her mind off the maniac in the driver's seat.

Tied in her own summer shawl, with her hands behind her back, she managed to wiggle one way and another until the soft cloth began to slip. Within minutes, she had her arms free. Danbury's red handkerchief slid from her mouth, and she belly-crawled toward the back of the wagon.

Danbury didn't see her snake over the tailgate or drop to the ground in a heap. He was a hundred yards up the rutted road, raving to himself, when he glanced over his shoulder and noticed the empty wagon bed. He bellowed, and yanked the mules to a stop, practically flying off the seat.

He was no mule-skinner. He couldn't turn the team on such a narrow road, so he leaped down to pursue her on foot.

Moll lurched to her feet, aching in every muscle, her heart pounding with fear. When she saw the wagon stop, she sped toward town, ignoring her ragged breath and the stitch in her side. Neither would matter if Danbury caught her.

The dress she'd worn especially for her Sunday picnic hadn't been designed for racing. Nor had her shoes. She briefly thought of the freedom of the comfortable knickerbockers. Then she didn't think at all but kept running for her life.

Danbury kept getting closer and closer. His aura of evil touched her skin before his hand did. It assaulted her nostrils with a gruesome stench. This man meant to murder her!

The vision of the skeleton at the bottom of the holding pond flashed into her mind. Was this the man who murdered the other teacher?

A scream began to build in the pit of her stomach, but she was running so hard, laboring for breath, that she couldn't utter a sound.

His dirty fingernails dug into her shoulder, pulling her off-balance. Her shoe hit a rut, and she stumbled. She could feel herself falling, feel his fingers clawing into her flesh like talons. She flung her arms up to protect herself as she hit the ground. The earth, packed solid by the weight of the logging wagons, was granite hard. A groan tore out of her, but she was unable to make any other sound.

He picked her up like a rag doll and began to shake her. All the while he babbled incoherently about evil women, the devil, and pain.

Adrenaline surged through her brain, and she was blazing angry. The bastard wasn't going to kill her without a fight!

She slashed her fingernails across his face and poked him in the eye. He howled, surprised at the pain, and hit her hard in the chest.

"Evil daughter of sin!" he howled. "They sent you away. . . . Your parents didn't want you."

"You! You went through my papers! You touched my clothes!" Moll was even more furious.

He aimed another blow, but she swung sideways, taking the crack on the shoulder.

Moll kicked out savagely. "You're the one who beat me. The night it snowed."

"No." He shook his head, refusing to take the blame for a crime he didn't commit, though he was trying to commit a far greater one. "Buckley. Brooks, he's the one. You knew his secret."

"What secret?" She didn't know anything about Buckley Brooks except that he had a dirty mouth and a dirtier mind. She wasn't sorry he'd been caught working for the Rockwells. She only wished he'd been stopped before he shot Win.

"Are you the Rockwells' assassin?" Given the circumstances, it was a strange conversation, but Moll intended to know who was doing her in. Her birth had been an accident, but by God, she was going to have all the answers to her demise.

"I'm God's assassin."

"Don't be dumb—it's the Rockwells who want me dead."

"You're not that important," he said, suddenly looking and sounding reasonable, sane.

It made her skin crawl.

Eddie Hodges carried a pistol in his saddlebag. He had it in his hand now as he thundered up the road. Spotting the teacher struggling in the middle of the road with Danbury, he fired. He missed by twenty feet, which was fortunate, since Danbury was holding Moll with his arm around her neck.

Win almost died of fright when he saw Danbury chasing Moll. Pleading with the Almighty to save her, he pushed the tired bay to run faster.

Patsy was shouting for the kid not to shoot and cussing the horse he'd chosen. The roan was a looker, but it didn't have much staying power, carrying a man of his size.

Danbury seemed oblivious to the approaching riders and continued to tighten his stranglehold on Moll. She stomped his foot, elbowed his gut, and bit two teeth into his wrist till she drew blood, but in his obsession he didn't notice.

Eddie was aiming again when Patsy pulled up beside him. "Let me have the pistol, Ed."

"He's hurting her."

"You might hit her. I can take him down and not hurt her."

After a second the boy handed over the gun.

"Hit the ground, Moll!" Patsy yelled. "Go limp! Drop!" Patsy roared the orders, as he jumped from his horse and took aim.

Whether she did as instructed or simply blacked out from lack of oxygen, Patsy did not know. She suddenly crumpled, and he squeezed the trigger.

C.J. and Jed were right behind him, and back down the road to town, other riders were coming.

The first bullet hit Danbury in the eye. The next two plowed into his chest. He fell and landed near Moll.

Win leaped off the horse and ran toward her, terrified of what he'd find. She stirred and murmured his name as he pulled her into his arms.

"I knew you'd come," she whispered and shut her eyes.

He buried his face in her dusty black curls, too overcome with emotion to do anything else.

C.J. looked down at Danbury's twisted body. "He was a strange one," he said. "Strange about women—talked about 'em real queer. Like they was all after him, and he was fightin' em off. I thought he was braggin'. He never slept, though, just wandered around at night, peekin' in windows."

C.J. didn't mention that he, too, had peeked in windows. It was sort of exciting, but a grown man didn't do that more than once, not when willing women were waiting for him. Now that he wasn't drinking, he'd found he was vigorous again.

Patsy looked over to where Jed was helping Win with Moll. He felt guilty as hell. She wouldn't have gotten into this mess if he'd been doing his job, instead of goading Jed into courting Hildy. He'd miss Hildy when he left, but the way old Jed was shaping up, Patsy thought she'd be happy.

"Eddie, will you bring that team back down here?" he called. "We'll load up Danbury's body."

"I wanta thank you—about the gun, an' all," C.J. said.

Patsy understood what he was saying. The other man was as rough as a cob, but there was no doubt that he loved his son.

"A boy shouldn't have to carry the burden of killing a man," Patsy said.

C.J. nodded. "It's a terrible load."

"Yes, it is," Patsy agreed. "Maybe you can help me get another wagon so we can take Miss Kennedy back to Hannah's."

*   *   *

The following day, Moll lay back on the horsehair sofa in Hannah's bright parlor, suffering the attention of the entire town. It was the first time in her life she'd entertained so many folks in her white cotton wrapper, but Hannah insisted that she rest.

"So what was Buckley's secret?" Selma Stoneleigh asked. There was no subtlety in Selma. She asked what she wanted to know.

"Patsy thinks he's wanted in Denver for robbing a wealthy businessman named Seamus Blade and later escaping from prison. Sheriff Hilbert has sent to Colorado for a description." Win watched Moll from where he sat, unable to keep his eyes off her.

"But Brooks disappeared."

"Patsy works for Mr. Blade," Moll told Selma. She didn't elaborate. Selma didn't understand the finer points of life or relationships.

Awed by these new developments, Moll wasn't ready to discuss them. It was enough to know her father had sent his own bodyguard to protect her. He actually cared enough to want her alive.

"Poor Mark," Hannah said, knowing it would distract Selma.

"Poor Mark!" Selma launched into a ten-minute tirade on what an evil sinner Mark Danbury was. Then, to everyone's relief, she remembered that she wanted a vanilla bean to make vanilla sugar and went off to the Emporium.

"Do you think it's over?" Bill asked Win. He had his broken leg propped up on a stool.

"Danbury's attack was just a fluke. My cousins are still going full-bore. Before the summer's over, we'll have more trouble."

"I don't think I can stand it," Hannah said. "They are so wicked."

"They don't run my life," Win said. "And neither does the damned legacy anymore. I'm telling you right now, from this day forward, my life belongs to me and I'm going to do what I want."

He got up and walked over to where Moll was resting.

"Moll Kennedy, will you marry me?"

"What?" She was absolutely stunned.

"Will you walk down the aisle of the town hall and tell the people of Summit you'll be my wife and love me forever?"

"Just as soon as my bruises fade." Her smile was one of pure happiness.

Everyone in the room laughed and cheered.

Win took a sapphire-and-diamond ring out of his shirt pocket and put it on her finger. "My grandfather bought this ring for my grandmother—I thought you might like an heirloom."

She threw her arms around his neck, ignoring the twinges of pain. "I love you, Win. I'll take an heirloom, or a cigar band, as long as I get you, too."

Win hastily unbuttoned his wife's frothy white petticoat, let it drop to the floor in a heap, and lifted her in his arms. In the two months since their elaborate wedding, his passion for her had grown by the day. He had no idea he could love anyone as much as he loved Moll.

Her fingers clutched his wide shoulders as he tumbled her onto the wide bed and sprawled on top of her. She groaned aloud as his greedy mouth found hers. Soon they were lost in their own private sensual world, as they'd often been since their marriage.

Much later, when her breathing returned to normal and she could think again, Moll snuggled against the warmth of his solid chest. "I'm glad we sent the wedding picture."

Win chuckled. "I gathered from the bundle he sent with his note that your father is fond of photographs."

Her hand stroked the smooth hair on his chest. "And we sent such a nice photograph back."

"Yes, since your poster caused your father to fall over in a heap."

She punched his arm, giggling. "Patsy assured me the stroke wasn't caused by the poster, Winslow. But the rest of the family might get the wrong idea if they saw it. I want them to like me."

"They'll love you, Moll. Neel said so in his letter. All of them—three brothers and two sisters. Do you think you can wait till the Christmas holidays to visit Denver?"

She reached up and kissed his wonderful mouth. "Some things are worth waiting for."

His answering kiss heated her blood yet again. She let herself flow into the sensual heat of his passion. She'd never believed that love like this was possible.

The pounding on the door came from deep within a dream. Moll was certain that she'd just drifted off to sleep. She tried to ignore the noise, moving closer to her husband's warmth. After their incredible night of loving, she wasn't ready for morning.

The pounding grew louder.

"Hey, you two. Open the door! Emergency!" This time the noise also came from the window.

Win grumbled, blinked, and began to crawl out of bed.

"Don't go." Moll grabbed his arm, not wanting to let go of the night's bliss.

"I have to. It's an emergency." His feet tangled in the petticoat he'd ripped off her last night, and in his effort to free himself, he tumbled back onto the bed.

Moll laughed at him, kissing his hair as he struggled upright, then watched him pull his clothes over his strong masculine body. She couldn't get over the fact he was her husband.

Overcome with curiosity, Moll threw on her robe and followed Win into the kitchen. Bill McDonald and Sheriff Hilbert had just walked in the door.

"What's wrong?" she asked when she saw their grim faces.

"The log dam at Folsom was blown up last night," Bill said. "Three years' worth of work for the whole logging camp was blown to hell!"

Moll's eyes flew to Win. He'd turned his back to her, apparently busy making coffee. Only the stiff set of his shoulders showed his anger.

"Win?"

He finished putting the pot on the fire. "It's over," he said finally. His face showed no emotion. "They won."

"By cheating and stealing," the sheriff said gruffly. "The dirty bastards. It probably cost 'em fifty dollars to hire some thug to blow all your work to hell."

"At least nobody was killed," Bill said. "I'm thankful for that."

Win poured the coffee when it was done, and they talked a little longer. Finally he shoved his chair back. "I know we can't salvage this, but I feel obligated to go to Folsom and look things over."

After Bill and the sheriff left, Win took Moll in his ʳms. "I'll be back as soon as I can."

She ached for him. "I am so damned sorry!"

"I'm not," he said. "I'm glad it's over. My cousins may get the money, but that's all they'll ever have. I've got you, Moll. And I've got my own dreams, a little money, and some big plans. We'll be all right. We've got a wonderful future ahead of us."

"I love you." Her eyes shone with unshed tears.

"And I love you, Mollene." He kissed her breathless. "That's all that counts."

Epilogue

September, 1897
Summit, California

Darkness had settled in around the house. Rain pounded on the windows and thunder rolled, but inside all was warm and cozy, with a fire burning in the pot-bellied stove. Win and Moll were oblivious to anything happening outside their sphere of love.

Win was gently soaping Moll's back with her bathing sponge, then letting the warm scented water sluice down her shapely body. She sighed with pleasure. The sponge floated away as Win soaped his hands and slid them around to her full breasts.

She looked back over her shoulder and gave him the smile that always threatened to stop his heart. "Oh, is my back around in front now?"

"Hummm," was his reply as he dropped a kiss on her delicious neck and moved his hands down to caress her abdomen—where his child was planted and growing. They'd just found out about the baby. At first Win had been stunned, then a feeling of blissful contentment swept over him, and sheer joy. He'd never thought he could be this happy.

"So they get no money at all?" Moll insisted. Win had promised to discuss Sampson's letter with her later, but at the rate his hands were moving and her body temperature was rising, the chance for talking would soon be gone if she didn't seize it now.

"Not even a nickel."

Moll clapped her wet hands in glee. "So tell me about it! How did they lose all that money?"

Win continued to stroke his wife's stomach, marveling that the seed of their family was sheltered beneath that almost flat surface. He wanted to fill not only his hands with her wonderful body, but his senses and emotions as well. She represented the promise of his life.

He did not want to talk about his rotten Rockwell cousins. But he knew Moll. All her passions ran deep and hot, including her hatred of the Rockwells. He sighed with resignation.

"I told you before that the log dam at Folsom had been blown up by an expert. But not Jed, of course. The charge took out the entire center section, causing a flume effect, sending the thousands of monstrous logs we'd stored there along with millions of gallons of water crashing down the Sacramento River like a flash flood, destroying everything in its path."

Moll dipped her fingers into the scented bathwater, then trailed them up Win's arms, causing his breath to catch before he could continue.

"When I saw what was left of it, I knew the property

damages were going to be horrendous. So I telegraphed
Sampson from Folsom, told him what had happened,
and asked that all the people along the river be reimbursed for their losses before the Rockwells got the
legacy."

Moll almost toppled Win into the small portable tub
with her. "And he paid out everything?"

"Every nickel. And that's not all. The moment he
learned that the ex-army munitions sergeant who
blew the log dam had been apprehended and was
only too glad to inform on the boys, he went to
court. Citing police evidence that Sheldon and Harlan had paid the man to blow the log dam, Sampson
obtained a lien against their property and other
assets in San Francisco, so that nothing they own
can be liquidated until all the damages caused by the
log-dam explosion have been settled. Which he figures will take years, and might totally bankrupt
them. He says sugar pine logs have ended up in San
Francisco Bay!"

Moll whirled around in the tub and threw her arms
around Win, her exuberance catching him off-balance.
He toppled backward, taking Moll and the tub with
him. Scented soapy water went everywhere. Win came
up spluttering, but after the initial shock, decided that
having Moll wet, warm, and clingy in his arms was
about all any man could hope for. To hell with the
Rockwells!

Later, when they were snuggled warmly in bed, their
naked bodies lovingly entwined, Moll nudged Win with
her elbow to get his attention. "So what happens to
your nasty cousins now? Will they be arrested? I want
to visit them in jail!"

Win chuckled. "I'm afraid you'll have to forgo that

pleasure, my love. It seems Sheldon and Harlan had some police informants who told them they were about to be arrested. They fled the country aboard a ship for Australia."

Moll's face fell. "They got away? Those dirty, rotten bastards!"

"Hey, hold on! Sampson figures my dear cousins won't find Australia much to their liking. As soon as they spend whatever money they escaped with in their carpetbags, they're going to have to *work for a living!*"

They collapsed in laughter at that thought and were still chuckling when they were interrupted by a loud banging on the door.

"Oh, what the hell now?" Win threw back the covers.

Moll put out a hand to stop him. "Shush. Maybe they'll think we're asleep and go away."

"No such luck," Win grumbled. "The light's on, and I recognize Murphy. A couple more thumps from that paw of his will probably break the door down."

He reached for his pants, stepped on the bar of soap from Moll's bath, and went down with a crash. Moll screamed. The front door banged open, and Patsy Murphy burst into the room prepared to do battle to protect her. But the sight of Win sitting naked in a pool of bathwater, looking thunderous, stopped him cold.

After a couple of seconds, he gave Win a hand up and Moll's unused bath towel from the arm of a nearby chair. "It seems I've interrupted something. My apologies. I'll just be goin' now . . ."

"No," Win said as he wrapped the towel around his waist and looked for the treacherous bar of soap.

"You're here now. You might as well tell me what's on your mind. Just watch where you step. We had a slight accident with the tub."

Patsy kept his thoughts about that to himself as he eased his bulk into the armchair. "C.J. just got back from Placerville, and he brought me a telegram from Neel Blade."

Moll emerged from the bedroom, tying her robe around her waist. "What's happened, Patsy? Is my father worse?" She feared that her father would die before she ever got to actually meet him.

Patsy's blunt features softened. "Ah, no, love. Seamus is doin' fine. I tell ya, he's got the constitution of an ox! No, it's Celestine. The chit went off ta visit friends months ago. The housekeeper in Denver's a tad concerned because Celestine hasn't written."

"Is this unusual?" Moll asked.

"I don't know. Celestine's never been away from home without a chaperon before. The old man always likes to keep track o' his chicks. But in the confusion of the last few months—his stroke an' all—the little heathen slipped through his fingers. Neel wants me ta come home." He paused. "It's time I took things in hand. And I'm a thinkin' the two o' you will be all right now. The Rockwells are outta your hair, and the men are arrivin' any day now to start puttin' that cable across the gorge. What a fine idea that was to build a tram to carry those logs to the sawmill on yonder ridge! So I'll be going in the morning."

"We'll see you at Christmas?"

"'A course, darlin'. By then I'll have me hands on that scamp Celestine. I knew it wasn't safe to let her out o' me sight."

Win laughed and clapped Patsy's beefy shoulder. "You're a brave man, Patsy."

"So are you, lad. Females who act first and think later run in the Blade family!"

COMING NEXT MONTH

RAIN LILY by Candace Camp

Maggie Whitcomb's life changed when her shell-shocked husband returned from the Civil War. She nursed him back to physical health, but his mind was shattered. Maggie's marriage vows were forever, but then she met Reid Prescott, a drifter who took refuge on her farm and captured her heart. A heartwarming story of impossible love from bestselling author Candace Camp.

CASTLES IN THE AIR by Christina Dodd

The long-awaited, powerful sequel to the award-winning *Candle in the Window*. Lady Juliana of Moncestus swore that she would never again be forced under a man's power. So when the king promised her in marriage to Raymond of Avrache, Juliana was determined to resist. But had she met her match?

RAVEN IN AMBER by Patricia Simpson

A haunting contemporary love story by the author of *Whisper of Midnight*. Camille Avery arrives at the Nakalt Indian Reservation to visit a friend, only to find her missing. With the aid of handsome Kit Makinna, Camille becomes immersed in Nakalt life and discovers the shocking secret behind her friend's disappearance.

RETURNING by Susan Bowden

A provocative story of love and lies. From the Bohemian '60s to the staid '90s, *Returning* is an emotional roller-coaster ride of a story about a woman whose past comes back to haunt her when she must confront the daughter she gave up for adoption.

JOURNEY HOME by Susan Kay Law

Winner of the 1992 Golden Heart Award. Feisty Jessamyn Johnston was the only woman on the 1853 California wagon train who didn't respond to the charms of Tony Winchester. But as they battled the dangers of their journey, they learned how to trust each other and how to love.

KENTUCKY THUNDER by Clara Wimberly

Amidst the tumult of the Civil War and the rigid confines of a Shaker village, a Southern belle fought her own battle against a dashing Yankee—and against herself as she fell in love with him.

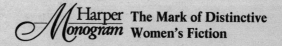 **The Mark of Distinctive Women's Fiction**

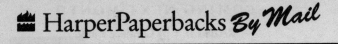

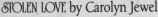

YESTERDAY'S SHADOWS
by Marianne Willman

Bettany Howard was a young orphan traveling west searching for the father who left her years ago. Wolf Star was a Cheyenne brave who longed to know who abandoned him—a white child with a jeweled talisman. Fate decreed they'd meet and try to seize the passion promised. 0-06-104044-4

MIDNIGHT ROSE by Patricia Hagan

From the rolling plantations of Richmond to the underground slave movement of Philadelphia, Erin Sterling and Ryan Youngblood would pursue their wild, breathless passion and finally surrender to the promise of a bold and unexpected love. 0-06-104023-1

WINTER TAPESTRY
by Kathy Lynn Emerson

Cordell vows to revenge the murder of her father. Roger Allington is honor bound to protect his friend's daughter but has no liking for her reckless ways. Yet his heart tells him he must pursue this beauty through a maze of plots to win her love and ignite their smoldering passion. 0-06-100220-8

ANALISE

Analise Caldwell was the reigning belle of New Orleans. Disguised as a Confederate soldier, Union major Mark Schaeffer captured the Rebel beauty's heart as part of his mission. Stunned by his deception, Analise swore never to yield to the caresses of this Yankee spy...until he delivered an ultimatum.

ROSEWOOD

Millicent Hayes had lived all her life amid the lush woodland of Emmetsville, Texas. Bound by her duty to her crippled brother, the dark-haired innocent had never known desire...until a handsome stranger moved in next door.

BONDS OF LOVE

Katherine Devereaux was a willful, defiant beauty who had yet to meet her match in any man—until the winds of war swept the Union innocent into the arms of Confederate Captain Matthew Hampton.

LIGHT AND SHADOW

The day nobleman Jason Somerville broke into her rooms and swept her away to his ancestral estate, Carolyn Mabry began living a dangerous charade. Posing as her twin sister, Jason's wife, Carolyn thought she was helping her gentle twin. Instead she found herself drawn to the man she had so seductively deceived.

CRYSTAL HEART

A seductive beauty, Lady Lettice Kenton swore never to give her heart to any man—until she met the rugged American rebel Charles Murdock. Together on a ship bound for America, they shared a perfect passion, but danger awaited them on the shores of Boston Harbor.